AN ELEMENT

OF CHANCE

Historical Fiction Published by McBooks Press

BY ALEXANDER KENT
Midshipman Bolitho
Stand into Danger
In Gallant Company
Sloop of War
To Glory We Steer
Command a King's Ship
Passage to Mutiny
With All Despatch
Form Line of Battle!
Enemy in Sight!
The Flag Captain
Signal–Close Action!
The Inshore Squadron
A Tradition of Victory
Success to the Brave
Colours Aloft!
Honour this Day
The Only Victor
Beyond the Reef
The Darkening Sea
For My Country's Freedom
Cross of St George
Sword of Honour
Second to None
Relentless Pursuit

BY DUDLEY POPE
Ramage
Ramage & The Drumbeat
Ramage & The Freebooters
Governor Ramage R.N.
Ramage's Prize
Ramage & The Guillotine
Ramage's Diamond
Ramage's Mutiny
Ramage & The Rebels
The Ramage Touch
Ramage's Signal
Ramage & The Renegades
Ramage's Devil
Ramage's Trial
Ramage's Challenge

BY DAVID DONACHIE
The Devil's Own Luck
The Dying Trade
A Hanging Matter
An Element of Chance

BY DEWEY LAMBDIN
The French Admiral

BY CAPTAIN FREDERICK MARRYAT
Frank Mildmay OR
   The Naval Officer
The King's Own
Mr Midshipman Easy
Newton Forster OR
   The Merchant Service
Snarleyyow OR
   The Dog Fiend
The Privateersman
The Phantom Ship

BY JAN NEEDLE
A Fine Boy for Killing
The Wicked Trade

BY IRV C. ROGERS
Motoo Eetee

BY NICHOLAS NICASTRO
The Eighteenth Captain

BY C. NORTHCOTE PARKINSON
The Guernseyman
Devil to Pay
The Fireship

BY W. CLARK RUSSELL
Wreck of the Grosvenor
Yarn of Old Harbour Town

BY RAFAEL SABATINI
Captain Blood

BY MICHAEL SCOTT
Tom Cringle's Log

BY A.D. HOWDEN SMITH
Porto Bello Gold

BY DOUGLAS REEMAN
Badge of Glory
First to Land

BY R.F. DELDERFIELD
Too Few for Drums
Seven Men of Gascony

BY V.A. STUART
Victors and Lords
The Sepoy Mutiny
Massacre at Cawnpore

An Element of Chance

**DAVID
DONACHIE**

THE PRIVATEERSMAN MYSTERIES, NO 4

MCBOOKS PRESS
ITHACA, NEW YORK

Published by McBooks Press 2002
Copyright © David Donachie 1991
First published in the United Kingdom in 1991
by Macmillan London, Limited

Cover painting by Geoff Hunt

Library of Congress Cataloging-in-Publication Data

Donachie, David, (1944–
An element of chance / by David Donachie.
    p.   cm. — (The privateersman mysteries ; no. 4)
    ISBN 1-59013-017-0 (alk. paper)
    1. Ludlow, Harry (fictitious character)—Fiction 2. Great Britain—
History, Naval—18th century—Fiction. 3. British—West Indies—
Fiction. 4. Privateering—Fiction. 5. Impressment—Fiction.
I. Title
PR6053.O483 E44 2002
823'.914—dc21   2002000137

Distributed to the book trade by
LPC Group, 22 Broad St., Suite 34, Milford, CT 06460
800-729-6078.

Additional copies of this book may be ordered from any
bookstore or directly from McBooks Press, 120 West State Street,
Ithaca, NY 14850. Please include $3.50 postage and handling with
mail orders. New York State residents must add sales tax. All
McBooks Press publications can also be ordered by calling toll-free
1-888-BOOKS11 (1-888-266-5711).
Please call to request a free catalog.

Visit the McBooks Press website at www.mcbooks.com.

Printed in the United States of America

9 8 7 6 5 4 3 2 1

To the memory of my brother
JOHN DONACHIE

AUTHOR'S NOTE

THOUGH this is a work of fiction, if you care to read *The Social History of the Navy,* you will find that it is, actually, based in part on a series of events which did take place.

PROLOGUE

SHORT OF gunners, the artillery salvoes were too weak to halt the French advance. Worse still, the smoke from the guns, billowing over the attacking infantry, obscured their movements as they approached the opposite bank of the Rivière Salée. Harassed by their officers, the redcoats, under continuous fire from skirmishers, tried to form up at the water's edge. Forced out of its prepared position, the state of the Guadeloupe garrison was now fully exposed. More men had dropped from sickness or fatigue brought on by the West Indian climate than fell to musketry. Behind them their comrades lay in serried rows, some dead, others dying, with those who would survive now useless as combatants. An army that had been numerically superior was now outnumbered two to one. Hence this advance to the river-bank. If the enemy could be kept in the water, hampered in their movements by the tug of the current, then perhaps the situation might be saved. Fresh from Europe, the Frenchmen suffered none of the handicaps that fell on the more exposed British troops, a difficulty which had been compounded by their commander's decision to bivouac them, prior to the battle, next to a fetid swamp.

By the command tent, the staff officers looked towards General Trethgowan, each mentally composing the letter that would exonerate them and place the blame for any possible defeat firmly at the door of the man responsible. Advised to intercept the French invaders on the beach, he'd chosen instead to draw them into a set-piece battle. Any hint that the armies of Revolutionary France would not abide by the standard rules of warfare fell on deaf ears. Indeed, he'd scoffed at their being led by a typical example of the scum thrown up by the Revolution, an ex-baker called Victor

Hugues, and promised his subordinates an easy victory over what could only be a poorly led rabble.

Captain Elliot Haldane, liaison officer with the local militia, spoke very forcibly, in a tone that very nearly breached the bounds of military discipline, pleading that his men be allowed to attack the enemy.

"They are the only troops we have, sir, who are not affected by the climate. I repeat my request that they be allowed to—"

"Damn you, sir!" shouted Trethgowan, his red face colouring an even deeper hue at such insubordination. "I have told you before, they are Frenchmen, and not to be trusted. Don't be fooled by those white Bourbon uniforms and that damned Bourbon flag. As soon as they cross the river, they'll turn coat and join our enemies."

"They despise the Revolution as much as any Englishman, sir. And being planters whose families reside on Guadeloupe, they have a great deal more to lose than us. These are the very same men who helped Admiral Jervis take the island in the first place."

"You have your orders, Captain. They are to stay on the defensive. And please ensure that they do not break and run at the first hint of danger."

"Where would they run to, General?" said Haldane sadly. "This is their home."

The Frenchmen knew by the look on Haldane's face that his efforts had failed. Being a local force, their discipline was not that of any regular army. So, for all the regard in which he was personally held, he was forced to suffer an abundance of abuse regarding the qualities of Trethgowan and the troops he led. He took it all silently, seeing little point in any attempt to defend his fellow countrymen to these colonists. Most odium was heaped on the general, who'd pointedly ignored any advice they'd offered. Deep down, for all their insults, they knew that the redcoats, better led and healthy, were a match for the men across the river.

"I must ask you formally, Messieurs, to take up the position allotted to you, and defend this bank of the Rivière Salée to the best of your ability."

"*Regardez!*" One of the colonists, who being on the seaward edge of the position had a clear view of the bay, was pointing out to sea. The joyous nature of his response was echoed by others, as they gesticulated wildly. Haldane pushed his way through the throng, his heart pounding at the sight of the man-o'-war's billowing sails. Before the wind, she was a magnificent sight, with an admiral's red flag streaming forward.

"Monsieur de la Mery," cried Haldane, addressing one of the white-coated officers, "you are a sailor by profession. What help can we expect from that ship?"

The captain knew by the glum look on the Frenchman's face that the reply was not a cheering one. "They may arrive too late to land a force to help us."

"What about the cannon? Can they not play on the enemy flank?"

"There are shoals by the river mouth that will keep them well out to sea. Unless they carry larger cannon than any frigate I know, they will lack the range."

The sudden rattle of the drums, coming through the smoke, alerted the defenders to the imminent assault. Haldane fought to inject a positive note into his voice. "I doubt our enemies know that, Monsieur. I suspect the mere sight has led them to launch a pre-emptive strike. I urge you, Messieurs, to take up your posts."

For all the individual nature of their enrolment, they were an efficient body of men. Emboldened by the sight of a British warship, they ran to the river-bank with a heartening degree of *élan*. Haldane was set to follow when de la Mery restrained him.

"Captain Haldane. My men and I did not enlist to end up as prisoners. And Guadeloupe is not our home."

"I know, Monsieur," replied Haldane. He'd heard from more than one source how this man and his contingent of sailors had been forced to flee St Domingue after the slave rebellion. Trethgowan had provided an added insult when he refused these sailors leave to patrol the coastal waters.

"What do you anticipate will happen if your general realizes that the battle is lost?"

Haldane was tempted to lie to him, to say that all would be well. But the look in the Frenchman's dark, penetrating eyes precluded such a course. Both men knew the state of the army, knew that Victor Hugues had outmanoeuvred Trethgowan at every turn. If the ex-baker didn't triumph today, he would tomorrow.

"He will ask for terms."

"For his entire force?"

"Of course."

"His entire force of soldiers?" said the Frenchman, with heavy emphasis on the last word.

Their eyes stayed locked together for a few seconds before Haldane replied. "Whatever you do, Monsieur, provided it is commensurate with your own honour, will surely satisfy me and my countrymen."

The squeak from de la Mery's coat pocket, as his pet mongoose poked out its narrow little head, broke the stare. That was immediately followed by a fusillade of musketry as the French started to wade into the river. They ran to their allotted places, and joined the unbroken line of white-coated colonists. The smoke and noise of battle seemed to increase the heat. Soon every man on the river-bank who'd survived the fusillade was engaged in a personal contest. Bayonets jabbed forward, to be met and parried by pikes and swords. The cries of the wounded and dying lifted themselves above the clash of metal, only being drowned out by the thundering cannon as Hugues and Trethgowan aimed their field-pieces over the combatants' heads.

The great cheer from the inland flank, plus the merest hint of surging blue, was enough to tell Haldane that the weak and debilitated redcoats had failed to hold. The pressure on the colonists' front decreased as Hugues withdrew those opposite to exploit the breakthrough. Forewarned by de la Mery, Haldane and his men immediately fell back. With a wave of his sword towards the gallant British officer, the Frenchman led his contingent away towards the town of Pointe-à-Pitre.

◆ ◆ ◆

The drums beat a steady rhythmic tattoo that wafted across the bay towards the anchored frigate. Ashore the act of surrender was being carried out with strict military precision, even if the surviving British redcoats could barely stand. In front of General Trethgowan stood the author of this singular defeat, the corpulent figure of the man who'd been sent from Paris to recapture the French sugar islands. At two cables' distance, even through a telescope, his face was a blur. But his uniform said everything. Victor Hugues was dressed in black, unlike his gorgeously attired military advisers. Round his waist he wore a thick tricolour sash. His tall black hat was set off with a huge cockade: red, white, and blue, the colours of Jacobin Republicanism. Behind him, in neat ranks, his small army, preceded by the company of artillery, crossed the pontoon bridge which straddled the Rivière Salée. A substantial body of troops remained behind, guarding a large rectangular object shrouded by a tarpaulin. This piece of equipment aroused a great deal of curiosity. Under the awning, the officers gathered on the quarterdeck of *Diomede* speculated openly about what it might be. Bessborough stood rock still, as if by his immobility he might mitigate this blow to his country's esteem. He didn't react to the sudden activity behind him, keeping his telescope trained on the events unfolding ashore. To turn and enquire would be beneath his dignity as a vice-admiral of the red. Not that such a thing was necessary. The midshipman delivering the message to Captain Marcus Sandford had a clear voice and a penetrating delivery.

"There's a water hoy full of Frenchmen come out from Pointe-à-Pitre harbour, sir. Their leader says that they are sailors, not soldiers, therefore they are spared the obligation to surrender."

"How many?" asked Sandford.

"Forty in all, sir. Must have been hanging off the sides."

"Do you think they were observed from the shore?"

The voice that answered, in heavily accented English, finally gave Bessborough cause to turn around. The party had come aboard without waiting to be invited, their leader stepping forward with his hat in his hand. The admiral saw before him a tall young man in a white frock coat, dark-skinned and handsome, with deep brown eyes and a steady gaze. His attention was then taken by a sudden movement and a mongoose, obviously the man's pet, poked its head out of his coat pocket, jerking left and right as it gazed around the deck.

"We were not seen by the *canaille* on the beach, Captain."

"General Trethgowan made the terms of surrender, Monsieur," said Sandford. "They quite specifically included all the Frenchmen who'd fought on the British side."

"To be exact, all the French soldiers, Captain."

Sandford looked pointedly at the uniform coat, which was of the same cut and colour as those of his fellow countrymen lined up behind the redcoats on shore.

"Time did not allow us the luxury of an identity separate."

"Dillon?" said Bessborough, as Sandford looked to him for a decision. The admiral's political assistant gave a slight cough before replying. He was a tall man, thin and wiry with narrow features and slightly protruding blue eyes. His fine ginger hair was carefully arranged to cover encroaching baldness and his voice was soft, southern Irish.

"It seems to me, sir, that the soldiers have given enough away for one day. I think General Trethgowan should have held out a bit longer. At least until Monsieur Hugues agreed to allow the Royalists to depart with our men. He can only wish to retain them for the purposes of humiliation, which is not something we should be a party to."

Bessborough didn't give a toss for French humiliation. His mind was concentrated on the way that Trethgowan, and the army, had let him down. "Well, he didn't, Dillon, which has landed all of us in a fine mess. God only knows what their lordships will make of this fiasco."

Trethgowan was most certainly finished as a soldier. The Horse Guards would never forgive him for such a defeat. But it was more than just a disaster for the army. As the naval commander on the spot, he wouldn't escape without a blemish. Questions would be asked: like how a man with a force of two frigates, a brig, and five transports could have been allowed to sail unmolested all the way from France to the West Indies and, once there, land troops without any interference from the Royal Navy. There were circumstances that would mitigate the strictures of the Admiralty: Admiral Lord Howe, with his hatred of close blockade, had contrived to let this fellow escape from Brest; Hugues had arrived at the beginning of the hurricane season, a most unusual thing for a Frenchman to do, thus taking everyone in the region by surprise, then on landing he announced that all the slaves were to be free, in line with the tenets of the Revolution, a pronouncement that caused no end of unrest.

But most of all, his troops were fresh from Europe, and everything Trethgowan had done only reinforced that telling advantage. Using the Rivière Salée as his main bastion he'd secured his right flank against the marshes and his left flank by the sea. It was too late now to tell the bonehead that in this part of the world to bivouac right next to a swamp was an elementary tactical error. By the time Hugues attacked, the August heat and the foul air from the marshes had left Trethgowan barely able to muster one tenth of his available strength. The troops Bessborough'd raised in English Harbour were still over the horizon, too far away to save the redcoats ashore, while the shallows of the river delta precluded the idea of using the frigate as a floating battery to harass the French. He needed the 32-pounder cannon of a 74-gun ship to achieve anything in that line. That too was some way off, escorting the lumbering troopships. It only added insult to injury that there was no sign of the two French frigates. The only vessels in the bay were Hugues's transports and they were covered by Trethgowan's truce.

As the drums beat out a final hurried tattoo everyone faced the shore, just in time to see the regimental colours dip in surrender towards the pale white sand. At the rear of the line, the fleur-de-lis of Royal France dipped too, this before the ranks of white-coated soldiers. Trethgowan presented Hugues with his sword, which the Frenchman accepted. But when the commander of the Royalists proffered his in a like manner, the Jacobin declined to take it. This was a bitter moment. There wasn't an officer aboard *Diomede* who didn't think that Britain had a duty to those Frenchmen. But General Trethgowan, more concerned for the health of his own men, and faced with the intransigence of Hugues, had agreed to leave them behind with a promise from the new governor of Guadeloupe that they would be well treated.

"You would imagine it couldn't be worse," said Dillon, as the troops marched down to the edge of the beach, their pace set by the regimental fifes and drums. "But Trethgowan has even asked the sod for the use of his transports. Could he not have waited for us to gather some?"

Bessborough scowled. The act of surrender had made his desire to sink those very ships impossible. "His sole aim, I imagine, is to get as far away from Guadeloupe, and as quickly as possible. After all, this fellow is allowing him to depart with his weapons and colours intact."

"It's a neat ploy," said Captain Sandford, gloomily. "We can hardly go after his frigates while our troops are in their transports."

"Best send your barge ashore, Sandford. Trethgowan will expect us to take him and his staff aboard."

This didn't please either man. Sandford had already given up his cabin to the admiral. With senior army officers aboard he'd likely have to shift again. Bessborough had no desire to spend a second with a man who, to his mind, deserved to swim to English Harbour. The sailors watched for an age as the troops, some walking, more carried, waded out into the surf and shuffled aboard the French transports.

"Sail ho," came the cry from the mast-head. "*Redoubtable*, sir."

"Thank God," said Bessborough. "Sandford, hoist the following signal. *Flag to* Redoubtable. *Depart from convoy and join flag with all despatch*. I'll shift into her as soon as she arrives. You can have the pleasure of Trethgowan's company tonight."

"Thank you, sir," the captain replied, making no attempt to disguise the irony in his tone.

"And on no account, Sandford, are you to surrender your cabin to him. That is a direct order. Make the general and his staff sling hammocks in the bilges if you so desire."

As if in agreement, the mongoose in the Frenchman's pocket added a loud and penetrating squeak.

An hour passed, with Bessborough pacing up and down the quarterdeck, only the occasional soft curse breaking through from his troubled thoughts. *Redoubtable* was still a mile away when the last of the French transports ran up a signal to say it was fully loaded. Any hope he'd harboured that he might avoid coming face-to-face with the soldiers faded away. He stopped pacing when he heard the whistles, set to welcome the general aboard with a salute that accorded with his rank. That, and the sight of the transports weighing anchor and beating out of the bay, deepened his frown. The same black look returned when the army commander finally came on deck. The first thing to take Trethgowan's eye was the knot of French soldiers. Their white uniforms made them somewhat conspicuous.

"What the devil are these fellows doing here?" he demanded, his high red colour increasing with anger.

It was Sandford who replied. "They came aboard from the port, sir, having rowed out in a wider arc. No one saw them."

"That is neither here nor there, sir," boomed Trethgowan, his blue eyes popping out of a face the colour of his tightly buttoned red coat. "I undertook to surrender all the Bourbon troops to Monsieur Hugues. I will not countenance the breaking of my solemn word."

Dillon cut in. "Pray, General, what difference would it make if he's short of a couple of dozen?"

"Why, damn you, sir! You're a civilian. You would do well to remain silent. This is a matter of military honour."

Bessborough exploded. "That word in your mouth, sir, on this day, is an abomination! How can you prate about military honour when you've just been soundly trounced by a tradesman?"

"Oh God! I was right," said Dillon, sharply, his soft Irish voice loud enough, for once, to attract everyone's attention. "It is a guillotine."

That dreaded word silenced Trethgowan's response. All eyes turned to the shore. The tarpaulin had been removed from that squat rectangular mass. The angled blade, at the top of the twin struts, shone dully in the sunlight. The soldiers who'd attended to its transportation were lowering uprights to hold the whole assembly steady.

"Look, sir," said Sandford, his arm pointing towards the lines of Royalist troops, now hatless and disarmed. Hugues's soldiers had hemmed them in, their muskets lowered threateningly. The new governor of Guadeloupe stood outside the circle as, one by one, a dozen men were dragged out, their hands tied, before being hustled towards the guillotine.

"What's he about?" demanded Trethgowan.

Dillon's words were no less effective for being delivered in his normal quiet way. "I think your man is about to show you, General Trethgowan, that he too is a civilian."

The first victim was pushed up the steps. Their companions, who'd come aboard earlier, pushed their way through the throng of British officers to witness this barbarity. No one spoke as the man was forced to his knees, his head thrust down to lie on the bottom of the infernal machine. Hugues stood, his cockaded hat raised in the air. As he dropped his hand the blade was released. Every man aboard had imagined that sound, the music of the French terror. But they were hearing Madame Guillotine's true voice for the first time. Nothing had prepared them for the reality. They gasped as the heavy blade swished down the wooden channels. The thud as it hit the bottom affected them all, as did the sight of the severed head dropping into the basket. A great fount of blood shot out from the trunk as the blade was raised, a grisly accompaniment to the cheer that followed his death. Two men grabbed the legs and dragged the headless body away as another victim was hustled up the steps to meet his fate.

"He gave me his word," said Trethgowan.

"You're a horse's arse, sir," said Bessborough, the only man senior enough to level such a vulgar accusation. That he'd used such a common expression only served to demonstrate the depths of his feelings. He was much taller than the soldier, a fact made more apparent as the admiral moved closer, to a point where they were practically touching. "You were an idiot to let him get ashore uncontested, a buffoon to wait for him to attack, a fool to fight him where you did, and a poltroon for accepting his word. This ex-baker from Marseilles has put you in the oven, Trethgowan, and baked your reputation to perfection."

"I will not be addressed so," he spluttered as another cheer came floating across from the shore.

"Ahoy, *Diomede*," called Captain Vandegut from the deck of the *Redoubtable,* which had sailed close without anyone noticing. "Why in hell's name are we letting their transports go?"

Bessborough spun away from the choleric soldier and grabbed a speaking trumpet from a midshipman. "Sandford, up anchor and get us out of harm's way."

"Harm, sir?"

Bessborough raised the trumpet. "Vandegut. You, sir, will mind your manners when you address a flag-officer. Now run out your lower-deck guns. I want you to shape a course across the bay. Get in as close as you dare and destroy that guillotine. If in the process you can dismember that swine in the cockaded hat, so much the better."

Trethgowan protested as he was shuffled aside, the frigate's deck now full of running men. "Admiral Bessborough. Might I remind you that my soldiers are in those French transports? Do you want to see them murdered, sir?"

Bessborough turned to yell at him, his whole frame full of the air he'd sucked in for the purpose. But nothing emerged and slowly his body deflated. When he did speak it was quietly.

"Sandford. Request Captain Vandegut to belay. And strike my flag. I'm shifting to *Redoubtable*."

Another cheer rent the air. Dillon approached the admiral and whispered in his ear. The older man nodded slowly then walked across to the knot of Frenchmen, taking the one he'd already spoken to by the elbow. He felt the cold nose of the pet mongoose touch the back of his hand.

"What's your name, boy?"

The young man spun round and pulled himself to attention, making no attempt to wipe the tears from his eyes. "Lieutenant de Vaisseu Antoine de la Mery."

"And these men?"

"Colonists turned common seamen, Monsieur. Artisans and bondsmen from St Domingue. We came to Guadeloupe after the blacks took over our island." Another cheer, another victim, as the young man nodded. He reached into his pocket and pulled out the mongoose, stroking its enquiring head. "One day, *petit ami,* we will get our revenge."

The cheering still echoed as the admiral shifted to *Redoubtable.* Those aboard the 74 were as appalled as the men of the frigate. But Hugues hadn't ceased to shock. Obviously too impatient for the guillotine to do its bloody work, he'd lined up the Royalists before the trenches they'd intended to defend. Then with another wave of his cockaded hat a fusillade was fired into the backs of the defenceless soldiers. Those struck by a ball pitched headlong into the trenches. It was only then that the watchers realized the men had been roped together. Those untouched by musket fire were dragged down by the wounded or the dead. The next line of wretches faced the void. They were shot down in turn, to fall upon the bodies already there. Some would die from the wounds, others from suffocation, but it was clear they were all doomed. Victor Hugues had arrived in Guadeloupe, and he had signalled his intentions from the very first day. The full rigour of the revolutionary terror had come, at last, to cast its shadow over the West Indies.

CHAPTER ONE

THE POUNDING rain washed across the forecastle, acting like a curtain to cut out all trace of the French ship, labouring a mere two cables ahead, just inshore of the *Bucephalas*. A true white squall, a downpour so heavy that it could deaden the waves on the sea itself. Harry Ludlow, holding the wheel, bowing under the weight of the water that lashed his oilskins, sought to do no more than hold his course, for this was a dangerous shore. It was harder for the men aloft, their feet precariously balanced on the slippery wet ropes, the horses, slung below the wooden yards. They had to fight this teeming cascade, and the howling wind, to reef the topsails. If they failed their captain would struggle to keep his ship under proper control. The shifting, variable gale that accompanied such squalls ensured that anything less than perfection would mean their blowing right out of their robbands.

"How long for this one, Captain?" shouted Pender from under his sou'wester.

This was not the first such tempest they'd faced that day. And when the rain cleared away those with little experience of such conditions would be amazed, yet again, at the drop in the wind and the calm of the sea. Older hands, who'd served with their captain before and were accustomed to the Bay of Biscay, would merely shake their heads once more at the tricks the weather could play.

"Just hope it clears before he sights the Goulet." As Harry answered his servant, he lifted his head and allowed some of the rainwater to wash the salt off his face, ignoring the amount that made its way down the inside of his coat. "In these conditions I wouldn't chase him into that stretch of water if he was a Spanish plate galleon."

"It would be a pity to lose him after all this time."

"We shan't lose him, Pender, never fear."

Harry Ludlow sounded a lot more confident than he really felt, for this was a pursuit that should have ended hours ago. He'd been a canny opponent, this merchant captain, with a crew that had served him admirably. Even in his new ship, the *Bucephalas,* which was a flyer, fresh off the stocks at Blackwall Reach, the chase had managed to elude him. The Frenchman had used every trick in the sailing manual, and each fluke in the changing weather, to evade capture. He was clearly a mariner at home in these waters, perhaps a local seaman making for his home port.

They had sighted him well to the south, just as he opened the great bight of Douarnenez, sailing large on a north-west wind, with his bowsprit set towards the Pointe du Raz, possibly making for the mouth of the Loire and the port of Nantes. The deep-laden merchantman, probably a West Indian trader, on sighting the *Bucephalas* across his path had not waited to discover if he was friend or foe. He'd put up his helm and worn right into the wind, tacking and wearing till he cleared the head of the bay. The shoreline, as the day wore on, changed from long golden beaches backed by low, grassy dunes to grey jagged cliffs, with needle rocks poking out of the tumultuous off-shore spume. If the Frenchman knew anything about the perils of the coast of Brittany, it didn't affect his actions. He disdained safety and stayed close inshore, either oblivious, or prepared to accept the danger he was courting. Taking him on would be no easy matter, which was very different from the way it had looked that morning.

"We shall have him before dinner, James."

Harry had passed this remark to his brother when the sun shone in a flawless sky, at a time when the chase was still fresh enough to be exciting. The younger of the two Ludlow brothers sat in his shirtsleeves in a captain's chair near the skylight, enjoy-

ing the fine autumn weather. Even so dressed, James Ludlow managed to look slightly out of place, very like a man who was too
refined for life aboard a ship. He smiled in response, wishing to
underline the fact that he had great faith in Harry's seamanship.

"I think we need a flag, James. I wouldn't want our quarry to
doubt that we're British."

There was nothing hurried in his brother's response, which
caused Harry to smile himself. Aboard the *Bucephalas,* when the
captain issued an order men rushed to obey, the pounding of their
bare feet thudding out an urgent tattoo on the spotless planking
of the ship's deck. But haste was anathema to James Ludlow. He
carried out his self-imposed task as keeper of the flag-locker in a
naturally elegant manner that was deeply incongruous aboard a
privateer, a ship designed solely for war.

"Let us hope that he carries a decent cargo, brother, one that
will serve to line all our pockets with gold."

The remark, deliberately loud, was greeted with a grim smile
from the crew. They'd seen precious little of that commodity since
they'd set sail from the Downs in July. Each man had signed on
with Harry as a volunteer; paid a wage, but really aboard for a
share of the privateer's booty. Many, not least the naval officers
with whom they stood in direct competition, considered their trade
mere piracy. But Harry Ludlow carried letters of marque, bearing
the royal seal of their sovereign, King George III. These documents
permitted such men to pursue the ships of his enemies, to take
them and destroy them if they wished, or to sell any captures, with
their cargo, for a profit.

The mood on deck stayed buoyant as the morning wore on.
Every man aboard knew that their vessel was a fine sailer on a
bowline. *Bucephalas,* beating up into the wind on a closer heading than their quarry, was narrowing the gap at a steady pace.
Harry, watching the Frenchman closely, and observing the action
that would bring him round on another course for the tenth time,
was mentally counting off the number of tacks he'd have to complete before he could put a shot across the Frenchman's bows. But

then the chase surprised him by declining to tack, instead holding his course and running inshore towards the grey, threatening rocks.

"Damn it, Pender, I don't think very highly of this manoeuvre. If he doesn't bear away from the shore, he'll rip out his bottom on some reef. It might be wise to clear away the boats in case, otherwise we'll have to stand off and watch his crew drown."

Harry addressed these remarks to the man who stood beside him, holding the wheel. Small, compact, with a dark complexion and a ready smile, Pious Pender was happy to be titled Harry Ludlow's servant, though he was a great deal more than that— something known to every member of the crew. He'd come into his service by accident while serving aboard a man-o'-war, a course he'd adopted to evade the long arm of the law. Few men aboard the ship knew Pender had been a thief, and a good one, who'd only fallen foul of the authorities through the jealousy of others. Since first meeting with the Ludlow brothers he'd rendered invaluable service, even to the point of saving Harry's life. Thus there existed a bond between the three men that transcended the normal relationship of master and servant. He was also their friend and confidant, as well as the man the captain of the *Bucephalas* trusted to command his boarding parties.

The crew, appraised by Pender of the new orders, wondered at their need. Nevertheless, they rushed to do their captain's bidding, while at the same time keeping a weather eye on the Frenchman. Each hand was certain that their quarry would see sense, haul off the shore, and put himself out of the rocky frying pan into the range of their deadly fire.

Yet it soon became clear that the merchant captain knew his business. He'd calculated, expertly, the rise of the tide as he edged inshore. Now, having peaked in the last half-hour, it was falling. This set up a leeway that, time and again, kept him out of harm's reach. And as the day wore on, matters steadily took a turn for the worse. It was as if by some sixth sense he'd anticipated the wind shifting into the west, had foreseen that the weather would change from brilliant sunshine to a grey overcast sky filled with sudden downpours, squalls of such intensity that they drove James

Ludlow, and anyone else unemployed, below decks. For all Harry's seamanship, which was of the highest order, the Frenchman had taken advantage of every one of them to fox the pursuit. Obviously the man knew the waters of this jagged coastline like the back of his hand. And it wasn't all mere evasion. He was forever trying to lure the *Bucephalas* into striking on unseen rocks, the fate that Harry had earlier assigned to his opponent.

Bucephalas had been forced to haul off three times now, as Harry'd been set to pin the chase, the lookout's sharp eyes and his own nose for danger spotting the hidden hazards of submerged reefs and rocks just in time. Frustration was mingled with admiration. The Frenchman's skill was awesome. If anyone doubted that it was skill and was tempted to term it luck, they only had to recall one fact: that this ship had already sailed through the entire blockading squadron of the Royal Navy, set to guard the approaches to the main French naval base of Brest. Now, having turned back towards them, he was approaching the Goulet, that treacherous passage that led into the port, dragging the *Bucephalas,* and Harry Ludlow, in his wake. The crew glanced at him occasionally, wondering what action he would take. But their captain was not one to discuss matters on his own quarterdeck. Only Pender, standing beside his captain, was close enough to be privy to his intentions.

"I'm praying that he will haul himself off when the tide has fallen. It's not a passage any sane man would risk at slack water. I wouldn't enter the Goulet without something under my keel, even if I knew the place as well as an inshore shrimp netter."

Harry had no need to explain to his servant that this was truly an iron-bound coast. In the past three months Pender had seen enough of the rocky shore, and been regaled with enough tales of disaster, to know that it ranked as a ships' graveyard. But Pender also knew how much Harry Ludlow needed this capture. For a privateer who'd enjoyed unbounded success at the outbreak of the Revolutionary War, the pickings, in this third year of conflict, had been slim indeed.

But then, two years earlier, he'd arrived off this coast before most of the incoming ships knew that England was once again at war with France; that the Jacobin despots in Paris had chopped off the heads of their king and queen, and were now extending such a fate to an increasing number of their titled fellow countrymen. Two years earlier, with several captures already sent in, and given the competence of his quarry, he might have let this fellow go.

He was, of course, operating in a narrower band of water now, avoiding the Royal Navy ships cruising off Brest and La Rochelle. Beating a hasty retreat every time he spied their topsails wasn't merely a ploy to evade their disapproval. Every man-o'-war afloat was short of trained hands. Harry Ludlow carried written exemptions, a legal document barring his men from being taken up by the press, but he was loath to put such a legality to the test in open water, far away from any other authority than the muzzles of a warship's broadside.

His crew had with good cause rated him lucky at the start of the voyage. Now, after three months of fruitless cruising, most were beginning to wonder if Lady Fortune hadn't deserted their captain. Some even suggested this new ship carried some kind of curse. How could they lack success when it had everything a privateer captain could want? *Bucephalas* was like a cut-down frigate, smaller in everything but the height of her masts. She had speed for the chase and guns to call any sensible fellow, save a naval ship, to spill his wind.

The men, labouring under this latest downpour, were as keyed up as Harry Ludlow, their eyes fixed on the point at which they'd last seen the chase, hungry for the weather to clear so that they could get a proper sight of their potential victim. The sky grew a little lighter to larboard, taking on a silver sheen, a sure sign that the rain was easing. Harry, in anticipation, put his helm down a touch. He wanted to come out of this squall much closer to his enemy, alongside if humanly possible. It seemed his wish would be granted quicker than he thought. The speed with which the first sail appeared out of the rain shocked him to the marrow.

"Let fly the sheets!" he yelled, as he spun the wheel to bring his ship into the wind.

He didn't have the means, in speed or wind-power, to come right round on to a larboard tack, a fact that made him curse himself under his breath. The Frenchman had obviously decided to ram him, a potential hazard that he should have foreseen. But he hadn't. So he adopted the safest course to ensure that such a manoeuvre failed. Yet, even with a well-trained crew, his response seemed painfully slow to take effect. Time seemed to stand still as the ship they were pursuing loomed large, a monster in his imagination.

"Man the starboard braces and haul away."

The yards, first loosed to spill the wind, were hauled round and bowsed tight so that he could pull away from the shore on a starboard tack. The ghostly shape of the merchant ship seemed to tower above him, close enough to scrape the paint off his side. Then the first gun spoke out. Only when he heard that familiar sound did he realize that, whatever this ship was, it was far too big a vessel to be his quarry.

It was as though the boom of the guns was a signal for the weather to clear. Suddenly the sky was visible, as the rain fell off to a steady drizzle, moving away towards the rocky shore and exposing the first of the three ships that occupied the small area of spume-flecked inshore water. It gave Harry no pleasure to see the flag at the main that identified the third ship as a frigate of the Royal Navy. It pleased him even less to see that the gunports were open and that the ship's cannon were aimed in his direction.

CHAPTER TWO

THE GUNS went off again, but not on the side facing *Bucephalas*. Smoke billowed up and flew on the wind towards the merchant-man. With eighteen-pounders a man-o'-war could threaten the Frenchman in a way denied to him. His twelve-pounders lacked the range, and his carronades, set amidships, were smashers, only useful at close quarters. But the ball from an eighteen-pounder could travel half a mile and still cleave its way through six inches of solid oak. The Frenchman knew that as well as anyone afloat. He put down his helm, aiming for calmer waters. Then he struck his flag, well before the shots from the frigate churned up the waters around his ship.

Harry observed, absent-mindedly, that the gunnery was very poor. His attention was concentrated elsewhere. He searched the sky anxiously, hoping to see evidence of another impending squall, which would hide his departure. The Frenchman was no good to him now. He could not dispute the prize with a frigate. The crew of the *Bucephalas* would get nothing out of the capture, which would be claimed by the Royal Navy. For all that such an out-come galled them, it was clear from their worried expressions that, exemptions or no, they were as eager to be off as their captain. Most had served at one time or another aboard a man-o'-war. It was clearly not an experience they wished to repeat. Failure to get away might end with them trading the comfort of a privateer for the hell of a king's ship, with flogging a daily occurrence and food to eat that had been so long in the cask that it was foul before war even broke out.

Whoever was in command on the frigate's quarterdeck must

have guessed his intention, for the voice boomed out through the speaking trumpet, so loud that it stopped James, emerging from the companion-way, dead in his tracks.

"Keep station under our guns, sir, and stand by to receive a boarding party."

"Harry?" said James, but his brother's upheld hand stopped his questions. Pender, ever alert, pressed Harry's own speaking trumpet into his free hand, then quietly ordered the crew to man the yards.

"We are the *Bucephalas,* sir. Letter of marque, out of Deal, cruising these waters with the permission of the king himself. We do not require a boarding party."

"Damn you, sir," replied the gruff voice, the Hibernian accent very evident. "It's not for you to decide the actions of a king's offi-cer."

"Sounds like a Scotchman," said James acidly. It was a race he had little time for, a nation that had rebelled twice since the Union and been so comprehensively forgiven that, in James's jaun-diced view, they practically ran the entire country. Having a brother-in-law of that persuasion whom he disliked had fuelled his prejudice. Given the rude way they were now being addressed, it looked as if such feelings were about to be vindicated.

Harry raised the speaking trumpet once more. "I carry exemp-tions for all of my crew, sir, properly signed by the Secretary of War himself."

"If you was a gentleman, sir, I might take credence. But see-ing you're a damned privateer, no commissioned officer could accept your word."

"Can I borrow the speaking trumpet?" asked James, his nor-mally calm face suffused with anger.

"No, James, you cannot."

"Get your crew away from those braces, laddie, or I'll put a ball in your hull."

Harry fought to keep his voice calm. He was as angry as James. But no good would come of trading insults with a naval officer.

They generally hated privateers, whom they saw as dedicated to taking what little profit existed out of their profession while disdaining the risks they had to run in fighting a well-armed enemy.

"You are welcome to come aboard, that is, if you are the captain."

"Oh, don't worry about my rank, laddie. You shall be served out in the proper manner."

"I don't like the sound of that, Harry. What does he mean by served out?"

Harry didn't reply, turning instead to address his next words to Pender. "Fetch the papers from my cabin, and line up the hands to be listed off by name."

Then he turned to look down the deck, at the anxious faces of his crew. "No violence or harsh words, d'ye hear? Our papers are in order and he, for all his manner, is duty bound to respect them. But if one of us so much as raises a hand to any of his men, then he'll call that an offence and clap the miscreant in irons."

"Boat putting off, Captain," said Patcham, one of the men Harry had elevated to a position of authority. He'd come down from the tops, where he'd been set to watch out for danger. Obviously he'd been so intent on the French merchantman, and the hazards of the inshore waters, that he'd missed sight of the frigate in the offing. It was the occasion for a severe rebuke, but that would have to wait till they'd seen off the approaching threat.

"Cutter and barge," added Patcham. "With a party of armed marines aboard each one."

"Should we arm ourselves, brother?"

"No, James. That is the very last thing we should do."

He could see the figure at the rear of the barge, wrapped in a boat-cloak, which was a necessary precaution given the sloppy, uncoordinated rowing of the boat crews; his hat, worn fore and aft, had the gold lace that marked him out as an officer. He took the telescope from Patcham and trained it on the passenger. As the barge came closer, the features came into focus. A scowling face, dark skinned, with heavy black eyebrows that seemed to join in the middle. This over angry eyes and the kind of blue-black jowls that denoted a troublesome growth of beard. The lips moved soundlessly, but the words were emphatic. Harry was enough of a lip reader to work out that the captain was cursing his inept crewman, a well-deserved tongue lashing that was being received in stoic silence.

James had taken another telescope from the rack and followed suit. Being a portrait painter of some repute, a man to whom the human form was the subject of professional scrutiny, the face conveyed more information to him than it did to his elder brother.

"He's in a fine lather, Harry. And by the miserable cast of his features, it would appear to be his natural state."

That supposition was borne out as the captain came aboard, followed by a spotty midshipman and his file of marines. He eschewed any courtesies, not even touching the rim of his hat, and he glared at everything with that same black look. Most sailors coming aboard a well-run ship, regardless of their purpose, managed a compliment of sorts. Not this fellow.

"Toner," he barked. "Captain of the *Endymion,* 32 guns, fifthrate."

The unfriendly cast of his square-jawed face when silent was enhanced by his upper teeth. Slightly too large for his mouth, but regular and even in size, they assumed an unnatural prominence in speech, then seemed to grind on his lower molars when he wasn't talking. The bloodless lips were stretched in what looked like a permanent grimace.

"Harry Ludlow, owner and captain of the *Bucephalas.*"

The black eyes narrowed under that single heavy eyebrow, making him look like some Hogarthian demon. "Ludlow!"

"This is my brother, and my partner in this enterprise, James Ludlow."

The eyes flicked towards James, then back to Harry as if noticing the likeness between them. The teeth ground against each other audibly, and their owner emitted a low, angry growl.

"Upon my soul, Captain Toner," said James, in a soft, languid voice, "you seem to have an exceedingly bilious countenance. No doubt it befits the nature of your occupation, where terrorizing innocents is a daily occurrence. But please remember that, as a guest aboard our ship, we expect better manners."

James's barb had no effect. It was impossible for Toner to look any angrier than he did already. He spat out his next question.

"Y're never Thomas Ludlow's brats, are ye?"

"This is intolerable!" snapped James, stung out of his elegant air by the evident displeasure in Toner's remark.

Harry held up a restraining hand. "Please, brother. Can you not see that it pleases the captain to anger you? It would be better not to oblige him."

James recovered himself, forcing his voice back towards the languid tone he could use to such devastating effect. "Of course, Harry. Silly of me. I'd forgotten how hard it is, in these troubled times, for the navy to man its ships with proper gentlemen. Such a want of manners is only to be expected when you elevate bare-arsed crofters to senior rank."

Toner's teeth ground so hard that Harry wondered how they stayed in one piece. But his true bile was directed at James, and the look in his eye demanded that this brother desist with his insults.

"You asked a question, Captain?" Harry said, holding out the letters of marque. "Albeit in a most offensive way. We are indeed the late admiral's sons."

Toner barely gave the parchment scroll a glance, his eyes flicking once more between the two brothers. "I dinna ken what old Foulweather Tom Ludlow would say to find his bairns engaged in this game. He'd spin in his grave, I'll wager."

It was a long time since Harry had heard anyone use his father's nickname. And usually when they did, this allusion to the late admiral's fondness for rough weather had a quality of affection in it. Toner managed to make it sound like a fault. So much so that Harry's voice, in response, sounded a great deal less accommodating.

"Our father's opinions about us are none of your concern, Captain Toner. It is intrusive to even allude to such a thing. If you wish to inspect our papers please do so. There's little to be gained from wallowing about here."

That produced a smile. The bloodless lips stretched out even further. "Oh, I think there's gain to be had, for those wi' the luck to warrant it. Yon prize is a fine catch, would you no' say?"

"Unless you intend to share its value, Captain Toner, it is of no concern to me."

"Share, damn you!" he barked, pushing his face forward.

He grabbed the papers from Harry's hands and read them quickly. The red ribbon, set in the great royal seal at the bottom, flapped in the increasing breeze. Harry glanced out to sea. The squall he'd needed earlier was coming now, racing down upon them from the grey horizon, a great sheet of teeming rain.

"So y're a letter o' marque, right enough," said Toner. He looked down the deck at the numerous crew, before turning back to look at Harry. "And well manned, an' all. Trouble is, laddie, that I have a king's ship that's short on its complement. So it will be necessary to relieve you of a few of yer crew."

"I'm sorry I'm unable to oblige," Harry replied coldly.

The teeth flashed as the lips stretched again, in what passed for a smile. "Are ye now? Well so am I, laddie. But the king's needs come first."

"Every man aboard this ship is exempt from impressment, sir. And, I might add, my ship does not require a naval boarding party to prove its function."

"Exempt," snapped Toner, thrusting the authority that allowed Harry to sail as a privateer back into his hands.

Harry pointed to Pender, standing in the bows beside the very first man lined up along the deck for inspection. "My servant has them. He will read them off to you."

Toner glared at him for a full ten seconds, then spun on his heel and walked noisily across the deck. He had a stride that relied on a great quantity of heel, which, thudding off the spotless planking, only added to his angry comportment. He snatched the papers out of Pender's hands just as Harry's servant read out the first name.

"Benjamin Flowers of—"

"Forgeries!" barked Toner, waving the list furiously. He turned to shout up the deck at Harry. "Do you expect me to faw for such crude stuff as this, laddie?"

"If you look at the bottom of the list, sir, you will observe the name of a fellow countryman of yours. You may have heard of him, for it is the signature of Henry Dundas."

"Do you rate me gleckit, sir?"

It was James who replied to that, the words clipped, precise, and potent.

"If you would care to translate that Celtic barbarism into plain English, sir, we will provide you with an answer. But if the word, as I suspect, refers to a want of intelligence, then I fear the answer may displease you."

Toner, without thinking, had opened his mouth to explain. James's well-aimed riposte snapped it shut again. But in turning to face the younger Ludlow he'd seen what Harry had observed moments before. The approaching squall.

"Forgeries, sir. I stake ma name on it." The voice rose to a shout and he called to the spotty midshipman. "Hemmings, caw the boats alongside. Marines, every second man's a volunteer."

"Belay!" yelled Harry, in such a commanding tone that the redcoats hesitated. "You do not have the right."

"Don't I, man? I'm short o' hands to fight a war. And here you have all these skulking scullies hiding behind this." The list was raised in the air, then Toner took it in both his hands and ripped it in half. "Well, that's how I rate yer damned exemptions, sir. They dinna any longer exist."

For all the marines had hesitated at Harry's command, they had lowered their muskets, threatening every man aboard. To fight them, unarmed, would be folly. They could claim duty as an excuse if they caused any casualties. But any injury to a serving man at sea could result in a criminal charge that would be decided in an

Admiralty court. Harry had no faith that justice would issue from such a source. Toner noticed the hesitation. His hand, with its thick mat of black hair, shot out, taking Pender unawares. He had him by the jacket and had thrown him across the deck before anyone could intervene.

"We can start with this one."

Harry might have counselled caution but he was not immune to sudden fits of temper. Renowned for the care he took with his crew, he couldn't stand by to watch a man he considered a friend so roughly manhandled. Reacting with instinct rather than reason, he ran down the deck, grabbing a marlinspike as he went. It was raised in the air as he careered towards Toner. The naval officer stood his ground, letting his boat-cloak fall open to reveal his pistol. Harry might be furious, but thankfully, he wasn't completely out of control. To strike an armed man at such close quarters would be madness. He stopped in front of the captain. Toner pushed the pistol forward into his stomach. The words, coming out through the clenched teeth, sounded as though they were being wrenched from his throat.

"Your father was a greedy bugger, just like you. The likes of me could have starved for aw he cared. Nothing would please me more than to air the guts of his son, with the power o' the law on my side."

"That is my own servant. You have no right to a single man aboard this ship, least of all him."

The first spot of rain bounced off Toner's hat as he replied. "He's been pampered, then, just as they aw have. Time they served aboard a proper ship. I'll only press half your men, laddie. The law disna permit me to leave you short-handed. You'll have enough to sail your pretty wee boat back to Deal."

Harry had to shout, for the rain engulfed them both. "I'll see you court-martialled for this!"

Toner shouted back, his bright red tongue spitting saliva.

"Dinna threaten me, Ludlow, or I'll put you ashore on the coast of France, then sink this damned barky as if it were a Frenchie!"

CHAPTER THREE

THE MARINES had fixed bayonets before the rain fell. That, coupled with the speed at which Toner's sailors came aboard from the boats, established, to Harry's way of thinking, that his actions were premeditated. He wanted hands and he was going to take them whatever proof was presented. Harry Ludlow was outnumbered, unarmed, and still very close to those eighteen-pounders. The desire to strike Toner, regardless of the consequences, was unbearable, and it was Pender, back on his feet, an observer of this exchange, who provided the balm that eased his rage.

"Easy, Captain." The west-country burr added to the soothing effect of the words. What followed was delivered as much to Toner as to his own captain. "There's an admiral hard by to sort this out."

Toner looked at him with a stony glance. He saw a small compact man, in oilskins, with lively intelligent eyes. The defiant grin that Pender added was like pouring fuel on an already violent blaze.

"Hemmings!" he shouted.

The midshipman's "Aye aye, sir" was muted by the rain thudding on the deck.

"Take this man's name. Addressing an officer without permission is the charge." Toner pushed past Harry and made for the entry port. "And Hemmings, if anyone offers resistance, or tries to save his fellows, he's to be bound tight. He'll be flogged for insubordination as soon as he's fetched aboard."

"I would challenge you to do that to me, sir!" shouted James, stepping forward to intercept him. "Not even a villain like you, a Celtic oaf, would stoop to pressing a gentleman."

"I wouldna have you, laddie. You're a Ludlow, which is as good as to say useless."

James slapped him hard, with enough force to jerk his head back. The pistol came up under his chin and Toner pulled the trigger. The click of the striking hammer was audible, even in the thunderous downpour.

"Thank your lord God my powder is damp," hissed Toner. "If you ever do such a thing again, I'll take yer heid off wi' ma bare hands."

He was through the gangway before James reopened his eyes, as surprised as anyone to find that he was still alive. Men from the *Bucephalas* were already being hustled into the boats, with the others, including their captain, standing uselessly in the face of the marine bayonets. The rain suddenly eased off again, settling to a steady drizzle. The red-coated lobsters departed last, with one contingent standing off in the cutter, muskets raised to cover the withdrawal of the remainder. As soon as the last man left the ship Harry shouted out: "Stand by to get under way."

"Harry?" snapped James, clearly intent on insisting that they take action.

"Get out of the way, brother. I can't fight Toner, but I can go above his head."

"The admiral?"

"Yes. But we have to get to him before that bastard does. I want our side of the story told first." He shouted out the commands to brace the yards as he took the wheel from Patcham. "If I can't have him up for attempted murder I'll make sure he's beached for the rest of his natural life."

He turned back to Patcham, standing sheepishly by their side. "Get aloft, Patcham. And turn your head this time. I want to find the *Queen Charlotte*. If I miss her, I'm very likely to blame you. In which case you'll wish you'd been pressed into the navy."

It was hard sailing, with only half the normal crew and the wind dead foul. The sudden squalls made the weather freakish, which called for constant attention to the trim of sails. Tack upon tack they bore up for the Brest approaches. The frigates were inshore, to guard the Goulet, but the ships of the line were far out to sea, beating to and fro in all weathers to keep the door locked on French ambitions.

"I just hope that Bridport hasn't retired to Torbay."

James merely nodded. That particular subject had been a running argument throughout the whole sea-going community while they'd last been ashore. The best way to maintain a blockade caused as much debate as the prospect of a regency. Harry inclined to the views of admirals like Jervis and Middleton, who insisted that constant vigilance, which meant a fleet of line-of-battle ships permanently at sea, was the only way to keep the French bottled up in their harbours. Admirals like Bridport, and his predecessor Lord Howe, maintained that such a course put too much pressure on both ships and crews; that it was better to anchor in Torbay or Portsmouth, leaving a screen of frigates to watch the enemy, and await the news of definite French offensive action before weighing to intercept.

The French had duly escaped on several occasions. Despite the overwhelming evidence of a failed policy, Admiral Lord Howe's victory on the First of June, lately termed "Glorious," had stilled any criticism. No one wanted to point out to the old man, or the delirious nation, that in fighting the French fleet he'd failed in his primary task: to stop the American grain convoy from landing its cargo in a country on the edge of famine, which would certainly have brought France to her knees, ended the Revolution, and possibly decided the war.

"What was Toner's ship doing so close inshore?" asked James, interrupting Harry's train of thought. "Surely he should have been out at sea with the rest of the frigates."

The remark certainly struck a chord with his brother. Harry looked at him strangely, clearly troubled by the same thought. But any deliberations he might make on that score were interrupted by the cry from the mast-head.

"Two sail fine on the starboard bow."

"James, if those are our ships, we daren't risk being called on to explain ourselves. Break out an Admiralty flag."

"Have we got one, Harry?"

For the first time in hours Harry smiled. He'd paid good money for the means he now intended to employ, buying a copy of the private signal book from a penniless midshipman in a Deal tavern. The flags he carried as a matter of course. The Admiralty signal was designed to speed a vessel's journey, and it forbade any naval ship, even a flagship, to impede her progress.

"It pays to be prepared, brother. There's also a flag to say that we are carrying despatches, the private signal is listed in the day book, and we can send aloft a ship's number. All of it strictly outside the law, but it could be enough to get us past those frigates."

"How do you know what those sail are? They could be merchantmen."

"Humour me, James."

"Two frigates, Captain. I think they're *Pallas* and *Naiad*."

"Jump to it, James. If we can get those signals aloft they won't dare try and stop us."

James called to a pair of sailors and rushed for the flag-locker. Within minutes he'd read from the signal book and had the flags bent on. They hauled them aloft and then tugged at the halyards, sending the tightly bunched cloth streaming out to windward. The frigates had altered course to intercept, and having the weather-gage they closed quickly.

There was just a chance they wouldn't be fooled, and insist on coming alongside to investigate. Yet everything was in order. The private signal, supposedly a secret from the enemy, which was designed to foil French attempts at deception, was the correct coded message for the day; but having been at sea for three months, he had no idea if it had been changed. He watched carefully as the warships came closer. Suddenly a whole host of flags broke out at the mast-head, acknowledging the private signal and wishing him godspeed.

"James. Let's push our luck. Hoist a query. Ask them if they have the position of the *Queen Charlotte*."

"That's going to be a long message."

"Try 'flag,' then."

The frigates, who'd borne away to resume their cruising, obliged in the most handsome manner. But James drew the line when Harry suggested they inform the pair that the *Endymion* had been taken by the French and should be intercepted and engaged. "If you can think of no other reason, Harry, just remember that our men, including Pender, are aboard."

Having taken possession of the French ship, Toner put a prize crew aboard then went himself to examine the ship and its cargo, leaving Harry's men until this task was complete. While they awaited his return the ship's surgeon examined them, looking in their mouths for signs of scurvy and enquiring closely to find out if they were poxed. Judging by the sullen, dispirited look of the Endymions, his standards didn't run very high.

There were clear signs of undernourishment in quite a few of the hands. Any curiosity they had about these new arrivals manifested itself in a dull-eyed indifference. They'd taken a prize, which would mean money for the whole crew, yet they showed little sign of being pleased. But the most telling aspect of their behaviour was that so few, in contrast to Harry Ludlow's men, carried themselves like proper sailors.

Pender, standing by the rail, had watched Harry depart with a heavy heart. They'd barely been out of each other's sight for the last two and a half years. Now he was left behind, while the *Bucephalas* headed for the nearest superior officer. Being a realist, he had few illusions about his situation: he'd known men pressed into the fleet who'd not set foot on English soil again for ten years, going halfway round the world in the process. He shook himself out of his pessimistic torpor and turned to walk amongst the men, doing his best to raise their spirits, assuming quite naturally the leadership he'd exercised aboard the *Bucephalas*.

This behaviour didn't go unobserved by the *Endymion*'s officers, and one took pains to inform the captain on his return, making no attempt to disguise the object of his interest when he did so. This was underlined when Toner took station by the mizzenmast to read these new hands the Articles of War. There was little doubt that the captain had marked him out as a natural leader. As he read from the book, he seemed to direct his words almost entirely towards Pender.

The Articles of War covered every conceivable sort of behaviour at sea, and applied to officers as much as to the men. The list of offences was as daunting as the punishments that could be inflicted, since these, short of an actual death sentence, were entirely at the personal discretion of the captain. A formal execution required a proper court martial, with an array of officers combining to make the decision, but all the hands who listened to Toner knew one fact: there were more ways to kill a man than by hanging him from the yard-arm. Constant bullying could reduce even strong men to physical wrecks. An officer could select any member of the crew he wanted for a dangerous task. Or the sailor, at the mercy of an all-powerful authority, could die at the grating, if the captain was minded to flog him enough. No superior, in the Admiralty or aboard a flagship, would question an entry in the ship's log which read "expired while in receipt of punishment."

The few words the newly pressed men had exchanged with the Endymions had been enough to let them know that Toner was a tyrant, a man who used flogging for even the most trivial misdemeanour. They weren't slow to tell them of the first flogging they'd seen, of a poor wretch fresh from gaol who had little blood or spirit to spare, and had died before they lost sight of England.

Toner's officers, both warrant and commissioned, who would be hand picked by their superior, looked and acted as though they shared his tastes. The *Endymion* was still hove to, with the hands tidying up the decks under their watchful eyes. The guns were run in now and the decks were being cleared after a successful action. But even so the rope's end was never still, laying into bare shoulders right and left. Men were started aboard this ship, it seemed, even when they were doing their work efficiently.

The hands might glare at their tormentors, once their back was turned, but there was no redress for this. Captain John Toner set the standards of discipline. He was, in the time-honoured phrase, a god on his own quarterdeck; a god with a deep voice and a dark, choleric appearance. His word was law and he uttered the law through clenched teeth. He even gnashed them as he read out the Articles of War, giving his deep voice an extra element of terror.

He warned against everything from insolence, through mutiny, bestiality, and sodomy, to murder, each one bringing down upon the offender the prospect of death. Finally he reached the closing sentence.

"And whosoever shall contravene these articles, set down by the Lords Commissioner of the Admiralty, whatever his station, will answer at their peril."

There was a moment of silence when he finished. He cast his black eyes around the assembly, as if he needed to exchange visual contact with each pressed man. Before him stood a group of individuals bred to the sea, nearly all of whom had served aboard a king's ship at some time in their lives. These men returned his look with equal curiosity and that didn't please him. He was a man who was used to a bowed head and no eye contact from his inferiors.

"You've had an easy life," he growled. "Shirking yer duty. Well, that ends now. You will learn that I will brook no dissent, nor spare a man who fails his work. Nor will I stand to be stared at. So learn this, and learn it well. You will address no officer who hasna spoken to you. And aboard this ship a bold look, one that even hints at a challenge to authority, counts as insolence."

Then Toner looked round the men again. One by one they dropped their eyes, for he seemed ready to flog them to gain a quick ascendancy. The last person he glared at was Pender. It went against the grain of his character to succumb, but he did so. He'd attracted enough unwelcome attention already, with what had happened aboard *Bucephalas* and here on this deck. There were more ways to undermine a captain's authority than by providing him with a willing victim. Pender surmised, from the atmosphere that pervaded the *Endymion,* as well as the way Toner had marked him out, that he'd be lucky to escape the lash if he was confined in this ship for as much as a week.

"We have done well the day. That barky carried enough sugar to sweeten London's tooth. There will be gelt for you when you return home." The heads stayed down, so that Toner was denied the smiles of gratitude that he expected. But his next words sent a shudder through their ranks. "Some men behaved discreditably though, what wi' the sail drill, the gunnery, and in handlin' o' the boats."

Toner paused for several seconds, savouring the terror caused by expectation. "But I'll no' spoil the mood. Let us rejoice in having taken a prize, and put away punishments that can be laid at the door of an over-eager crew."

This statement was followed by another long pause.

"Mr Dunlop!" Toner shouted, his hand sweeping over Harry's men. "You will assign these men to their watches, which by their appearance should be in the tops. Stand doon the present topmen's watch and we shall ha' a wee look at how the scullies perform. And, Mr Dunlop, you will introduce them to the manner in which I expect them to perform. Stand by to increase sail."

The first lieutenant barked out a series of commands. Harry's men were ordered aloft, their backs lashed with the ropes' ends he and his underlings carried in their hands. The *Endymion* had been hove to in the rocky bay, held steady by the topsails and the rudder. Down below men were ready on the maincourse braces and the frigate started to move as soon as they brought them round to take the wind. Once they'd set the courses they were ordered to proceed still higher, to loose the topgallants. Pender and his men clawed their way up the shrouds, then fanned out from the masts along the narrow footropes, leaning over the yards. Clews were loosed on command and the king's ship, which had started to claw its way out to sea, picked up speed, heeling over under the press of the wind. Looking down, all the men could see beneath their bare feet was the grey, heaving water. But it wasn't that which upset them. It was when they lifted their eyes to the horizon, to the sight of the *Bucephalas,* visible in the far distance, tacking into the wind on its mission to rescue them from what looked like a floating hell.

Harry's men were allowed no rest until the watch changed. Then they were hustled below. Over the next hour the men were split into their various divisions, with a lieutenant in charge of each. Pender tried to keep them together, but either because they were acting from orders, or because they apprehended the dangers, the *Endymion*'s officers went out of their way to split them up, scattering them amongst the existing messes. Hammocks were provided, along with their numbered space. Here they would sleep in a space fourteen inches wide marked on the deck head. The working of the ship doubled this, with one watch always on deck, but even in twenty-eight inches, you couldn't sleep without coming into contact with your neighbour.

"Welcome to Hades Hall," growled a voice in the hammock next to Pender.

He looked to find the source. He saw a large man with a dark, saturnine complexion, leaning half in, half out of his hammock, a mocking smile playing about his thick red lips. In his hand he had a couple of dice which he was rolling in a slow continuous motion. Pender was too shrewd to open his mouth to a perfect stranger. You could never tell, aboard a new ship, who was on your side. He merely grunted in reply.

"I hear you was exempt, an' all?"

"Not according to your captain, we weren't."

"He's your captain now, mate. An' I wish you joy of him, for there was never such a bastard in a king's coat."

"You're taking a chance, friend," said Pender. "That's no way to talk to a man you can't be sure of."

That provoked a low chuckle. "It's not hard to be sure of a man aboard the *Endymion*, mate. Abaft the mast they're all bastards, before the mast they're all scarred. There's not a hand below decks who hasn't felt the lash since we came aboard, most of them before we ever raised our anchor."

"Well, you'll forgive me not talking till I've seen that for myself."

"You'll see, all right. You'll see the skin stripped from the back of every man that came aboard, including your own, if'n you've got eyes in the back of your head."

Pender remembered the way that Toner had looked at him with his black, steady gaze. The knowledge that he'd dropped his own eyes stung his pride and made his reply a trifle injudicious.

"We don't plan to be aboard that long."

The thick lips parted in a disbelieving grin. "I heard that from one of your mates. Said your captain had gone to see the admiral off Brest, so's to get you all sent back again."

There was little point in denying it, if someone had already opened their mouth. "That's right!"

"Fat lot of good that'll do you, mate. He's not under Bridport's orders."

"Makes no odds," said Pender. "If the admiral tells him to do it, he'll have to obey."

The man pushed himself up a bit higher with one elbow, to look the recumbent Pender in the eye. "Only one problem, friend. He ain't ever going to see Admiral Lord sodding Bridport again. We passed the blockading squadron two days ago, exchanging salutes an' the like. We even asked them for hands and were told to try coming inshore for a few Frenchmen. That's what we were doing when we came across you an' that prize."

There was a long pause while his neighbour waited for him to ask the obvious question. But Pender declined to do so, not even turning his head to look.

"You're a tight-lipped sod, an' no error. Don't you want to know where we're headed?"

"If you want to tell me, you will."

"We're off to the Caribbee, mate. Your captain can moan all

he wants. But unless he's got wings to fly, he's seen the last of you lot till the peace. Like as not you'll die aboard. If you're lucky Johnny Crapaud might get you with a musket ball or round shot. But you'll likely expire from Toner's cat o' nine tails. That is, if the yellow jack don't get you first. There's a rate of deadly air in them West Indian islands."

CHAPTER FOUR

WITH THE tropical sun shining in the clear blue sky, the captain of the *Ariadne* did nothing to make the other vessel suspicious, nor attempt any friendly gesture, even though they both flew the Stars and Stripes of the young American Republic. Instead of bearing down to intercept, he edged his ship away slightly, displaying a caution that any captain sailing the Caribbean would find natural. The gaff-rigged Yankee ketch, now hull up, did likewise. It was a very long time, some hundred years, since the buccaneers had ruled these waters. But the Caribbean was still dangerous, with the competing interests of France, Spain, and Great Britain to contend with. Each nation took great trouble to ensure that their colonists would be supplied from the mother country, so that the wealth of the West Indies, used in payment for these essentials, flowed back to their native coffers.

No one assumed another ship to be a friend unless absolutely certain of their identity. The ketch would, as a precaution, load her swivel guns. The crew would be issued with weapons until their captain considered himself out of danger. Stroking the head of his pet, which was precariously balanced on the rim of the steering wheel, de la Mery ran his eye over the ship to ensure that all was in order. As he looked forward towards the bowsprit of his schooner the Frenchman imagined what his quarry would see. A few men on the slightly untidy deck, seemingly intent on repairing sails and tidying the falls. They would observe that his schooner mounted small cannon in both the bows and the stern. But they were bowsed tight against the side, with no appearance of being loaded, seemingly harmless.

What they would not see was the canvas-covered gunports with gun crews crouched under the bulwarks on either side; nor the crowded companion-ways, full of armed men. These hidden attackers, Frenchmen like himself, were in a high state of excitement. Each brandished a favoured weapon, either cutlass, axe, or boarding pike. They were whispering to each other, gesturing and rehearsing for the coming action. Still well out of earshot, he called to them, reminding them for the hundredth time that their aim was a swift attack followed by a quick surrender. He wanted to take the ship and its cargo, not human life.

But he worried that, offered any real resistance, his men would not obey such an injunction. The things that had happened to them in the last three years had brutalized them long before they'd been presented with this opportunity to indulge in seaborne larceny. Changed them to the point where spilling blood meant little or nothing. They'd seen their world collapse twice. First St Domingue, torn apart by slave revolt. In the process of fighting the blacks and mulattos they'd witnessed atrocities and seen sights of such carnage that they beggared description. In turn, their own humanity had evaporated, along with their hopes. In retaliation they'd committed acts of such callous cruelty that their souls were doubtless scarred for all eternity.

Most were *engagés,* bondsmen who'd come out to the West Indies on three-year contracts, peasant farmers, fishermen, or small tradesmen who'd been ruined by the depression that preceded the Revolution. What irony that the same event had fired the slaves to seek their freedom. Alone they would not have succeeded. But there were others on St Domingue who thought themselves dispossessed. The mulattos, descendants of the numerous liaisons between owners, overseers, and their female slaves. They too had taken up arms against the settlers. The colonists had laughed at their rag-tag army, led by an ex-coachman called Toussaint l'Ouverture. How could any force consisting of slaves and half-breeds overthrow Europeans? But, by sheer bravery and weight of numbers, they'd succeeded, throwing the white men off the island. Antoine de la

Mery had also lost everything he possessed: family, home, and plantation, burnt to the ground by his own slaves. Only his pet remained, descended from a dead original, as an echo of that previous life. He had few skills that would earn him his keep, except the fact that he'd once served as an officer in the French navy.

Circumstances on St Domingue made him a soldier. He gathered a group of settlers together to fight for control of the colony. No help had come from France, itself caught up in the turmoil of the Revolution. Slowly, inexorably, the insurgents had prevailed. Commandeering a ship from the harbour at Port-au-Prince, he'd got away with the last of his men just before the final collapse. They sailed for Guadeloupe, taking service with the Royalist settlers, men who'd assisted the British to wrest control of the island from the representatives of Revolutionary Paris. Yet even that success had turned sour. He'd watched from the deck of a British man-o'-war as those they'd fought alongside were butchered, their deaths a combination of British military stupidity and a barbarity as fierce as anything they'd witnessed in St Domingue.

To lose everything once makes a man angry. But to lose twice can destroy his beliefs, breaking the ties that bind him to both his humanity and his religion. His *engagés* had lost twice, and would have starved if the British had not provided for them. But charity leaves a bitter taste and, quietly informed of his intentions, they'd flocked to rejoin him, hoping they'd been given the chance to make something of themselves again. Now, after three months, they had their ship, a secure base from which to operate, and last but not least another quarry in sight.

Handing over the wheel, he picked up the mongoose and headed for his private quarters. Once inside his pet was confined to a small basketweave cage, which de la Mery placed in the quarter-gallery, one of the two smaller cabins that abutted the main accommodation. A glance along the inner wall reassured him that all the glass-fronted cases were securely closed. A brass-bound chest took up the whole of one end of the room, secured by a stout padlock. The sound of biting and scratching, as the animal tried to escape from its cage, brought a smile to his lips as he went back to the main cabin. But that evaporated as he turned to pick up the black coat that formed part of this deception. Underneath, looped across the back of the chair, the tricolour sash that would adorn his waist seemed to mock him—that and the tall black hat with the red, white, and blue cockade. He put the coat on, stuffed the sash into the hat, and returned to the deck, placing that part of his disguise under the binnacle. Taking the wheel again, he looked forward over the bowsprit.

Beating up towards the American left all the options to the other helmsman. But the captain of the *Ariadne* knew they would come on, just as he knew their name, destination, and cargo. The whole intelligence network of the British navy, set up over many years, had combined to put him in exactly the right place to inter-cept these vessels. If his target proved over-cautious and chose to run, it would make little difference to the eventual outcome. In a stern chase his schooner could outsail any gaff-rigged ketch. But since that would entail a battle, he'd do everything he could to avoid such an eventuality. In any fight he could suffer damage and perhaps casualties from gunfire, however light; it also made board-ing perilous since he would be opposed by men prepared to fight. Partly it was because he cherished his crew. They'd been through a great deal together in these last two and a half years. Death or injury was a risk they all ran, but more importantly, diminished numbers would make it harder for him to achieve the required level of success. He had similar information about other merchant ships, and needed a full complement to man his captures. Each cruise had to be a success or there would be no others. Nothing would annoy his partner and benefactor more than an early return to port and an opportunity for plunder missed.

Whoever was in the tops had obviously informed the deck that the *Ariadne* posed no danger, and the ketch swung back on to its original course. De la Mery did likewise. The hands who'd been working on the deck now lined the side, waving occasionally to their opposite numbers. The two ships closed the gap between them, with the schooner beating up into the steady Trade wind while his quarry sailed easy. The point arrived when they were set to pass by within hailing distance. A gesture ensured that the men below were silent. Then de la Mery indicated to another sailor in the bows. This fellow, a Quebeçois who spoke excellent English, raised a speaking trumpet to his lips.

"Ahoy, *Brandon!*" he shouted. "What news from New Bedford?"

The voice of the man who responded from *Brandon,* likewise using a trumpet, floated across the water.

"Who are you?"

"Is that Abel Rolfe who's a-hollering?"

"It sure is."

"Are you saying you don't know who I am?"

"Can't say as I do, friend."

"Well, put your helm down, man, and take a closer look."

The effect of these words was all that they could have hoped. Not only did the *Brandon* edge closer, but Rolfe eased his braces to take some of the way off her. The Frenchman waited for the appropriate moment, then spun his wheel. Simultaneously, the men on deck came alive, hauling round on the yards. Now the *Ariadne* was heading straight for the *Brandon*'s side. The canvas screens dropped away as the gunports flew open, showing a row of cannon ready to fire. The man with the speaking trumpet called out once more.

"Heave to, *Brandon,* or we'll favour you with a dose of some grapeshot."

Abel Rolfe, yelling at the top of his voice, tried to escape. His men rushed to bowse his yards tight as their captain eased his rudder to take full advantage of the wind. The six-pounders on the *Ariadne* spoke out together. Not that their fire did much damage, but the grape sweeping high across the deck stopped the Brandons from completing their tasks. *Ariadne* swung broadside on, with the captain at the helm calling to the men below to come on deck. The two ships crunched together as his boarders rushed to the side. They were leaping the gap on to the *Brandon*'s deck before the Americans had time to recover. Ropes flashed out and the two vessels were soon lashed tight, swinging round with both sets of sails flapping uselessly.

Rolfe made the mistake of trying to fight, even though most of his crew had wisely backed away from this sudden, over-whelming assault. But he was up against ten men and soon succumbed to the numerous blows. Antoine de la Mery yelled at them to desist, as he struggled to fasten the tricolour sash around his waist. But fired by a blood-lust too long ignored they paid no heed to his commands. Jamming the black hat on his head he ran for the bulwarks. His men didn't stop as Rolfe fell to the deck, continuing to hack at his defenceless body. Axes and cutlasses swung relentlessly. The sound of metal crushing bone, the squelch of blood as the attackers slipped in his visceral gore, made the others in his crew drop to their knees and beg for mercy.

It took all the power in the Frenchman's voice to stop his men from slaughtering them right away. Frightened, they were herded into the waist. He jumped aboard and stood silently over the remains of their master. He was dead, of course, his eyes staring lifelessly at the blue sky. The captain of the *Ariadne* nearly crossed himself, stopping just in time as he remembered who he was sup-posed to be. But he mouthed a silent prayer, before looking up, his dark eyes sweeping the deck. Everyone aboard watched him, waiting for his response. They couldn't know how such an out-come depressed him. Taking cargo was one thing, cold-blooded murder quite another. It was small compensation that another would take the blame. Two and a half years of warfare had not made him immune to the effect of an unwarranted death. As on previous occasions, every precaution had been taken to avoid such an outcome, but this time he had failed, forcing him to rack his brains to find a solution that would protect both the remainder of the crew and himself.

"Lash the body to the end of a boom."

There was a moment when his men hesitated to comply. But

the eyes flashed angrily and, aware that they'd already disobeyed him, they consented to do his bidding.

"Now haul it up and swing it out over the water."

The ropes creaked as his men hauled them through the blocks. The inert body swung out over the blue sea. Blood dripped into the water, creating a black stain just below his one remaining foot. He jumped on to the side of his ship and called out to the prisoners in his heavily accented English.

"That blood will bring the sharks. Some of them will feed on what they can reach. As long as he bleeds they will stay with your ship. If you try any tricks, my men will throw you over the side. I don't think I need tell you what your fate will be."

The shiver that ran through his audience was all he could have asked for. He couldn't let them go, to tell of what had happened here. There was a British frigate just over the horizon, patrolling the approaches to Martinique, sent to capture exactly the same ships that he intended to intercept. Normally he would sail towards his next rendezvous and then put the crew over the side, setting their boat in a current that would carry them towards land, but away from the frigate. Now, with Rolfe dead, murdered by his *engagés,* he must keep the crew in captivity for a longer period. That would require leaving sufficient men aboard to subdue the prisoners, which in turn made any future action more hazardous. But there was little choice. Once he'd taken the rest of his captures he could rendezvous with the *Brandon* and set a course for Puerto Rico. If he put them ashore there it would be a long time before the Spaniards, notoriously suspicious of intruders, released them. Till then he needed to instil fear in the Brandons to stifle any thoughts they might have about retaking their ketch while they were still at sea. He wouldn't be around to protect them if they did, and he knew what his men would do under such circumstances. They'd butcher everyone aboard. He pulled himself up to his full height, hooking his fingers into the sash that identified him as a full member of the bloodthirsty Revolutionary Convention.

"If you doubt my word, then let me tell you this. My name is Victor Hugues. I am the Governor of Guadeloupe. If you've heard of me, you'll know what to expect."

De la Mery knew he'd made a mistake by the time he'd taken his next prize. While no one died in that encounter, due to his short-age of men, the captain, another American, had also attempted resistance. For that, he'd received a nasty wound to the head which the Frenchman felt obliged to dress, taking him into the quarter-gallery to do so. At least his patient didn't move, his attention entirely taken up with staring at the brass-bound chest that occu-pied one end of the room. That concentration was shattered when his pet mongoose, having gnawed through the bindings on his cage, escaped. Mistaking the American's colourful tassled boots for a snake, it nearly inflicted another wound on the invalid. The creature scampered out of the cabin, making for the rigging, which only added to his frustration. The whole enterprise was behind schedule, and he was obliged to put the crew over the side imme-diately, giving them the position of the British frigate, since the current would not take them anywhere near land.

"I never thought to meet Victor Hugues in the flesh," said the American, coldly.

De la Mery hitched his tricolour sash a little higher. "Only you can decide, Monsieur, if that is an honour or a curse."

"Can't see it being anything more'n a curse when you robbed me of my ship and the cargo."

"The misfortune of war, Captain Caufield. Now please, join the rest of your men in the cutter."

Oliver Poynton, captain of his Britannic Majesty's 28-gun ship *Andromache*, paced the windward side of his quarterdeck. His hands were clasped behind his back, the knuckles showing white as the scowl on his face grew deeper and deeper. He was a small man, with a round, pale face, small brown eyes, and a hooked nose. In his deep blue coat and his snowy-white waistcoat, buttoned tight over an ample stomach, he was apt, in such a pose, to remind those of his crew who'd been whalers of the penguins they'd seen in Antarctica.

The first lieutenant, Bryse, well aware of his captain's mood, approached him formally, standing to attention and removing his hat. "Permission to go about, sir."

Poynton looked at him for several seconds with a vacant stare, as though Bryse didn't exist. Then he glanced towards the island of Martinique, faint in the distance, with the smoke of the volcano of Montagne Pelée rising into the blue sky above the town of St-Pierre. His head swung back as he looked aloft, as if hoping by this mere display of interest that the lookout would sight something in the empty waters around them.

"Is there any point, Bryse, I ask you?" he snapped.

The first lieutenant wisely declined to answer, remaining stiffly at attention, gazing over the top of his captain's head. Poynton fixed his attention forward, on the crew, who were waiting for orders. Normally that was a cause for quiet satisfaction. Despite his losses to the notorious West Indian climate, he commanded a very efficient ship, with a crew that had served together for six years. Commands aboard the *Andromache* were so familiar that they could be issued in a whisper.

Every man knew his station and his job. They took great pride in their sail drill and gunnery. They also knew the ship's course and the task in which they were engaged. Likewise they were as aware as the premier that the time had come to go about on an opposite heading. Without orders the men had taken up their stations, then looked aft, in anticipation of the requisite commands. Their silent stares infuriated Poynton. His anger boiled over, causing him to yell at them to get on with their duties. No one moved, quite simply because no one had to. He spun round and snapped at his first lieutenant.

"Humbugged at every turn, Bryse. What do you have to say to that?"

Such a direct question from his superior demanded that he

reply. He tried a soothing response, even though he knew that it would very likely prove futile. "There could be any number of reasons, sir. Freak weather conditions, for instance."

Poynton was about to blast him when the lookout hailed the deck. "Deck there. Ship's cutter, fine on the larboard bow. Single gaff sail and low in the water."

Poynton's shoulders seemed to slump and his voice was soft enough not to carry past Bryse. "Not again."

The premier cupped his hands and called to the lookout. "How many men aboard?"

The lookout, knowing that his emotion would be shared by everyone on deck, allowed himself to deviate from the strict rules governing the making of reports to officers. The sour, angry note in his voice was a mile away from the mere relating of the facts.

"Just like the others, sir. Overflowing like a free bawdy house!"

"Shape a course to intercept, Mr Bryse," said Poynton, squaring his shoulders again. He turned and looked over the bulwarks, to a sea still empty to an eye at deck level, and slowly extracted a telescope from the rack by his elbow.

The men that came up the ship's side had been in the cutter for a mere four hours, which meant that their ship had been taken just below the horizon, out of sight of the *Andromache*. They were Danish and their vessel, the *Ecklandsal*, had been captured without a fight. The captain, Gunnerstrom, was confused, not only by what had happened, but in the manner of the loss.

"A Dansk flag they fly. My name is to them known as well. They call to me, hello *Ecklandsal*." Then he jabbed his finger into his chest. "Hello, Ole Gunnerstrom too."

Poynton made a polite face, but declined to say anything. He could see no point in letting on that he knew the name of their ship, and this captain, as well. In his cabin he had a list. The *Ecklandsal* was on it, with a description of her tonnage and her cargo, as well as precise instructions relating to her course and illegal destination. This was the fourth time he'd heard such a tale in as

many days. But good manners obliged him to invite Gunnerstrom
to his cabin and offer him a drink, some food, and an ear willing
to suffer his woeful story. The Dane was long-winded and graphic
in his description, both of the ship that had taken the *Ecklandsal*
and of the man who commanded it. Listening to this took a great
deal of patience. Once Poynton had consigned him to the gunroom, Gunnerstrom would find there three other merchant
captains who could relate exactly the same tale.

"For my life I feared a lot, French pigs."

The Dane turned his head to spit on the deck. But he stopped
on seeing the rich carpet that covered the planking in the *Andromache*'s great cabin. Likewise the glass that he held was of the
finest crystal and the furniture that filled the room, as well as the
gilt mirrors on the wall, created the air of a rich man's study rather
than a cabin of a man-o'-war. It was no place to go spitting on
the floor, however angry you were.

Poynton longed to puncture this injured innocence, to tell this
uncouth villain what he knew: that Gunnerstrom, just like the
other three captains sharing the officers' quarters, had been intent
on selling their goods illegally into a British possession. If this
"French pig" hadn't got him, then he himself would have done
so. And then he would have lost not only his cargo, his liberty
would have been forfeit too. He'd have been confined to the cable
tier, instead of enjoying the hospitality and the comforts of the
gunroom.

"Did you by any chance catch the fellow's name?"

"Catch? He introduce himself to me, the swine. Hand me drink
and say he's sorry. Sorry, with that damn it hat and sash."

The Dane stood up, wide eyed with disbelief at the effrontery
of his captor, and essayed an elegant bow. "Victor Hugues, he say.
Heard of me you may. Known I am for my love of blood. How
wise are you not to resist. Me allow to help you, your sea-chest
load in the boat."

"And the ship? Did you get the name of his ship?"

Gunnerstrom shook his head and prepared to resume his seat.

"Stokes!" yelled Poynton. The steward appeared before the Dane was halfway to comfort. "Show Captain Gunnerstrom to the gunroom. Ask Mr Bryse to sort him out a berth, then compliments to the master, he's to report to me."

Poynton might have thought he was smiling at his "guest." But to Gunnerstrom he looked like a man who wanted to bite off someone's head. He uttered a quick thanks and hurried after the steward. The captain of the *Andromache* spun round in his chair and looked out at the wake. Quietly he repeated the name Victor Hugues, and in his mind went through the events of the last week. Five ships he'd been intent on intercepting, all taken like this last one from under his very nose. He had to assume that the first one, an American vessel called *Brandon,* had been taken as well, though he'd had no sight of the crew.

Victor Hugues? He'd given each captain a drink and an apology. Could this really be the same man who'd butchered three hundred men on the beaches of Guadeloupe, who'd set up the guillotine in the main square of Pointe-à-Pitre and continued his bloody work on the civilian population? Hugues had sent expeditions to try and retake both Dominica and Grenada, which had led to much fighting on both islands. There was no doubt he was a genocidal firebrand intent on setting the entire Caribbean alight. But none of that really mattered. It didn't alter the fact that Hugues clearly knew exactly where these ships were from, as well as where they were headed.

"The question is this," he said to himself. "Where, Monsieur Victor Hugues, are you getting information that tallies exactly with what is being given to me?"

The knock on the cabin door made him spin round quickly. The master entered on command and stood to attention before his captain. Poynton looked at the top of his desk, at the list which contained the names of another four vessels. Then he picked up his quill pen and with an angry flourish scored out the last of them, *Eckslandsal.* At the top the only name without a line through it seemed to mock him. *Brandon!*

"Shape me a course for English Harbour."

As the master went out, his steward came back in. "There's another one of them there captains seeking a word, sir."

"Which one?"

"Caufield, your honour. One of the Jonathans."

Poynton sighed. "Very well, show him in."

The American came through the door just as the first of the commands rang out on deck. A well-built individual with a scarred face, he wore a bandage over one ear, the result of a wound he'd received when he lost his ship. Caufield paused for a moment, crouched in the low doorway, his ear cocked to hear the orders, then turned to look at Poynton.

"Sounds like we're setting a brand-new course?"

"You wish to see me?" asked Poynton. Caufield just smiled and closed the door, cutting off the sound. He moved towards the desk and sat down without being asked. "Well?"

"It seems to me a mite lucky, Captain Poynton, that you have sat in the path of so many distressed sailors, and that in so short a space of time."

"Does it indeed?"

"It do. And I was wondering whether you was waiting for something."

"You may wonder all you wish, sir."

"The man who took my ship."

"Victor Hugues," interrupted Poynton.

Caufield looked away then. He fingered the bandage over his ear and his voice was low when he replied. "As you say, Victor Hugues." His eyes lifted to look at Poynton again. "He was sharp an' no mistake, Monsieur Hugues. Must be upsetting to you and the British navy to have so many ships taken from under your noses by a man like that."

"He was lucky," said Poynton.

"He was that. And if he hadn't been so lucky we might have sailed right on till we met the good ship *Andromache*."

Poynton's eyes narrowed. "You might."

"We would have been safe then, sir, right under the guns of King George's navy."

Poynton coughed loudly. Caufield leant forward, his elbows on the desk. "We captains have been a-talking. And it seems to us that you're just a mite upset. We was wondering if we had in some way offended you, or deflected you from your duty?"

It was Caufield's attitude that cracked Poynton's demeanour, especially the way he was leaning on his desk, like a man addressing a social inferior. "Let us say that I'm not fooled by your inventions. Every one of you pleads the innocent. Rest assured that if I'd met you, there would have been little doubt—"

Poynton stopped suddenly, not wishing to state openly that he knew they were illegals. To do so would only expose him to explanations, followed by further protestations of innocence. Caufield seemed somewhat abashed, because he'd dropped his eyes till they were staring at the desk. Then he stood up abruptly, bending over to avoid hitting his already damaged head on the deck-beams. When he spoke again he had a grave expression on his scarred face.

"Forgive me, Captain Poynton. I came here to thank you, not to annoy you."

"You have already done that, sir, several times. I had assumed you came to request something."

Caufield turned at the open door, through which the sounds of the ship carried once more. "I came to ask when we were heading for home. I guess what I'm hearing is the first part of my answer."

He was gone before Poynton could ask him how he knew they were heading for English Harbour. A mere change of course was hardly sufficient. Perhaps he'd bespoken the master as they passed in the corridor. The captain's eyes dropped once more to the list of ships on his desk. He grabbed the paper, scrunched it into a ball, spun round, then threw it out of the open stern window into the wake.

CHAPTER FIVE

ADMIRAL Bessborough fingered the knife that lay on his desk, his face creased with displeasure as he listened to Poynton's lengthy report. The coffee poured by his manservant Cram lay untouched by his side. He was a handsome man, despite his years, who'd been termed "Beau Bessborough" in his youth. The Gainsborough portrait in his drawing-room showed him to full advantage. Tall and imposing, with a smooth rounded face topped by a noble forehead, he had a strong nose and deep green eyes under an impressive pair of bushy eyebrows. The waist and the jowls had thickened somewhat since he'd sat for that painting and the air of confidence achieved with the brush had not carried over with age. He was vaguely aware that his officers didn't respect him, without being conscious of the reasons: that his preferred method of command alternated quixotically between flattery and bluster. And, especially since the loss of the island of Guadeloupe, he seemed to have let slip control of events.

His greatest fear was that another island would fall to the French. They'd already tried to retake Dominica, committing their usual barbarities in pursuit of their aims. That threat looked to have been contained, though all the military forces at his disposal were tied down on that island. That left all the other British possessions in the Caribbean exposed, a danger that could only be met by constant patrolling carried out with the limited means at his disposal. On top of that, he had a responsibility to stop illegal trade. This was a matter on which his second in command, Captain Vandegut, had pronounced views, which he freely and openly discussed with everyone but his commander. At this very moment Bessborough's noble brow was furrowed and his eyes were troubled. Finally, as Captain Poynton paused for breath, he interrupted, his manner abrupt and his voice harsh.

"What you're saying, sir, is this. That you have returned empty handed. That you have miserably failed by allowing yourself to be humbugged by some filibuster, who merely had to take station upwind of you to capture all the ships you were set to intercept."

Poynton flushed angrily. He was not accustomed to polite behaviour from his seniors, least of all Bessborough. But the man should have taken some cognizance of the other people present. Vandegut, the captain-of-the-fleet, might be a two-faced nuisance, but he was at least a contemporary. And since he and the admiral rarely saw eye to eye, it was a fair bet that he'd support him. Then there was Cram, a mere serving man, though many a ship's captain had been given cause to wonder if that appellation was appropriate. He had come into the household with Lady Bessborough, having served in a stratum of society that made his present appointment seem, to him, a demotion. If anything, when it came to naval officers he surpassed that lady in the depth of his condescension, which was no mean feat. But Poynton could console himself that he was a retainer, and therefore, regardless of his pretensions, of little account.

Dillon was Bessborough's political assistant; his presence offended him. The Irishman had his eyes on the floor between his feet, fixed there the entire time Poynton had been in the room. The animosity between the pair was well known. They'd rubbed each other the wrong way from their very first encounter, long before their present commander had arrived from England, and each subsequent meeting only made matters worse. There was no cause other than mutual antipathy. But the real problem for a man as proud as Poynton was that Caddick, the admiral's nephew, was in the room, ostensibly there to take notes. He was still in his formative years, and the boy had passed for lieutenant so early in life entirely because of his uncle's influence: the captains who examined Caddick saw Vice-Admiral Bessborough as their patron, and were more interested in pleasing him than in assiduously examining the boy. He was close to being the most junior commissioned officer on the station, yet he'd been given command of the brig *Percival*. This act was, in itself, scandalous enough and caused the usual moans from those who saw themselves as more deserving of promotion, officers who'd been at sea twice as long as this upstart. But they knew they could do little in the face of such potent interest. They consoled themselves with the fact that Bessborough had arrived in the Lesser Antilles with only one relation, instead of the customary half-dozen. Other officers of more senior rank, on observing that the *Percival* was kept safe in harbour under the admiral's avuncular eye, were less ready to indulge him. They wondered, sometimes aloud, why the brig and its commander were not, like them, almost permanently at sea.

Dillon, despite his dislike of Poynton, spoke out, seeking to calm things by introducing a positive note. If it was intended to aid the captain of *Andromache* it failed. All Poynton saw was an attempt to mollify his commanding officer, rather than him.

"We have acquired some hands, sir," he said. "And that is very necessary in this climate. Certainly equal to the interception of illegal cargoes."

Bessborough made no attempt to modify his angry tone as he rounded on his political assistant. "Nonsense, Dillon. What's fifty or sixty sailors compared to what those ships were about?"

The Irishman coughed gently and rubbed his hand across his thinning ginger hair, wondering if the admiral was referring to their activities or their value. Given the manifold tasks that fell to the Leeward Islands squadron, it was remarkable, if not uncommon, that the *Andromache* should be so engaged. It was an activity layered with excuses, not the least of which was the need to protect British vessels trading between the islands. But no warship so occupied set sail without a list of illegals, ships of other nations trading into King George's possessions in defiance of the Navigation Acts. This provided nearly everyone on the station with that most welcome alternative to dreary blockade duty: the taking of prizes for profit.

Despite the recent drought in captures, Poynton had badgered

Bessborough for the right to cruise independently, a privilege that the admiral normally reserved for his client officers. In a navy where advancement was dependent on interest, to be attached to a successful senior officer was paramount. This man had no need to win battles. The sole requirement was that he be gainfully employed, and therefore be in a position to pass such a gift on to those who'd supported him in the past. In turn, they could expect that anything going in the way of profit or glory would come to them. But this put a heavy responsibility on the commander, especially in a world where every officer, of any rank, felt he had a God-given right to inform the Admiralty of his feelings. Letters from disgruntled captains with no connection to the admiral could generally be discounted. But if he couldn't keep his clients happy, the rumblings of their discontent could do much harm.

Normally reliable in such areas, Bessborough had swung round on to the opposite tack, partly to offset the failure at Guadeloupe, and he'd given Poynton the opportunity to stifle accusations of blatant favouritism. That the man before him fell outside that category had something to do with his manner, but more to do with the fact that he'd been on the station when Bessborough arrived. He had, under Admiral Sir John Jervis, helped capture Martinique, St Lucia, and Guadeloupe. He was also tactless enough to refer, often, to the qualities of his late commander as well as those successful forays. If anything was designed to ruin Bessborough's day it was the slightest mention of his predecessor, coupled with the name of the last of those islands.

Furious despatches continued to flow back and forth between the Admiralty and Antigua, with those Bessborough received showing scant appreciation of the difficulties he laboured under. Everyone in London, down to the meanest, crab-handed clerk in the Admiralty Office, knew that ships on this station had too many tasks to perform, just as they knew that a French fleet could arrive in the West Indies before the commander on the spot even knew they'd sailed. But the loss of Guadeloupe had happened in his bailiwick, so Bessborough had to deflect the criticism heaped on

officers seen to have failed in their duty. His attempts to shift some
of the blame to Lord Howe had foundered on the Glorious First
of June. It was useless to point out that Victor Hugues had sailed
in April, while the noble Howe had been sitting comfortably at
anchor in Torbay. The Channel Fleet had been at sea when it really
mattered. Trouncing Villaret-Joyeuse had made "Black Dick"
Howe the hero of the nation. Any criticism levelled at him not
only fell on deaf ears, but seriously compromised the complainant.
On receiving news of the battle, and well aware of the damning
statements his despatches contained, Bessborough had feared that
he might be relieved. It was a situation which unsettled his supporters and encouraged those disinclined to show respect.
Vandegut was one who'd exploited it to the full, taking advantage
of his commander's uncertainty to inflate his own importance.

"While I don't entirely agree with Admiral Bessborough, Poynton, I'm forced to concede that you have performed in a manner
somewhat less than satisfactory. A few sailors to man our ships
hardly constitutes a return on such a heavy investment in time and
trouble, given the other difficulties we face on the station. Thank
God this fellow took none of our own ships, for if he had, we'd
all be called to account."

Bessborough glared at him, before transferring the look to his
nephew, busily scribbling away. He wasn't alone in his discomfort. The captain of the *Andromache,* who'd expected support,
knew he'd just become another pawn in Vandegut's game. The
second-in-command had already had his way in the matter of the
time the squadron's frigates spent in harbour, maintaining that the
crews suffered less risk of disease at sea. Forced to agree, Bessborough had none the less insisted on keeping Vandegut's own
ship, *Redoubtable,* tied up in Antigua. Thus he spoiled the true
aim of its captain, which was to get his own ship away from any
control, leaving him free to do as he pleased. Being the commander of a 74-gun ship, on a station where independent cruising
was confined mainly to frigates, clearly frustrated him. Many
concluded that this fact provided the main reason for his latest

campaign, which opposed the whole concept. His next remark certainly reinforced that impression.

"The loss of the prize money must have come as a grievous blow."

Irony not being his natural forte, this attempt fell flat, leaving him sounding piqued. Poynton ignored the implications of the remark, concentrating instead on the way Bessborough had insulted him, while at the same time ensuring that his remarks were addressed to the Irishman.

"As for my being humbugged, that is a matter of opinion. It seems to me something more than that when every ship was clearly identified by name."

Dillon responded sharply, well aware that the criticism was being levelled at him. "I need hardly remind you, Captain Poynton, that the Caribbean is not our private preserve. If we can come by information, so can others."

"You're right, Dillon! Any fool can with little effort discover where the illegals are going." Dillon's pale cheek took on the merest touch of pink, evidence of a discomfort that clearly pleased him enormously. "In fact, it may interest you to know the name of this corsair. He indeed has done that very thing."

Poynton's face took on a sour expression. He was still smarting from Dillon's earlier observation about acquiring hands, which he saw as condescension, while harbouring deep resentment against Vandegut. But his true aim was to pay the admiral back, both for his words and for the way he'd undermined him by allowing his nephew to be present. Vandegut, square of face, with blond, near white hair, looked at him keenly, as if sensing he was about to upset Bessborough.

"The schooner hailed, apparently, from Guadeloupe, sir. But the truly interesting part is this: that it was, according to those masters I rescued, under the command of one Victor Hugues!"

Even Cram stiffened at that name. Caddick's pen shot off the edge of the paper in his lap. Bessborough abruptly stopped fidgeting with his knife. He fixed the captain with a stare so malignant that he recoiled slightly. Vandegut, off to the left, had entered on the first trace of a smile. But the same look, transferred to him, wiped the temptation to gloat from his mind. The cold eyes swung back to Poynton.

"What did you say?"

"You may interview them yourself, sir. They will, to a man, inform you that the fellow who captured them wore all the regalia of his despicable murderous Jacobin tribe. They see themselves as lucky to have survived and are of the opinion that only their neutrality saved their lives."

A moment's silence followed that last remark. Poynton was unaware of the latest intelligence: under economic pressure the nature of Hugues's rule had changed. The guillotine, first used to decapitate French settlers, was now employed as a weapon of terror against the slaves. Having freed them initially, an act that helped him take the island, he'd swung right round to the opposite tack. Any protection they'd enjoyed under Bourbon rule was rescinded. Their masters were back in control of their lives with a vengeance, encouraged by the governor to repair the damage his previous acts had caused. The first priority was the production of a decent sugar crop, without which Guadeloupe could not survive.

"You're sure it was him?" asked Vandegut, cautiously.

"I am indeed, the fellow actually introduced himself. I think perhaps he wanted us to know."

Dillon looked up, opening his mouth to ask a question, but the admiral's furious bellow silenced him.

"Hugues!"

The satisfaction was only apparent in Poynton's eye. The rest of his countenance remained rigidly disapproving. "Yes, sir. It seems that the Jacobin has foresaken not only his governorship but his guillotine in favour of piracy."

"D'ye hear that, Dillon?" Bessborough shouted, throwing a newspaper across the desk at him. It caught the edge of his cup and sent his coffee all over the desk. "And on the day that I hear

Trethgowan has been cleared of any misconduct for the loss of Guadeloupe."

"Indeed, sir," said Dillon. He'd seen the most recent batch of mails, and the newspapers they contained, but had shown sufficient tact in not alluding to their contents.

Bessborough glared at Cram, busying himself clearing up the mess, before continuing. "Oh, yes. I had a letter from my wife's Sackville cousins explaining why. The Duke of York made such a hash in the Low Countries that they will whitewash any idiot to avoid the risk of a prince of the blood being impeached."

"Perhaps we should request that the Duke of Clarence come back on this station, sir," said Poynton, an observation made doubly malicious by the fact that the house in which they sat had been built to accommodate the king's third son. "The presence of a royal sapling, in wartime, obviously provides protection for all manner of misfortune."

"You do yourself no service by attempting to bait me, Poynton." The captain's look of injured innocence, along with Vandegut's smug expression, only added to the admiral's discomfort. It also left him pondering on the limits of patronage. Poynton would have been more circumspect before his cruise. Now that he'd been favoured, and had failed so abysmally, he'd know that there was little prospect of another opportunity. He therefore cared nothing for Bessborough's opinion.

"Please submit a report in writing. That will be all."

CHAPTER SIX

POYNTON left the room with some degree of satisfaction. He'd put Bessborough in his place. Certain things, however, still rankled. Vandegut was right. Because his illegals had been intercepted by Hugues he'd earned no prize money. But then neither had the admiral, who would whistle for his eighth share of the value. Four of the merchant captains had departed his ship and now filled the ante-room outside Bessborough's office. He scowled at their looks of keen anticipation and completely ignored the only civilian present. Norrington, the agent for the Lloyd's insurance syndicate, had arrived the previous day from Jamaica. Given the gossipy nature of the port, the underwriter knew who he was, that he'd just returned, as well as the nature of his recent travails. So his look indicated a desire to engage the captain in conversation. Poynton, who had no wish to repeat what he'd just told Bessborough, increased his step and went through the outer door before any one of those present could question him.

"You have four of the merchant captains in the ante-room, sir," said Vandegut, pursing his pale lips. "It might be wise to call upon them to confirm what Captain Poynton has said."

"I may not like Poynton, Vandegut, but I have never doubted that amongst my senior officers he, called upon to do so, will tell me the truth."

The other man wasn't wounded. He continued as if no insult had been intended, or received. "That, of course, is not the reason they're here. Even though our difficulties have been explained to them, they wish to protest at what they see as the forced impressment of their men."

Bessborough gestured to his nephew to cease taking notes. "A dull ritual, Captain Vandegut, and quite useless. Besides, all the crews volunteered."

This common fiction was frequently aired. The sailors, regardless of nationality, had been given a stark choice. Starvation or a chance to accept the king's bounty. More men died from the West Indian climate than from any other cause and Bessborough had to replenish the ships' companies from somewhere. Illegals not only provided the navy with prizes, they also helped him to adequately man his ships in a region where the climate was deadly. One of Vandegut's pet theories was that ships kept at sea suffered fewer casualties. That the admiral, much to the annoyance of his captains, had given way on this was just another manifestation of his diminished authority.

"I mention it only because one of them is an American. You will be aware of the particular difficulties that exist in that area. No doubt his protest will, in time, land on some desk in London." The look in Vandegut's eye was one to make Bessborough wonder, not only at the limits of patronage, but the skill of their lordships at the Admiralty. Whatever the circumstances, they seemed to be able to always provide a second-in-command who irritated his commander. Captain Vandegut's unctuous tone was right now doing that very thing. "I do not say that you should satisfy him, sir, merely that you should listen. Since they were not actually taken in the act of landing illegal cargoes, it is unfortunately a burden you must endure."

"Norrington is also waiting to see you," said Caddick.

Bessborough's eyes were raised to the ceiling at the mention of that name. "How many of Poynton's illegals did Lloyd's cover?"

"Two, sir," Dillon replied.

"But we didn't take the vessels, Dillon. It's no good complaining to me about insurance losses if I don't have them."

Vandegut adopted an arch tone as he cut in again. "He will, no doubt, repeat his general condemnation of independent cruising."

"He should have more care about those he does business with.

If he confines himself to insuring English hulls, I'm certain his profits will soar. After all, look at the lengths we go to in order to
protect them."

"Norrington is no fool, sir. He probably knows how much
effort we put into gathering intelligence about illegal cargoes."

"We put no effort into it at all, Captain Vandegut," said Dillon. "Such information comes as a result of our attempts to
confound the enemy by seeking information on their possible
movements."

Vandegut didn't respond to that, seemingly willing, as a serving officer, to allow another common fiction to be aired. Yet a
more independent mind might enquire just how much of Dillon's
time was devoted to a business which, properly handled, could
earn practically everyone on the station a lot of money. Dillon,
like Vandegut, was excepted from this profitable distribution, the
Irishman because he was a shore-based civilian.

"Norrington claims that these risks were occupied in normal,
legitimate trade," Vandegut continued. "This is an argument that
we are in no position to refute. He wishes to enquire if the Royal
Navy has any intention of protecting such a thing."

"Damned barefaced cheek!" snapped Bessborough, angry at
the audacity. He suspected that Vandegut might be an investor in
the insurance market, though he couldn't prove it. And clearly
he'd already discussed the whole matter with Norrington, which
bordered on gross insubordination. The mere presence of an underwriter, especially one making such an outrageous statement, only
added fuel to the admiral's natural inclinations. "Tell him to go
and jump in the harbour!"

"I'd see him, sir," said Dillon.

"Why?" asked Bessborough quietly, well aware that Dillon
would not advance such a course without good reason.

"How do you think such activities are viewed in London, sir?"

Bessborough looked hard at Vandegut before replying. "You
know that as well as I do. I am required, as part of my duties, to
stop illegal trading by neutrals with our island colonies."

"Even when there are, perhaps, more pressing tasks?"

Bessborough shot another quick glance at Vandegut, partly to see his reaction to Dillon's words, and partly to prevent him responding. His negative views on the subject were well known. "I perform those tasks, Dillon, everyone knows that."

The Irishman didn't reply right away. The mention of those responsibilities would bring home once again how vast they were. He had to protect legitimate convoys coming to and leaving the Caribbean, ensure safe passage for inter-island trade, and keep a watch on the French islands while protecting British possessions. The prevailing winds obliged him to be prepared to descend on Jamaica should that island be threatened, with no corresponding reciprocal reinforcements should a French fleet appear off English Harbour. Added to these cares was the possibility that the Dutch, having been over-run at home, might join his list of enemies. And finally there were his nominal allies, the Spanish. No one trusted them at all. Added to which the Dons on the Spanish Main hated the English more than any other nation. With the elephantine memories of their race they were still seeking revenge for the depredations of Drake and Hawkins nearly two hundred years before.

"What are you driving at?" the admiral asked finally, making no attempt to disguise, either by his tone or his look, his serious doubts as to which side his political assistant was on.

Dillon smiled and smoothed his hair. It was his turn to throw a look towards Vandegut, as if asking the wisdom of pursuing such a conversation with him present. Bessborough followed his glance. He frowned deeply, but then nodded for him to continue.

"You referred to the way General Trethgowan escaped any censure."

"I did."

"Does it not occur to you that the ministry may still be looking for a scapegoat?"

Caddick shifted uncomfortably, while Cram gave an audible sniff, no doubt meant to convey that such low-lifes as politicians weren't fit to wipe Bessborough's boots. His master, on the other hand, failed to produce any such air of assurance. His voice betrayed more than a hint of his prevailing anxiety.

"If they are, Dillon, and I'm in the firing line, there's precious little I can do at this distance to avoid it. I've written to my relations, of course." He brightened at that, producing a smile which took in Vandegut and Caddick. He himself was distinguished by his naval rank. But his wife was extremely well connected, a fact which had helped him to acquire this very lucrative command. It also helped to offset the malign strictures of his second-in-command. "I must rely on them to see justice done."

"It cannot help to have accusations of greed bandied about at the same time," said Vandegut.

"Greed!"

For once Vandegut managed the irony. "While we might be aware that you're performing your duty, sir, there may be others, ill disposed, who will see the pursuit of illegals as mere piracy."

"Like Norrington?" asked Dillon, softly.

"The Lloyd's syndicates have a strong case," said Vandegut. "One that I endorse. Might I be allowed to suggest a temporary suspension of independent cruising, sir, publicly stated in a written order, and for a specific period of time? Then we can concentrate on our true task, which is to keep the French from mischief."

Bessborough threw his head back and laughed. Dillon had drawn Vandegut out to a position where he was openly stating views that he'd hitherto confined to backstairs complaint. The man had also gone a fair way to admitting that he might well have an interest in Lloyd's. His next remark matched Vandegut's tone perfectly, in the way it was larded with false sincerity.

"You're worried that Norrington's letters, outlining the way I conduct myself, will be used against me?"

Committed, the other had no intention of withdrawing. Instead he sought to broaden the threat. "He's not the only one. The

planters whose goods are seized form a powerful lobby. The combination, in what I must stress are the present circumstances, could
be harmful."

Bessborough sat forward, choosing to ignore what his second-
in-command clearly implied: that if his commander was caught in
a wave of disapproval, then the backwash could harm others, not
least a man who could look forward to being an admiral himself
within a year or two. Instead of answering Vandegut, he chose to
direct his remarks to Dillon.

"I'm damned if I do, and damned if I don't. Stopping the illegals offends the planters and insurers. Failure to do so blackens
my name both with Billy Pitt and the Admiralty." He left out any
mention of his client officers, all of whom demanded, and got, frequent permission to pursue non-military targets. "And you can
imagine how many people are jockeying to have me replaced after
Guadeloupe. This command is one of the plums of the service.
There's not a flag-officer who's served here who hasn't gone home
rich, in peace and war, just from the proceeds of their eighth.
Damn Norrington and the planters! The danger to my tenure does-
n't come from that quarter. It's my fellow officers I have to worry
about." He spun to face his captain-of-the-fleet with a defiant look.
"Ain't that the case, Vandegut?"

That brought forth a startled nod from Vandegut, caught out
by the speed and directness of the question. But Dillon, by responding, saved him from the need to reply.

"It's better, if we have a concern, that it should be raised. No
good comes of bottling up such misgivings."

"Quite," said Bessborough, his eyes still fixed on Vandegut.
"We carry on as before. Now! We've been suffering a bit of a
drought lately, and that in itself is a worry. But what do you make
of the way this happened?"

Dillon shrugged. "As I said to Captain Poynton, Admiral, we
are not alone in this part of the world. These illegals sailed from
St Eustatius. If we can place people gathering information in a

place like that, so can the French. Naturally, our quarry go to great lengths to avoid us, so even the best information is no guarantor of success. The idea that Hugues has thrown his hat into the ring does startle me somewhat. I always rated him unpredictable . . ."

"Far from it, Dillon," said Bessborough wearily. "He has one aim in life. And that is to make me miserable."

Caddick spoke up. The youth either didn't know, or didn't care, that in such a gathering he was required to remain silent. In fact, given the subject under discussion, he shouldn't have been there at all.

"I'm inclined to look at it in a positive way, sir."

Bessborough, instead of slapping him down, replied softly. "I'm damned if I can, Charles."

"If Hugues has taken to piracy, then he's less likely to be plotting any attacks on another island. There are, if I may say so, other benefits."

"Go on."

"No British vessels were taken. While no one would upbraid this command for a failure to intercept illegals, any loss to our own merchants would cause no end of trouble. Almost as much as the loss of another sugar island. Therefore Monsieur Hugues, by transferring his activities, may have inadvertently done us a valuable service."

"And lined his own pocket."

"Is he engaged in such an activity for profit?" said Dillon, prepared to pursue what was obviously an interesting idea. "Or is it that life on Guadeloupe has become less pleasant without the kind of luxuries that his planters are accustomed to?"

Bessborough wasn't persuaded, though he looked as if he wanted to be. Vandegut, on the other hand, was looking at him as if he was mad.

"Given his reputation, plus the disaster his supposed reforms have engendered, few have been inclined to visit the island since his arrival. After all, he has nothing to trade with. Freeing the slaves meant no harvest. Any sugar or coffee they grew merely rotted on the stem."

"But you told me he's put them back to work," said Bessborough, with an air of confusion.

"It will be next year before that has any significant effect. Meanwhile he has a disgruntled set of colonists. He can't resort to the guillotine again, and taking another sugar island is proving difficult. So perhaps he's sought to alleviate the shortages by this piracy. He brings in goods to please his planters, and tweaks our nose at the same time."

"What utter nonsense!" said Vandegut.

"Is it, Captain?" Dillon seemed slightly nonplussed at the depth of Vandegut's response. As Bessborough's second-in-command he was privy to all the incoming intelligence. Thus, unlike Caddick, he could measure the idea against some positive information.

"If what you say is true what are we to do about it?" asked Bessborough, addressing the question to the Irishman and his nephew, and completely ignoring his second-in-command.

Dillon replied. "I would say this, sir. Our paramount concerns are always strategic, which means we have a duty to ensure that no other island falls to the French. That must be, and remain, a priority."

"So you suggest we carry on as before?"

Dillon nodded and Vandegut frowned. But the admiral's bumptious nephew had more to say. "I dare say the officers you despatch will make every effort to catch him, sir."

Bessborough coughed to cover his embarrassment, and fixed Caddick with a look. It was obvious he could not believe that his nephew was so naïve as to advance such a notion. Did he really not know that every captain on the station, given the choice of chasing Hugues or prizes, would plump for the latter every time, even if he ordered them to do otherwise? The problems that beset the admiral obviously depressed him, and he sighed.

"You will have to see Norrington, sir," said Vandegut, quickly.

He thought for a moment, then nodded towards his political assistant as if he'd asked the question.

"And the merchant captains?" asked the Irishman.

"Four, you say?"

Dillon nodded and Bessborough turned to his nephew. "Tell them to elect one of their number to act as a spokesman, Charles. I can't face four of them, either individually or together. Indeed I have little desire to see them at all. You deal with it."

CHAPTER SEVEN

"THERE IS nothing I can do for you, Captain Caufield," said Stephen Norrington, his gaunt face even more pinched than normal. "It is not my place to pay out claims on policies taken out in the Americas. You hail from Sag Harbor, I believe?"

Caufield nodded slowly.

"Then you must present that to the Lloyd's agent in New York. They may, if they accept your word, pay out on the spot. Or they may elect to send the papers for onward transmission to London. I will, if you call upon me tomorrow, furnish you with a certificate confirming the circumstances of Hugues's felony, which may assist in reaching a quick settlement. That, I'm afraid, is all I can do."

"And how, sir, am I to get to New York?" asked the merchant captain, the nasal Yankee twang very evident in his voice. "I don't even have the means to get back to Long Island."

Norrington was uncomfortable. Not because of his refusal to discount Caufield's loss of both ship and cargo, nor the circumstances. That was a probability which would be attested to by Captain Poynton and his officers. And given the other similar claims, fraud was unlikely. But with the shortage of coin in the West Indies he could not pay out on claims which he'd not personally underwritten. As to Caufield's crew, for them he cared nothing. It was the physical presence that really troubled him. Nathan Caufield was a big man, with powerful shoulders and a square, scarred face. The livid lump of his recent wound was still very evident. And he was too close for comfort, his eyes boring into the side of the insurance man's head, which was set resolutely forward.

"Kinda bothers me, the way we was taken, Mr Norrington. Don't seem to bother you none."

"Of course it does, sir," he replied, still refusing to turn and look at his interrogator. "Lloyd's may never demur when faced with a loss, sir. But the syndicates take no great delight when they have to pay out on claims."

"Is that what you're planning to tell the admiral?"

"What I have to say to the admiral is my concern, both before I see him and after."

Caufield nodded slowly, a smile playing about his thick lips. "I was kinda hoping, after you had words, that you'd have the answer to something that's been bothering me."

"Which is?"

"How in hell's name did that Poynton feller know where to find us?"

"Who says he knew?"

"He did, sir," replied Caufield, now so close that his hot breath played on the other man's ear.

"But he didn't find you, did he?" snapped Norrington, finally turning his head.

He was not a man made comfortable by close proximity to others. His anger at what he felt was an intrusion took his attention away from what the American had said. What he saw on his face angered him even more. It seemed as if Caufield, with his very obvious grin, was mocking him. "If you remember, you found him."

"That's right, Mr Norrington. Why, how could I possibly forget such a thing?"

The door of the office opened and Dillon came out. Norrington, catching the nod, got to his feet. Dillon held the door open and allowed him through, then turned to the rest of the occupants. "The admiral's nephew is in my office, which is next door. He will see one of you, who will act as a spokesman for all; the rest can wait outside."

"And what will the admiral's nephew say, sir?" asked Caufield.

"How would I know that?"

The American laughed out loud, a sound that was certainly heard in Bessborough's office before the door was closed. Norrington had taken a seat before the desk and was composing his features into the pinched expression of a man intent on launching himself into a lengthy complaint. Cram, deferentially pouring, and gently spilling, coffee, did nothing to dent this resolve. But Bessborough did!

"Can I save you some time, Mr Norrington?" The agent looked upset at the older man's abruptness. He'd obviously rehearsed his submission. Vandegut shifted uncomfortably in his chair as Bessborough continued. "I, sir, am a humble sailor. You are a man of business. It may make sense to you to insure the ships and vessels of illegal traders as well as our enemies, but I am at a loss to see the logic of it."

"We are not here to discuss our methods of business, sir," said Norrington.

"But you do insure French merchant vessels, as well as the illegals that breach the Navigation Acts?"

"Of course, if they pay the proper rate. And before you accuse us of abetting crime, sir, let me add that our clients are not required to tell us their precise destinations. They are merely required to inform us if they intend to sail into a zone of conflict."

"They pay an extra premium for the privilege," said Vandegut, trying to be helpful.

"Of course," added Norrington.

Bessborough glared at Vandegut, then at Norrington. "Then perhaps I might be permitted to observe this: that if you were to inform the navy of the dates of the cover, the nature of the freight, as well as those owners who choose to pay extra, then we could easily anticipate their landfall and clap a stopper, once and for all, on their activities."

Norrington's face had become even more pinched as each point was made. "Are you seriously suggesting, Admiral Bessborough, that we breach confidentiality?"

"I had in mind the needs of the nation. We are, after all, engaged in a war."

"And we, sir, are engaged in the kind of business that finances it. The next thing you'll be demanding is that we decline to insure French ships!"

"It might make their lives more difficult."

"On the contrary, sir. It would only bring irreparable damage to the London market."

Bessborough sat back, a slight smile playing on his full red lips. "There we are, Mr Norrington. You demand the right to be left to trade freely. So be it. But please allow us poor sailors to make war as we, and the needs of the country, demand."

Norrington's face took on a cunning look, as though Bessborough had walked into a trap. "Do such needs require naval officers to ignore their duty?"

The smile stayed on Bessborough's lips. But any amusement that had existed quite disappeared from his look. His heavy eyebrows twitched alarmingly. "Have a care, Mr Norrington. I dislike lectures from civilians on the nature of my duty."

"Yet you take ships off blockade and convoy duty, and allow them to act as licensed corsairs." That earned Vandegut another glare, with the clear implication that Norrington had come by that information from him.

"And now, these past months, despite your feeble attempts to blockade Guadeloupe, I hear that this fellow Hugues has taken a leaf out of your book. I have no need to wonder at the net result. Losses, sir, and a corresponding increase in rates. I am obliged to inform London, Admiral Bessborough. I might add that I cannot avoid the possibility that they may complain to the ministry."

"Let them do so, sir. And if my superiors see fit to alter my instructions, then rest assured I shall oblige them. As of this moment I cannot oblige you!"

Dillon, who'd been silently watching this exchange, cut in. "Especially since the suspicion exists, Mr Norrington, that your sole concern is to secure the profits of your syndicate, regardless of the effect this has on the success of the war against the French."

Norrington flushed angrily and stood up.

"Do not dare to term it a suspicion, sir, as though such an attitude is felonious. Rather call it a fact. My sole concern will always be for the profits of Lloyd's. If there is any larceny being practised hereabouts, it is in the way that naval officers seem intent on lining their pockets at our expense. Good day to you."

He spun on his heel and made for the door. Bessborough's final remark, delivered in a loud angry voice, pursued him. "You will just have to adjust your rates, sir, and suck a little more blood out of your victims."

Dillon had followed him out of the door and into the hallway. He was surprised to observe that it was empty. The door to his own office stood open, with no sign of Caddick either. He walked to the main entrance and looked both ways, before asking the marine sentry if he'd seen the merchant captains. The man looked right and left to check that his superior, Captain Metzerhagen, was nowhere near, then leant forward and addressed Dillon in a very familiar way.

"They's gone, your honour, an' not happy at that. They had quite a talk, and many a high word about the bairns they're draftin' into the navy. One of them, that tall American cove, Caufield he termed himself, who seemed to be the leader, said that it were bad enough being told to "sod off," which is easier to do to one man than four. But that to have it done by a whelp was a-doubling the insult."

The marine had noticed the frown that appeared on Dillon's pale face. He spoke hurriedly to cover himself against the effect of what he'd imparted. "Them was his very words, your honour, which he bade me pass on as they was spoke."

Dillon was still frowning as he replied. "Then we must thank Captain Caufield for his acute perception, as well as for saving us a deal of time."

As he turned back towards his office he passed the door which led to the admiral's room. Bessborough's voice, rising in anger, easily penetrated the two sets of doors as he berated his second-in-command in a manner that had become all too rare these last few months.

"If you cannot recall your duty to me, sir, I'd be obliged if you would remind yourself of the duty you owe to your service."

Norrington was back in his rooms at the Duke of Clarence with the quick tropical night taking the sun, if not the heat, out of the day, before the import of Caufield's words struck him. He knew his interview with Bessborough had gone badly. Losing his temper had prevented him from saying half the things he'd intended. Now he was writing to Vandegut, outlining what steps they could possibly take to limit Bessborough. It was reference to recent events which provided the trigger. He ran over in his mind the facts as he knew them. This fellow Hugues was nothing like the man he'd heard about. The Jacobin Governor of Guadeloupe had a fearsome reputation as a bloodthirsty tyrant. Yet he'd let go all the crews of the ships he'd taken without a scratch, with their ships' papers and clear instructions as to the location of *Andromache*. Was that what Caufield was implying? That Hugues not only knew the location of the illegals, but somehow had advanced warning of the position of the British cruisers? It was an intriguing thought, even if it was none of his concern. Still, it would do no harm to add it as a postscript on his note to Vandegut, who could at least be relied upon to take such concerns seriously.

It took time to compose, being of necessity couched in terms of some caution. After all, it was mere supposition. At all costs he must avoid the temptation of being seen to give it too much credence. As an endemic doodler, as well as a cautious correspondent, Norrington rarely delivered a note that didn't have some example of his thought process drawn in the margin. Thus this note had several outlines of ships, plus an unflattering ten-stroke sketch of Bessborough that he hoped would amuse Vandegut. The loud knocking on his door started when he'd barely sanded the paper. Irritated, he called to his visitor to enter, a feeling not eased when the door opened and Gracewell, the innkeeper, ushered Captain Nathan Caufield into his presence.

Norrington stood up, the letter to Vandegut in his hand. "And to what, sir, do I owe the meaning of this call?"

"You said something about issuing a certificate."

"If I recall, Captain Caufield, I also said something about the morrow."

"I'm leaving at first light, Mr Norrington. I can sail the cutter up through the islands without assistance."

"Can you indeed?"

"So I'd be obliged."

Norrington had it on his face to refuse, to insist that the American delay his departure. But the other man looked equally determined. The Lloyd's agent dropped his eyes. In the act of doing so he waved the letter in his hand, which reminded him of its contents. Needing a method to withdraw from confrontation, he held it up before Caufield.

"I have just written to . . ." Norrington paused, suddenly not wishing to use Vandegut's name. By doing so he would run the risk, however tenuous, of undermining what was a very useful relationship.

"To Dillon," he said quickly, "regarding what you told me earlier."

"Which was?"

"That it was singular, the way this Hugues fellow knew the location of the *Andromache*. I dare say that you're hinting at the same conclusion as I drew; that information about the movements of illegals could come from anywhere. But the orders given to Poynton originated here in Antigua."

"So you didn't mention it to the admiral earlier?"

"No, I did not," he replied testily. "I had other matters to bring to his attention."

"Well, that's as maybe, Mr Norrington. Happens I should have been a mite more clear about what I was saying. But, here and now, I am more concerned about you issuing me a certificate."

"The idea that there might be a leakage of information to a Frenchman doesn't alarm you?"

"Not at all. You seem to forget I'm an American."

The elegantly and expensively dressed Mr Norrington looked him up and down slowly, seeming to linger over the rough quality of his homespun clothes, with a special frown for his tassled leather boots, decorated with various Indian designs. "How could I do such a thing?"

"My certificate?" said Caufield sullenly.

The American's attitude stiffened his earlier resolve. "I am not subject to your whims, sir. It is no concern of mine if you have decided to depart at an inconvenient time. You may come back in the morning or sail empty-handed."

"You're a businessman, Mr Norrington, is that right?" The underwriter nodded impatiently. "Then I reckon that I have something to trade with you."

"Indeed, sir," he replied, as though such a concept was unthinkable.

"I have another piece of information about this which may interest you."

"Go on."

"I will for my certificate."

Norrington was about to refuse again. Then he recalled that it was Caufield who'd raised his earlier suspicions. Had he been more attentive, it would have been a telling card to play and the interview with Bessborough might have ended on a more triumphant note.

"Oh, very well," he growled, reaching into a large calf-skin bag and pulling out a ledger.

"What if I was to tell you this, Mr Norrington: that I have been to Guadeloupe; that I have seen the governor in person, as he superintended the execution of a few blacks who took his ideas of freedom too seriously. Now I grant that he wore a black hat and coat, and decorated himself with sashes and cockades. But he's a small man, with quite a belly on him, eyes like a wild hog, and a skin more pockmarked than any I've seen. And given the pleasure he took in murderin' those niggers, I don't reckon that an ounce of pity occupies his soul."

"I cannot see what this has to do with the subject at hand."

"It has everything to do with it, friend," replied Caufield, his hand going to the livid scar on his forehead, with the black stitches still plain to see. "The man who took my ship not only doctored me, he poured me a drink and said he was sorry."

"That, I admit, is singular, in so bloodthirsty a tyrant."

"Except for one thing, Mr Norrington. Whoever it was who took my ship was of medium build and straight. And though his skin carried the marks of the pox, it was of a light variety. He was handsome and every inch a gentleman."

"You make him sound like a paragon."

"Not quite that, Mr Norrington. He took my ship and every cent I possess."

"Do you have any idea who he is?"

"Nope. But he had a pet mongoose, which is a damned odd thing to cherish. Thing'd got out of its cage and damn near bit my leg while he was a-fixing my head."

"Have you any idea what are you saying, man?"

"I do. I'm saying whoever he was, his name is no more Victor Hugues than that damned rodent."

Norrington sat down abruptly at his desk, pulling the ledger towards him. With swift strokes he wrote the details of Caufield's loss on the outside of the page, copying the same information on to the inside half. Then, having signed both, he authenticated the American's section with a heavy embosser, the seal sitting square in the middle of his florid signature. Finally he sliced out the necessary certificate and handed it to his visitor.

"That, I think, concludes our business. If I may be permitted to bid you good day."

Caufield just smiled at the implied insult, took his certificate, and left. Norrington sat down and reread the note he'd penned for Vandegut. The implications of what it contained, added to what the American had said, were obvious. He was tempted to write to the admiral direct. What a fine thing it would be to present that pompous oaf with the knowledge that something was amiss. Yet, on reflection, that would never do, since there was always the possibility that everything Caufield had told him was false. It would be no good making wild claims about spies in Bessborough's headquarters if he couldn't, at the same time, put his finger on the culprit. That was no easy matter, even with Vandegut's active assistance.

Few people could have known about Poynton's orders. The clerks, with scant regard for discretion, and inclined to leaving things lying about for all and sundry to see, would be barred from their composition. Poynton may well have talked himself, though given the jealousy amongst officers he would perhaps have felt it better to remain silent. There was the discrepancy in the name of the corsair. If this fellow wasn't Hugues, who was he? The governor of Guadeloupe might, like the British, have spies all over the Caribbean. He could, therefore, have advanced warning of potential illegal traffic to match that gathered by Dillon. But someone else? Was he merely a deputy acting in Hugues's name? And his knowledge could have been mere luck. There was the distinct possibility that this fellow had seen *Andromache* cruising on her station and that sending the crews towards the frigate had either been fortuitous or a fluke. Perhaps, if he enquired, it would be best to be circumspect. Whatever he decided, he saw, with his prickly pride, a chance to wipe the smile off Bessborough's face. Even the letter he'd just composed, without alteration and from such a source, would be most unwelcome. But with a postscript added, it was even more satisfying.

Norrington laboured as usual over the contents, this time seeking the right tone, one that would wound while expressing concern. His pen flicked in the normal fashion, as though it had a life of its own. The words he needed wouldn't come, but while he sought them he'd inadvertently drawn a fair likeness of a mongoose on the copy of Caufield's certificate. He'd intended to send a messenger to deliver his original note. But on reflection, given the added information it obtained, plus the difficulty of communicating it in writing, he felt a personal call to be necessary. There was an almost jaunty air about him as he put on his hat, picked up his cane, and descended the stairs. Norrington, letter in hand, made his exit through the crowded tap-room, just for the satisfaction of glowering at the owner, Gracewell, who'd admitted Caufield. He didn't notice the American, who was seated in one of the high-backed chairs. Smiling, the underwriter made his way out on to the street. Gracewell looked at his watch, which said seven o'clock, and wondered, idly, where Mr Stephen Norrington was off to at this time of night. Bridge, who handled the post, would have shut up by now. Then his attention was caught by the back of another customer departing the inn. His suspicion that it was Caufield was confirmed when he turned round in the doorway, scanning the room before he finally departed.

CHAPTER EIGHT

THE NOISE of the crickets covered Caufield's approach to the veranda surrounding Admiralty House. At this time of the morning, the hour before dawn, the marine sentries would be at their most lax, more interested in sleep than security. He watched them circle the building twice, silently calculating the amount of time he'd have available. Not that anything was certain. First he had to force an entry. Once inside he couldn't be sure of his whereabouts, never having got beyond the ante-room outside Bessborough's office. But it was of a style that matched many houses in Long Island, with large sash windows designed to admit a quantity of light, and having been in the ante-room he suspected the main office backed on to this rear portion of garden. The best guess was the room with the pair of French windows that stood central to the entire ground floor. The occupants would, presumably, be asleep upstairs. He checked his pocket, touching the sand-filled canvas tube for reassurance, then checked that the small metal crowbar was safe in his inside pocket, before moving forward.

He had one leg over the rail when one of the long windows to his left suddenly filled with light. The American threw himself against the cool white wall, his breath still and his heart pounding in his chest. If they caught him at this the British would not be forgiving. It might not stand up as common theft, especially with him being American, a nation which the British felt had more sympathy with the French than with their kith and kin. In this naval port, Bessborough was the fount of justice, able to have him shot as a spy, without reference to any civil power. Carefully he inched along the wall till his head was right at the edge of the lighted window. He saw Dillon through one eye, sitting at his desk, rifling through a deep pile of papers. The chest that acted as his strongbox was wide open, the glow from the oil lamps illuminating the neat racks of scrolls that made up the political assistant's world. Was the Irishman looking at the very thing he sought? If not, then the answer might well lie in that strongbox. He'd intended to search through the admiral's papers. But this early riser was, no doubt, privy to the same information. And his strongbox was already open. Could he take Dillon instead of wasting time trying to force open Bessborough's cabinets? It was a tempting prospect, made more so by the lack of time. The marine sentry would come round again shortly, so he tiptoed back to the next darkened window and forced the slim knife up into the crack between the two sashes.

The catch, on a window that was opened frequently, slid along easily. Likewise the lower frame, which opened without a sound. The sudden flash of white, the moon reflecting off a marine belt, had him diving through the gap. The clunk of his crowbar, jammed in his coat pocket, as it hit the sill seemed to echo round the whole building. He pulled the window shut and lay flat on the bare oak boards, praying that the sentry hadn't heard the noise. In his head he tried to count the footsteps, doubling the number for safety. Caufield stood up slowly. His breath, held throughout the moments of danger, escaped in a hiss as he made his way to the centre of the large room. There was sufficient moonlight coming in through the French windows to make out its shape, and given the geography of the building and the size of the room it looked as though he'd been lucky enough to get right into Bessborough's office.

A pair of chronometers hung either side of the double doors opposite the French windows, which he assumed led to the anteroom he'd occupied earlier that day. Another set of four doors covered the whole of the left-hand wall. They would open to make a ballroom. Huge mahogany cabinets, their brass locks throwing out a dull gleam, filled each exterior wall. There was a single door in the centre of the right-hand wall. The thin strip of light underneath stood out in sharp contrast to the rest of the room. Dillon's office! Carefully he calculated the odds. It would be difficult to force the admiral's cabinets open with someone next door. The Irishman might hear a noise and come to investigate. Better to seek what he wanted from that open strongbox. If he tried the door and it was locked, Dillon might hear him; if he didn't hear the latch being tried and Caufield still went after him he'd have to go out through the ante-room into the hallway, with no idea about the internal security arrangements. There could be, probably were, armed guards out there. Gently tiptoeing round the room, he ran his hands over Bessborough's mahogany cabinets, before turning to the huge desk. The locks on the drawers were stout affairs, though forcible. But it wasn't something that could be done without noise.

His feet made no sound as he moved across to Dillon's door, pressing his ear to the panel in case he was no longer alone. The soft humming worried him at first, till he identified it as singing; some kind of soft lament. It decided him: it was the sound of someone off guard, perhaps a man creating enough noise inside his own head not to hear the handle of his door being turned. Caufield took out the canvas bag filled with sand. Slowly, with his free hand, he turned the brass knob, exerting slight backwards pressure to ensure that the door remained closed. As soon as it had reached the limit of its turn he gave a gentle push with his shoulder. The thin crack of light made him smile. It wasn't locked. He coiled himself, creating a mental picture of the interior of the room. Dillon was at his desk, which lay on the far wall some ten feet distant, so he had his back to the door. If he was still engrossed in his work Caufield could cover that before the Irishman knew he was in the room.

The sudden increase in light as he threw open the door caught him unawares, making him pause for a split second before he rushed forward. It didn't save Dillon. But it did mean that Caufield caught him on the front of his head rather than the back, since his victim was given time to turn round, his arm coming up swiftly to defend himself. But the sand-filled sack was through the

Irishman's guard. The blue eyes, wide open with alarm, which had fixed on Caufield's face, went opaque immediately after he struck. The American leant forward to catch the body, intercepting it before it left the chair. Gently he eased Dillon down on to the floor, allowing the inert form to roll on to its back. Then he dashed across to the window and closed the shutters.

He had to lean over the body to examine the papers on the desk, rifling through the pile. The lettering he recognized, but being in a strange language the words made no sense. So he turned to the strongbox, pulling roll after roll out of its slot. Caufield started to curse in frustration. There were letters in French and Spanish, neither of which he could read. The only scroll of interest to him related to the recent actions of the *Andromache*. He scanned it with a mounting sense of frustration. Here, in writing, were the interceptions that Poynton was supposed to have made, with names, dates, probable courses, and exact landfalls. But what of the information that determined such a course? There was nothing in the strongbox about future intentions. Nor did what he have in his hand give him the identity of Dillon's spies. Perhaps the Irishman only carried such information in his head. Having emptied the strongbox, he spotted a small brass ring in the base, which when he pulled it opened to reveal another chamber. The leather-bound journal lay on top of a thin metal box. He opened the box first, quickly counting the coins it contained, a mixture of guineas, moidores, and Spanish eight-real pieces. Caufield hadn't come here to rob anyone, but to seek information. Yet given what he'd lost, the danger he was in, and the fact that Dillon might well have recognized him, it made sense to remove the money. At the very least it provided those who would investigate with a motive for his forced entry. But it didn't really help him with the main purpose of his nocturnal visit, which was to find a clue to the routes of the next group of illegal cargoes.

The answer was probably locked away in Bessborough's desk. But having chosen to take on Dillon, and spending so much time with his papers, there was none left to look next door. In fact, it was already time to leave. But he could not bear to do so. Instead he carried the leather journal to the lantern on the desk. It was some kind of diary, with each date of entry marked out at the top of the page. But the actual writing, being the same as the papers on the desk, defeated him. A letter, neatly folded, dropped out as he turned a page, landing on Dillon's chest. As he bent to retrieve it the Irishman stirred slightly. Caufield cursed, at the same time noting that the man's clothes were covered in dust. He would either have to go now or give him another belt with the sandbag. The idea of striking a defenceless man being repugnant, he threw the journal back into the strongbox.

The letter was about to follow, not even rating a cursory glance, when he hesitated. He opened it up, registering that the writing was different and some of the language comprehensible. It was dated two weeks before from an address marked St Eustatius, the port from which he'd so recently sailed. And at the bottom was a scrawled signature, hard to decipher, but which definitely contained the initial C. followed by another initial letter. The actual surname was a scrawl, but he thought he could make out an O followed by an apostrophe. The remainder was an indecipherable line which tailed away towards a common seal. Above that, in code, was some kind of list, including names. Most of the words made no sense. But the names did! With the exception of one, *Brandon,* it was the name of every vessel that had been taken by the man calling himself Victor Hugues. He looked at the words written in English, which referred to something called the League of United Irishmen. But that didn't interest him. He looked at the scrawled signature again, concentrating much harder on the tail. The smile grew slowly on his weatherbeaten face. Nathan Caufield had sailed these waters all his adult life and had made St Eustatius his base on more than one occasion. This letter came from that port. He now reckoned he not only knew where to look, but who it was who supplied the British with their intelligence, the last link being provided by the fact that Dillon was Irish. Then he realized that the journal he put aside must be written in the

Erse. Who, apart from another Irishman, could tell what information it contained?

Dillon groaned, his arm lifting to try and reach his swollen temple. Caufield was in a quandary. There was someone, somewhere, to decipher that journal, whatever the language. But by removing it, or the letter in his hand, he'd alert Dillon to his real reason for the break-in. If he just took the money it would look like plain robbery, by a man down on his luck, which might lessen the pursuit. Dillon must have read the letter, perhaps even translating it for Bessborough. He would certainly know where to look for his attacker if it disappeared. He threw it into the strongbox, emptied the money into his coat pocket, and ran out through Bessborough's office.

The eastern sky was tinged with the first trace of dawn as he raced across the lawn heading for the brick wall enclosing the admiral's garden. The postern gate lay off to his right, but that, he knew, was locked. On the left of that lay a clump of bushes that would hide his climb. The bricks on the inside were worn, providing a good purchase for his feet. In seconds he was slithering down the outside, to a point where the wall turned, providing a conveniently dark corner. His foot caught on something, twisting his ankle, and he careered headlong into the ground, cursing as the pain of contact shot through his shoulder. The impact winded him too, causing him to slump at the base of the wall until he could recover his breath. As he lifted his eyes the dark lump took shape and he pulled himself across to carry out a closer examination. He knew it was a body as soon as he touched the yielding cloth. A sharp tug on the shoulder and the cadaver rolled on to its back. The top of the man's head was a mass of sticky gore, already attracting the attention of the flies. The sightless, glassy eyes of Stephen Norrington, pulled out from the shade, picked up either the last flicker of starlight or the first hint of dawn. Caufield didn't wait. With an energy born of terror he leapt up and ran, cursing as he heard the crowbar, which had worked itself free from his pocket, clatter along the ground.

* * *

"There was nothing else missing, sir, may God be praised. It was plain robbery and no more."

Bessborough paced up and down, still in his nightgown and cap, his hands behind his back. Caddick had been sent out with a party of marines to search for the culprit and a messenger had been despatched to find Vandegut, who'd recently begun a liaison with a local widow, something which had prospered so heartily that he was often absent from his quarters.

"Are you sure you can identify him?"

Dillon raised his hand to touch the lump on his temple and he nodded. The surgeon had bathed it in some cooling alcohol, and the odour of the spirit filled the room. He could hear the faint sound of a commotion outside the windows and he spun his head at the knock on the door, which caused him to wince with pain.

"Enter!" shouted Bessborough.

The door flew open and young Caddick came in holding a crowbar in his hand. He addressed his uncle without any hint of formality. "We've found Mr Norrington in the street."

"What!"

"Dead, uncle. His head has been shattered by a heavy blow." He held forward the blue-grey crowbar. "We found this beside the body. It's what killed him for sure."

The colour left Bessborough's face as he took the instrument out of his nephew's hand. Then, as he looked at it, and saw the blood at one end, he muttered an almost inaudible, "My God."

The silence descended after that. Everyone in the room would speculate privately as to what this portended. There was also the creeping realization that Dillon was lucky to be alive. Captain Vandegut, his clothing in some disarray, came in through the ante-room as the surgeon exited to look at Norrington's body. He was followed almost immediately by the marine captain, Metzerhagen, who'd been sent to search the harbour.

"Caufield took his cutter out of the naval yard yesterday and tied it up at the public quay."

"Have you looked for it?" asked Bessborough.

"Yes, sir. He was observed rowing it out into the roadstead at around dawn. Those I spoke to said that he was not in any great hurry."

"But he's not out there now, I'll wager," said Dillon, with a bitter tone.

"Unlikely, Mr Dillon. His cutter most certainly will have sails aboard. He'll be well out to sea by now, with a rich choice of destinations to choose from." Vandegut was looking at his superior, and using a tone of voice that somehow indicated that such an outcome was his fault.

"They've just found the body of Mr Norrington in the garden," said Bessborough. "I regret to inform you that he did not expire naturally. My nephew tells me that his head's stove in."

Vandegut's square face had gone chalk white, matching his hair. Plainly, he could not make the connection. "Did Caufield murder him, too?"

"So it would seem, Captain, unless we've had two intruders on the same night."

"He must be brought to justice, sir, and swiftly."

The admiral came between the two others in his pacing and turned and looked at Dillon. "I cannot sanction a pursuit, not for one man in a boat who could have gone anywhere."

The Irishman nodded, slowly, to ease the pain. "I understand, sir."

"But, sir," said Vandegut, as Caddick slipped out on to the veranda, "we must do something. A ship's boat, well manned, might catch him."

"And which direction would you choose?"

"I repeat, sir, some action must be taken."

"I will make sure the governor circulates the entire Caribbean with a warrant. If this Caufield ever turns up on British sovereign territory, he'll hang, for certain. Now forgive me, gentlemen, while I get dressed."

"This has been a terrible night, Dillon," said Vandegut, glaring at Bessborough's retreating back. "You have no idea how I esteemed Norrington."

"Do you wish to take charge of the body?"

Vandegut hesitated for a moment before answering. "Yes."

Caddick reappeared as Vandegut left the room. "My uncle?"

"Getting dressed," replied Dillon, pulling himself slowly to his feet.

"I've had a look through the telescope. There's plenty of shipping out there. A good half a dozen of them could be Caufield's boat."

"Or none of them."

"Quite."

"Do we know where Norrington was staying?"

"At the Duke of Clarence, I believe."

"I will go down there and look to his things," said Dillon wearily. "There may be something amongst his papers which will help us. Unless you'd rather?"

"No," Vandegut replied. "You go."

CHAPTER NINE

IT WASN'T the first time that Lord Bridport had shaken his head, the slow movement matching the motion of the flagship as it rose and fell on the swell of the bitterly cold English Channel. It was as if he wished Harry to be in no doubt of how he viewed Toner's behaviour. Yet it had a contrived quality. There was a suspicion in the air that the admiral believed the opposite of his words: that the men of the *Bucephalas* had got what they deserved, and their captain along with them.

"The *Endymion* was not under my direct command, sir."

"Those exemptions were issued by the Secretary of War himself," snapped Harry. "Their validity is beyond question."

"Quite!" The long thin nose, in the spare face, swung round to face the speaker. "Though I'm bound to observe that it hardly aids the cause of naval recruitment if every government minister feels he can exempt men from the service."

"It could have been signed by the Admiralty ten times over, sir," replied James. "It would have made no difference. Toner is a thief by nature and would have taken them regardless. Perhaps it is a feature of his Celtic blood."

Lord Bridport frowned, his thin grey eyebrows knitting together.

"I should take care, Mr Ludlow. It does you no credit to go bandying around accusations of thievery. Apart from any other consideration, they can land you in the dock on a charge of slander."

"Damn slander!" snapped James. "This officer indulged in criminal behaviour. It is to be hoped that there is a naval law against such acts. There is most certainly a civilian one."

With "Black Dick" Howe retired ashore after the Glorious First of June, Lord Bridport held the premier appointment in His Majesty's fleet. He was very senior in the service, accustomed to deference as a right. It was evident that he disliked James's bellicose tone. But, for all his prestige, he was at a loss to know how to chastise an irate civilian, even in his own great cabin. Instead he glanced at his flag-captain, Parker, who sat to the right of the desk, indicating that he should reply on their behalf.

"There is, sir, most assuredly, a law against such things, clearly stated by the Lord Commissioners. Captain Toner will face a court martial for his actions."

"When?" asked Harry coldly. He knew that no court comprised of naval officers would do overmuch to punish such an offender, especially when he had taken the hands he needed out of a privateer.

"I cannot see anything happening until he returns from the West Indies," said Parker.

James, normally the soul of urbanity, who'd already allowed his own high standards of behaviour to be comprised by his earlier outburst, now felt his jaw drop. Harry's stomach contracted. "The West Indies?"

"Yes," replied Lord Bridport. "He has orders to join Admiral Bessborough on the Leeward Islands station." The old man's eyes brightened at the mention of it. "Damn me, Mr Ludlow, I envy him, for all the perils to a man's health. It cannot be worse than this station, beating to and fro, frozen to the marrow in a permanent gale of wind. You're lucky to have found me, sir. I am on the point of giving the orders to bear up for Torbay. All this nonsense about a permanent blockade is so much stuff. If we stay on station, and the French come out, our ships will be in no state to fight them. Much better to stay at anchor, preserving our spars and canvas, and then—"

Harry ruthlessly interrupted the older man's peregrinations on naval strategy. "I would appreciate your lordship's advice on how I'm to get my crew back. Especially if they are, at this very moment, being carted off to English Harbour?"

"Ticklish, I grant you," replied Bridport, after a short pause. This was necessary to recall what it was his unwelcome guest was talking about.

"Perhaps you can overhaul him in that ship of yours," added Parker, pointing out of the great stern windows towards *Bucephalas,* which was following in the *Queen Charlotte*'s wake.

"To what purpose? He's not going to surrender my crew without a direct order."

Bridport cut in, his long face, under the heavy wig, deeply sorrowful. "One which I cannot provide. As I said, Captain Ludlow, Toner is not under my command."

"You are saying that only the Admiralty can give him such an instruction."

"I am indeed."

Harry sat silently for a moment, with his brother watching him closely. The two other men exchanged glances. It could not be said that they smiled. But they shared satisfied expressions that this minor problem, which didn't really concern them, was about to be so deftly resolved.

"Can I have a word with you alone, my lord?" said Harry.

The thin grey eyebrows shot up. "Alone, sir?"

Harry's voice was hard and cold. "Yes, my lord. I have things to say that you may not wish to share with the rest of the ship."

"I dislike the implication, sir," snapped Parker, the only other member of the ship's company present.

But Bridport, who was staring at Harry, held up his bony hand to stop the flag-captain saying more. He was no stranger to the name Ludlow. The father of these young men sitting before him in the great cabin of the *Queen Charlotte* had been a contemporary of both himself and his brother, Admiral Lord Hood. Indeed, Hood and Admiral Ludlow had been exceedingly close. Bridport was also aware that his brother had a great affection for his late friend's offspring, an affection that had manifested itself in several ways, not the least of which was his attempt to reverse the withdrawal of Harry Ludlow's naval commission.

These youngsters were rich and well connected. James Ludlow, slim, handsome, and dressed to perfection, looked what he was: a man of the town. He was much esteemed as a portrait painter by London society, even if his personal morals, and his very public affair with another man's wife, had led to a scandal. He oozed a social confidence that was in sharp contrast to his elder brother. Not that Harry Ludlow was cowed by his surroundings; it was merely that he was so obviously a sailor, with a girth and physical presence lacking in his more elegant sibling. The likeness was there, right enough. But Harry reminded the fleet commander of his father. And Bridport, who'd had dealings with Admiral Sir Thomas Ludlow, knew that he was not a man to bluff, being famous for two things: his love of a blow and his directness when addressing superiors and inferiors alike.

"I cannot think that you can have anything to say to me that cannot be uttered in front of Captain Parker."

"Then you are not the man you're reputed to be," replied Harry curtly.

The thin eyebrows shot up. "What, pray, am I reputed to be?"

"A man of keen intelligence, sir."

Bridport drummed his thin finger on the polished surface of his desk, his eyes locked on to those of his "guest." There was no smile when he spoke, for it required little intelligence to guess that what would follow was likely to afford unpleasant listening.

"Leave us, Parker, if you would be so kind."

James required no separate injunction. He stood at the same time as Parker, and they filed out of the cabin. Neither of the protagonists at the desk spared them a glance. Their eyes were still locked in that cold mutual stare.

James hauled the collar of his boat-cloak tightly round his head to avoid the spray shooting over the bows of the barge. They had left the *Queen Charlotte* and were making their way towards their ship in a wicked, choppy sea.

"You must tell me what you said to make him change his mind, brother!" he shouted.

But Harry merely smiled and indicated that they were close to the gangway. James would have to wait for an explanation. He was forced to further patience once they were aboard. Harry would not consent to speak until he got the *Bucephalas* clear of the fleet. That was no easy task. None of these ships of the line, sailing in strict attendance on the flagship, would alter their course by a hair's breadth to accommodate a privateer. Then he locked himself away, studying the charts, and the lists of the ship's stores, with instructions that he was not to be disturbed. Finally, after an hour, during which his brother chafed with impatience, he came on deck again. The orders rang out that put the *Bucephalas* on to a new heading, with all canvas set to take advantage of the westerly wind. Harry, at the wheel, set sail after sail, topgallants, royals, and kites, followed by spanker and flying jib. *Bucephalas* raced through the water, with the log showing a touch over thirteen knots and great spouts of water breaking over the cathead.

This new course had brought a few curious glances from the men. Several of them, between hauling on ropes and bending on sails, had sidled up to James. Even with an overcast sky they guessed that the ship was headed due south. But he was in no position to enlighten them. Whatever their private thoughts, they said nothing to the man at the wheel. Their captain liked to run his ship navy fashion, which precluded the asking of questions on the quarterdeck. Finally Harry pronounced himself satisfied and, calling for his dinner, went below. Both brothers had changed into dry clothes and were comfortably reclining in front of the stove, nursing a glass of delicious Chambolle-Musigny, before Harry could be brought to explain. And even then it was only when James insisted.

"I cannot abide this smug air, brother. You have the look of a man who's just sold a spavined horse at full price."

"It's been a rare event these last months, James. But if I'm smug it is because I have achieved something. Ever since I was a nipper aboard Father's ship, I've longed to beard an admiral and put him in his place."

"Which you did today?"

"Politely, but firmly."

"And what polite expressions did you employ?"

"I merely laid out the alternatives for Lord Bridport to examine. One of which was that I return to England and inform Dundas that neither his signature, nor his elevated position, meant anything to the temporary commander of the Channel Fleet. I also reminded him of the difficulties, for someone of his seniority, of obtaining and holding his present position. Then there is the matter of the policy of retiring to Torbay, which does not enjoy universal approbation. There are admirals ashore who think such a policy mistaken, who also see themselves better suited to the task of confounding the French. They are, no doubt, exerting every ounce of their influence to have him superseded."

"All of this is common knowledge."

Harry gave his brother a wolfish grin. "Then I enquired this of him: how he would react to a group of Members of Parliament demanding his removal every time there was a maritime debate in the House."

"Could we muster such a group?"

"I don't know, James. But then Lord Bridport is in the same boat as we are. He doesn't know either."

"I take it you offered him an alternative?"

"I did. Since Toner's criminal actions took place in an area under his command, he has the right to order the return of our men. So, to facilitate me, and also to minimize the trouble I could cause, he wrote such an order, with a copy to the Admiralty."

"It's a nice idea, brother, though I think rather hard to enforce, since we have no idea where Toner is."

"We know where he's headed, James."

"And what about our present course?"

Harry glanced over the stove at James and smiled. His brother was a surefire conduit of information aboard the ship. Men who would not come within ten feet of Harry with a question had few qualms when it came to collaring the younger Ludlow. They knew that when enough of them hinted at the same disquiet, James would seek an explanation on their behalf.

"We are in his wake, brother. He's on course for the West Indies. Toner will head south to pick up the Trade winds. So will we."

"Can we catch him?"

"If we crack on we might. But having looked at the state of our stores we will need to victual at the Canaries."

Harry's air of confidence suddenly evaporated and he sat forward in his chair, his knees nearly touching the stove. "I know you didn't sign on for this, brother. Your short cruise has already gone on a lot longer than I anticipated. I thought you'd be home in a prize long since. I cannot spare the time to touch in England, so if you wish I will leave you in the Canaries. It will be easy to find a passage home from there."

"What? Are you suggesting I leave the ship and miss settling that Scotsman's hash! Take me to the ends of the earth if you must."

Harry smiled warmly at that, as though the mere presence of James would ease his burden. "We might come up on him mid-ocean."

"It's a chancy thing to call on a warship to heave to, Harry. Even I know that much. And would he treat Bridport's orders with any more respect than he treated our exemptions?"

"I need to know where he is, brother. But I shan't go calling on him to heave to. I think he'd rather sink us than admit his error. So I shall be content merely to sight his topsails. If we are then favoured with a wind we could arrive before he does. But since he's on the same course I shall not worry if we arrive a few days behind him."

"You obviously feel, since we are going all this way, that we have a reasonable prospect of success."

"I do," replied Harry, recovering his composure. "We must get him in the presence of another senior officer, one who would not dare to question Bridport's instructions. That person can then command Toner to comply."

"And where is this wondrous personage to be found?"

"English Harbour."

"Antigua?"

"Yes, brother. That is where Admiral Bessborough is stationed, and that is where we must go. So you can tell the crew, when you go on deck, that we're heading for the middle passage, bound for the West Indies."

"For the sole purpose of rescuing our crew?" asked James.

Harry lost his self-satisfied air, looking suddenly angry. "Have you forgotten that Pender is amongst those men?"

"No, Harry, I have not. I merely enquired if there was another reason for your decision. And if you are curious as to how I come to ask, then let me say that knowing you, as I do, leads me to suppose your answer superfluous."

Harry tried to maintain his sour look. But he couldn't hold it in the face of James's quizzical expression. The grin broke through. "We've had few pickings here, brother. It will do no harm to go fishing for prizes in fresh waters."

"I thought as much."

"Do you disapprove of the idea?" asked Harry.

"Certainly not. And your reasoning will make the crew doubly happy. They are sick of our lack of success."

"Why doubly happy?"

"Most of the men who've spoken to me had a terrible fear that you were going to let that bastard Toner get away with it, and leave their mates to the mercy of the navy."

The weather cleared the following day and as they sailed south it became blissful. Long days of unbroken sunshine with a blue, empty sea all around them. Harry took great trouble in the setting of his sails. For once in his life, he needed to care for his masts and canvas. The way he sailed *Bucephalas* the day before had helped to ease his temper, but it was not something he could sustain. They were all going to be away from home for a long time, with no sure knowledge that he'd be able to replace anything severely damaged. Besides, with half his crew gone he was a touch short-handed for the kind of racing process which would easily overhaul *Endymion*. The only article in which he was profligate was powder and shot. He prized fast, accurate gunnery above all things and now, under-strength, he needed even greater efficiency on the guns than he'd demanded before. Every empty cask and barrel was put to use as a target, the air filled with smoke and sound as the crew fired off their cannon in competition, with a guinea on the scuttle for the winning team.

It was as though the gods of the sea, having been so cruel for so long, now saw fit to favour them. The wind was in the right quarter, steady and strong for days on end. They sighted the occasional ship on the horizon, but few afloat had the curiosity to come and investigate in the middle of a war. Besides, *Bucephalas* was clearly no merchant vessel. Her row of gunports denoted that she was well able to defend herself. With topgallants aloft and drawing she was a handsome creature, a hundred feet long, with three high masts. Some might mistake her for a warship, since she looked very like a cut-down frigate of the 22-gun variety. Fast and nimble, especially on a bowline, able to keep stays in tight manoeuvres. But she flew no man-o'-war pennant at her mast-head, nor the national flags that would mark her out as Royal Navy. Brand new, she was a dry, weatherly vessel that could fight anything short of a sixth-rate. And even then, if he got near enough, Harry's carronades could blow a hole in the foot-thick planking. Not that he would get that close. He was a privateer, who owned the deck on which he stood. Fighting warships was something he trained for, but sought to avoid. His business was the chasing and capture of merchant cargo, which could be sold, along with the ships, for a handsome profit.

They raised the mountains of Grand Canary within a fortnight, black and menacing, with a ring of white cloud around the summit. Harry put into the harbour to make up his stores. His crew, denied shore leave, didn't complain. Instead they laboured to bring aboard water, firewood, hogsheads of beer, rum, lime juice, and cases of wine. There was fresh bread and biscuit, fruit and vegetables, casks of beef and salt pork, powder and shot, and extra bolts of canvas to replace damaged sails.

Harry worked his crew double tides, and ordered all his stores from the tenders that surrounded the ship as it anchored, despite the fact that such chandlers charged premium rates. The only person allowed ashore was James, burdened with the task of sending Harry's letters as well as his own, so that those in England, friends, family, and business associates, would know their intentions. Despite what he'd said to James, the confident way he hinted that they could arrive at practically the same time as Toner, Harry Ludlow knew the sea to be a fickle mistress. The weather could favour one ship quite easily against another, even if they sailed exactly the same course, giving Toner a wind denied to the *Bucephalas*. The *Endymion* could arrive weeks before him, or, if things proved especially foul, and forced the frigate south into the Doldrums, months behind.

As James returned, laden with books describing their destination, the lights were coming on in the lower town, beckoning the sailors to taste the delights of the bawdy houses and taverns. But Harry's men barely spared them a glance. They knew as well as their captain what could happen at sea. The only moans that could be heard were from those complaining thus: that taking on so much in the way of stores would make them too low in the water and slow the ship down. As they cleared the harbour all eyes were turned to the west, wondering how their shipmates were faring. Every man aboard felt, in his bones, that they were in peril.

CHAPTER TEN

"YOU'LL LEARN the cost of stubbornness here, I swear!"

Dunlop's angry face was less than an inch from Flowers's. Pender, standing next to Callander, the midshipman who had charge of the party, was set to move forward to intervene. His shipmate from the *Bucephalas* was known to like a scrap and he might just forget himself and belt the premier, which would result in a hanging. There were few officers aboard the *Endymion* who turned a blind eye, but when it came to a zealous pursuit of duty, the first lieutenant was the worst. Flowers hadn't got himself into this predicament by being stubborn; it was merely his inability, in these new surroundings, to adjust his way of doing things. Accustomed to Harry Ludlow's methods, in which a trained man was allowed to work without fuss, he could not accommodate the constant presence of carping officers. Nor did he see that an unimportant task had to be carried out speedily, as if the ship was in mortal danger. Flowers was one of the few aboard who'd never served on a king's ship, and the ways of the navy were a mystery to him.

Young Mr Callander, a Scotsman like his captain, with his baby face and kindly demeanour, had been content to let the men work at their own pace, something which earned him a rebuke from his superior. Dunlop had undertaken to show how an officer should command his men, and when Flowers had failed to increase his pace, the premier had exploded.

"I was doin' the job right, your honour."

The seaman's face didn't help. His head was an odd shape, in some ways like a crescent. And he talked out of the corner of his mouth, like a man imparting something secret, which made his reply seem all the more insolent. The premier's bloated purple face seemed to swell even more, the cratered nose twitching as though it had a life of its own.

"How dare you answer me so!"

The rope's end hit Flowers on his left ear. He crouched down and away from the blow. But Pender could see that he was bunching himself up to retaliate. He shot forward, put one foot behind the man's heel, then grabbed Flowers by the back of his shirt and yanked hard.

"Ain't you got no manners, you swab?" he yelled, as his shipmate fell backwards. "Don't you yet know how to go about addressing a gentleman?"

Pender threw Flowers to Jubilee, a barrel-chested Pole who had the strength to contain half a dozen men, then turned to face Dunlop, his expression that of a man both confused and sorry. What he was presented with didn't do much to reassure him. If ever a man could be judged by his face it was the first lieutenant. He had bushy ginger eyebrows over a pair of tawny eyes. Every vein in his swollen, purple face was broken: the effect of over-indulgence in drink, abetted by wind and weather. His nose had erupted in all directions, the cratered lumps giving it the appearance of some diseased tree trunk. When he smiled, which was rare and never humorous, his yellow teeth only added to the impression of some animal without a trace of human pity.

"He don't yet know his duty, your honour," said Pender, touching his forelock hastily. Inside, he was as angry as Flowers. But he'd set himself the task of keeping his men away from the grating, and if that meant a pretence at servitude, so be it.

"And neither, Jacko, do you," hissed Dunlop, looking over Pender's shoulder at Flowers, Jubilee, and the silent midshipman. "Is this the way you command your men, Callander, so that they feel free to question the premier?"

Pender took a deep breath. He was committed. Silence wouldn't get him out of trouble, only words.

"It's strange surroundings for all an' no mistake, sir. Even those that's been aboard a king's ship before. But if you give us time, we'll come to your ways. An' you'll find that you got a good bargain. Willing sailors, instead of pressed men."

Dunlop was just about to explode again, about to tell the whole group that they'd be willing or be flogged, when the trembling voice of Mr Callander cut in.

"I take full responsibility, sir. Being that these men are proper sailors, who needed no telling to do their duty, I left them to work at their own pace."

Dunlop's tawny eyes never left Pender's face and the smell of his rotten breath was strong as he replied. "Then you are not behaving like an officer should, sir, which is what I expect you to do. Quite apart from the point that it is your sworn duty."

The premier pressed his own knotted rope into the boy's hand. "Take this, sir, and use it freely."

Pender couldn't see the boy shaking, but the fact that he was quivering was reflected in his voice. "I shall attend to that duty more assiduously, sir, should I be granted the opportunity."

The young man had, either by accident or design, made it impossible for Dunlop to issue punishment. By taking the blame upon himself, Callander would be undermined if the premier went further. Dunlop walked past Pender, pushed both Flowers and Jubilee out of his way, and spoke softly to the midshipman, who, with his fair complexion, long red-gold hair, and blue eyes, all aided by an untimely blush, looked something like a girl in a man's suit.

"You'll get the opportunity, Mr Callander. Just as I dare say, at some time soon, you'll need to bring some defaulters before the captain. Put aside your inclination to kindness, sir, for it will be abused by these people. And should you not fancy the notion of flogging, be advised that it is the only true method of discipline."

Callander tried to keep his gaze steady, but the mention of his responsibilities as an officer of the *Endymion* made him drop his eyes. He looked very much like the insecure young boy he truly was, even in the blue uniform, with its white facings, which was designed to give him presence. Dunlop's voice, as he continued, had the soft insistent tone of a concerned parent.

"Don't let the idea of a little blood put you off, sir. You will grow accustomed to that. Just as you will come to realize that a ship that sheds no blood is useless to king and country. These louts will dun you at every turn. They are scum without brains, but they're not short on cunning."

Callander lifted his eyes to Dunlop's. He could hardly say what he felt; that these men were not stupid, even the Pole, Jubilee, whose English was confused; that they worked well if left in peace; and that brutality would destroy their efficiency, not enhance it. The young man, instead, said what the bounds of naval discipline demanded.

"Aye, aye, sir."

The premier spun on his heel and marched off down the gang-way. Pender turned and winked at Flowers, then spoke softly to the young Scots midshipman.

"For God's sake, Mr Callander, belabour us with some abuse. It don't matter what you say, if you shout loud enough. We'll do the work, and your yellin' will keep the likes of the premier off our backs."

"Get working, you damned swabs," piped Callander, with a feeble swipe that hit the bullwark.

This remark was accompanied by another untimely blush. The voice was too high to sound threatening, but the men under his command, who like all sailors loved to beard authority, cowered away as though he was Lucifer himself. They scurried about their tasks, favouring each other with sly winks and covert grins.

"You sailed close-hauled there, mate."

Pender looked up into the dark-complexioned face, which bore a knowing grin. It was Garmond again, the man who'd addressed him in his hammock on their first night aboard. He'd put flesh on that voice the following day, since they shared a mess table. Gar-mond always had an amused expression, enhanced by the look in his eyes. This contrasted oddly with his gravelly, nasal voice. He smiled often, but it was the follies of his fellow seamen that amused him more than any joke. From Warwickshire, he'd been some kind of clerk in civilian life. How he had come to the navy was a secret that he wasn't prepared to divulge. All that anyone knew was that he'd been taken up for the navy as part of the new law that obliged each inland parish to provide a levy of men for the fleet.

Clearly he was a man educated well above the norm, which indicated that he was either from a debtors' gaol or the local Bridewell prison for convicted felons. Most of the others aboard the ship, who'd been recruited from the same source, were vagrants or ex-farm workers who'd lost the means to survive due to the increasing enclosure of common grazing lands. Every non-maritime parish in the land had decanted the contents of its workhouse into the fleet, which served a double advantage. It absolved them from the need to provide useful citizens and it cut the local poor rate by removing those who subsisted on it. That such a draft did nothing for the efficiency of the king's navy was not held to be a matter of much concern. If these men knew nothing about how to set a sail, tie a knot, or fire off a ship's cannon, then the navy would teach them.

The *Endymion,* apart from the commissioned and warrant officers, was now split into three factions. By far the smallest was those men who'd been aboard when Toner took over the ship: these were the men that the previous captain didn't want. Being a person of some influence he'd been allowed to shift as many hands as he wanted to his new command, and naturally that meant he took those men who performed well. What he left behind were the dregs that could be found in any crew. They might look like "tars," with their decorated pigtails and lofty manner, indeed some served afloat most of their lives, but they were either dimwits, drunkards, sodomites or hard bargains who could not be brought, by kindness or the lash, to the proper execution of their duty.

The problems of crewing the ship had been eased by the men taken from the *Bucephalas.* Disgruntled they might be, but they knew their jobs. And they were men that Harry Ludlow had

selected from a much larger pool of volunteers. They could all
hand, reef, and steer with a professional ease which they applied
to all their tasks. A wise head would have let them be and sprin-
kled them amongst the crew in such a way that they would teach
those less able landsmen, so that they, too, could contribute to the
running of the ship.

The third group, those landsmen, were the most numerous.
Life ashore had been, for them, no bed of roses. The Poor Rate
didn't run to two square meals a day, with clothing provided and
a promise of money to be paid at the end of their commission.
Never mind that the cost of their pursers' slops was taken out of
their wages and that such payments often came to them years late.
It made no difference that their first experience of life afloat was
a sickness so debilitating that they fully expected to expire. Time
would grant them sea legs, just as it would make familiar that
which was initially strange. Any decent captain would have treated
them kindly and eased them into their new life. But Pender had
already heard the tale of their first days at sea. Toner would not,
or could not, abide their inefficiency. His orders had sent him off
short of his proper complement, with those hands he had either
truculent or untrained. He'd used the lash to cow them, and rope's
ends to drive them to their duties. Pender had heard that one man
had died at the grating, though he didn't know the circumstances.

All of this was fertile ground for a sea-lawyer like Garmond.
Here was a man who could read and write fluently, something
which elevated him in the eyes of his fellows. He was as useless
as the next man drafted from parish or gaol, but he had the ability to be in the background when matters took a nasty turn so
had, as yet, avoided his share of punishment at the grating. What
he did share, and freely, was his opinions regarding their officers.
Given his abilities with pen and book he was right to see himself as their equals. Toner, with his background, had not attracted
any aristocrats, or wealthy officers, to his command. So, to Garmond's way of thinking, the only thing that those who lorded it
over him had was a blue coat with some brass buttons and a piece

of parchment with a seal. Tom Paine was his hero, so knowing how to sail a ship gave them no power to chastise their fellow man. What he really meant, of course, was himself. Punishments inflicted on others only served as fodder for his opinions. There was no charity, as far as Pender could observe, in his concern.

"You should've stayed back and left Flowers to take the lash."

Pender answered warily. If taxed to explain his reservations, he could not have stated exactly why he mistrusted Garmond. Perhaps it was because the fellow was too smooth, to ready to smile at another's misfortune. In the main he agreed with the sentiments he expressed. But Pender had the feeling that this was someone with more behind his words than he was prepared to say openly.

"You attend to your concerns, Garmond, an' I'll see to Flowers', and mine."

"An' what am I to do if'n they're the same?"

"Can't see how they could be, mate."

Garmond snorted derisively. "You'll know soon enough when your skin's introduced to the cat."

Pender was tempted to say that he'd met that problem before, but that would smack of boasting. Nor was he willing to divulge the fact that he'd been in the king's navy, though someone like Garmond would doubtless guess that from his behaviour.

"I intend to spare myself that pleasure, mate."

Jubilee, the Pole, who worshipped Pender, had obviously seen that Garmond's presence was unwelcome. He stepped between them, imposing the considerable bulk of his squat frame as a barrier that could not be breached. Garmond laughed out loud, taking care to turn his head towards the bows so that he would not be observed by the officers on the quarterdeck.

"Don't you go a-thinking that little play-act will save you. If you knew Dunlop better, you'd not be so cocky. You caught him when he was sober. Later, or some other night, when he's in his cups, he'll remember you and the way you addressed him. Then he, and that bastard of a second lieutenant McPartland, will get to egging each other on. Mr Callander won't be forgotten either.

He'll be seen to have embarrassed his premier, will have his arse stretched over a gun barrel, and his seniors will take turns with a sapling to remind him of his proper duty. And then he'll come after you, with all the other drunks in the gunroom to aid him. An' in case you think I'm gilding it, let me tell you it's something that's happened more'n once."

Pender sought to make his voice relaxed, as though Garmond's words had no effect. "If I have to bear a floggin', so be it."

"Floggin', mate? I should pray for that. If the officers come out full of that blackstrap claret they're so fond of, it will be with cudgels in their hands. When they gets like that, broken skin is no substitute for broken bones."

CHAPTER ELEVEN

STRUAN CALLANDER, standing at the taffrail, looked up at the clear night sky, marvelling at the stars which filled the heavens. The *Endymion* was on a south-westerly heading searching for the line of latitude which they'd sail. Following this would take them across the wide Atlantic until eventually they raised the island of Antigua. The Milky Way lay like a gossamer blanket above the masts. The North Star, so far south, was a mere speck, with none of the brightness it had in more northerly climes. To the south new stars and constellations provided the means of determining the ship's position. There was a slight feeling of pride that they were no longer a complete mystery. He was fresh to the subjects of astronomy and navigation, yet pleased that they held no terror. He might have reservations about his instructors but the boy enjoyed his lessons, just as he took pleasure in the way that the complex task of sailing a ship seemed to seep effortlessly into his brain. Actions which had been incomprehensible a few months previously were now second nature, part of his very being. The social aspects of life afloat were less so.

He'd come up on deck to get away from the noise and ribaldry of the midshipmen's berth. There his fellow "youngsters" seemed intent on aping their elders in the gunroom, both in their capacity for drink and in the base nature of their conversation. The talk was all of the whores they'd bedded. Even Overton, younger than Callander and half his size, intimated he was a great bawdy-house athlete. And if they were to be believed some of these ladies had hearts of pure gold: his fellows were so accomplished in the rogering line that the doxies, in a state of ecstasy, declined to be paid. It was either that or crude allusions to sodomy and bestiality, with many an injunction aimed at him to cease his constant attempts at self-abuse.

That part of the naval life didn't suit him, and his first days aboard had been hell. Every ship subscribed to its own ceremonies of initiation. *Endymion* was no different. He'd been sent aloft, to the very top of the mainmast, to fetch a sky hook, the terror of his passage to these dizzying heights bringing delight to those below. On returning to the mids' berth he'd found rats in his sea-chest, trying to eat the lace of his best linen shirts. His breeches had been torn off him on the first night, exposing to many a salacious eye that he was not yet fully grown to manhood. This had earned him his nickname, Daisy Callander. This shortcoming was referred to endlessly, along with enquiries as to whether he'd yet enjoyed his "first spurt." The gunner's wife, Mrs Wallington, who had charge of the midshipmen's welfare, blithely informed him he was fortunate; that this particular mids' berth was a lot better than others she'd known. In some of the ships she'd served aboard such a pretty boy as he would have found himself in deep water, vessels that positively crawled with persistent and uncontrollable pederasts.

Young Struan Callander ascribed the absence of such problems to her presence. From the oldest to the youngest, the midshipmen went in mortal fear of Mrs Wallington's wrath. With twice the girth and three times the strength of her husband, she was not afraid to box their ears if the need arose. And the good lady saw the welfare of the newer recruits as a particular concern. So bullying, goosing, and attempts at seduction were rare. There was a hierarchy, of course, which had nothing to do with Mrs Wallington. This placed Midshipman Hemmings at the top. His elevated status was nothing to do with age, ability, or experience, since he was a mere fifteen years old and not overbright. It was accorded to him because he was expected to pass for lieutenant at an early age, and rise rapidly in the service, being a distant relative of Admiral Colpoys, who could be expected to use his influence on the boy's behalf.

The youngster stayed near the edge of the rail that ran round the quarterdeck, not wishing his footsteps to be heard by the captain, who was in his cabin right beneath his feet. The loud noises coming from the gunroom, one deck below on the upper deck, were sufficient to penetrate both the planking and the thick casement windows. It was not till he was right by the taffrail that he heard the murmuring voice coming through the skylight of the main cabin. The voice was angry, obviously haranguing someone. He recognized Toner's low growl, having been exposed to it many times, chastised for skylarking or some dereliction of duty. With a quick glance at the marine sentries, he edged closer to the skylight, wondering who his captain was berating. He could only hear the one voice and it was a moment before the boy realized that Toner was talking to himself, though there were clearly two sides to his conversation, with one half being carried out in a jocular tone.

"Now that your debts are settled, Captain Toner, and you have a wee bit of gelt to spare, can I interest you in a small investment that will see you an amazing return?"

The voice changed from a wheedling one to the familiar grating tone he knew so well. "Oh, aye, John Toner. They'll be after you, projectors and the like. As soon as you've got a spare bob in yer poke they'll be there, with schemes aplenty to dun you out of your money."

There was a long pause, during which the noise from the gunroom increased perceptibly. They'd started to sing what sounded like a snatch of opera, with the purser's fine tenor voice rising clear of the rest.

"Listen to them," growled Toner. "No' a gentleman among them and the purser an indictable thief, for all his pretty bel-canto. How can a man progress with such a set of officers? Low-lifes and drunkards to a man, an' very likely poxed into the bargain."

The sound of footsteps as one of the marine sentries moved had Callander stepping away smartly from the skylight, his mind full of what he'd heard. It had never occurred to him that Captain

Toner might despise his officers. The natural order of things almost demanded the opposite. Certainly he was a remote man, who entertained rarely, but the mids' berth had put that down to his lack of means. Perhaps he didn't entertain because he had no desire for the company. Idly, as he made his way below decks, he wondered if his captain was drunk, since he could hardly encompass the idea of a sober man talking so earnestly to himself.

"Mr Callander." The midshipman turned to face the third lieutenant, Wheeler, who was the officer of the watch. Alone amongst those with commissions, this officer seemed disinclined to use excessive punishment. "Mr Hemmings gave me a message for you. You are to report to Mr Dunlop in the gunroom."

"Aye, aye, sir," the boy replied crisply as he turned towards the companion-way. He smiled. What would the premier say if he heard his captain's low opinion of him? He hated Dunlop, as much for his ugliness as his methods. The way he treated the crew disgusted him, since the premier saw no difference between the good and the bad. He was equally harsh with everyone. McPartland was no better. Callander had learned more from these new hands in two weeks than Dunlop had taught him in two months. He'd been worried the other day when he'd intervened to protect Pender. But Dunlop had let it pass. If he alluded to it at all, it was only to wonder when Callander was going to finally bring a man up on a flogging charge. The blast of hot, fetid air hit him as he opened the gunroom door, as did the bellowing voices of the singers. Dunlop, at the head of the table, held up a hand, which brought immediate silence.

"Ah. It's Mr Daisy Callander, the common seaman's friend. Do enter, young sir."

The boy looked around the assembled faces, red, perspiring, and grinning, wondering what it was about his person that seemed to amuse them so.

Pender woke the instant the hand touched him. He was halfway out of his hammock before the whispered voice reassured him he was in no danger. As he steadied himself he realized that he'd been woken by the young midshipman, Callander. The boy spoke in his usual careful way, a clear method of speech which Pender now knew was the accent of the Scottish Highlands.

"You must get Flowers out of his hammock, at once."

Pender took the youngster's arm to pull him away from the ears of the others. As the boy moved he emitted a slight gasp before clenching his teeth.

"Dunlop?"

"Not just him, Pender. I was called up to the gunroom. They're all as drunk as lords. I was tied to the table. Even the purser took a hand in whipping me."

"Why?" asked Pender, though he feared he knew the answer.

"What happened the other day. I thought he'd forgotten or let it pass."

"And they're coming after me and Flowers?"

"When they've treated themselves to another bottle."

"You best get back to the mids' berth."

In the light from the tallow wads, the older man could see the glistening wetness on the boy's cheeks. "I'm sorry, Pender. I cannot aid you further."

"Never fear, Mr Callander. The likes of Flowers an' I have been in hot water all our lives. If we're set to take a beating then so be it. But I reckon, myself, that we're wise enough to outwit a parcel of drunken swabs."

"But . . ."

"Go, Mr Callander. You've taken your whipping. If you hang around here, you'll only leave yourself open to another."

The boy, propelled by the force of the older man's arm, walked away slowly, his body unnaturally upright and his gait stiff. Pender made for Flowers's hammock and pinched his snoring nose.

"It's me, Pender. Get out of there, damn quick. Dunlop and the other officers are coming after us, probably with cudgels if Garmond's to be believed."

He then raced back to his own hammock, to wake Garmond.

But there was no need. The man was lying with his eyes wide open, his thick red lips parted in that infuriating smile. "I won't rouse myself to say I told you so."

"I need your dice," whispered Pender.

Garmond grinned then, his teeth shining in the faint tallow light, which made Pender wonder if he'd guessed his intentions. His hand went over his head to pull the bag that hung from the same hook as the head of his hammock. He delved inside and came out with a closed fist, which he thrust towards the other sailor. Pender took the small metal cup containing the dice without a word and ran back to Flowers. The man was still half asleep, but the sound of footsteps, and the kind of carrying noise that a drunken man mistakes for a whisper, soon woke him up. They ran for the furthest companion-way, their bare feet making no sound on the smooth planking of the deck.

"Where are we going, Pious?" asked Flowers softly, so alarmed that, for the first time in his life, he'd used Pender's nickname.

"Where drunken men might fear to follow, mate. We're goin' into the tops."

"What if they come up there after us?"

They were at the bottom of the companion-way, with the moonlight streaming through the gratings to make a criss-cross pattern on the lower deck. Flowers saw the flash of Pender's white teeth as he smiled. "I hope they do, Flowers. For nothing would please me more than that I should aid Mr Dunlop and his ilk in slipping from the shrouds."

The sudden commotion behind them, raised angry voices mixed with protestations of ignorance, was ample proof that their disappointed assailants had found the empty hammocks.

"We're in trouble now," said Flowers.

Pender laughed, though not loud enough to be heard by anyone other than his companion. The effect on Flowers was immediate. He too had realized the absurdity of what he'd just said. "Come on, you daft bugger," said Pender, taking his arm to drag him up the ladder that led to the deck.

No one noticed them as they scurried towards the foremast shrouds. Pender leapt up on to the bulwarks and slipped his foot into the cat's cradle of ropes that stretched taut, from the side of the ship to the cap. Flowers followed and they raced up into the night air with the confidence of experienced topmen, to whom such an avenue was commonplace.

The platform at the join of the lower mast and the topmast was not spacious. But it would provide enough room for two men to be caught doing something illegal. And should the drunken officers pursue them, then they could always go further aloft, and out on to the yards, where a man intent on swinging a cudgel would have to be very seriously inebriated to follow them.

Pender had one hope: that Dunlop didn't want the captain to know what he was about. Toner wouldn't care about his officers beating his men with ropes' ends, he watched that every day, but cudgels were a different matter. Their new captain might be a tyrant, but he was, according to some of the hands, a punctilious one, who insisted that everything be done within the regulations. A serious injury with a heavy club inflicted in the heat of the moment would entail awkward entries in the log.

That bible, which recorded every action that occurred to the ship and its crew, was a sacrosanct source of the truth. It could be embellished, of course, just as certain actions could be made to look unimportant. But the ship's log, along with the muster books, accounts, and inventories, were carefully scrutinized by the clerks of the Admiralty Office. Such men had a sharp eye for dissimulation, allied to an abiding distaste for serving officers, who, to their mind, did nothing but waste money and stores. The information the ship's books contained had to tally. While euphemism was rife, no captain dared to enter a deliberate falsehood, since discovery would entail a court martial and could, in extreme cases, cost him his commission.

Pender found he was holding his breath, waiting for the sound of the officers coming on deck to find them. But there was no noise to indicate such a thing and he began to relax. He opened

his hand and looked at the dice, the ivory picking up the glim
from the moonlight. His mind went back to the look that Garmond had given him as he had handed them over. It was a memory
that, for reasons he couldn't fathom, made him uneasy.

"Are we safe?" asked Flowers.

"I don't call being rigged to the grating safe."

"What do you mean?"

Pender explained what had happened, how Garmond had forewarned him. He said nothing about Callander, for that was a secret
best kept safe. Then, as gently as he could, he told the other man
what they had to do. "If there be such a thing as the lesser of two
evils, mate, then this is it."

Flowers replied with a gentle curse.

CHAPTER TWELVE

THEY WAITED until the officer of the watch, doing his rounds, was right beneath them. Then Pender rattled the cup containing the dice. The officer stopped and looked round. Pender rattled the cup again and shot back out of sight as the pale face, looking up in the air, was suddenly illuminated by the moon. He recognized Wheeler, the most junior lieutenant.

"You men. In the cap. On deck, at the double."

"Bastard's too lazy to come and get us," said Flowers.

"Come on. I know you're up there. And bring those damned dice down with you."

Slowly, with the attitude of men caught red-handed, they made their way down on to the deck, there to stand before the irate lieutenant. Pender knew that Wheeler was less imbued with the spirit of the *Endymion* than the other officers. That still made him someone who would certainly do whatever Dunlop ordered. But he had certain advantages over the premier, as far as these miscreants were concerned. He was fair-minded, sober, on duty, and probably totally unaware of the first lieutenant's plans. They held their breath, praying that such thoughts were true. Wheeler was glaring at them in the most unfriendly way. Suddenly, he called to the marines and ordered them to lock the two sailors in the cable tier until defaulters in the morning.

"Damn fools you are, too," he hissed, as they were led below. "Only an idiot gets caught dicing."

Toner had not yet read the specific Article of War that related to gambling, a clause which deemed it prejudicial to good order and discipline. But he'd arrive at that point in a few minutes, which would be the moment to call forward the two malefactors to face their "just" punishment. Garmond, standing just behind Pender and Flowers, whispered in the first man's ear.

"Fine world, ain't it, mate, when officers can dice away, if they please, while the likes of us are flogged for it?"

Pender, right at the front of the crowded assembly, couldn't reply. But he tried to kick Garmond discreetly by lifting his heel.

"Strikes me," Garmond continued in his nasal voice, "that the Frenchies might have the right of it. Happen it's time we did something about the men that lord it over us. Ever ask yourself, Pender, why someone like you has to bow the knee to a pup like Callander? Your blood's the same, and you've got a better brain . . ."

Pender heard the man gasp, as his heel got him on the shin at the second attempt. But Garmond refused to be quiet. "All I ask is that we talk, man to man. 'Cause you and I have it in us to ease the lot of every poor sod aboard . . ."

Garmond obviously had his eye on Toner. As the captain's eyes swung round to look at the two defaulters, the voice behind Pender's ear fell silent.

"Step forward, defaulters," said Dunlop, his voice thick and his eyes puffed with lack of sleep.

Pender and Flowers did as they were ordered. Toner looked them up and down, his black eyebrows twitching and the ever-grinding teeth gnashing away.

"Mr Callander, do you wish to plead for your men?"

The young midshipman's response earned him a hard look from Dunlop.

"I do, sir."

"Then proceed, Mr Callander."

"I would plead, sir, that the men are new to the ship and its ways, let alone the discipline of the Royal Navy. No doubt, on a privateering ship, gambling is permitted . . ."

Callander stopped, not because he'd run out of words, but because of the black look in his captain's eyes. The boy realized then that the more he pleaded for Pender and Flowers the greater his commander's anger would be. That would increase the level of punishment Toner would inflict. All the lines he'd so carefully rehearsed were worse than useless. Indeed, they were positively dangerous. Yet he was committed to saying something, so he decided on a complete change of tack. The words, delivered in his clear, Highland accent, didn't emerge smoothly. He stumbled over every sentence, and kept his head down lest by a stare, or a blush, he might increase his captain's anger.

"Yet they knew enough to avoid a public place . . . so they are aware that they were committing an offence . . . against the articles that were read to them when they came aboard."

His tongue seemed stuck to the roof of his mouth, and he didn't have the saliva to wet his parched lips. "Perhaps they thought the officers slack, sir . . . Perhaps, hearing the revelry emanating from the gunroom, they felt immune from discovery."

He heard Dunlop grunt at that point, but the premier couldn't interrupt. Somehow, the thought that he'd upset the first lieutenant, who'd taken the lead in beating him over the gun, made the rest of his impromptu speech easier to deliver.

"Imagine, sir, the shock when their felony was uncovered. I think they realize now that they are commanded by most diligent officers; that they cannot transgress without certain punishment; that they have partly taken on board the lesson; and that you, sir, in a spirit of magnanimity, should punish them accordingly. For you have their souls in your charge as well as their bodies. I request, for their own salvation, that you make an example of them, sir. And in doing so you take the opportunity to demonstrate to the newer members of the crew the depths of your benevolence, as well as the unbending standards that you exemplify."

The last words had come more easily, and so delivered with a flourish, brought forth a murmur from the crew, standing behind the two silent offenders. The less able brains were incensed, thinking that they'd heard a young gentleman, previously deemed kindly, demand the lash when he should have being seeking leniency. But those few who had the power of thought, saw that the youngster had boxed his commander in. Many of those present had served under hard captains, a few had even met tyrants like Toner in their life at sea. What all these commanders had in common was one thing. Regardless of how they were perceived by others, they all saw themselves as fair, upright men, imposing proper discipline, to maintain clear standards.

Pender had listened harder than most. He knew that young Callander had changed tack, realizing that a plea for leniency was wasted on Toner. The boy had appealed, just in time, to the one part of his captain's nature that might produce the result he desired. Pender had never envisaged that he might get off without a flogging. He, at least, was grateful to the young Scotsman, whose aim had been to diminish the sentence, on a ship where fifty lashes was a common punishment for a minor misdemeanour.

Callander had dropped his head again, so that the blush caused by his own eloquence was hidden. But finally the boy lifted his eyes to look at Toner. The captain's countenance was still hard, the teeth still as they'd been before. But there was something behind the eyes, almost a softening, that raised Pender's hopes. It was almost as if, by speaking so, the midshipman, who was after all a fellow countryman, had caused Toner to doubt the rightness of his actions.

"Eloquently put, Mr Callander. I have mind to hearken to what you say."

"If I may be allowed a word, sir," said Dunlop.

"Later," snapped Toner.

His premier flushed at this, but it was his own fault that he had suffered a public rebuke. He'd spoken too late to influence matters. The captain could hardly contend that he'd listen to Callander, then allow his second-in-command to interfere, and probably press for the maximum punishment. Once Dunlop had done so, he'd be obliged to agree. And his reasons for heeding Callander were complex, too tangled to even attempt a public explanation.

It was nothing to do with the connection between them, though it would doubtless be perceived as such. The boy's presence aboard was a way of repaying a favour to Callander's uncle, an Edinburgh moneylender who'd advanced him credit in the past. Toner saw an opportunity for a little popularity here, and though not normally a man to court such an ephemeral thing, he was not so insensitive a soul that he despised the notion of being liked. Then there was the pleasure to be derived from doing the unexpected. Circumstances, added to his own inclinations, had imposed the need to flog freely, hardly surprising given the crew that the Admiralty had saddled him with. But the hands were still divided into the Endymions who'd come aboard at Portsmouth and the Bucephalases. A proper flogging would only drive them together, possibly making an already sullen complement dangerous. Far better to favour the newcomers, and cause resentment amongst the original crew members.

He looked at Pender and Flowers, with what he supposed was a smile. To them, with his lips stretched and those teeth grinding against each other still, it had the appearance of a man preparing to deliver a death sentence.

"I'm no' a cruel man," he said, "who flogs his hands for mere pleasure."

There was hardly a look on that deck that didn't shift at those words, not daring to be observed in eye contact with one another, lest they be seen to be shocked at such a blatant falsehood.

"And a good captain should hearken to his officers, however young. But he should also seek to guide them, since their souls are as dear to him as those of the crew. There are times when a harsh benevolence is unfitting. I must also demonstrate that I can see the sense of leniency. I will impose a punishment of a mere twenty lashes per man. Boatswain, rig the grating. Mr Callander, seize them up."

Garmond had time for just one more opinion, before the two men were hauled forward by the marines.

"He's got a silver tongue, that lad. Last man to be caught

dicing was treated to a hundred. Died before we cleared the Needles."

Pender, prey to enough anxiety as it was, felt the blood drain out of his face. He'd heard about the man who'd died, everyone had. But no one had told him that the charge was gambling. If Garmond knew that, and had guessed what Pender was about last night, why had he so readily given him the dice?

"Sir," said Dunlop, quickly. "I most humbly submit that these men are insolent, and that an example be made of them."

Toner had a permanently angry face, so fixing the degree of his passions was confined to the eyes. These now flashed dangerously at his premier, causing Dunlop to pull himself very erect.

"Might I remind you, sir, that I command here. And if we are to discuss examples, Mr Dunlop, then you, by your actions, would ensure that we have a crew that is even more dissolute than any I've served with."

"Sir," stammered Dunlop.

"I have allowed you licence, sir, in your drinking and your revels. But remember that I berth above the gunroom the next time you choose to lift a bottle."

Dunlop pulled himself upright. His eyes had gone blank in the face of this reprimand. Only the involuntary twitching of his cratered nose testified to his discomfort.

"Carry on," he croaked.

Men rushed to lay the canvas that would protect the planks of the hallowed deck. The grating was lashed to the shrouds, angled so that the cat could sear across the naked victim's back, tearing the skin as it rose. Pender, hauled forward first, felt the ropes bite into his wrists. He took the leather strap in his mouth and bit hard. It was a small mercy to be spared eighty lashes, except that a dose like that could kill. But the nine-tailed whip, with knots along the length of each strand, would, at twenty blows, still rip his skin to shreds.

It was a pain he'd suffered before, so what was coming was made worse by the memory. That induced a sudden feeling of terror that he fought to suppress. He tried hard to focus on something good, like his children. Their faces filled his mind, smiling and happy, so different from the way he'd found them on his last run ashore, undernourished and in rags, the victim of their mother's love of gin. Pender had buried her. He'd saved the children, though, from their life in that Portsmouth hovel, just as he'd saved himself from a life of crime. Now they were safe and happy at Harry Ludlow's house in Kent, well fed and cared for.

The picture of his two girls and the boy, playing in the grounds or at their lessons, of his eldest perhaps writing him another letter in her crabbed young hand, dissolved at the first blow. All the strands of his mind were torn towards the searing heat that starting in his naked back seemed to spread through his whole being. The stinging sensation that preceded the pain had no time to disperse before he was struck again.

Blow landed on top of blow, each one a clearly audible crack. He could hear, faintly, his tormentor counting off the numbers. Three . . . Four . . . Five. Spittle dribbled over the leather strap and ran down his chin. It wasn't a stinging sensation now. It was agony, made worse by the certain knowledge that his skin was broken, and that each blow was now opening up a previous cut. For all that he suffered at this grating, Pender knew that worse was to follow. When they ceased this, and threw the bucket of salt water over his lacerated back, the real torture of a constant pain would begin.

He fought to keep from collapse, determined to deny Toner and his officers that pleasure. Thirteen . . . Fourteen . . . Fifteen. Pender felt his knees begin to go and hauled hard on the rough ropes that bound his wrist, so as to remain standing. His world and his mental vision shrank to that small expanse of ragged flesh. He had no memories now, happy or painful. No other thoughts penetrated his world. They were overborne by the sequence of seemingly continuous sounds. There was the swish that preceded each blow of the lash. The squelch as the ropes sunk into torn and bloody flesh. His laboured breathing as he exhaled, then the high pitch as he sucked in another deep lungful in anticipation, just as the last numbers were reeled off.

"Eighteen . . . Nineteen . . . Twenty."

"Punishment completed, sir," said Dunlop, stiffly.

"Very well. Cut him down and seize the other man up," Toner replied.

The salt water hit his back like a hammer, immediately stinging the open wounds. The hands that held him were very necessary, since his knees would not. The surgeon's voice was faint. "Permission to take the man below, sir."

"Denied," said Toner, without emotion. "Hold his head up so that he can see. By looking at the other fellow's back he will understand what we have done to his own. Perhaps it will keep him from transgressing again."

The two men held him upright. An unseen hand gripped his hair and pulled his head back. But Pender shut his eyes. The last thing he wanted to look at was Flowers's back. He heard the same sounds coming from both the boatswain's mate and the victim, but this time they were distant, as though belonging to another world. It was a measure of Pender's distress at his feelings of failure that in order to cut them out he tried to concentrate on his own pain. But the image of Harry Ludlow swam before his eyes, a vision that made him pray that his captain would rescue them from this ship before Toner, and his methods, killed one of the men from the *Bucephalas*.

CHAPTER THIRTEEN

THE ROUTINE aboard *Bucephalas* was the same every morning. Having raced on through the night, Harry shortened sail and took in his topgallants before first light. He was in the crosstrees with his telescope as the first rays of the sun shot over the edge of the eastern sea, scanning the western horizon for a hint of a sail. All he saw, dawn after dawn, was an empty ocean, with no sign of *Endymion* or any other ship. Back on deck, he would order his sails reset. *Bucephalas* took maximum benefit from the steady Trades, racing along with the sea spray breaking over the bows and flying up in the air, only to be blown away to leeward. Once or twice they espied the odd merchant ship, possibly an enemy or a neutral, but more likely British. Harry didn't even bother to investigate, his sole purpose being to raise the wake of Toner's frigate and sit just below the horizon until they reached Antigua.

He was enjoying a late breakfast with James, discussing the merits of various marine artists, when the cry of "Two sail, dead ahead!" came through the open skylight. Harry drained his coffee and walked out on to the quarterdeck, glad to observe that his own upper sails were already gone, hopefully making him invisible to the other vessels. He made for the tops as soon as the lookout identified them as warships. As he climbed the ratlines he heard the dull boom of the guns echoing across the water, which caused him to pause. He called down to the deck and ordered the ship cleared for action, observing how swiftly this command was obeyed, before resuming his ascent. Once in the crosstrees and following the direction indicated by the lookout, he quickly fixed the two sail on the western horizon, established that they were on the same course, and heading away from him. The gunfire echoed across the water again, but it was too far away and too bright to observe either the flashes or the direction of the shot. Also with the smoke of the guns being blown forward he had no idea if these two ships were consorts operating together, firing at something he couldn't see, or enemies engaged in battle. Neither could he tell their nationality. One of them could be *Endymion*, but the temptation to crack on and investigate was one he must resist. He was in no fit state, with only half his crew on board, to take a chance on their being French, a distinct possibility, this being the time of year, just after the hurricane season, when the enemy chose to despatch warships to the West Indies.

Even if they were British, he should avoid them. After what had happened with Toner he had no intention of exposing more of his men to the risk of impressment. His exemptions, ripped apart by the Scotsman, looked a sorry sight. Certainly they appeared less convincing now than they had before he came aboard. Even with a naval captain less jaundiced than Toner they might not pass muster. Set against that was his need to know the nature of what lay ahead. If it was *Endymion* and the frigate was engaged in a fight, then so was half the crew. Harry recalled the poor gunnery he'd observed off the French coast and wondered how the frigate would perform against a well-armed enemy. Would Toner have the sense to put the Bucephalases, well trained and competent, on the upper-deck guns? The other thought was equally worrying. If they were enemy ships, then he'd have to give up his habit of cracking on at night to try and catch Toner. If he continued to follow that course he could find himself one fine morning with two frigates close by, with very little prospect of either victory or escape.

He listened carefully to the sound of the guns, sensed that they were fired individually. Also, given the set of sails, with their courses still rigged, he surmised they were firing forward. So bow-chasers aimed at the stern of some other vessel. Then he picked up the first flash of the third sail. He concentrated hard, and slowly it took shape, a smaller ship, its topsails a mere speck on the horizon. The two frigates were gaining on their chase, while he, in turn, was holding his position on them. Which almost certainly indicated that the chase was a merchantman, slower than its pursuers, which would soon be overtaken and forced to strike. Harry looked down to the quarterdeck to see James with his head back, his eyes fixed on his brother. Doubtless he was wondering what lay ahead. That decided him. He too, for his own peace of mind, had to know exactly what dangers he faced. He called out the orders to reset the upper sails and slid down the backstay to the deck.

James was favoured with a brisk explanation while the men ran to their allotted stations. No sooner were his topgallants aloft than one of the frigates came about to investigate, leaving her consort to continue the chase. Being on the larboard tack his flag continued to blow directly away from *Bucephalas,* making it impossible to tell his nationality. They closed each other rapidly, indicating that the other ship was fairly good on a bowline. The trim of the sails told him nothing. Harry ordered the private signal, which he'd last used when trying to find Lord Bridport, to be hoisted. As soon as it was aloft he trimmed his braces and spun the wheel so that they were readable from the other ship's deck. The lack of response sowed the first seed of doubt. The second was the other ship's determination to stay on her present tack, which hid her flags from Harry's gaze.

"All hands," he said quietly. "Stand by to wear."

The frigate breasted the swell at exactly the same moment as *Bucephalas* and for the first time Harry could see her hull and figurehead. It was as if the other captain heard his shouted orders to come about. At that precise moment he swung his ship on to the starboard tack and, plain as day, blowing away from the mainmast, Harry spotted the tricolour flag of the French Republic.

◆ ◆ ◆

Harry Ludlow demonstrated some cunning in the way he outran the pursuit, making it look as though darkness was his saviour. Sailing into the wind, he'd had the legs of that French frigate. So he set no more canvas than was necessary to stay clear. The *Bucephalas* had unlimited sea-room and a steady breeze, with no change of weather apparent. Little more was needed to convince the Frenchman that there was no point in continuing the chase. Harry held his course throughout the night then bore up at first light. Finding the sea as empty as it had been on previous dawns he returned to his course. As he explained to James, with aid of charts, sailing on this latitude his destination would be as much a secret as theirs. They were unlikely to be cruising, with a return to their home port in France their final aim. They were, he suspected, heading west, making for the French West Indies, picking up what they could on the way. The frigate had got close enough to *Bucephalas* to mark her type. They might think her a warship, or guess that she was a privateer. Whichever, on this heading, he was clearly aiming to make the same journey's end.

"So, brother," asked James. "Given all this, and knowing that we are a desirable prize, how would you go about effecting our capture?"

"They'll sail in close company at night. But my guess is they split up at daybreak and take station just within sight of each other, thus covering the maximum amount of ocean along the median line."

"So they will wait for us?"

"Not just us. They'll be on the lookout for anything that happens along. And as to waiting, I doubt they'll actually heave to, though they will certainly sail easy, especially during the hours of darkness. They have to continue to make their westing if they wish to reach the Antilles and be of any use. Against that, they stand a very good chance of picking up a merchant prize by using their superior speed to overhaul the slower ships."

James frowned deeply, evidence that he had just formed an unpleasant thought. "Will they catch Toner?"

Harry was frowning too as he fiddled with his dividers, measuring the distance between their present position and the Canaries. But it was more the look of a man struggling with a new idea than someone harbouring a deep anxiety. He turned to walk back on to the quarterdeck, closely followed by James. He remained silent, well aware that his brother was ruminating on some plan of action. Finally, as though there had been no gap in their conversation, Harry answered the query regarding *Endymion*.

"Anything is possible at sea, James. The problem we face is our need to keep up. Otherwise I would change course and give those Frenchmen a very wide berth. But if I did that we could be at sea for a long time."

"So?" asked James.

Harry smiled suddenly. "That merchant ship they were chasing yesterday . . ."

"What about it?"

"We have to presume that they took her. The question is what they have done since. Put a prize crew aboard, certainly. Then they have a choice. Either they sail in company, matching their pace to the slower ship, or they part company."

"Leaving her to make her own way to the West Indies."

"Look at the chart, James. They are sailing on latitude seventeen degrees north, which is the proper course for Antigua. That is the most likely place to repeat their success of yesterday. But there's little point in their prize following the same course. The French retook Guadeloupe last year, which is, as far as we know, their only major possession in the region."

"So if they parted company, which is the option you clearly prefer, the prize would be on the latitude for Guadeloupe."

"Bravo, brother. Is that mind reading, or an indication of a precocious talent for naval strategy?"

"Are you not forgetting one thing, Harry? A prize will slow us down as much as it would them."

"The logical conclusion of that being?" asked Harry, wearing a wide, confident grin. James thought long and hard, but eventually acknowledged his difficulties with a shrug. "We need to achieve two things, brother. We must crack on to stay close to Toner. At the same time it would be an advantage to know that any suppositions we have made about those frigates are correct."

James looked unconvinced. For a moment Harry wondered if he'd overplayed his hand and his brother was going to raise objections. The illogicality of what he was saying seemed very obvious to him: that his objectives were mutually contradictory. It was typical that he didn't explain the other reason, which was too flimsy to bear close scrutiny. They'd want to know about those frigates in English Harbour, welcome sound intelligence about their names and capabilities, so the Ludlow stock would rise accordingly if they could provide it. That in turn could help him get his men back. He tried to look cunning, as a way of deflecting James's evident doubts.

"That requires us to retake the prize. It does not mean, however, that we must keep it. If the original crew is aboard, then we can hand it over to them."

"Will the French commodore not draw some of the same conclusions?"

"He might," replied Harry, his eyes going back to the chart. "It's fashionable these days to deride the French Navy. But I shall treat them with respect. I know from my own experience just how devious the Gallic mind can be."

Harry turned south as soon as he set his mind to the pursuit, with just the nagging suspicion that James had the right of it and the enemy would not only guess his intentions, but anticipate them. Once on latitude 12° N he turned due west again, the lookouts straining for the first sight of a sail. The horizon yielded nothing that day so he was left with little choice but to keep up his speed throughout the hours of darkness. Dawn saw him in his usual place, with his topgallants struck down, scanning the ocean as the

sun rose. Below, *Bucephalas* was cleared for action, with the
gunports open, the cannon run out and the smell of slowmatch
drifting up into the cool dawn air. The light increased, showing the gun crews, ears bandaged, crouched ready for the first
indication that those French frigates were close by. He called down
to the deck to inform them that they were safe. There was an audible reaction, half relief, half disappointment, which he registered
as he slid down the backstay.

By his reckoning they would either find the merchantman this
day or be forced to abandon the idea. Every man aboard was as
keen as their captain to see some success. After the run of misfortune that had attended them these last months they needed
something to go right, just to demonstrate that their luck had
turned. So they were all a-chatter with the prospect of some action.
The changing mood throughout the morning and afternoon stood
testimony to how fragile such optimism could be. Glum faces and
bitter laughter became the order of the day as their hopes faded.
To match the mood the weather clouded over, taking the blue out
of the sea as well as the sky and surrounding their ship with various shades of grey, which exactly suited their feelings.

The first blaze of red, as the sun sank into the thin band of
clear sky on the western horizon, did nothing to raise their spirits. Soon the whole flaming red mass stood just above the rim of
the earth's circumference, its glow turning the crest of the waves,
and the edges of the clouds above their heads, pale pink. The sails
of the *Bucephalas,* stretched taut by the Trade wind, took on a
reddish hue as the sea cut into the bottom of the sinking sun.
Whatever hopes they still harboured sank with it. All eyes were
now cast forward as it disappeared. Most turned away at that
point, but the cry from the lookout brought them back again.
Harry was halfway to the tops before the man finished what he
was saying. He made it to the crosstrees at a pace he'd not matched
since he'd been a skylarking midshipman.

"Where away?"

"Just on the rim of the sun, your honour, with a bit o' southin'. When she lifts on the swell you'll catch sight of the top of her poles."

It was the merest speck, a black thread against the glowing western sky. Harry had the impression of a sail as well, though that disappeared. Reefing topsails; it was the act of a merchant-man, something a ship with a small crew would do at night. He called down for a small alteration of course, one that would bring him into the other ship's wake, gazing steadily into that strip of sky which showed the last colourful effects of the dying sun. Finally only its reflected light remained, turning the massed stratocumulus from pink through indigo to pale blue. Then the last glow of light faded and complete darkness overtook them. They ploughed on through the inky-black ocean, without the benefit of a single star or a ship's light, until the sharpest eye aboard picked up the faint glint of a lantern dead ahead. Harry then ordered a reduction in sail. He had no desire to overshoot his quarry; he wanted the advantage of the weather-gage at first light.

The whole crew was in a high state of excitement, wide awake long before the call came to clear the ship. This was done with the minimum of noise, as though those taking down the bulkheads and striking the ship's furniture into the hold had a suspicion that their quarry was close enough to hear them even if they whispered. Again the smell of slowmatch filled the air as the tubs were placed alongside the guns, though the men had strict orders to keep their cannon inboard, bowsed tight against the gunports. Their captain, who'd stayed awake until the final change of watch, slept like a baby, snoring in total ignorance of the impatience he created, until those who wanted to shift his cot could wait no longer. A sharp nudge and a "begging your pardon" did the trick. He woke to find James already up, dressed, and on the deck. Harry ignored the black looks of his crew and carried out his routine of shaving and dressing as normal. He ordered that his breakfast be fetched, ate it slowly. Then, taking a cup of hot coffee, he went out on to the deck to join his brother just as the false dawn added a first touch of grey light. James had a telescope to his eye, aimed just to larboard of the bowsprit, to where the other fellow's lantern would be.

"Still there?" asked Harry.

James just nodded.

"Cook wants permission to douse the galley fire, yer honour?" said Dreaver, who'd temporarily taken over Pender's duties.

"Has everyone been fed?"

The flicker in the man's eyes nearly produced a laugh, since it was clear they'd only been waiting for him. "They have, sir."

"Then carry on."

"I fear your popularity has taken a turn for the worse," said James. "I was asked to rouse you out at least a dozen times."

"It is remarkable, to me, to find you awake. Has anyone bar me slept a wink?"

"If you can tell me how to remain comatose when half the crew are creeping round your cabin, removing your possessions, I'll be obliged."

Harry had James hoist a British flag. If it was the French prize it would make little difference; if another merchantman, a neutral, then they'd quickly respond with their own colours and perhaps save everyone a deal of time. There was no need to climb into the tops this morning, since the chase was dead ahead. But he had lookouts aloft nevertheless, with orders to ignore their quarry and concentrate their attention on the surrounding sea.

"He's doused his lantern, your honour," called a voice from the bows.

"Right, topmen aloft. Let's have more sails bent on."

"Is that not unusual, brother?" asked James. "Do you not normally reduce sail before an action?"

"Natural caution. I'm still half convinced that when daylight comes I will find myself with an enemy frigate on either beam.

Catching that merchantman presents no great difficulty. My first priority is to have the means of escape if it turns out to be a trap."

James had obviously picked up the note of anxiety in Harry's voice. "What's troubling you?"

"It's that lantern, James. On all night, acting like a beacon to draw us on. Imagine you're aboard that ship, which has just been taken as a prize. They must know we are about, perhaps even suspect that we'll try and effect a recapture. Yet they've taken no precautions. It smacks of carelessness, or a well-baited snare."

The *Bucephalas* picked up speed as each extra sail took the wind. Harry, at the wheel, listened carefully to the man casting the log, noting each increase as he added yet more canvas. The wind was strong without being overly so, which provided perfect sailing weather. Something of his mood communicated itself to every man still on the deck. Once they knew he was satisfied that *Bucephalas* was sailing at her best they remained on deck till the first hint of true daylight appeared. It was still overcast, so the seascape was dull grey to begin with, and much less likely to reveal anything than a shaft of sunlight. But slowly, as more and more of the ocean was illuminated, their tension eased, there being no sign of any warships close by. They were quickly spotted from the deck of the merchantman, a mere two cables' length ahead. Sails were being set in great haste in what would be a vain attempt to get away.

"Topmen on deck," he called, aloft. "Let's get the guns manned and run out." He turned to his brother, to include him by explanation, aware that at a time like this he was reminded forcefully that he had no function aboard the ship.

"We'll keep our sails set, James. They'll have no guns to speak of on a merchant ship, so they can hardly damage our rigging. It'll be safe enough to just let them fly."

"Why do I get the impression that you're not satisfied?"

Harry, whose attention had been taken up by the opening of the gunports, grinned at his brother. But that disappeared when he heard the sound of the cannon. The flash was clearly visible from the stern of the merchantman, bright orange in the grey light. A ball whistled by, to land harmlessly in their wake. "That is heavier metal than I anticipated, brother. I have no desire to sit in the wake of that for the next hour."

He shouted out a string of orders. Men rushed to the falls, loosening them off so that the wind, accompanied by Harry's spin on the rudder, brought them broadside on to the sternlights of the chase. Another command followed and one by one the long cannon spoke. For the first time on this voyage they were firing at a prize, a live target. In the excitement it would have been easy to blast away, wasting powder and shot as well as time, and merely sending spouts of water to wash the target's deck. But these men knew what they were about, knew that if they failed to silence the stern chasers then their ship would suffer damage as she continued the pursuit. Their aim was careful and their firing controlled. They treated the wood of the ship as if it were just another barrel in the water. Shot after shot struck home, shattering the deadlights and sending showers of splinters in all directions.

"That's settled that," cried Harry happily. "I don't think those stern chasers will be troubling us much more."

"Sail dead astern, your honour. She's setting her topsails. I think it's one of them damned frigates."

"Get those yards braced tight!" yelled Harry as he spun the wheel to resume their previous course. "And keep a sharp lookout forrard."

"A trap?" said James, calmly.

Harry rattled out another series of commands before he replied. "The guns were probably the signal. You can hear cannon fire across miles of water."

"We've outrun them once."

"We outran *one* of them, James. Remember they're a pair."

"Ship fine on the larboard bow."

"That will be the fellow who chased us the other day."

"And behind us?"

"The better of the two, with the weather-gage, a whole day to engage in his pursuit, and a consort to shepherd us off our best point of sailing."

"We've been humbugged, brother."

"Not yet, James. Not yet."

Harry had a look of pure pleasure in his eye. This gave the words a ring of confidence they would certainly have lacked spoken by another man.

CHAPTER FOURTEEN

JAMES LOOKED aloft. Even in his lubberly fashion he could see that sails were coming in, not going up. The question he was about to ask died on his lips as he glanced at his brother. Harry, judging by the look in his eye, was in no mood to indulge in polite conversation. They were gaining on the merchant ship and his brother, once he was satisfied with the trim of his sails, called all his men back to their guns. Close enough now to see clearly what was happening on deck, the evident panic which greeted this move made Harry smile.

"They're expecting us to shear off, James, and make a run for it. For all their calculations they never thought that I'd still try and take the prize."

"What is the purpose of that?"

"Confusion."

"Allow me to congratulate you, Harry," said James in a languid tone. "For you've most certainly succeeded with me."

Harry called for another to take the wheel and headed for the bows, speaking trumpet in hand, giving orders for the short-barrelled carronades to be run out as he did so. These had little range, but they fired a large ball over a short distance, which could inflict such serious damage that they were known as "smashers." Men were busy with their rammers and spikes, heaving on the twelve-pounder carriages to train them forward. *Bucephalas* was gaining rapidly on the prize, now close enough for Harry to read the name, picked out in gold lettering on her stern.

"Ahoy there, *Penchester Castle*," he shouted. "Heave to or I'll favour you with a broadside."

There was no reply, even after he'd repeated the words in

French. Harry turned and ordered his larboard guns to fire. At this range the gunners couldn't miss, since Harry had ordered them to concentrate on the shattered sternlights. The twelve-pounder balls followed each other through the already splintered wood, striking the interior bulkheads and making the merchantman shudder. The gunners were rapidly reloading as they overhauled her. As soon as they could bear, Harry ordered the carronades to fire. The huge balls ripped into the ship, removing half of the side of the cabin. Whoever was in command had seen enough of what this enemy could do. Clearly it was no part of the French commodore's plan that he and his prize crew should commit suicide. The tricolour flag was cut from its halyards. From standing stiff before the breeze, it dropped like a felled bird and drifted slowly down to the deck.

"Stand by to board," shouted Harry, as the *Bucephalas* came alongside. Then he rushed back along the deck to take the wheel. As soon as he'd head-reached the prize he issued his next command and spun the wheel. "Let fly the courses and the mizzen topsail."

With only the main and for-topsails drawing, the *Bucephalas* crunched into the side of the *Penchester Castle*. "James, take the wheel and hold her steady."

Harry grabbed a cutlass and ran for the bulwarks, pushing his way through his waiting crew so that he could be the first to jump aboard. Grappling irons whistled across and pinned the merchantman fast. There was no sign of any prepared resistance. The prize crew had cleared away from the side, loosed their braces, and taken station around the mainmast. Harry leapt effortlessly on to a clear deck, followed by twenty armed men.

"Secure the prisoners and find out if the original crew are aboard."

A youngster in uniform stepped forward. He was slim and dark skinned, and looked about fourteen years old. But he had an air of assurance about him that belied his years. In his hand he had his sword, held out for his captor to take.

"Keep your sword, Monsieur," said Harry, indicating the

frigate to the east, now coming up hand over fist with everything aloft that the ship could bear. The other enemy vessel was beating up into the wind with the same sense of purpose. "Perhaps I wouldn't have it for long anyway."

The hint of a smile played on the youngster's face. Obviously he too considered this a temporary set-back.

"God bless you, sir."

Harry turned at the sound of the gruff English voice to find himself facing an elderly grey-haired man in a long green coat stained with damp. Behind him, rubbing their eyes in the daylight, stood his crew. "Captain Jeremiah Postlethwaite at your service. To whom do I have the honour . . ."

"Harry Ludlow, Captain, Letter of Marque, *Bucephalas*. Your reference to the Almighty is apt. We'll need all God's help today, sir, if we're both to avoid your recent fate." He raised his hand, indicating the approaching frigates.

"Damn their eyes," replied Postlethwaite, as his look of happiness turned to one of renewed despair.

Harry had already turned back to his own men. "Get the Frenchmen aboard the *Bucephalas,* at the double. Captain Postlethwaite, I return your ship to you, with my sincere apologies for its condition. Let us hope that by our subsequent actions we can confound the enemy sufficiently to allow you to keep it."

"How so, sir? You may have firepower, I have none."

"We must split up. I would ask you to adopt a northerly course, sir, while I head due west. I shall slip past that frigate ahead, even though he will try to stop me. And I hope I have the legs of the other fellow, who does not yet know the abilities of my ship. I cannot swear to which of us they will value most. If it is you, sir, then your freedom will be brief. But my belief is that they will choose to pursue me. Even if my hopes prove misplaced, and that fellow to windward is faster than me, he cannot overhaul me this side of noon. If I can draw them away, you may, by changing your course, avoid recapture altogether."

Postlethwaite was seaman enough to know that the odds were stacked against him. He was being offered only the slimmest of chances and the fact showed on his face.

"It grieves me that I can offer you no more, sir," said Harry, softly. "But if I attempt to fight these two I will not save you, and I will most certainly be forced to strike myself."

"Aye," said Postlethwaite, shaking his head. Then he looked up and held out his hand. "I wish you good fortune, Captain Ludlow. And I thank you heartily for the charity that fetched you on to this deck."

Harry nodded his thanks and turned to depart quickly, hoping that his blush was not apparent. It had been something less than charity that had brought him here. He had his braces taut in seconds and looked over the side to wave as the grappling irons were released and the gap opened up between the ships. He allowed himself a quick word with the French officer, during which the young man, whose name was Thierry de Brissot, imparted some very interesting details about the ships he faced. This was done with some relish, since he clearly believed Harry's position to be hopeless. He said as much to James. "That young man's air makes me think that Captain Postlethwaite might get away after all."

James replied with mock alarm. "Do you mean I'm on the wrong ship, brother?"

Harry smiled, for he knew that in a situation like this his brother reposed great faith in him. James probably thought that he'd foreseen all this and already had a plan of action worked out. Nothing could be further from the truth. The *Bucephalas* was in a degree of danger that would require luck as well as ability to redress. He'd known the risks beforehand. But he'd not counted on the two enemy ships separating. Operating together he felt he could outrun them, either sailing large or on a bowline. But by setting one across his course and one behind, the French commodore had shown a shrewd appreciation of the capabilities of a vessel he'd barely seen.

It was time for him to return the compliment. He grabbed a telescope and went aloft to see what he could make of his opponents. The frigate to windward, sitting across his course, was the *Marianne,* 28 guns, with a Capitaine Villemin in command; the ship in his wake was named *Persephone.* She carried 32 guns, including eighteen-pounders. Young de Brissot had also named the commodore of the pair, a Monsieur d'Albret, with the confident assertion that Harry would soon have the pleasure of a personal introduction.

The problem was simple: to avoid a fight. It wasn't just the number of guns that counted against *Bucephalas,* the difference in weight of metal was enormous. Yet how to get past that frigate without being exposed to a broadside? Most worrying of all was the French habit of firing for the rigging. Given that the fellow chasing him was probably the better sailer of the two, it wouldn't take much damage to spars or rigging to slow *Bucephalas* down. Even if he could outsail the *Marianne,* the *Persephone* would overhaul him. If that happened then those 24-pounders were enough to make capture certain. The only thing he had in his favour was the sailing quality of his ship, therefore it must be used to the full. There was also the distinct possibility that they'd try and retake their prize rather than pursue him. He'd added little to the sails he'd had aloft to catch the prize and the *Persephone* was quite clearly gaining on him. He spun the glass to take in the *Penchester Castle,* which was doing its best to open a gap between itself and the frigates. If Monsieur d'Albret's priority was recapture he'd have to change course soon. It came as little surprise to Harry, as he sat and watched, that the Frenchman ignored Postlethwaite. No doubt he felt that he could take the *Bucephalas* with daylight enough to come about and chase the merchant ship.

It was time to forget about them and concentrate on the *Marianne.* He trained his glass on her, noting the figurehead that was a fair copy of the heroine of the Revolution. He also noted that she was in no great hurry, with just enough set to maintain decent progress. Sailing into the wind, she had to keep changing tack, which gave him a very good idea of the capabilities of her crew. What it didn't tell him was the nature and competence of her captain, and that, along with his orders, was the vital ingredient that would spell the difference between success and failure. She handled well, without being startlingly efficient. While he had a crew that would perform better, he was too short-handed to manoeuvre with ease and man all his guns. He looked around at the grey sky, noting that it was clearing to the east, as the steady wind brought in a change of weather. The gap was closing rapidly, since Harry made no attempt to change his course. That alone would give his opponent pause. He might have heavier guns, but Villemin would know that in a fight he could suffer just as much as a smaller ship. Being on his way to the West Indies, where the French had no dockyards to effect repairs, it might induce him to show some caution.

Back on deck, with time to spare, Harry had all his guns housed, taking care to leave his larboard carronades loaded, even if they were bowsed tight against the ports. With the galley fire out he couldn't feed his crew, so he gave them a tot of rum and an explanation of their position. Then he increased sail to close the gap at greater speed. He set his course to pass the *Marianne* to windward, a standard tactic for a ship contemplating battle. The smoke from his guns would blow over the enemy deck, obscuring their target. James had listened silently to his explanation. But as soon as the crew were out of earshot he could not resist asking questions.

"I'm hoping his orders are to keep to windward," said Harry.

"How does that aid us?"

"If his orders are at odds with his instincts, James?"

"We are relying on confusion again?"

The way James said that annoyed Harry, and he replied a trifle more sharply than normal. "Precisely."

James was not one to be silenced by that tone. He knew well

how to make his brother squirm. "Or on what you choose to call a fine calculation of chances. I seem to recall that such methods have seen us in difficulties before."

Harry hated that expression in James's mouth, a standing reminder of the way his sanguine temperament had come close to costing them both their lives. "Am I to be hounded by that remark?"

"Not if you admit your true reasoning, brother. All that stuff about the intentions of the French was eye wash. You are a man who loves action and danger. You seek a fight rather than avoid one. While it may not be sensible, it has the merit of being the truth."

Harry gave a wry smile. He found it hard to be angry with James, especially when his devious nature was exposed. But even if his brother had guessed the truth, he was not about to openly admit it.

"I should have left you in the Canaries."

"What! And deny me the opportunity to witness your military genius? I have a duty to pick up my brush and record such things for posterity."

"All hands," shouted Harry, to drown out the effect of James's sarcasm. "Stand by to go about."

They'd had their explanation, so they knew what he was up to. But those telescopes on the *Marianne*'s deck would twitch with surprise. The last thing this privateer should be doing was putting herself in a position to offer battle to one heavier ship, let alone two. Harry noted that they were about to increase sail and smiled to himself. He'd taken round one of the contest. He yelled the commands that had *Bucephalas* tacking into the wind. Nothing fancy, no attempt to show off the quality of his crew. But a manoeuvre carried out with reasonable efficiency that would sow some of the confusion he'd mentioned to James. He held his course for a mere ten minutes before he wore round, coming back on to his original course. Immediately Villemin shortened sail, which confirmed in Harry's mind that he had orders to stay to windward.

"Starboard guns!" yelled Harry.

The crew on deck left the braces while half his topmen came down on deck. The running out of the guns was an unhurried affair, and the loading was all dumbshow. The tubs of slowmatch were set to both sides, even though the larboard guns were still bowsed tight against the ports. He set his bowsprit straight for the Frenchman, who obliged him by holding his own course. A quick glance over the stern was all he needed to confirm that the *Persephone* presented, as yet, no danger. Then all his attention was concentrated on the man ahead, and the split-second timing that would be necessary to bypass him. The faces in the other ship's bows were turning from mere white blobs to true features, when the first of Villemin's bow-chasers fired.

Harry heard the ball whistle overhead, thankful that it missed anything vital. As if in response to that cannon shot he tacked again, this time juddering as the *Bucephalas* nearly missed stays. It had the deliberate appearance of a ship trying to escape danger. Both the *Marianne*'s chasers now opened up together. But on a mid-Atlantic swell, with the bowsprit punching into the run of the equatorial current, it was hard to take decent aim. The manoeuvre, as Harry tacked, had closed the gap even further. Silently he gestured to his men, who'd remained in position, to stand by. He gave the signal and gently eased the wheel to starboard, as though he was about to tack again so as to get to windward of his enemy. It looked like a shrewd tactic. This close, the Frenchman would overhaul him, opening up the possibility that after an exchange of gunnery he might be able to shear off and attempt an escape. Villemin had his orders. D'Albret, in *Persephone,* was still too far away. So *Marianne,* following Harry, started to tack so as to stay ahead of their quarry.

That was when the true quality of both crew and ship came to the fore. His men, in the act of loosening the braces, hauled them tight again. He spun the wheel back to larboard, called out his orders and the hands eased the braces inch by inch, so that the yards stayed true to the breeze. He wore round until the wind was on his starboard quarter, just abaft the beam, and shot off like a racing pinnace. Villemin, still tacking into the wind, should have held his course, and finished his manoeuvre. But clear evidence that Harry had surprised him came in the way he sought to reverse his heading and wear instead. For the vital minutes that he needed to wound *Bucephalas,* and so damage her rigging as to render her vulnerable, it left him stranded. Harry's larboard gunports, closed over the carronades, flew open. It wasn't much to rub salt into the wound. But at close range these two guns, fired by the best gunners aboard, removed a great section of the *Marianne*'s bulwark. More than that, the flying splinters took the minds of those French seamen off their task, giving Harry more time to escape. He yelled to his men to set more sail, fearful that the bulk of the other ship might take his wind. No command was necessary for the gunners. They housed the carronades and ran for the stern chasers. Before the enemy had come round to pursue, the first twelve-pound ball had smashed into the bows.

Once clear Harry eased his braces a fraction. The *Persephone* would still have to be dealt with. But Captain Postlethwaite and the crew of the *Penchester Castle* deserved as much help as he could give, so that they too could outwit Monsieur d'Albret. He tried his best, as the day wore on, to overhaul *Bucephalas.* They raced through the morning and afternoon, as the sun showed through the clouds, making the sea blue and the wavetops sparkle. For all the wind was steady, it had flukes that could be used to gain advantage. He tried a little southing, hoping to increase his pace, and lost a whole cable's length of distance when that proved unhelpful. Behind him Villemin laboured to hold station, until d'Albret remembered himself and detached her to search for the prize.

As soon as he gave that command, Harry set everything he could, and with an ease that must have depressed his enemy, opened up the gap that lay between them.

CHAPTER FIFTEEN

ANTOINE de la Mery stroked the head of his pet mongoose, once more balanced precariously on the wheel, as he conned the prize into the bay. The last to be captured on this trip, she was a Swedish cat full of valuable ships' stores which he'd taken at first light, ten miles off Barbuda, from right under the nose of an English frigate patrolling the approaches to the island. But this capture, like the *Brandon,* had gone horribly wrong. The decks were still streaked with the dark stains of dried blood. The crew, for reasons he would never know, were in no mood to respond to his Swedish flag, or his cheerful shouts of recognition. Perhaps they'd looked more closely at his disguise and seen something amiss. Was he, after months of easy captures, becoming lax? More likely, his success was beginning to count against him, with his description and methods becoming common knowledge, a sure sign that the time was approaching to retire.

There were innumerable reasons why a halt would need to be called, not least the state of his own ship. When he'd purchased her, from a Portuguese Jew in Curaçao, she'd already sailed the triangular passage more than once. In tropical waters the bottom of the ship fouled at twice the rate of colder climes. Worse, sections of copper had fallen off, allowing the weed and worm to penetrate and attack the hull planking. Careening would alleviate some of the problem, but he feared spending too much time on the island. The control he had on his men, as had just been proved, was tenuous. Who could tell what mischief they would create, unoccupied, on land with few distractions? Besides, that would

merely provide a temporary respite. The *Ariadne* needed the attentions of a proper dockyard to put things right. Nothing had
established that more clearly than the taking of this prize.

Having failed to stop the Swede, de la Mery was in no position to sheer off, leaving his quarry to tell of their escape. As a
consequence he ended up in a long stern chase. The way his ship
had laboured to catch up told him all he needed to know about
the state of her hull. A pursuit that a few months before would
have ended swiftly now took most of the day. And when he finally
caught the Swede he'd no option but to board in the teeth of fierce
opposition. If anything, his disguise had inflamed rather than
cowed them. He told himself for the hundredth time that he could-
n't have foreseen the outcome. It was as if his men, who'd behaved
well these last months, had been waiting for just such an opportunity to demonstrate their blood lust. Perhaps it was the sheer
frustration of the time it had taken to bring them to. Whatever
the cause, they'd shown no mercy, nor paid attention to his
attempts to interfere, shouted commands that were lost in the heat
of the encounter. Every member of the Swedish crew had died on
this deck, but not before they'd killed two of his own men, and
wounded four more so seriously that they would surely expire.

Up till now, given the number of vessels he'd taken, and due
to the care and control he'd exercised, he'd got away with very
few casualties. This was a product of both his instincts and his
needs. Intercepting illegal traders who would otherwise be taken
by the British cruisers was one thing. But killing the crews was
quite another. De la Mery abhorred the waste of a human life. His
own men could not be replaced, since the maintenance of secrecy
was a paramount concern. But he had the same attitude to others. Ever since his men had murdered Abel Rolfe, he'd managed
to continue his activities without spilling any blood. Eventually, if
he continued, his disguise as Victor Hugues must be exposed. His
own name would be added to the list of corsairs and filibusters
who'd made a fortune in the Caribbean. He wished to join the
group which included men like Morgan and d'Ogeron, who had

gone on to achieve respectability, not the likes of Kidd and Teach, who ended their days at the gibbet. Antoine de la Mery had no objection to a posterity that labelled him clever. But he hated the idea of one that would term him a cold-blooded murderer.

His greatest problem was the sheer quantity of specie he now had aboard his own ship. The secrecy surrounding his operations meant that he must keep it aboard, since only in his cabin was the money safe from awkward questions. Often, when placing his proceeds in the great brass-bound chest, his mind would go back to the day he was first made aware of what was being proposed. The approach was so subtle that it had taken him some time to discern it as such. Slowly, with much reference to his previous losses, he'd been persuaded that his present occupation provided the only means of repairing them. Finally, it was the position his benefactor occupied, plus the limited nature of what was required, the knowledge that the provision of intelligence, for fear of discovery, could not be indefinite, that had persuaded him to agree.

The method by which the proceeds disappeared was just as sound. The ships themselves, renamed, were sold on the Spanish Main, a ready market since the colonial Dons were not great boatbuilders. The cargoes went to a variety of pre-arranged destinations along the same coast, sold to discreet traders who could be relied upon to ask few questions when offered a quick bargain. Everything de la Mery disposed of he traded for gold or silver coin, a commodity of which the Spaniards, with their mines and gubernatorial mints, had a ready supply. On top of that, every vessel he took had a quantity of money aboard, the funds necessary to purchase fresh stores and to pay for emergency repairs. Rarely vast in themselves, they had accumulated till the total amount now exceeded five thousand guineas. But that sum was dwarfed by the proceeds from the sale of ships and cargoes. Time and again he requested some method, or a period of time, during which he could unload this responsibility. Despite repeated promises none had been forthcoming. All he received was another list of potential targets.

De la Mery pushed these worries to the back of his mind and concentrated on the needs of the ship. The entrance to the tiny bay was through a gap in two unmarked coral reefs, constantly growing and now only navigable when the tide peaked. This afforded his anchorage an initial line of defence. On first arriving here de la Mery and his band of Frenchmen had overawed the local tribesmen with a combination of threats and gifts, then they'd built themselves a makeshift stockade, a jetty, a warehouse, and finally a separate pavilion for their captain. These stood at the mouth of the river that provided them with fresh water, their walls in constant danger of encroachment by the dense surrounding jungle. Gruelegra, which lay to the north of the Lesser Antilles, was an island that had been ignored by nearly everyone who'd settled the Caribbean.

Really the tip of a single small volcano, it was bypassed by the followers of Columbus. Later settlers had, in the main, deemed it too mountainous for any form of large-scale cultivation. Then the Irish came. Military followers of Oliver Cromwell, stripped of virtually everything they possessed and banished by a vengeful King Charles, they'd tried to settle in the Caribbean after the Restoration. With no funds to purchase land, they'd been forced to try and make this island their home, only to find that the soil was poor and the fresh water too limited to support their number. Then there was the ever-increasing coral reef, difficult to navigate, which discouraged trading ships from delivering the staples necessary to the maintenance of a decent life. The Irish colonists had abandoned Gruelegra and dispersed southwards through the more fertile islands. The jungle had long since reclaimed their smallholdings but evidence of their previous occupation, and the preponderance of males, was clear in the hybrid features of the local tribe. These were basically of Carib stock, but intermingling with the settlers had created a quite distinctive cast of feature. Their dark skin had a grey, translucent quality and many of the men had crinkly ginger hair.

There was a small aviso rocking gently in the bay, which he recognized immediately. This was his contact with Antigua. The carefully sealed letters it carried would contain another list of ships to be captured. So be it. Despite what had occurred on this very deck, his men were better off at sea. There was nothing to do on the tiny island except drink rum and break the rules regarding relationships with the local women. Such taboos made the crew idle, and idleness led to excessive drinking. That in turn caused fights, which tended to be terminal, threatening his already depleted strength. De la Mery had arrived on Gruelegra with a mere 48 men. His strength was now under forty. Being ashore with little to do would turn some of the less bellicose minds to contemplation. No one was privy to the information they received except himself. Yet his men must know why their raids were so successful, guess why they had the name and course of nearly every ship they'd intercepted, wonder at the regular visits of the small aviso, manned by the silent mulattos who never came ashore. Then their minds might turn to the quantity of booty de la Mery had accumulated and the way it was destined to be shared. There was precious little loyalty or love in their service. Their leader ruled by a combination of material success and fear, allied to the prospect of a return to France or St Domingue with enough gold to ensure a better life than the one they'd left.

As soon as he'd anchored the prize he went back to the *Ariadne*. This came as something of a relief to his crew, who hated to be aboard without him present. He never locked the door of his main cabin, sure none of his rascals would venture inside despite the fact that stored therein lay the entire proceeds of his depredations. There was no laxity in this. He knew his crew were not the type to handle cane toads, or let a tarantula run across the back of their hand. Not one amongst them would go anywhere near a venomous snake, especially a fer de lance. That de la Mery did so, with seeming equanimity, enhanced his status. To them it was remarkable, almost mystical. To their captain it was

something that was easily accomplished, provided care was taken.
And if things looked bad, he always had his mongoose to hand,
ready to fight a reptile that proved dangerous.

He'd witnessed any number of people handling snakes, the first
time as a child. Such things had been a regular occurrence on the
plantations in St Domingue, part of the religious rituals imported
along with the slaves from Africa. Many times, before the revolt,
he'd had the local vaudoux shaman who was one of his father's
slaves show him the art of snake handling. The young Frenchman
had then gone to Paris to benefit from a rational European education. The combination of the two, plus an early introduction to
the great scientist Lavoisier and the physician Breconet, aroused
an interest in all things venomous, not least in their effect upon
the human frame. He believed firmly that just as smallpox could
be avoided by exposure to the less dangerous cow-pox, man could
survive the toxins from poisonous creatures. One kind of venom
must cancel out another. It was merely a case of marrying up the
two correct poisons to achieve the desired result.

The spread of venomous creatures throughout the islands, especially snakes, was haphazard. Some islands teemed with them;
others, a few miles distant, had none. St Domingue had them in
abundance, but his early experiments had been confined to sick
slaves who would probably have died anyway. It was much better here, on the island of Gruelegra, with the dense, mountainous
jungle to explore and an Indian culture that had been on the land
before the arrival of Columbus. The island had scorpions and
tarantulas as well as an infestation of fer de lances. De la Mery
was fascinated by this, the most deadly snake in the West Indies.
He would watch them kill a ship's rat, gasping at the speed of
their attack. And then, with their venom spent, he could handle
them, often taking them out on deck, much to the discomfort of
his crew.

The two messengers from Antigua were no more comfortable in
the presence of snakes and spiders than his own crew. They were

an unsavoury pair, scarred uncouth ruffians of mixed blood, the kind of men found all over the Caribbean. To a Frenchman the word mulatto covered all the percentages of blood, unlike the Spanish, with their exact shadings, their octoroons and quadroons. People like these were easy to hire, since they had little concern for the way they earned their money. Running between Antigua and Gruelegra for a fixed fee was better than the small-scale smuggling and piracy by which they usually made their living. If they were curious, they hid it well. The letters they carried in the oilskin packet were in code and comprehensively sealed. Not that this pair could read. But as a precaution, de la Mery, having as usual hidden his mongoose, had introduced them to his collection on their first trip, making only the slightest allusion to the fate that would follow if they tampered with these despatches. Certainly it worked. They rarely took their eyes off the bulkhead that separated the main cabin from the coach, as though the creatures contained therein, safely housed in glass-fronted cases, would burrow through the wood to get at them.

The messages they'd delivered were simple enough, to anyone who could comprehend them. The code would not have troubled a reader serious about deciphering their contents. They came in the form of a letter, written in Latin, between two priests, the subject being the conversion of the heathens to Rome Christianity and the missionary work of a band of itinerant Irish fathers. It contained a list of names, dates, and destinations, which apparently detailed masses to be held and the names of the officiating priests. In reality this was the information by which he took his captures. Educated by Jesuits himself, the translation posed no difficulty. Nor did the code, since he'd read it dozens of times. But this time the contents provided him with a surprise. His correspondent acknowledged the complaint about his ship and agreed that their activities were in danger of becoming common knowledge. But God's work must be done, indeed extended. They had always agreed that the most difficult conversions would lie amongst the English colonists. But that was no reason to avoid the attempt.

Quite the contrary. As a brotherhood, in the way that they'd avoided such a task, they'd been lax in their efforts. The day would come when they must cease to minister to those in need. Perhaps it would be soon, very soon. But it had not come yet, and if an English soul was to be saved, then the time in which to achieve it was short.

Antoine de la Mery read these words with mixed feelings. The idea of avoiding English ships, the most numerous in the area, had been sound. Time, distance, and parochialism were their main asset. People involved in the illegal trade avoided British ports since there was no advantage to be gained by trading into them: the Navigation Acts, where they allowed it at all, imposed high tariffs on foreign freight. Speculation about his activities was probably rife in places like St Eustatius. But the English, if they heard of his successes, would merely shrug as long as their ships were safe. That reluctance to enter a British port was multiplied a hundredfold when it came to places like English Harbour. Being a purely naval base, with an admiral as the sole arbiter of justice, illegal traders, even under legitimate disguise, could not be sure that if they did anchor there they'd leave with their ship, let alone their crew. Even British merchant vessels tried to avoid them. Thus the differing interests of the various parties worked in de la Mery's favour, allowing him to operate in an area where there was no one to oppose him. Now he was being asked to increase his level of risk substantially. Once English ships went missing, the navy, appraised by its own kind, would be obliged to come after him. The question this posed, and which he couldn't answer, was simple enough: was this extension of his targets prompted by greed, or the knowledge that the time was fast approaching when he would be required to disappear?

The events, plus the poverty that had set him on this path, that had sustained him originally, seemed somewhat distant now. Contemplating the prospect of calling a halt, he wondered yet again what would become of him and his men. His sugar plantation was probably still in ruins. There seemed little prospect of St Domingue being retaken from Toussaint l'Ouverture and his ramshackle army. France was in the grip of the Revolution, though the situation had eased with the fall of Robespierre. Perhaps that was what he should do: go back to France, and use his new-found wealth to persuade the present rulers to take back St Domingue from the rebellious slaves. Yet he wasn't sure he himself wanted to go back to the island. His entire family had died in the holocaust of the slave revolt. Both his parents, his wife, and children slaughtered in the most gruesome manner. Could he live and work with the memories of what he'd seen, on the very land where those atrocities had taken place? He knew he did not have to make a decision yet. But this latest message probably meant that the time was fast approaching when the luxury of procrastination would evaporate.

De le Mery crossed to his writing desk and penned a reply. This, as usual, contained an acknowledgement of his instructions plus the present total of their combined wealth. It also listed all his anxieties, especially those in regard to English targets, as well as a description of what had happened off Barbuda. He made such points for form's sake. The man he corresponded with knew the problems as well as he, and would have already weighed them in the balance. Triple sealed, his reply was delivered into the hands of the mulattos, along with several gold coins that had come from the Swedish cat. He saw the pair over the side and stood watching as the aviso tacked out of the bay. His pet, released from his sleeping cabin, had jumped up on to the bulwark to join him and he picked it up and went back into his quarters.

Gingerly he opened the door to the coach, the side cabin which, being the same size as his sleeping quarters, provided ample space to house both his reptiles and his loot. Seeing nothing, he slipped the mongoose into the tiny room, leaving the door open a fraction. When he had to leave the ship, and the huge brass-bound chest that held the profits of his cruising, there was nothing like the presence of a snake to deflect the curiosity of those left aboard. Most of his crew believed they could run faster than a man and kill instantly. Even he feared to enter a room in which a fer de lance was on the loose. Hence the mongoose, which would flush out the snake and kill it. The natives of Gruelegra would provide him with a replacement before nightfall and the carcass would be dissected, with the venom extracted for his experiments.

CHAPTER SIXTEEN

FROM THE top of the island the lookouts could observe a vast amount of the surrounding sea. The aviso was heading south, well away from the lugger near the northern horizon. The presence of such a small vessel excited little attention. Frequently there would be some kind of ship sailing by, heading along the line of latitude to Hispaniola. As long as they were merchantmen, they were ignored. The primary task was to keep watch for warships. They'd only ever spotted one on the horizon. That put the entire settlement on alert for a hurried departure, a panic that had subsided just as quickly when they'd established that it was on a course which would keep it well clear of Gruelegra. In daylight, such a watch was easy. Even at night the moon often bathed the sea in a blue light strong enough to provide equal security. When it was cloudy they mounted proper guards, to protect themselves against the possibility of a sudden attack.

Out at sea, Nathan Caufield laid aside his telescope and dropped his head into his chest. He uttered a soft curse. His efforts to find the corsair's base had borne fruit, but it was more by luck than guile. O'Dwyer, safe in his factory in St Eustatius, had lied to him originally, sending him off on a wild-goose chase. By the time he found out, and returned to confront him, a poster had arrived on the island which had his name and description. Nathan Caufield, thief and murderer, with a reward on his head, was in no position to threaten anyone with exposure, especially a prominent member of the trading community. The only pleasure lay in the way that the Irishman felt duped. He'd discounted the certificate Norrington had supplied, giving the American the equivalent of thirty cents on the dollar. Being now worthless it provided yet another reason to refuse any information. Nathan Caufield, short of hope and funds, had to resort to desperate measures.

Going home was an option, but not a happy one. He had debts in abundance and creditors whose patience had only been sustained by the expected profits from his Caribbean venture. He'd sent his son a letter telling him what had happened, and giving an outline of his intentions, with an injunction to Matthew to stop his mother and sister from worrying. He also instructed him to inform those seeking payment that his ventures had prospered, before signing off with the promise that soon their futures would be secure. Would Matthew find that hard to swallow, or see the opportunity it presented? The things he'd borrowed to sell in the Caribbean were now the property of the unnamed French filibuster, sold long ago and converted into coin. How many more ships had the man taken in these last three months, to add to those who'd taken refuge with Captain Poynton? How much treasure had he accumulated? Whatever he had, it must be kept somewhere. The most likely place was on his ship, since no man in his right mind would let such a fortune out of his sight. Weeks of lonely speculation, added to the awareness that he was being hunted, had turned such thoughts into an obsession.

Here was the stroke he needed to repair his fortune, destroyed twenty years earlier by the success of the American Revolution. In the grip of that growing obsession he'd even risked a return to Antigua, with the idea of repeating his break-in. O'Dwyer wasn't Dillon's only correspondent: there must be others in places like St Thomas and St Croix. But security had been tightened since his last effort, and he'd found himself skulking opposite the postern gate, trying to decide what to do. It was near the other side of that gate that he'd discovered Norrington, a memory that brought on a shudder. What would they say if he was apprehended here? No doubt it would add to the proof of his guilt, with the villain, full of remorse, returning to the scene of the crime.

Perhaps they'd even allude to the full moon that lit up the sky as part of the reason.

A trickle of people passed him as he nurtured these thoughts and concerns, racking his brain for a way to proceed. Two mulattos who'd merited barely a glance as they shuffled up the hill stopped by the gate. One pulled a watch from his coat and peered at it. That in itself was unusual. If men like these ever had a watch it would be stolen. And the chances of it being kept, when it could be traded for a drink, was slight. Stranger still was the way he executed a gentle tattoo on the studded wood. The door opened immediately. Even in the moonlight he'd observed that they were the kind of scum generally termed wharf rats. What were two individuals of that kind doing visiting Admiralty House in the dark, able to open a locked door by means of a knock that could only be a signal?

Dillon's spies! Throwing caution to the winds he jumped up and tried to scale the wall in an attempt to confirm his suspicions. The outside, rendered smooth, was too slippery and Caufield gave up lest he was observed trying. But his thoughts remained in turmoil. It had to be Dillon. He could receive such people without exciting comment. But why? Surely he didn't use such creatures to carry intelligence? He was still there, half an hour later, hiding across the street, when they came out. He followed them down the hill and witnessed a heated argument as one of them waved an oilskin packet at the other. This brought forth a string of negatives and an emphatic shake of the head, this followed by the clinking sound of shaken coins. Finally, the packet was grabbed out of the protester's hand and stuffed inside a shirt. The two continued their progress down to the harbour and on along the coast to the open beach where he'd landed earlier. Caufield was right behind them, able to see clearly when they waded out to their aviso. The moonlight showed them casting off the rope they'd tied round a palm tree as well as the sail being hauled up. Without further delay, he rushed along the shore to the point where he'd beached his own boat.

The whole of the next day was spent in their wake, but even though they made little attempt at haste, he lost them the next night, as they ran to leeward of Saba. Their aviso had just got too far ahead. They were easily able to outsail him in the cutter, and he had little chance of overhauling them. But Nathan Caufield reckoned they had no reason to dog-leg, so, with typical determination, he had held his course. The outline of the ship that had taken his was etched in his memory. Spotting it in the company of a damaged cat caused him some confusion. But the possible solution, as he eased round into their wake, wasn't long in coming. Could it be that those two wharf rats had despatches, not for one of Dillon's spies, but for the man who'd captured his ship? Now, as he sat off Gruelegra and watched the aviso clear the reef and shape a return course to the south-east, he was in no doubt. Luck, which had seemed hard to come by all these years, had favoured him at last, putting him within striking distance of the French filibuster—and of his treasure.

The *Ariadne* jerked, suddenly pulled up on the anchor cable that held her to the jetty, adding the creaking noise of strained hemp to the sound of the night. The other noises were constant. The sighing wind as it ruffled the palms, the deep grunts of the bull-frogs set against the ever-present background of the cicadas. Darkness had brought forth myriads of fireflies, which danced on the hot tropical wind. The lights were still on in the pavilion that stood at the point where the jetty joined the shore, but none penetrated to the still waters of the creek. Caufield, convinced that if this man's treasure was to be found anywhere it would be aboard his ship, glided gently towards the stern windows of the cabin. He hooked on to the rudder stanchion without making a sound and reached up to take a grip on the gilded decoration that covered the stern. It wasn't an easy climb, made even harder by the need to maintain silence. But the schooner had a low freeboard, which helped considerably. The long thin blade slid easily into the gap between the frame and the casement and Caufield heard the slight rasp as his knife forced up the metal catch. The creaking hinges, being so close, sounded deafening to him and made him halt his labours till he was sure that no one had been alerted.

The last heave, which carried him over the sill, was also noisy. The damask hanging that covered the rear of the cabin was no obstacle and once through he quickly pulled the window shut behind him. He'd observed the owner ashore, occupied at a table, cutting up something. He had no need to make a positive identification: the caged mongoose by his side sufficed. So he was safe. The door from the quarterdeck that opened into the captain's cabin would be locked and once the curtains were back in place he was hidden. His boat, on a long line, would drift on the current into the heavy undergrowth that lined the river-bank. So even if the anchor watch had heard him and looked over the stern to investigate, they'd have no way of knowing that he was beneath their feet. Mentally he tried to recall the layout of the cabin. The Frenchman had been so polite, commiserating with him over his recent loss, plying him with wine while he deplored the necessity that drove him to deprive a fellow sailor of his cargo. He knew that there was a large round table in the centre and several elegant cabinets lining the bulkheads, some containing the ship's documents while others were used to store the owner's crystal. There was also a mahogany wine cooler by the door to the sleeping cabin, with a matching writing table by the opposite door. He opened the door of the sleeping cabin first, to be presented with an empty cot swinging on the tide. The strongbox was in the cabin opposite the coach, so he closed that door and moved gingerly, hoping to touch the table with his fingertips. The height was wrong and it was his thighs that made contact first. The table shifted, making some of the objects it bore rattle noisily.

He edged around the rim, then extended one hand towards the panelled bulkhead. The distance was too great, forcing him to raise both hands and walk forwards. His left hand touched one of the brass sconces on the wall, the cold metal making him withdraw in sudden panic. But that adornment was enough to fix his position. He put his palms on the polished wood and inched his feet towards the door of the coach. The feeling of something running across the back of his hand made him freeze, a low gasp forcing its way out of his open mouth. Yet the sensation had been so soft, and so fleeting, that Caufield couldn't be sure if it had been real or imagined. He stood rooted to the spot for an age, waiting to see if it was repeated. Finally convincing himself that it was the product of his high state of tension, he began to move again. His left hand felt the moulding that surrounded the door and he slipped it down to the height of the handle with renewed confidence.

The pain in his index finger was so intense he responded with an audible gasp, shaking his arm before shoving his finger into his mouth. He had no idea if he'd been stung, bitten by something, or caught his finger on a protruding nail. His whole hand seemed to be afflicted by a numbing sensation. Casting aside caution he scrabbled around for the door handle, finally grasping the lever. He pushed down and forward, relieved that it wasn't locked. The sky had cleared again and the moonlight shone through the small panes of glass in the tiny windows, providing ample light to make out the silhouettes of the coach's contents: a cot strapped on one wall, a spare bed to accommodate a visitor, and various glass-fronted cases lining the inner wall, their surfaces reflecting the glim, itself bouncing off the calm water of the creek. That extra light helped him see what he was after. It stood at the very end of the small cabin. A huge chest, brass-bound at every edge and across the middle, with a great gleaming hasp at the front, secured with a stout padlock.

The numbness seemed to be spreading to his wrist. Using his good hand he reached into his coat and pulled a crowbar out of the large inside pocket. His heart was pounding now, in an excited manner the like of which he hadn't experienced for years. He could feel the sweat trickling down his brow, cooling slightly in the air. Kneeling down before the chest, he couldn't quite grip the padlock with his left hand, so he just stuck the crowbar through the hasp and stood up, putting his feet on the lid to provide purchase. As he wrenched at the hasp his foot slipped, throwing him back against one of the clear-fronted cases. The glass cracked and fell like a thousand church bells pealing at once. He spun round to try and catch the last shards. The streak of greenish silver that shot out of the case hit him almost before he noticed it, a flash of reflected light so small that it was gone in the time he took to blink. But there was no mistaking what had happened, nor the twin punctures on his wrist, which were already oozing blood. He screamed and dropped his jemmy, the sounds reverberating in the confined space, then staggered back into the main cabin, blundering into the edge of the door in his haste and calling out for someone to come to his aid.

The sound had already alerted the watch and one of them had run to fetch the captain from the pavilion. De la Mery reacted instantly. Grabbing the caged mongoose, then a lantern, he ran down the jetty and up the gangplank. Caufield's distressed cries, his urgent demand for assistance, were clearly audible through the door. The Frenchman, having relieved one of the guards of a cutlass, declined to be rushed. First he released the mongoose, which, sensing the presence of its natural enemy, began to scratch at the bulkhead. He took a firm hold of the weapon, then opened the door. The mongoose shot through the gap. With great care he shoved the lantern through, following it with nothing more than his head. The light showed a man lying across the table, his body shaking violently, his cries now reduced to incomprehensible grunts. The fer de lance was far enough away from the entrance for him to enter in safety. One of his crew immediately pulled the door shut behind him. The snake faced the mongoose, its swaying head off the deck. The lantern light played on its patterned skin, while it tried with its hiss and motion to frighten the rodent off. De la Mery inched forward with the cutlass raised till he was level with his pet, now standing on its hind legs. The cold, expressionless eyes of the fer de lance never left the main threat as the

Frenchman eased the cutlass to a point a foot away from the snake's head. With a sudden swipe he decapitated the creature. The mongoose shot forward and grabbed the writhing carcass with its sharp teeth. De la Mery rushed to look at the victim, who'd now slid off the table and on to the floor.

He searched for the twin puncture marks, finding them just inside the right wrist. He dashed into his sleeping cabin and grabbed an ampoule from one of the shelves that lined the walls, before returning to kneel over the man. The mixture had a foul smell, which filled his nostrils; as he spread it on to the wounds, the victim seemed to swell out of his skin. His bloated face was bright red and his lips were drawn back in a horrible rictus. His body was convulsed as though it was being torn apart. Finally he gave one great heave, as though his soul was trying to depart from his venom-filled body. Then he was still.

De la Mery put a small mirror to his lips and noted that he still had breath. Then he shouted for the anchor watch to fetch a stretcher. Not one of them would enter the cabin until they saw the mongoose carrying out the remains of the fer de lance. Even then, there was little gentility in the way they bundled their charge on to the canvas. He took time to check his strongbox, noting that the lock was intact, then he lifted the lantern to examine the glass-fronted cases that lined the walls.

It had been the American's misfortune to smash the one that held the fer de lance, one of the world's deadliest snakes. The creatures in the other cases reacted to the sudden examination: the poisonous cane toads trying to blend in with their background, the scorpions standing rigid, and his tarantulas clinging, still but deadly, to their thick webs. It was only then he noticed that the door was slightly ajar. A quick count established that there were two missing. He knew he'd have to find them. But first he had to see to the victim, who might very likely be dead.

CHAPTER SEVENTEEN

CAPTAIN Horace Effingham was the sixth commander in as many months to return to English Harbour completely empty-handed. But for once, this officer had something to add. One of Bessborough's most ardent supporters, who first served with the admiral as a midshipman, he was well known for his blatant avarice. He'd turned up on his first rendezvous off Barbuda and awaited the arrival of the promised illegals, only to find that no ships arrived. Frustrated by this total failure, he'd gone one stage further. A party of marines was put ashore, under the command of his first lieutenant. They'd confirmed that the beach designated as the illegals' landfall was full of barter goods. Sugar cane, molasses, coffee, and rum. The colonists obviously expected the same vessels as Effingham. He was back at sea, still cursing at what he'd had to leave on that beach, when he was favoured with what could only be described as a stroke of extreme good fortune.

Finding the heavily laden ship's boat, in such an expanse of ocean, was just that. The master had declined the invitation to come alongside, let alone board a British man-o'-war, fearing to expose his crew. The shouted exchange that followed had confirmed not only that his vessel was one that Effingham had been set to intercept, but described the man who'd taken them, then set them adrift. The name Victor Hugues had them returning to English Harbour earlier than anticipated. This, in turn, meant Effingham had met up with Poynton, preparing his ship for a refit in Jamaica. Kept apart by the exigencies of constant patrolling, plus Vandegut's insistence on vessels remaining at sea, they were, for the first time, able to compare notes. Their crews were exposed to the gossip of the port, as well as the gibes of the men of the *Redoubtable,* who'd already had the pleasure of jeering at several other prizeless frigates. It wasn't long before both men were appraised of such gossip. Nor did it take them long to realize what it portended. Together they'd gone to Bessborough, insisting that the situation be thoroughly aired.

This gathering was the result. Admiral Bessborough looked down the long table at the small group of officers, with his nephew at the end, once more taking notes. The spacious room at the back of the building, with windows opening on to a sunlit veranda, might be blessed with a cooling breeze, but there wasn't a man in the room who wasn't sweating profusely, due to a combination of tropical heat, anger, and professional apprehension. Then the old man's eyes lit on Dillon. His political assistant wouldn't sweat, regardless of temperature or pressure. Alone amongst the assembly he was without wig or uniform, the thin ginger hair carefully arranged, as usual, over the top of his head. His loose calico coat and nankeen breeches, which hung on his spare frame, were well suited to the climate, unlike the heavy blue broadcloth worn by the admiral and the ships' captains. Dillon's lack of discomfort, plus his ease in a situation he knew to be tense, obviously needled Bessborough, who accompanied his opening remarks with a chilling glare.

"Well!" he snapped, the bright blue eyes piercing and angry. "If what we hear is correct then that damned Frenchman is running rings round us."

Dillon, who had been quietly fingering the papers on the table before him, didn't react to this sudden verbal assault. He knew the true nature of affairs. Bessborough was deflecting any criticism on to him, while being all the while aware that the only evidence they had of Hugues's involvement was the reports provided by these two officers. All the commanding officer got for his manufactured bellicosity was a thin smile. The voice, when the civilian replied, was soft and gentle.

"The manner in which Monsieur Hugues located his quarry is not something on which I can enlighten you."

Poynton cut in, ignoring the strict protocol of naval manners, which insisted that he should ask the admiral's permission. "This is no longer mere rumour, Dillon. Hugues is out there, and he seems to be able to operate at will."

It was Vandegut who replied, adding an even deeper hue to the flush of anger that reddened Bessborough's cheeks. "No doubt, Captain Poynton, having identified the problem, you have also formulated a solution."

"I have. He must be confronted and destroyed. I say the best way to stop him is at source. Take him outside his home port."

"I doubt he actually sails in and out of Pointe-à-Pitre," said Dillon, "and Guadeloupe has no shortage of bays in which to land illicit cargo."

"Then we must concentrate our forces, and blockade the whole island. Then we could clap a stopper on him in no time."

Bessborough looked at him coldly. "You're suggesting that I denude the entire Caribbean of defence in order to pursue a single dubious menace?"

"Considering the harm he does, Admiral?" said Effingham.

"I can just imagine the harm such an action would do me, sir. The lack of warmth between London and this station is bad enough after the loss of the island. Until we have troops enough, any attempt to retake it is doomed to failure. Yet you want we instigate a close blockade, of indefinite duration. What happens if the French suddenly appear, in strength, off St Domingue, while we're beating back and forth off Basse Terre? I'd be lucky to avoid the fate of Admiral Byng."

That name sent a shiver through the entire assembly. Byng had been shot by firing squad, in '57, on his own quarterdeck. His crime, what the government called a gross dereliction of duty. In truth the man had been sacrificed to save the reputations of his political masters, and to encourage others to be more zealous. For all the chicanery of the primary reason, the subsidiary effect had been profound. There wasn't a senior officer in the fleet who didn't recall Byng's fate before initiating any action.

With too many tasks for their numbers, it seemed as if every event in the region contrived to make matters worse. The French island of St Domingue, having succumbed two years previously to a slave revolt, should have eased matters. But the leader, Toussaint l'Ouverture, had finally shunned the hand of English friendship, and professed himself wedded to the ideas of the Revolution. Dillon had garnered limited information about l'Ouverture's intentions. But it seemed that the fellow was busy seeking an alliance with the very people he'd fought to gain freedom. What if the former masters, taking advantage of this, decided to use that island as a base? Troops from Europe, allied to the slave army, would become a substantial force. They might choose to attack nearby Jamaica. This obliged Bessborough to keep a major part of his force as a screen to the east of Hispaniola, further depleting his resources, while his counterpart in Kingston, Admiral Bollom, enforced a close blockade of Port-au-Prince and the harbours on the other end of the island.

"What I want to know is how he's getting his information," said Effingham.

"This is a matter which must be addressed, Admiral Bessborough," said Vandegut, his eyes gleaming. "Especially in light of what has happened to our other cruisers."

"Something of which Captain Effingham and I are unaware," said Poynton, with equal force. "Just as we have been kept in the dark about the low rate of captures. Might I add that a more open approach to that would have saved us the indignity of hearing about matters from the lower deck." Poynton made a dismissive gesture towards Caddick. "Why, I dare say your nephew knows more than we do."

Vandegut pursed his lips as he replied directly to Poynton. "The question this begs has nothing to do with success or failure. I think you know my views on the subject of independent cruising, sir. The sight of our ships returning to harbour empty-handed only reinforces that opinion. It should be discontinued forthwith."

Dillon tried to cover it, since Bessborough, having blasted Effingham, seemed either incapable, or unwilling, to do so.

"We hold a prominent position in the area, we do not hold a monopoly. I can think of two sources for anyone seeking such intelligence. One is, of course, the harbour from which the illegals sail. But the other is their island destination. With the amount of goods being shifted in one consignment, keeping it secret poses a problem. Added to that, we are required to wait until the illegals make a landfall before we can take them. We must, in short, catch them in the act."

"Even if he is not required to wait till they land their cargoes, Hugues is taking them mighty close to their destinations," added Effingham.

Poynton cut in. "Indeed he is! Need I remind you that I actually picked up the crews of the ships I was sent to intercept. Instead of clapping the sods in irons, I was obliged to feed and berth them."

All eyes were on Poynton now. He was still smarting from that particular indignity. The natural sympathy was somewhat muted by the knowledge that one of the men he'd fetched back had turned out to be no more than a common thief and murderer. Also, having served on the station for three years, he'd already made a considerable sum of money.

"I think the circumstances of that were somewhat unusual."

"I'll say they were, Dillon," said Effingham. "That is one instance where we had a definite indication that something was seriously amiss. I have just provided another."

Dillon didn't react angrily to the implication that he was being stupid. He was not a man to raise his voice at any time, something which often infuriated those who dealt with him.

"The information given to Captain Poynton came from St Eustatius. Yours from St Croix. Neither is under our control, gentlemen. The destinations were Martinique and Barbuda respectively, both places where the French could be expected to have spies."

"No one is saying that your information is at fault," said Bessborough, finally coming to his aid.

"Have you considered that it might be compromised?" asked Effingham.

"No, sir!" replied Dillon sharply. "I have not. Nor will I do so in the face of mere speculation. And I would remind this gathering that what we are discussing now is of secondary importance."

Bessborough, who'd lost control of the meeting, tried to reclaim his prerogative, raising his voice to do so, though nothing that followed could truly be said to address the subject under discussion.

"Does it occur to you, gentlemen, that I too have suffered? Quite apart from the loss of prestige." This did little to dent the others. They all knew that Bessborough wasn't short, and could afford to go without his eighth share of the proceeds.

"Besides that, I have superior officers in London who will want to know what the deuce is going on." He emphasized his discomfort by slapping the table. "Am I so damned with incompetent officers that, free to sail where you will, not one of you can take possession of so much as an illicit bumboat?"

Their commander stood up, knowing that his height and figure would add to the effect. He was an imposing creature, both physically and by virtue of his connections, his whole bearing enhanced by the full-dress uniform of his rank. Bessborough's wife had cousins scattered through the peerage and many other family members occupying positions of influence. There had been a time when all these qualities combined to make him an object of some fear to his subordinates. Now what they saw was a man clearly lacking confidence, and trying to cover the fact with bluster.

"It is our job to confound the enemy. Surely I need hardly remind you of your duty, gentlemen."

"We are aware of our duty, sir," replied Poynton, with a corresponding level of hyperbole. "We have performed it in the past, even against well-armed enemy warships. Given sound, accurate intelligence, we will do so in the future."

Bessborough frowned. The allusion would penetrate his thinking quickly enough, the implication that under a more active commander, like Jervis, this discussion would be superfluous.

"We have already established that the intelligence we receive is sound."

"With respect, sir," boomed Poynton, "we have done nothing of the sort. All we have had is soft soap from Mr Dillon."

The Irishman replied in his usual gentle manner. But there was no doubting the steel in his expression, since his opinion of Poynton was several degrees below that of the admiral. "If you wish for hard tack, instead of soft soap, Captain Poynton, you can have it."

"Please, Mr Dillon," said Bessborough, waving a calming hand.

"No, sir," snapped Poynton. "Let him speak. I have never once felt that Mr Dillon utters the unvarnished truth. Perhaps the world he inhabits precludes that. It would be edifying to know, for once, what he truly thinks."

"That unvarnished was a well-chosen word, sir," said Dillon, his eyes hardening. His hand went to his temple at the same time, as if to say that while evidence of the assault was long gone, the memory was still fresh. "Had you failed to include it I might have found need to show you the truth by a recourse to arms."

"I would not shy away from that, sir," said Poynton coldly.

It was Vandegut who interrupted. "Gentlemen, we are not here to either indulge in, or pursue, private quarrels. We are here on the king's business."

Dillon looked around the table, seeming to take in each angry glare in turn. Clearly Poynton had got under his skin. For once his voice was harsh and uncompromising.

"We have agents all over the Caribbean, who send us information at great risk to their own personal safety. They are not there to provide fat purses for naval captains, yet they do so. I cannot guarantee that others are not active in the same field. These men provide you with the name of the ship, the cargo, the destination, and the time of departure. I leave to you the wind, the weather, and your crews, which, I readily concede, are outside my competence."

There was a sharp intake of breath at that last sentence. The

implication was obvious. Dillon was accusing them of being nothing less than indifferent sailors and poor commanders, who'd
failed because of their own incompetence. Vandegut, his square
face pale, yet furious, was the one who spoke out, just ahead of
a crimson-complexioned Poynton.

"It is easy for someone to impugn us sailors, sir, less so that
we should do the same to you. I would ask you to withdraw those
last words."

Dillon responded with a wolfish smile. "If they require to be
withdrawn, then I do so readily."

"You do so when the harm is done, sir," hissed Poynton.

"Be quiet!" shouted Bessborough, his handsome face also red
and suffused with anger. "I will remind you that I command on
the station, and I will see proper behaviour. This is not a fishwife's
combination, where anyone is free to speak as they wish, even
senior captains."

"My apologies, sir," said Poynton, with an air of indifference
that could only multiply his commander's anger.

"We have things to be proud of, as well. I would point out to
you that not only have we contained the French incursion on
Dominica, but that not a single English ship has been lost these
last three months. That duty ranks a close second to the primary
task of containing the French. The question now is this, what
would you have me do?"

No one spoke, for they'd been ordered not to. Partly it was
because they'd observed the cavalier way the admiral had treated
Poynton. But more important was the way that Bessborough
seemed to be ignoring his responsibilities, forgetting that he was
there to lead, not follow. The silence seemed to make their commander even angrier, smacking, as it did, of indifference. All
present fully expected him to take his bile out on the same can-
didate. Instead he looked right to the bottom of the table, to his
own nephew.

"Well, Mr Caddick. Can you throw some illumination on this,
or are we all to sit here like stuffed Italian dolls?"

There wasn't a single person in the room, except his uncle, who didn't show their displeasure at the inclusion of Caddick in the discussion. That a young man who'd never been on any kind of cruise should be asked to comment on the activities of his superiors was galling enough. But to that you could add the young man's demeanour. You couldn't say Caddick slumped. But, at ease in his chair, he put one hand to his mouth, then moved his shoulders to adopt a deliberately thoughtful pose. Being slim, with pale gold hair, it gave him the appearance of a particularly louche poet. And the voice, when it came, had all the torpor of the well-bred scion of noble blood, called upon to descend from Olympian detachment and deal with the cares of lesser mortals.

"This didn't happen in the past. So we must conclude that the intelligence collated by Mr Dillon is no more than common knowledge. All that has happened is that this fellow, with the means at his disposal, has decided to act on it."

"Could that be true?" asked Bessborough

Dillon was angry. "I find the expression 'common knowledge' to be offensive, sir, and must insist that it be withdrawn. Does your nephew seriously imply that the people we employ do no more than pick up gossip? If that's the case, perhaps Mr Caddick can explain to me why we take so much trouble to confine its distribution here in English Harbour."

Poynton, presented with the chance to blast three enticing targets, couldn't resist the temptation. He was, of course, voicing a possibility that had occurred to others. But a combination of hierarchy and caution had kept this particular genie in the bottle.

"I take it you're sure that there is no leakage at this end, Mr Dillon?"

The sudden grin with which the Irishman responded warned Poynton that he had gone way beyond the limit. Only three people were privy to the entire file of incoming intelligence, and they were all present.

"Damn you, sir, how dare you!" shouted Bessborough.

Poynton tried bluster, appealing to a pale-faced and angry

Vandegut. "I meant only that some genuine mistake could be made, sir."

"You did not, sir!" snapped Vandegut. "I do not know what Mr Dillon and Admiral Bessborough intend. But if you do not provide me with an apology in writing, I will take the matter further."

"I have impugned no one," said Poynton, softly. "I have merely exercised my right to allude to a possibility. I do not know the details of your precautions, nor am I aware of who might have sufficient access to breach them. After all, I do not reside in Admiralty House."

"I see," replied Dillon. "You wish to include Lady Bessborough, her daughters, and the admiral's servants in this fiction?"

It was Effingham who came to Poynton's rescue, using his long acquaintance with the admiral to get his fellow officer off a very nasty hook. "Come, gentlemen. A chance remark, maladroit I grant you. But no insult was intended and none should be taken."

"I agree with Captain Effingham," said Caddick, an intervention which earned him several malignant looks.

Poynton might resent the young man's cheek, but he grasped the lifeline nevertheless. "The question we must now ask is this: what do we do henceforth?"

"I don't think that is a problem you need concern yourself with, Captain Poynton," said Bessborough, coldly. "The solution will fall to others. Hugues has luck, but it could run out at any time. The Caribbean may be large, but it is not the Atlantic. One day he will be in the wrong place . . ."

"It may be fruitless, sir, and it does our ships no good," protested Vandegut.

Bessborough went red in the face again. "Is every order I issue to be questioned, sir?"

Vandegut was not to be cowed. In fact, he plainly took a savage delight in reminding his commander of his prerogative. "I have the good of the service as my concern, sir, and I will not be denied my right, as the senior captain on the station, to an opinion."

Bessborough's dander was up, his colour high and his gaze stern. "That is a statement, Vandegut, that would carry more weight if your opinion ever coincided with mine!"

Dillon moved to smooth matters, his soft Irish voice in sharp contrast to Bessborough's angry growl. "It may be that Captain Vandegut is right, sir. After all, we have to answer to the Navy Board for the state of our vessels. If ships' captains cannot produce results, then it is hard to see how we can justify sails and spars, not to mention extensive repairs, even refits in the Jamaica dockyard. Why, we would be accused of milking the public purse."

Dillon could not have produced more embarrassment if he'd accused them all of avarice to their face. And that applied especially to the admiral. The eighth of every penny his captains earned in prize money was something he'd sorely missed, even if he never alluded to the fact. It was no secret that much influence, plus a fair number of bribes, had been expended to get him this command. His extended family would expect him to return, like his predecessors, with a deep purse, ready to spread the rewards of his posting to their mutual benefit. This hope was much diminished by the loss of Guadeloupe, which still hung like a sword of Damocles over his affairs.

"Dammit, Caddick!" yelled Bessborough. "Will you sit up in your chair, sir. Must I remind you that you are the junior officer present at this table."

Caddick shot bolt upright, his discomfiture made all the worse for being rebuked by a normally kindly uncle. It provoked smiles on the faces of those who did not see the shout for what it was: a way of avoiding a direct response to Dillon's gibe. The sound of the signal gun made them all look towards the open French windows. Cram, the admiral's servant, appeared suddenly on the veranda, his hand up to restrain an impetuous midshipman intent on entering the room. The youngster was instructed to stand to attention and wait, while Cram, in his most unctuous tone, announced him. Bessborough growled at his servant and barked at the boy to report.

"There's a frigate in the offing, sir. *Endymion,* 32. Captain Toner. She's made her number, hoisted a signal to say she bears despatches, and requests permission to take aboard a pilot and enter the roadstead."

"Permission granted. Signal the captain to report to the flag forthwith," replied Bessborough. Then, with a gesture that dismissed both Cram and the boy, he turned back to the assembled officers. "That will be all, gentlemen. Mr Dillon, you will remain."

The officers had stood up, making their preparations to leave. But their admiral, who had suffered much during the meeting, could not resist a parting gibe at those under his command. "Perhaps this is the fillip that we need. There's nothing like a dose of new blood, eh! Toner is by reputation a zealous officer. I've a mind to give him the next opportunity to cruise, as a way of introducing his men to the climate."

The blue eyes blazed now, as he cast his gaze round the assembled officers. "It may be that he can succeed where others have failed."

CHAPTER EIGHTEEN

THE SIGHT of land afforded some relief to the crew of the
Endymion, though if they'd been taxed to explain why such a
thing brought them cheer they would have been hard put to
advance a convincing reason that did not in the end come down
to mere change. The voyage across the Atlantic had been a living
hell for the whole crew. Generally the sun had shone and the wind
had stayed fair. Most captains would have contented themselves
with such an easy passage. Not Toner. He had every watch on
near continuous drill, driving them to their stations time and again
to rehearse the same manoeuvre. Captain John Toner had one aim:
that he should by the time they reached Antigua be in command
of a crack frigate. His crew had to walk a flawless deck, past newly
blacked cannon and neatly arranged piles of shot. Every rope must
be perfectly flemished and lie in a neat loop. The topmen, generally the cream of any naval crew, needed to set or take in sails
faster than any competitor, so that their captain could manoeuvre
with the grace to make admirals gasp. The guns' crews were
required to serve their pieces so that they could fire off two broadsides in a minute. But if anything exposed the fallacy of Toner's
regime it was this: the gunnery was all dumb show, mere running
in and out. Their captain lacked the means to purchase a private
supply of powder.

Those of the hands who'd served in such ships could attest to
only one fact: that the level of efficiency the captain sought could
only be achieved after years of sustained effort. A crack frigate
required an extended commission; a committed, long-serving captain, prepared to provide all manner of things out of his own

pocket; and dedicated officers, a willing crew, and an accepted code of discipline. *Endymion* was deficient in every single area except the last, and that was so harshly imposed that it created a disgruntled crew, not a willing one.

During the crossing, most of Harry Ludlow's men had been flogged, several more than once. Yet, in the main, they could count themselves fortunate. It was much worse for the rest of the crew, especially those landsmen who'd come aboard at Portsmouth and could not adjust to naval life. And after that one example of Toner's leniency, when he'd doled out a mere twenty to Pender and Flowers, he'd never again spared a man his full measure of punishment. The officers, with the exception of young Callander and Mr Wheeler, took their cue from him. Below decks, in the nature of things, the strong tended to play on the weak, making matters worse.

Some of the inexperienced hands could not bear the continual bullying. They retreated into themselves, scarcely speaking from morning till night, skulking round the deck, grey-faced and watchful. They gulped their food in corners lest they expose themselves, by mere association, with the more defiant members of the crew. It was useless to take them to task, to inform them that this behaviour instead of easing their plight only brought out the worst in their superiors and made them the butt of every perceived mistake aboard ship. Even Harry Ludlow's men were becoming obstinate and fractious, ready to do violence to anyone who trespassed on what they saw as their rights, and Pender's task had changed. He no longer sought to protect them from the excessive discipline— punishments were so regular as to render that a waste of time—but he sought to keep up their spirits, constantly reminding them that they were different, that their impressment was illegal, and whatever else happened the man they'd gone to sea with was not one to leave them in the lurch.

Despite these efforts, some were inexorably sucked in, which would eventually lead to their loss of a separate identity as their attitudes became those of the most disgruntled Endymions.

Garmond was at the centre of this. Slowly, by adding the answers he received himself to the information gleaned by others, Pender had established that Garmond had indeed been a clerk. But he'd also been free with his master's funds and found himself in trouble. Peacetime would probably have seen him hanged, or at the very least transported to the new convict settlements at Botany Bay. From the way he talked, either fate would have had more attraction than serving in the king's navy. He was often surrounded by willing listeners as he recounted, again and again, the rights they should have, contrasting them with the life they led. Pender had done his best, but it was hard when he agreed with so much of what the man was saying. In other circumstances he'd have openly supported him. In truth, Harry's servant was caught between two stools, a position made all the harder by Garmond's inventiveness when it came to finding new grievances. They all knew the food was rotten and the water foul in its casks. The ship's biscuit was full of weevils which the hungry midshipmen used to fatten up the rats for consumption. But most of all it was the punishment. Garmond had even used the nature of their destination to suborn the crew.

"Did you know that where we're going there is a limit to the number of lashes that an owner can give his slave? Twenty is the maximum permitted by law! Now think on that, shipmates. You, serving king and country, can be flogged as many times as it suits your captain. Not so a black. And why? 'Cause he's a slave and has a value. Not us. We're not valuable, we're expendable."

"There he goes again, using 'em big words no one can figure."

"It means that they don't care if you live or die, mate. But they do care if a black man does. Now don't that just tell what your officers think of you."

"Some officers," said Pender.

Garmond knew that Pender had authority amongst the Bucephalases. He was careful never to blackguard him, even to those of Harry's men seduced by his vision of a more equable world. He also spent much time trying to win Harry's servant over to his cause. Pender had one aim: to get his men off this ship in a group, so that they could return to their proper station. But he could see the way the wind was blowing. Under the combined pressure of Toner's discipline and Garmond's sedition, the crew were working up a head of steam that threatened catastrophe. In order to counter Garmond's baleful influence, he'd secretly drawn up a petition, to be presented to the admiral when they arrived on the Leeward Island station. After fulsome expressions of loyalty to both king and country, and a carefully expressed willingness to fight the enemy, it explained the illegal impressment of the Bucephalases. Pender then went on to describe life aboard the ship for all of the hands, pleading with the admiral to intercede and put an end to this tyranny.

Writing such a petition was one thing, getting it ashore quite another. For that he'd need help. With a captain like Toner, it was a fair bet that none of the hands would be permitted leave. But all the officers and young gentlemen would take it in turns to go ashore. He took the opportunity, while fetching the food for his mess from the galley, to approach Mr Callander.

"How's Flowers?" asked the young midshipman, looking left and right to ensure that they were not being observed by another officer. They'd had the unfortunate duty that morning of watching him receive forty lashes for what Dunlop termed insubordination.

"Bearing up, your honour. Flowers is a tough bird, though his skin had barely recovered from his first flogging."

"And what about your own back?"

"Healed now, sir," replied Pender. "Though how I've avoided a repeat visit to the grating I'll never know."

Callander pulled a face. "Odd that such a thing should depend on luck."

"It does that in the best of king's ships, never mind—"

Pender stopped, for even with the midshipman he was unsure of how far he could go. Callander had no doubt, which was evident both by his word and the expression which accompanied it.

"I hope to God there isn't one worse."

The youngster looked closely at Pender, once more taking in
the lively dark eyes and the ready smile which seemed to hover
just round his lips. He admired the man's self-assurance, and wondered, even with his inexperience, what could be achieved with
such men by the application of kindness rather than cruelty. The
men under his command had shown endless patience with his frequent hesitations. They went even further when the eye of the
premier was upon them, undertaking their tasks long before
Callander had a chance to issue the correct orders.

Many a time he'd cursed the connection that had put him
aboard this ship. Yet he'd badgered his guardians to let him go to
sea. The boy was an orphan from the landlocked hills of north
Perthshire, who, sailing and fishing on the lochs, had dreamed of
wider horizons. One uncle, who lived in Edinburgh, had favoured
Toner in the past, allowing him extensive credit on advantageous
terms. Struan Callander, fourteen years old, was now aboard the
Endymion to settle that debt of gratitude, though the sums of
money were still outstanding. He felt personal guilt for the original flogging Pender and Flowers had received, which was odd.
Every man in his watch had suffered worse and not produced quite
the same emotion. Deep down he cursed himself for not having
the eloquence to save them, or the courage to challenge Dunlop,
to explain what had really happened. No one could blame them
for the hatred of officers that such punishments engendered, a
hatred he assumed included himself. Mr Callander would have
been nonplussed by their true feelings. Both men, and more beside,
held him in some esteem. They knew, even if he did not, just how
much he'd achieved in easing their lot.

To the topmen Callander had become something of a mascot.
Since he understood the rudiments of sailing, learnt before he ever
came aboard, he'd absorbed quickly any lessons he was taught.
Others were responsible for his studies in mathematics and navigation. But there existed a mass of detail in the mere handling of
a ship that the crew were happy to help him with. Here was a

young officer who could both accept advice and indulge in the proper degree of dissimulation so beloved by tars.

On watch, or giving orders to his men during the interminable sail drills, he was every inch the tyrant. No action was undertaken without an accompanying curse, delivered loud and clear. The rope's end seemed to be in constant use. But those before the mast knew well that when Mr Callander swung his starter, it connected with wood, not flesh. And all had heard him speak quietly, so that only his correspondent could hear, urging a man to see to his duty, lest he be forced by watching eyes to go further than his own inclinations could bear.

"I have come to ask a service," said Pender.

Callander knew, by the way the older man held his breath, that what he was about to be asked was no small thing. This knowledge halted his breathing as well.

"I have written two items, one petition and a letter, to the owner of the *Bucephalas*."

"Then take care that they are not discovered."

Pender grinned. "They're well concealed."

Callander didn't respond to the grin. If anything his frown deepened. "Don't assume that the captain or his officers are unaware of the mood below decks."

It was now Pender's turn to close up. He was not going to discuss what happened out of sight of the officers, even with Midshipman Callander. The young man couldn't miss the change of mood.

"There are those who seek to curry favour, Pender, by trading information."

Pender doubted if the officers truly knew as much as they supposed. If they did, they'd clap half the crew in irons. Loose tongues were a known hazard aboard ship. Any sensible man didn't mention anything seditious unless he was very sure of his audience.

"There's always men like that, Mr Callander. If you lived in my world you'd learn to spot them, real quick."

"What do you want me to do with your letters?"

"Post them."

"You're so sure I'll get the opportunity?"

"I'm damn sure I won't," said Pender angrily.

"I will do what I can to get you some shore leave."

Pender tried to hide it. But he gave the young man a look which left him in no doubt that his efforts would be wasted.

"Very well," said Callander. "Where are they?"

"I'll pass them to you when the right time comes, Mr Callander. I've no mind to put you in danger by making you responsible for 'em. Besides, where would you hide them in that bearpit they call the mids' berth . . ."

Pender knew that Callander had spotted someone coming, just by the way his eyes changed. His voice became harsh and his expression hard. He lifted the kid that contained the food and peered into it.

"Dammit, man, do you think you would get such food ashore? No, you'd very likely starve, and the world would be a better place for it. Think yourself lucky that the king sees fit to feed you, at all. Now get back to your mess."

Pender turned away quickly and slid past the approaching bulk of the first lieutenant. He heard Callander behind him, addressing Dunlop.

"Damned oaf. Said the salt pork was a wee bit off. As if someone like him could tell."

"Nose too close to his arse, most like," growled Dunlop.

Callander laughed loudly, the sound filling the narrow space between decks. "Damn good, sir. Why, that is very droll."

Pender, as he hurried away, wondered if the youngster would pull it off. It was a terrible over-reaction to such an old, well-tried joke.

Every officer was on deck, in full dress, as they came in sight of the main signal station. Toner paced the windward side of the quarterdeck, his face set hard, and his eyes flicking constantly to ensure that everything was perfect. He desperately needed to make a good impression on Bessborough. He didn't know the admiral and that was a worry. The commander would have his own adherents, men he would favour over any stranger. Toner must try to overcome that, not least because it could mean he'd be allowed to cruise independently among the islands, with the prospect of prize money to make it all worthwhile.

Toner wasn't safe yet. That merchantman they'd taken off the Brittany coast would only go part way to a settlement of his debts. These, which had been a worry before he had a ship, had rocketed to alarming levels after he'd taken command of the *Endymion*. No officer could go to sea wholly devoid of private stores. He needed wines, spirits, cheeses, and livestock, all of necessity bought on credit in Portsmouth. Then there were new uniforms, travel, accommodation, and douceurs to be paid for the smallest service.

Posters calling for volunteers had been printed then distributed around the Hampshire countryside, with an accompanying posse of officers and hardcases, the first to persuade men to enlist with pots of ale and charm, the second to abduct by force the hands he needed to man his ship. The expenses fell on him, and the constant demands from the Admiralty to make up his complement and get to sea showed little cognizance of the fact that, after two years of war, the natives of Hampshire were immune to blandishments and too sharp to be taken up by the press. Finally he had been given a draft from the reserve tender, made up of useless landsmen, who'd "volunteered" to serve in the navy. Still, for all those difficulties, it was better to have a ship than not.

The years before the war had been very lean, Toner forced to exist on half-pay in dour, stinking Edinburgh lodgings. The constant effort to juggle the small sums available made him morose. It was an endless, soul-destroying task just to hold off his creditors, whilst simultaneously keeping up the appearance required of his rank. He attended every social function that offered the prospect of meeting anyone influential who could assist him, gatherings where he was required to give the impression of wealthy indifference to the prospect of command.

How often had he lost money at cards, in the hope that the man taking his money would look kindly on any application he made for assistance? How many women had he paid court to, laughing at their stupid fripperies, so that their husbands would favour him? Not that many of the ladies were fooled by his masquerade. Mothers with eligible daughters made sure that this half-pay captain with the forbidding countenance and prominent teeth had little opportunity to pay court to their offspring. Widows with a portion left by their late husbands barely spared him a glance. They concentrated on the army officers. After all, someone who had to purchase his commission was far more likely to be a man of parts, and have the merit of an independent income.

The reality of his situation was never more obvious when he left these glittering assemblies to walk home, his cudgel at the ready lest some footpad mistake him for a worthwhile victim. Home to a cold, damp attic in a mean part of the old town, with the ever-present smell of human filth and a shrew of a landlady demanding her rent. That would entail another grovelling visit to young Callander's uncle, who at least didn't press him for immediate repayment. But such calls did little for his self-esteem, something he was constantly reminded of every time he saw the young man on his deck. Letters to the Admiralty, begging for their indulgence, had finally borne fruit. But Toner knew he was of no real account to those scribbling clerks and secretaries, let alone to their lordships. He'd only got this command through the rapid expansion of the fleet.

As he looked along the deck, towards the bows, he saw Pender, going aloft to take in sail. That brought back to him what he'd done off the Brittany coast. For the hundredth time he reminded himself that it was necessary. There was a war on and he had a fighting ship so short of hands that it was near useless. Those he'd found aboard the *Endymion* were the scum of the earth. The previous captain, promoted to a '74, had taken all the good men to his new command. But even the dross he'd left aboard looked like promising material when compared with the draft he'd received from the hulk. He'd been supplied with men who'd either been had up for debt, or convicted of every crime known to man, not one of whom had ever set foot in so much as a river ferry. There were thieves, debtors, and fraudsters, plus a rapist and an inveterate gambler so undernourished that he'd died at the grating on their first day at sea.

The trip down the Channel, once they'd cleared the Needles, had been a nightmare. Toner and his officers had been on deck the whole time, lashing about with their rope's ends in an attempt to get these lubbers to perform even the most simple task. How they'd stayed afloat, never mind made any progress, was a mystery to him. And all the time he'd asked himself, "What will I do if I run across an enemy warship?" And then he'd happened on the *Bucephalas*.

He recognized that signature on those exemptions right away. Not only had he met Dundas on several occasions, he'd written to the Secretary of State for War numerous times, asking him, as a fellow Scotsman, to intercede with the Admiralty on his behalf. He felt he'd done right, but a nagging fear persisted and would not go away: fear that he had committed a grave error that would return to haunt him. Such thoughts just added to his determination to make a success of his commission, so much of one that he would never be beached again. Some telling stroke, like a single-ship action, would wipe his slate clean. It was easy, as they drifted in towards the shore, with a local pilot conning the ship, to day-dream. He would be given a whole *Gazette* to himself, perhaps even be knighted by the king. Hostesses would vie to have him at their table. Offers of marriage from titled ladies would abound and his crew, who were wary of him now, would idolize him for his bravery and huzzah him every time he came aboard.

"Admiral to *Endymion*, sir. Anchor under instructions of pilot and captain to report to flag."

Toner, still in his reverie of unbounded success, replied to the young midshipman with surprising gentleness. "Very well, Mr Overton. Acknowledge and prepare to launch the barge."

"What about the crew, sir?" asked Callander, who was close enough to his captain to hear this exchange.

Toner had hardly used his barge since he'd come aboard; consequently he'd never assigned men to the duty. The implication was obvious. Neither the captain nor the premier could be sure of mustering a reliable crew. They would touch the shore and disappear.

"Never fear, Mr Callander. Let us have a couple of armed marines in the bows. Antigua is a small place. Much as the men might want to run, they will soon find that there is nowhere to go."

"Might I suggest that I detail some of the men that came aboard from that privateer, sir?" said Callander.

Toner glared at the boy. "Why them?"

Callander looked at a point above his captain's head and replied crisply. "Because they are the men in my division, the best sailors we have aboard, sir. Indeed one of them has served as a coxswain before, and I would not like the dignity of the ship, or my captain, to be impaired by being rowed ashore by a band of lubbers."

The silence lasted a full minute while Toner digested this information. Callander was in an agony of suspense. He'd promised to aid Pender. This, short of his doing something directly himself, represented the best chance the man had to communicate with either his original captain or those in authority. And the youngster wanted to avoid, if he could, becoming personally involved. Such assistance, exposed, would mean him being dismissed from the navy.

"A wise thought. Make it so, Mr Callander."

"Might I also suggest that the marines are unnecessary, sir. If you show trust in the men, I'm sure they will respond in kind."

There was almost a look of sadness in Toner's face as he replied to that. But his voice was as harsh as the thought was unbending.

"If you believe that, Mr Callander, you mix wisdom with stupidity in equal measure."

CHAPTER NINETEEN

"I MUST SAY, Captain, I find your eagerness to be at the enemy most gratifying. I fear some of your fellow officers' zeal has been sapped by the tropical climate."

The heat, or rather the humidity, was taking its toll on both men. Toner had come ashore in the middle of a downpour, which as usual ceased as abruptly as it had begun. The sun was out again, causing clouds of steam to rise from the earth. Bessborough was sweating profusely, even though he was sitting under a great fan. He also had the advantage that, as the senior man present, he had no need to create an impression with the punctiliousness of his dress. He wore a loose coat, an open-necked shirt, and had left off his wig. Toner had no such luck, smartly attired as he was in his blue broadcloth coat and thick waistcoat. The tight stock round his neck was disintegrating as it soaked up the perspiration running down from under his wig and there were two bright red spots on his normally grey cheeks.

"Might Ae suggest, Admiral, that they'd be cooler out at sea."

This apparent witticism was delivered with Toner's habitual glare. Coupled with the grinding of his teeth this smothered any element of drollerie, making the remark sound like unbridled criticism. Bessborough only knew the Scotsman by reputation. He'd been told he was humourless, something certainly borne out by that last remark. Stiff was another word applied to the man, which also, in these circumstances, seemed apt. Anyone with any sense would have asked permission to remove his coat as soon as he arrived. The admiral wasn't aware that Toner ascribed to him the same qualities attached to his own name, in particular that of

being a strict disciplinarian. Bessborough had consulted a written
report delivered as part of the despatches, the sum of the opinions of those who had him as a subordinate. The Scotsman was
called a proper Tartar by some who knew him, a bit free with the
lash. Not that the admiral disapproved of such a thing. Quite the
contrary, proper discipline had to be maintained, and in wartime,
with pressed men aboard ship, a firm hand was something he
deemed a necessity. Toner had no idea what had occurred before
his arrival, and was surprised by the warmth of the reception Bessborough afforded him.

"If you wish to remove your coat, Captain, please feel free to
do so."

He felt his heavy black eyebrows twitch slightly, but it pleased
him that his voice was even as he replied, "That won't be necessary, sir."

Toner had no idea that he'd managed to make that sound like
a rebuke. Bessborough looked ready to snap at his inferior when
the slight knock at the left-hand door distracted him. He looked
up to see Dillon enter.

"You sent for me, sir?"

"Yes, Dillon. Allow me to name Captain Toner, of the
Endymion. You will have seen her come in, no doubt. Captain,
this is my political assistant, Mr Dillon."

Bessborough saw Toner's face freeze. His eyebrows, which had
registered mild disapproval at the suggestion that he remove his
coat, now seemed joined to his wig. Dillon's mode of attire was
the cause. He was dressed in a one-piece garment, made of loose-
fitting linen, which covered him from neck to floor. The Irishman
noticed the evident disapproval and smiled slightly, his soft voice
seeming to mock the upright officer as he spoke. "You would do
well to remember you're in the tropics, sir. If you don't undo that
stock, Captain, you won't survive the day."

"I don't take cognizance of civilians, sir, in matters of dress or
behaviour."

Dillon shrugged and sat down. But he could not resist the

obvious pun, which he delivered with his usual disregard for rank or station. "Suit yourself."

Toner turned to see if Bessborough was going to rebuke his assistant and was dismayed to observe that the admiral seemed not to have noticed anything untoward.

"Captain Toner has brought us some news, which may prove to be of value. You will know, Dillon, that the Netherlands have been overrun by the French. They've slung out the House of Nassau and declared a republic. What is it called, Toner?"

"The Batavian Republic, sir."

Bessborough seemed to ruminate on the word for a moment, as though it confused him. "Odd name, Batavian. Can't say I smoke the provenance. Anyway, Dillon, Toner thinks they might go to war with us, in support of their new allies. If they do, we'll be able to sort out that hornets' nest of thieves in St Eustatius."

"I'm sure that's something that would afford all your captains great pleasure, sir."

"Rodney did it, you know, Toner," said Bessborough, his blue eyes alight with an inner fire. "Didn't say a word, either. They reckon he took four million pounds in booty out of there. He even left the Dutch flag flying for months and trapped any ship that hadn't heard the news."

The amused look on Dillon's face at such openly stated avarice produced a hasty change of subject from the speaker.

"Captain Toner is keen to get to sea and blood his crew. I've explained that barring Hugues the enemy has for the moment surrendered the Caribbean to us. So there's scant prospect of glory. But there is nevertheless fruitful employment. I called you here to give him a review of the situation and the latest intelligence of possible illegals."

"Illegals?" barked Toner, like a dog responding to an intruder.

"There's no end of neutral ships breaking the Navigation Acts, Captain. They provide the most pressing targets at present. Indeed they are the only ones. But care must be exercised. They cannot be taken in open water unless you have proof positive that they are trading in defiance of the Acts. And once they've handed over their manifests, the cargo becomes the property of the colonists."

"Surely that still makes it forfeit," said Toner.

"Technically, yes," said Dillon. "But the reality can be somewhat different."

"Have you ever met Captain Nelson, Toner? He has the *Agamemnon* at present, I believe?"

"I have, sir. An odd wee man, who, for my money, pampers his crew. He is, it is true, a competent officer. But I've heard it said he's a mite too keen on his own glory, and less concerned with the needs of his king. Did he not marry the present Mrs Nelson on this station?"

"That's the one," Bessborough beamed, which confused Toner. But Dillon understood, having heard him before on the subject of officers like Nelson. To the admiral, Captain Nelson was a sad case. His favourite saying was that "he was a man who longed to strut like a peacock, even when he so clearly lacked anything approaching plumage."

"Nelson was sued for a hundred thousand pounds by the planters of St Kitts. He took some ships in the harbour, illegals of course, but with cargoes for which they'd already paid. They issued a writ in the local court. Fool couldn't leave his ship to go ashore lest they throw him in gaol for debt, and he couldn't leave the harbour lest they retake their goods."

"They appealed against his actions to the crown and it was upheld," said Dillon.

"The West Indian sugar lobby is very powerful, Toner. You will forget that at your peril."

Bessborough's eyes took on a cunning look, which Toner missed and Dillon spotted because his head turned towards the doorway behind the Irishman. The admiral then waved his hand, beckoning whoever had entered.

"Come in, Charles. We have some mail from home and I'm

nearly finished with Captain Toner." The Scotsman turned his head as Bessborough made the introduction. "Allow me to name my nephew, Captain. Lieutenant Caddick of the brig *Percival*."

The young man was favoured with a critical look, followed by a grunt that stated neither approval nor disapproval.

"Where was I?" said Bessborough.

"The West Indian sugar lobby," Dillon replied.

"Of course. It's not that I want to curtail you in any way, d'you understand. If you feel your duty requires you to act, then you must do so. Just don't hang about. Fetch the miscreants to English Harbour and let me deal with the planters."

A glance towards Dillon, a sight of the amused look in his assistant's eyes, made him change the subject abruptly. "Anyway, you go off with Dillon and he will give you all the latest information we have on illicit cargoes."

"All the information. And Captain Effingham?"

"What about him?"

"Since he came in early?"

"Effingham has other duties to perform."

"Then I'm to brief just Captain Toner, sir?"

Bessborough frowned but got no chance to reply.

"You will be brief, sir, I trust," snapped Toner, standing up and glaring at Dillon with the teeth parted in what passed for a smile. The captain's eyes took in the man's eccentric dress once more and his teeth ground together as he continued. "I can see nothing to be gained by hanging aboot in port when there's work to be done."

Bessborough and Caddick sat on either side of the admiral's desk, engrossed in the pile of letters from England. It seemed every member of their extended family had been in touch with anyone who could aid the cause, and that such correspondence had borne fruit.

"Things seem to have swung round in our favour, uncle."

"Thank the Lord!" said Bessborough with feeling. "I might

put on a bold face to the others, Charles, but I think you know how worried I was."

There had been a time, last year, when he'd feared he might be caught up in the backwash from Trethgowan's failure at Guadeloupe. The man should have been court-martialled, of course. But given the other military failures of the last few years, not least those perpetrated by the king's own son, he'd suffered no penalty. The Horse Guards could hardly chastise him when the Duke of York, the titular commander-in-chief, had made such a hash of his own campaign. That, despite the anger at the Admiralty, had deflected any action against him. It seemed, finally, that the matter was to be laid to rest. Caddick put down the letter in his hand and picked up another heavy piece of parchment. His uncle raised his eyes, clearly noticing that his nephew was holding one of the official despatches addressed specifically to him, an action which caused the youngster to hesitate. But it was only for a second, since his uncle went back to his own reading.

"No sign of any French ships on the way, uncle," he said.

"Don't you believe it, lad," Bessborough replied, without looking up. "That's just what they said before Hugues arrived."

Two doors away Dillon was closeted with Toner, who still declined to alleviate the distress caused by his heavy uniform. He listened while the Irishman outlined the potential location of a group of three ships expected to make a landfall on Martinique within the week. This was followed by the details of a number of vessels said to be heading for Guadeloupe and a pair of illegals on their way to Dominica. The information was comprehensive: ships' names, masters' names, tonnage of each vessel, and even a list of their cargoes. The Scotsman could hardly believe his luck, a fact which was evident in the sour expression on his face and the way he questioned Dillon.

"This all looks very bonny, I must say. Too bonny, perhaps. Is it not just pious hopes you're feeding me?"

"No, Captain. Someone has gone to a great deal of trouble to ensure that this is accurate information."

"And where does all this information come from?"

"Only people who need to know are vouchsafed such things."

Toner's reserve was understandable. What was on offer was quite a windfall. As a new arrival he was wondering why, when he wasn't a client of Bessborough, such plums were being offered to him and not the other captains. But Dillon went on to inform him that things were not as simple as they seemed, as well as to warn him to have a care to keep his actions legal.

"You will be aware of the possibilities of error at sea?"

Toner's eyes flashed angrily, and his eyes took in the top of Dillon's one-piece garment.

"More perhaps than me," said the Irishman in a conciliatory tone. Toner opened his mouth to interrupt, but Dillon held up a hand to stop him. "I will not dare even hint at a lecture on navigation, sir. No doubt you heard of the gentleman called Victor Hugues before you left England."

"I read about Trethgowan's failure."

"The recapture of Guadeloupe was quite a shock, not least when our troops outnumbered his by three to one."

"I heard he slaughtered his own countrymen before the admiral's very eyes. Right there on the beach, too."

"And mine, Captain Toner. I, too, witnessed that atrocity. Hugues didn't stop there. He set up his infernal guillotine in the market square and proceeded to behead anyone who questioned his authority. His control of the island was soon as absolute as anything they have seen in France."

"Has the admiral no' considered an attack on the place? If I've heard ye right, there's nothing in the naval line to defend it, barring the odd brig. The frigates he came out with were sighted in Brest."

"We lack the means, Captain Toner. There's little point in destroying ships and harbours if we cannot land troops. Hugues knows this as well as anyone."

"You don't need bullocks. What aboot marines?" said Toner, sharply. "A'm amazed no one has seen fit to stretch their orders a wee bit. A surprise could work wonders."

"Before you allude to the possibility of sudden attacks, let me tell you that Guadeloupe has a high peak. They can see for miles around and spot any ships over the natural horizon."

"They're Frenchmen, are they not?" stated Toner, as though the conclusion that they were inferior to the British was obvious.

"I think it would be best if we return to the business at hand," said Dillon coldly. "Hugues has set himself up as a buccaneer. We have to respect neutrality. No such constraints are placed on him. Thus, recently, a certain number of ships we'd hoped to intercept have been taken by him. He captures them at sea, while we are forced to wait until they make an illegal landfall."

Toner looked at the list in his hand for a moment, which is all the time it took him to make the connection. "Are you telling me these illegals might no' be where they're supposed to?"

"It's possible."

Toner stood up abruptly. "So that's it, is it?"

"That's what?" asked Dillon calmly.

"Why I'm being sent out. Bessborough disna know me from Adam. Yet A've no sooner dropped anchor than he's telling me to put to sea again. There are two other frigates out there. Why not send those that are already here, tell me that? Poynton Ae danna ken aboot, but Effingham has served under him for years and has a right to be favoured. It's a wild-goose chase, isn't it? Those damn ships you're on aboot won't be there, so let's send out Toner. Let him fail instead of his friends."

Dillon's eyes flashed. Obviously he had no intention of telling Toner if he was right or wrong.

The look reminded Toner that he did not cut a very prepossessing figure, that he had about him a meagre air, with his pinchbeck shoe buckles and worn linen.

"It is my task to provide intelligence, sir. It is your job to execute it. If you have reason to doubt that your orders have been issued in good faith, then I suggest you return to the admiral and decline the opportunity."

Toner had leant forward to put Dillon in his place. But the words he intended to use died in his throat. He could do as the Irishman suggested. But if he followed such a course, he'd be cutting off his own nose to spite his face. Bessborough probably had little regard for him now. If he declined to do his bidding he could kiss goodbye to any prospect of being favoured in the future. The *Endymion* would find herself on permanent convoy duty and any prospect of taking a prize, of clearing his debts, would evaporate. He fought to control his features, bending them into what he thought was a friendly smile. To Dillon it had the appearance of a man suffering from a serious disorder of the bowels.

"You have their course and destination, you say?"

"Not yet, sir. But if you're lucky, I will have them tonight."

CHAPTER TWENTY

PENDER sat in Toner's barge hard by the Admiralty quay, sweating in the full glare of sunlight and silently cursing the presence of the marines. It was just possible that they were like the rest of the crew, sick of the captain. But since it was a matter of policy to keep sailors and lobsters apart, he didn't know them well enough to find out. And Toner had left them orders to shoot anyone trying to leave the boat. Not that anyone would "run" in this heat. The sun beat down on them with its relentless glare, baking them alive inside their blue pea jackets.

"Ahoy there, *Endymion*."

The whole crew looked round to see Midshipman Callander standing in the bows of the launch. He too had a complement of marines in the boat.

"We've just had a signal to make up our wood and water and prepare for sea." His eyes seemed to be fixed on Pender as the boat drew closer. The sailor shook his head almost imperceptibly and indicated the silent marines.

"Tie up alongside, men," he called, as the launch drifted slowly into the side of the captain's barge. It was only then, as the boat spun sideways, that Pender saw the glowering, purple face of Dunlop astride the rearmost thwarts. He called loudly to the midshipman, too loudly, since the boy wasn't far away.

"Mr Callander, you are over prolix. It's no concern of the lower deck what we are about. You will instruct the men to wait here while you and I go to the master attendant."

"Aye, aye, sir," said Callander. He leapt nimbly across the boats and jumped up on to the quayside. Dunlop followed at a more sedate pace, glowering at the barge crew. Once he was on the quay he spoke softly, and impatiently, to Callander.

"I shall partake of a little relaxation while I'm ashore. See that building yonder, with the Boar's Head sign? I'll be in there. You take this list to the master attendant, ask him to be zealous, and come straight back to the quay. If you catch sight of the captain approaching, fetch me out of there double quick."

"What if the captain returns before I do, sir?"

Judging by the crowd of women outside the Boar's Head, his premier's pleasure was not to be confined to a mere drink. And Dunlop, desperate to be off and, after months at sea, to pleasure himself on a whore, was practically hopping from foot to foot in his eagerness.

"Perhaps I could detail one of the men to keep a lookout."

The premier was walking away as he replied, "Yes, yes. Some-one reliable, mind. They are not to set foot off the quayside. If anyone runs Toner will have both our hides."

Callander looked down into the barge, full of sweating crew. "Pender. Up here, at the double. And I think it best if the rest of you find some shade, otherwise you won't be fit to row the captain back to the ship."

Pender jumped up on to the quay to stand beside Callander. They watched as the barge fended off, followed by the launch, gliding in the shade cast by the huge bulk of the *Redoubtable*. Immediately dozens of heads poked out through the gunports, to start a conversation with these new arrivals, people who had news from home.

The young midshipman stood close and explained the task, and the constraints, to Pender. Then with a worried look, he added a warning. "You mustn't run, Pender, you understand that, don't you?"

"I can't, Mr Callander, can I? There's forty of my shipmates still aboard the ship. When I leave, they all leave. But I have still got to get word to my captain, which I cannot do stuck here on the quay."

"You said you put something in writing?"

"Yes."

"Then give it to me."

"You've already got it, Mr Callander. It's in your coat, the inside pocket on the left, with what I hope is enough money to send the letter to England. The other packet is for the admiral here in Antigua."

Callander's hand went to check, and his eyes showed the surprise that he clearly felt when his hand touched the two folded packets. "Where did you learn that trick?"

Pender just smiled at him, not willing to reveal that he'd been a thief in the past, and a good one. "You'd best be on your way, sir, or we might run out of time." He watched him leave, then saw him stop and talk to the black street vendor plying his trade outside the tavern. He was grateful when the negro came towards him, with a scooped-out coconut full of cool lemonade. He reached into his pouch to pay, but the vendor just grinned.

"Officer, he pay already."

"God bless him," said Pender. "I hope he lives long enough to be an admiral."

Dillon caught Bessborough just as he was about to leave for dinner with the governor, who resided to the north of the island, in the capital, St John's. His carriage, with his wife and two daughters already aboard and Cram scowling on the box beside the driver, stood by the front door.

"Well?" he enquired testily. "Our newcomer must be a happy man."

"I have little faith in the venture, sir," said Dillon. "Though I hope, profoundly, that I'm wrong. I see no reason why Toner should do any better than the other captains."

"He's commendably eager," replied Bessborough, with a foxy air.

"Can I speak freely, Admiral?"

"Do you not always, Dillon?"

The Irishman gave him a thin smile and rubbed a hand across his thinning ginger hair. "Toner is eager for wealth, or glory, or both."

"That is no bad thing."

"I feel you should impress on him, sir, that there are limits beyond which he cannot go."

Bessborough frowned. "I should think he's aware of that."

"I fear he will test those limits."

"Let him, Dillon. I am sick of sitting here with nothing coming in." He must have realized the dual nature of that remark and spoke hastily to lay the suggestion of pecuniary interest. "What do you think they will say at the Admiralty to my despatches? They won't thank me for failing to stop the traffic in illicit goods, nor will they think to blame my officers. No, Dillon. Call it speculation or rumour if you like, this Hugues is having some success. I, for one, have not sought to exaggerate it. But even with what is certain they will lay the responsibility squarely at my door. So, if Toner bends the rules a trifle, it can only be to my advantage. He has been sent to this station by their lordships, so I owe him nothing. If he's in the wrong I can disown him. If, on the other hand, his actions are upheld, then it will look as though I have ordered it so. My stock will rise accordingly."

"There is a third possibility, Admiral. And it is this: in his desire to prove himself, Toner will so exceed the bounds of his authority that he will bring a heap of ordure about all our heads."

Bessborough was already halfway into the carriage when he replied, "No, no, Dillon. You will have warned him against that, I'm sure."

Which, translated, meant that Bessborough didn't care if Toner got into trouble. The Scotsman, and if necessary Dillon, would bear the brunt of any opprobrium that followed in the wake of Toner's actions. If the admiral, as he seated himself, noticed that his assistant was displeased, it didn't show. He had a grin on his face like a Cheshire cat.

"Just think, Dillon. If Toner surprises us and has some luck—

imagine the looks we'll get from the likes of Poynton and Vandegut."

"Come along, husband," cried Lady Bessborough, her substantial chest swelling under the shade of her parasol, "or we shall
be late."

Later that day Dillon was on the same road, making what had
become a familiar journey, and a welcome break from the stuffy,
inward-looking atmosphere of Admiralty House. He flicked the
whip to encourage his pony up the steep rise that carried him out
of English Harbour and on reaching the summit turned to look
over his shoulder. Behind him the whole anchorage, said by some
to be the best in the Caribbean, formed a vast panorama. The
green landscape ran into the sliver of golden sand that ringed the
island, which fizzed with the stark white of the surf as it beat
against the shore. The different hues of the water, pale in the shallows above the coral reefs, deep blue over the trenches that went
down a thousand feet, showed clearly the changes that had taken
place in this, the tip of an extinct volcano.

The sun shone as always, that golden orb that so delighted the
new arrival in the West Indies. But few from northern Europe went
long in this climate without becoming bored by endless sunshine,
missing the variations of weather that they'd been raised with.
True, the sky, now its normal blue, flecked with towering clouds,
could change very suddenly. He could see a storm now, a huge
black mass on the western horizon, rain so heavy that it blotted
out every sensation but its own presence. Usually it would pass
over in minutes, leaving the ground steaming, and the men who
occupied the earth pulling at their clothes to relieve the discomfort caused by the humidity.

But like everything about the Caribbean, there was an obverse
side to paradise. Every regiment posted out from England lost
more men to disease than to enemy fire. Even those long resident
could succumb to the "yellow jack," so termed because of the
colour such an ailment tinged the victim's skin. In the hurricane

season, the wind could reach phenomenal strengths, a power potent enough to beach the largest sailing ship, or to lift a palm tree out of the ground and send it, like some great primordial spear, hurtling through a solid brick wall.

Right now it was calm, with the *Endymion* already moored in the far reaches of the outer bay, her topsails catching the last sunlight and turning a pale shade of orange. Toner must have declined to revictual in his eagerness to be off. Moored so far out, he would not be at the mercy of the tide if Dillon returned with confirmation of his orders. The rigging was full of men and below them, on the quarterdeck, stood a knot of officers, their dark blue coats standing out against the bleached planking. Toner was amongst them, scowling in his habitual manner at his officers and crew.

The interview with Toner had left an unpleasant taste. The Scotsman was one of those men who considered all other humans to be an inferior breed, set upon the earth to meet the demands of serving naval officers. He despised soldiers and civilians alike, and had given Dillon the impression that his regard for his fellow captains was extremely limited. Time and again he demonstrated all the arrogance and hypocrisy of his type, men that the likes of Dillon would have despised, if they could have summoned up the energy. Unbeknown to the captain of *Endymion* the Irishman had realized that his performance was false; had seen that underneath he lacked, to a marked degree, the confident manner he was so intent on creating. Toner, in anticipating condescension, had armoured himself to head it off, creating a shell of apparent self-assurance to defend his weaknesses. The matter of his coat revealed more than he knew; it wasn't that he didn't want to take off the heavy broadcloth garment to relieve his discomfort. He was afraid to do such a thing, since he might be seen as something less than the perfect officer.

Dillon, who'd been ruminating on that interview, suddenly shouted, even though he must have known there was no chance of Toner hearing him. "It will kill you, Toner, if you don't learn, which will be no loss!"

The sudden noise startled his pony, forcing him to pull hard on the traces to keep it from wandering off the track. But he got it under control, and set off with the trap jogging along at a fine pace. Dillon began to sing to himself, his gentle voice caressing the Gaelic words of an old Irish ballad. The two flagons of rum in the bottom of the trap clinked together, providing a rhythmic accompaniment to his singing. To the west the black storm cloud had moved on to the north, leaving the sun to set into the mass of conflicting colours that made up the horizon.

Bessborough paced back and forth at the bottom of the staircase, fuming at the way his wife and daughters kept everyone waiting for their dinner. The fact that the governor, a civilian with the lax attitude of the islands, forgave this lapse of manners made no difference. The admiral was, like all naval officers, a punctilious time-keeper. Besides that, he was used to taking his dinner at three. It was now past five and he was sharp set and rumbling to prove it. Finally his wife appeared at the top of the stairs, dressed in white and looking, with her ample figure, like a 100-gunner under full sail. Bessborough was known to wonder in the company of close friends if his daughters, thin creatures with rather pinched faces, would end up looking like their mother. Being girls, they were almost strangers to him. For all his *bonhomie*, appearance, and manifold social graces, he was prone to admit he found his own girls hard to talk with. To his wife's mind, that applied to her as well.

"I will not have you frowning at me like that, sir," she boomed, well before her feet reached the parquet flooring. "If we are delayed, you are the culprit."

"Damn me, madam, that is not so."

"I would urge you to modify your language, husband," Lady Bessborough replied in a loud whisper, "if for no other reason than your daughters, innocent creatures, can hear you."

"Then don't presume to land your lack of time-keeping at my door, madam."

"It is either firmly at yours or of that toady Dillon, sir."

"Lady Bessborough," cried the governor, advancing to meet her. "If I'd known what wonders you could have achieved by such a short delay, I would bid you return to your toilet. Why, madam, you are the very picture of elegance."

Lady Bessborough accepted this flowery compliment as nothing less than her due and, taking the governor's arm, swept into the dining-room.

"Damn him, the fat red-faced toad," said Bessborough, softly. "We dine with this poltroon twice a year, and twice a year I have to listen to the same nonsense."

"Why, Papa," said his eldest daughter, Emily, "do you not take pleasure from hearing Mama praised?"

The admiral just glared at her and followed his wife into the dining-room. The meal that came after, though substantial and delicious, was ruined by the conversation. If Bessborough had hoped to get away from the name Victor Hugues he was to be disappointed. The governor had seen fit to add a group of local merchants, as well as ships' captains, to the normal complement of army officers and civilian officials. In the isolation of English Harbour this was a breed of people he rarely met, for which the admiral was truly grateful. Worse still, they had plenty to say to him and were not to be restrained by the company of ladies. News had come in of several British ships lost, of crews set adrift, with the name of Victor Hugues on every tongue. Rumours that they'd hitherto ignored as not affecting them were added to their grievances, so that he was regaled with what it seemed was common gossip in St Eustatius, St Thomas, and St Croix. The governor, though an admirer of Lady Bessborough, felt no need to shield her husband, who was subjected to a barrage of complaints. He was finally handed a comprehensive list of ships that had been taken in the previous months.

The journey home to English Harbour was accomplished in near silence, as the daughters, looking at their father, realized he was in no mood for small talk. Lady Bessborough, still basking in the attentions she'd received, felt no requirement to ruin her mood by easing his. But he did growl one emphatic remark, which was to the effect that he'd never had a meal in which both the food and the conversation had been so indigestible.

Dillon sat in the bright moonlight that bathed his surroundings, a small bay on the northern coast of the island fringed with palm trees. His coach lantern, shaded on three sides, shone brightly towards the surf, creating a small arc of golden light that attracted endless flying insects. His attention was concentrated on the inky blue sky, slashed across with a single shaft of glaring white moonlight, waiting for the return signal that would announce the arrival of a messenger from one of his agents. There was no impatience in his eyes, even though the men he was anticipating were late. The Irishman knew this was a game for stoics, an activity in which passion was an enemy, not a friend.

The pinpoint of light fixed his attention. He lifted his hand and placed it in front of his own lantern, holding it there for several seconds before removing it again. The light out at sea responded in similar fashion, so Dillon got down from the box and grabbing hold of the two flagons of rum made his way towards the water's edge. Out at sea there was a single sail, the huge triangle of the lateen rig that dwarfed the tiny boat beneath it, just dark enough to contrast with the slightly blue sea. Then it was gone, run down on its boom, as the aviso headed in towards the shore.

Dillon was close to the waterline when the boat touched, its keel grinding noisily on the sand. The two negroes in the bows leapt ashore, one coming towards the Irishman, the other holding the boat at the shoreline. They exchanged their greetings in Erse. The use of this language acted as a form of security, since no Englishman would comprehend it, and the Scots Gaelic variety was noticeably different. Dillon accepted the two oilskin packages, one large, the other small, proffering one in exchange. Then the negro, who was head and shoulders taller than Dillon, held his hand out for the rum, his teeth glinting as he gathered them into his arms.

With one flagon in each hand, he turned and bounded down the beach. Within seconds he was gone, pushing his small sleek boat out into the surf, his wet body suddenly illuminated by the phosphorescence. His companion waited till he'd leapt aboard, then hauled on the ropes to raise that triangular sail again. Its shadow faded as the boat headed out to sea, the bows crashing into the waves and sending a flash of white spray into the dark night air.

Dillon pushed the larger of the two oilskin packages into his coat pocket and got back on to the box of his trap. As soon as he was into the line of trees he unshaded his lantern, which cast just enough light for him to see the papers he extracted from the smaller packet. He read the words easily, having learned the Erse before he ever spoke English. The news from home was good, the cause of Irish independence seeming to prosper under the leadership of Lord Edward Fitzgerald. Wolfe Tone, leader of the United Irishmen, was facing the threat of being banished to America. O'D-wyer informed him that the need for funds was still acute, though the money raised in the Caribbean out-weighed that from any other source.

Engrossed as he was, and with the pounding of the surf, he didn't hear the sound of the boat scrunching into the beach. Nor did he observe the young man who approached within ten feet of his shay. Hidden behind a tree this stranger watched him closely, before ducking back as Dillon finished his reading. The Irishman flicked his whip and set his pony in motion. The young man hesitated for a moment, unsure what to do about his boat. He ran back quickly and lifted the rolled blanket that contained his few possessions, then set off at a trot after the carriage. The track was rough, slowing the pony's progress. But that track in turn led to a junction. Here one road led to the main commercial Antiguan port, St John's. The other took Dillon south on the well-worn thoroughfare to English Harbour. On the smooth surface the young man could not keep up with the shay. But it didn't matter. He was sure he knew the driver's destination. Once he arrived there, it would be easy to learn the identity of the man who'd received those oilskin packages from St Eustatius.

Out at sea the two huge negroes had started on Dillon's rum, lashing off the tiller on their boat so that the aviso sailed itself, its course west by north-west in the direction of St Eustatius. Clouds now obscured the moon and the stars, which made little difference to the pair. They'd sailed this route many times before, to meet the man without a name, who spoke Gaelic, on that same beach.

The master of the *Lady Barraclough, en route* from Bristol to St John's, was drunk in his cabin. Taking advantage of this, the few members of the night watch, given the steady trade wind, had lashed off the wheel and picked a convenient spot to lie down. According to their captain's calculations, they would raise Antigua at first light. They couldn't miss it, running along the island's line of latitude. Navigation being an imprecise science, they were slightly off course, some five miles to the north of their assumed heading and several miles further west than the master had reckoned. In the darkness the two negroes, too busy talking and drinking, didn't see their nemesis until the bows were practically above them. On board the merchant ship those who should have been looking out, who would have heard their cries of panic, were sound asleep.

The *Lady Barraclough* had a displacement of eight hundred tons and was fully laden with cargo. The small aviso, built for speed, was a flimsy affair. When the cargo ship struck, the boat nearly broke in two. Perhaps it would have been better for the men aboard if it had. But enough strakes of wood held to pin it, for a moment, to the ship's bows, driving it under water, and propelling the two occupants out into the warm enveloping sea. The barnacles that encrusted the *Lady Barraclough*'s bottom tore the dark skin of their outstretched arms, filling the water with blood. The remains of their aviso, now in two sections, thudding down either side of the ship, careered into them, the jagged edges of wood cutting flesh and the sheer force of the impact breaking bones. The noise of human screams, added to the drumbeat of wood on wood, woke those on board the merchant ship. They leapt at first to their stations. Then, drawn by curiosity, were in time to line the side just as the wreckage, and the two broken, lacerated bodies tumbled into the creamy wake.

The master came staggering out of his cabin, clutching at the binnacle for support, demanding to know what was going on. To a man, his crew denied all certain knowledge, offering opinions that ranged from an uprooted tree to a sleeping whale. He cursed them roundly, before returning to his bottle. Once he was gone, his men rushed to the stern rail. But there was nothing to see in the stygian darkness. The two halves of the aviso had sunk. And at night, who could be expected to see the remains of two dark-skinned negroes, floating face down in the black water?

Toner had a boat by the quay, with his second lieutenant, Mr McPartland, swaying drunkenly above it. Dillon pressed the confirmation of *Endymion*'s orders into the man's sweating palm. He fell into the boat rather than lowering himself, and the crew pushed off from the harbour wall to a chorus of drunken commands.

"Naval officers," said Dillon to himself. Then, gently, he spat into the harbour.

CHAPTER TWENTY-ONE

HARRY MADE his landfall 36 hours after Toner had weighed anchor. They were at a late breakfast, once more entertaining the young French naval lieutenant, who'd turned out to be a pleasant youth, when the cry of "Land ho!" interrupted them. After three thousand miles of ocean it was a welcome sound. All three rushed on deck, napkins in hand. The low shore came in view with the hills behind, its line of palm trees bent by the wind. James professed himself disappointed. Antigua, for all that it was their first sight of *terra firma* for weeks, did not inspire the lyrical side of his nature. He'd grown up with tales of the fabulous West Indies. He expected to see a riot of colours, both flora and fauna, with some notion of the natural power of the elements thrown in. There was nothing of that nature on the eastern shore: just low, rather bare hills, dotted with windmills and houses. But as they rounded the island, weathering the point that led to the bay that enclosed English Harbour, his heart lifted.

This was truly a beautiful vista, set off by the distant sight of a frigate, heading east, under sail. The outer roadstead was a great horseshoe surrounded by golden sands, then a narrow bottleneck that led to the inner harbour and the town. The red brickwork of the naval buildings' rope walk, sail loft, and hospital, seemed, in both their colour and design, entirely appropriate to their setting. The settlement itself rose in haphazard tiers, a mixture of styles, with large white houses at the uppermost levels, with the battlements of Shirley Heights above to provide protection for the entire anchorage. The place also had an orderly air missing from a European harbour. It was as if the sun, shining in the clear azure sky, imposed a discipline in the way men lived their lives. The few ships were anchored in neat lines, the houses behind all in a seemingly pristine condition, nestling between the blue of the sea and the deep green of the landscape. And then there was the smell of myriad perfumes, of frangipangi and flame of the forest, so strong that they overbore the normal odours of a seaport. From being disappointed, James swung round with the unpredictability of a tropical storm to a sense of delirious happiness.

But it didn't last. For one thing the French lieutenant, Thierry Brissot, of whom they'd become quite fond, would be handed over to the naval authorities, there to await an exchange of prisoners. At least they could provide the young man from Artois with the wherewithal for a comfortable confinement and they pressed a goodly sum on to him despite his very vocal protests. The other problem was finding a berth for the *Bucephalas*. This was a much more tedious affair than it had been for the *Endymion*. Harry Ludlow had to deal with the rapacity of the local dockyard commissioner, who would not consent to provide a berth without the clear hint that a personal gift would follow. This fellow, a half-pay naval captain of advanced years who'd stayed on in the West Indies, operated through his agents in crime, the local pilots. It was from one of them that the Ludlow brothers learnt of Toner's arrival, plus the nature of his hurried departure. James, on receiving this intelligence, was more deeply affected than Harry. His mood of enchanted wonder evaporated abruptly.

"This Toner has taken on a diabolical hue, brother. Not a sniff of him over the entire Atlantic and now we find him gone from here without the time to dry his stockings."

Harry answered half-heartedly. He was more concerned with the pilot, who'd come aboard inebriated, then sunk a pint of claret in a bare four minutes. He'd then been somewhat rude to their prisoner, though he had no knowledge of the way he had been captured, an act which had earned him a stiff rebuke from James. Surly, as well as drunk, it was necessary to see him over the side with some care. His attention then shifted to conning the *Bucephalas* in towards their allotted buoy. Harry took up the conversation where James had left off.

"If I didn't know better, I'd assume he knew we were in his wake. He certainly made off with unseemly haste."

"Do we know why?"

"Oh, yes. The pilot, as well as being venal, was quite a talkative soul. And Admiralty House leaks like a sieve when it comes to rumour. Apparently Bessborough dislikes his captains lounging about in the harbour and puts them to sea with only 24 hours to revictual. The one in the harbour is off to Jamaica for a refit and that fellow we saw heading east had only just come in before *Endymion*. Anyway, it seems Toner pressed for action, dressing it up in a lot of rhetoric about duty. Claimed to be afire to seek out and destroy the enemy. But that won't wash out here. Everyone knows that he's after some quick money. He also had a degree of luck. Bessborough is, apparently, at loggerheads with one or two of his officers. Toner's arrival gave the old man a chance to remind the fellow of his powers of patronage."

"All that in such a short time," said James. "Your pilot was somewhat more than talkative. Do they know about Monsieur d'Albret's frigates?"

Harry grinned. "No, James. They do not. I intend to keep that as a surprise."

The commands ran out to back the topsails and the way came off the ship. They'd launch a boat with a cable to tie up to the buoy. Harry looked around, to make sure that he had room to swing round on that cable, before calling for his boat crew to row them ashore. As they made their way towards the harbour entrance they passed several dozen boats heading the other way. There were the usual doxies, tinkers, charlatans, and traders, intent on separating the crew of the *Bucephalas* from their money. But they were not all like that. Every ship in the harbour had put off a boat to investigate.

"We are subject to a degree of scrutiny, Harry," said James, as a naval cutter slid by, full of officers who were naked in their curiosity of the other boat.

"Hardly surprising, James. The *Bucephalas* will never be mistaken for a merchant ship. When king's officers see a well-armed British vessel in these waters that does not fly a warship's pennant, they smell competition. And I dare say the pilot, in his own drunken way, has let on all he knew as he sailed by. They will all have learned that we have a French officer aboard and be wondering how we, a privateer, came across him."

"From that I deduce we are, as is usual, unlikely to be welcome."

Harry just smiled, as though the prospect of being unwelcome pleased him.

Bessborough, sitting at his desk, took the news of Monsieur d'Albret and his frigates with surprising equanimity, while being careful enough to congratulate them on their escape. The other news they bore seemed to affect him much more deeply. He read Bridport's words for the tenth time, yet still he did not speak. The Ludlow brothers, unaware that he had Pender's petition by his left hand, sat waiting patiently, well aware that to interrupt now could only weaken their case. Finally the older man lifted his handsome head and looked at them with his steady blue eyes. There was no real friendliness there, but nor did he show repugnance. James didn't notice, but the lack of the customary official distaste surprised Harry. The admiral reached out for the bell on his desk and rang it. A servant appeared at once.

"Ask Mr Dillon to join me, would you?" As the servant left he turned to the brothers and smiled for the first time. "You would oblige me, gentlemen, if you would step out on to the veranda for a moment. I require a private word with my assistant."

Both brothers stood up immediately. Bessborough beamed at them, obviously going out of his way to be pleasant. "There is a most heartening view of the harbour and the surrounding hills, and rest assured I will send you out something cool to drink."

"Thank you, Admiral."

"You are Tom Ludlow's boys, are you not?"

"We are," replied James.

Bessborough looked at Harry, who was waiting to see what the older man would say next. He'd never met the admiral, nor heard his father talk of him. But mention of their parentage usually led to some indication of the enquirer's views on their father. This time Harry was disappointed. Bessborough's next words were clearly addressed to him alone.

"Then you will be no stranger to these parts, sir. Perhaps the view will revive a few agreeable memories rather than astound you with its beauty."

"Do I know you, sir?" asked Harry.

Bessborough shook his head. "I think not. But if I may allude to something more unpleasant than the prospect from the veranda, I was at your court martial in '82."

Harry's face creased up. He was clearly perplexed. "I recall the name of every captain who sat on that court."

"I was not a member of the court, merely an observer, Mr Ludlow. You will recall as well as I do that we'd just thumped the French at the Saintes. I received my step after that, from Admiral Rodney personally, so I was the newest post captain in the fleet. Suddenly, I realized, I could find myself sitting in judgement on my fellow officers, even my recent contemporaries. I attended to learn what I had in store. I must say, the trial, and its outcome, still intrigue me."

"That chapter of my life is closed, sir," said Harry coldly. "It is not something I take pleasure in discussing."

Bessborough paled slightly, Harry's tone being harsh. He stood up, a clear signal that they should depart. But there was a glint in his eye that made both brothers suppose he'd set out to discomfit them. And at least, in Harry's case, the admiral had certainly succeeded.

"Then forgive me for raising the matter," he said smoothly.

◆ ◆ ◆

Dillon read Pender's petition, crabbed, careful writing on a single sheet. It was not the first document of its kind he'd seen. In fact, the opening was depressingly familiar, full of protestations of loyalty to both King George and the Lords Commissioners of the Admiralty, plus a promise that the authors would willingly fight the French, indeed die for their country, but they could not face another day aboard such a hellish ship. Then followed a tedious list of grievances about pay, and complaints against their officers, in particular their captain for his tyrannical ways. The second sheet was different.

It related the way that Pender and his mates had been hauled out of the *Bucephalas* to serve aboard Toner's ship, an act which was damned as illegal. Since they were aboard unlawfully, any punishment meted out to them was an assault, and would be the subject of a criminal charge once the men were back with their true captain. Bessborough, his pale blue eyes expressionless, waited until Dillon had finished the petition before handing over the orders from Bridport.

The Irishman was quick enough to make a connection without reading it. "That ship that berthed an hour ago, the one that looks like a small frigate?"

"*Bucephalas,*" said Bessborough.

"I had a message from the quay to say that they have a French officer aboard."

"Yes," said Bessborough. "They ran in with two French frigates, a 28 and a 32: they retook a prize and thus the officer who was sailing her. There's some crew as well. Had a narrow escape by their account."

"Do we know their destination?" asked Dillon.

"No, we don't. These fellows are too polite to demand that their prisoner tell them," said Bessborough with a sour look. "Though I'm sure that you can guess it as well as I."

"Guadeloupe or Dominica?"

"Hell's teeth and damnation," the older man snapped, his face colouring with suffused blood. "With Poynton in dock I'm short on cruisers as it is. And I've just sent Effingham to take station off Grenada. Not a word from England and a ship just in."

"Any troops on board these Frenchmen?"

"None, according to the Ludlows' other prisoners," replied the admiral. "Those confined to the cable tier were more willing informants than the fellow to whom they gave a cabin." He pointed to the papers in his political assistant's hand. "What do you make of those?"

Dillon read the orders through quickly, before looking at the two brothers, standing on the veranda with their backs to the room.

"Lord Bridport sent a copy to the Admiralty?"

The older man nodded. "Apparently the exceptions were signed by Henry Dundas himself."

"Jesus, Mary, and Joseph! He sits at the Prime Minister's right hand. Not a man to cross."

"Most certainly not," snapped Bessborough. "But can I strip forty-odd men out of *Endymion?* If I do, it will meaning taking hands out of the other ships on the station to make up Toner's complement, otherwise his ship will be near useless."

"An order which will be badly received."

"Very badly, Dillon. I will have protests in writing."

Dillon nodded towards the Ludlows. "What about an appeal to their better nature?"

"Damn it, man, they're privateersmen. The older one is also as stubborn as a mule."

"You know him?" asked the Irishman.

"I know of him. He's the son of an admiral and used to hold a commission himself. He was out here in '82. Did well at the Saintes, then challenged his first lieutenant to a duel. Fellow called Carter, I recall."

Dillon's eyes lit up at the mention of the word "duel." Being Irish, with a Dublin background added to the hot temper of his race, he was more attracted to that sport than others. "Did they have the encounter?"

"Oh, yes. Pistols at dawn. Ludlow put a ball in the other fellow's shoulder. There was a court, of course, which when it heard the evidence admonished Carter for bringing the whole thing on his own head. Apparently the fellow was a martinet in the wardroom. Had Ludlow apologized, he could have left the cabin without a blemish."

"I take it he didn't?"

Bessborough shook his head. "Point-blank refused. They stripped him of his commission. No choice really. Can't have junior officers shootin' their superiors, can we?"

Dillon grinned at that. "You said he's the son of an admiral, sir."

"Tom Ludlow, who was one of the hardest, most stubborn coves I've ever met." He noticed the lift of the Irishman's pale ginger eyebrows. "I know what you're going to say, Dillon. With such a father why wasn't he reinstated? The answer is I don't know. Perhaps there was more to the affair than meets the eye. But if this Harry Ludlow is anything like his pater, I would guess that he's in this position through his own stubborn refusal to bend. So if you wish to appeal to his better nature, you may go ahead. I for one will not expose myself to a snub."

Dillon held up Bridport's orders. "I cannot see how you can refuse this."

For once, Bessborough showed a flash of genuine anger. "I'm not under Bridport's command. And a fat lot of good he's done for me. For all I know these two frigates they talked about are out of Brest."

"I'm well aware of that, sir. But neither do you want to go making an enemy of someone like Dundas. He is Billy Pitt's best friend. It's only his efforts and patronage that keep the ministry in power. If he tells the Cabinet that we need a new commander on the Leeward Island station, it's as good as done, regardless of Lord Spencer's personal views."

Bessborough shook his head slowly.

"I know. I know. It's a fine state of affairs when you can't rely on the First Lord of the Admiralty to protect the navy from politics. But I don't have to tell you that due to disease every ship on this station is short of hands. And we're not taking deserters out of the American ships at anything like the rate we require, simply because we're not taking enough ships. If I make a move to lower the existing complements of the rest of the squadron, the commanders will use that fact as a stick to beat me with. They might even lay their present lack of success in suppressing illegal trade at my door. And how can I ask them to go into action against these damned frigates with a deficit in their muster rolls?"

Dillon nodded towards the Ludlows again. "I will talk to them, if you wish, sir."

"Do so, Dillon, do so. But whatever you attempt, for God's sake don't expose me to their condescension."

CHAPTER TWENTY-TWO

"**I AM AS** patriotic an Englishman as the next man, Mr Dillon. But you cannot ask of me that I surrender so much. Nor, sir, do I wish to expose men, who I would remind you signed up as volunteers with me, to the harsher conditions which prevail in His Majesty's ships."

Dillon had folded the recently delivered petition, which sat on the desk between them. He might be familiar with such documents. But the list of punishments inflicted by Toner on the *Endymion*'s crew was an outrage by any standards.

"All I am trying to say, Mr Ludlow, is that returning your men could render every ship on the station useless."

"You cannot ask us to shoulder such concerns," said James. "And if I may be permitted an observation, sir, it is this: that you would not be short of men at all if their conditions of service were improved. Their treatment is an abomination to any civilized person. Why, their pay has not risen since King Charles's time. And that, sir, is a scandal."

The Irishman's lips, which were as pale as his face, moved very slightly, as he favoured James with a thin smile. And his hand moved to the folded document in front of him.

"I must riposte with the obvious point, sir, that these are matters outside my purview."

Harry cut in, to bluntly expose the truth of this conversation.

"It is interesting that the admiral does not see fit to make this request himself, Mr Dillon. I can only deduce from that one thing: that he feels such an overture too absurd to contemplate."

Dillon, having no other cards to play, threw up his hands. He could neither threaten nor cajole. He took them back to see Bessborough, who saw from his expression that his assistant had failed. The admiral had already acknowledged that he would have to concede, but he was intent on doing so with ill grace. He beckoned for the brothers to take a seat, playing the one weapon he still had in his armoury. Procrastination.

"I must tell you, Mr Ludlow, that the *Endymion* was well victualled. I gave Toner the liberty, since he's new to the station, of complete independence. He could well be at sea for months."

Harry knew that was humbug. Toner might have a degree of freedom. But he'd also have a fixed rendezvous should the admiral need to change his orders. Presumably Bessborough intended to do something about Monsieur d'Albret, either before he got to Guadeloupe or after. He gave the older man a wolfish smile.

"If you issue me with instructions for Captain Toner, plus his likely course, it will give me great pleasure to deliver them."

"No, no, Mr Ludlow. That I cannot do. No naval officer would relish such a thing delivered of a civilian hand."

The sound of angry, raised voices, outside the office door, made them all turn. The voice rose as the door opened and closed. "I demand an immediate interview!"

"Poynton!" said Bessborough. Dillon nodded as Cram entered and whispered in the admiral's ear. He looked at Harry and James with a mixture of resignation and regret. "I'm afraid, gentlemen, that I must request you avail yourself of my panorama again. I have an irate officer who, by the tone of his remarks, finds your presence in these waters somewhat uncongenial. Cram will get you anything you wish."

The view from the veranda, with goblets of a fruity rum punch to drink, was everything the admiral claimed it to be. James seemed content with that, remarking on the sheer depth of colours that surrounded them. But Harry, while keeping his back to the room, had wandered closer to the windows as soon as Cram disappeared.

Not that he needed to, since the naval captain who found their presence unwelcome made no attempt to lower his voice for the sake of their dignity.

"Less than scavengers, sir. They are below dungmen, not fit to sweep a street full of open sewers."

"Nevertheless, Captain Poynton," replied Dillon smoothly, "quite apart from the fact that they engaged the enemy in the most handsome manner—"

"You have only their testimony for that."

Dillon carried on as though he hadn't spoken. "They carry letters of marque. The admiral does not have the authority to limit their activities."

"Quite so!" added Bessborough.

"I said we wouldn't be popular," said Harry. James cocked an ear to listen to the torrent of loud abuse aimed at "those damned privateers," this intermingled with complaints about the way Toner had been favoured.

"Then if they are to be allowed to proceed with their depredations, sir, I repeat my demand that something be done about the flow of information we receive, or that positive steps be taken to curtail the activities of this fellow Hugues."

"Everything that can be done, is being done." said Dillon.

"It is not," snapped Poynton.

Dillon looked at Bessborough, expecting him to interrupt, but he was looking at the ceiling. Poynton, aware of this, was encouraged to continue.

"Surely now that English ships have become a target we can no longer pretend that all is well. Your treatment at the governor's dinner must reinforce that."

That brought Bessborough's attention back to the matter. He glared at both men. Dillon responded with a confused look. Poynton had the good grace to blush. "What of the governor's dinner?"

"You, sir, were harangued by the mercantile interests."

"Was I, indeed!"

"So I was informed."

"By whom, sir?"

Poynton shrugged, clearly unwilling to say. But he kept talking, that being the best way to avoid revealing the source of his gossip.

"I would also add our failures are bad for morale, as well as discipline. The hands are as sick of this as their officers. The most useless waister has gleaned the simple truth, one alluded to by Captain Effingham at our previous meeting; which is, that this Frenchman has either suborned or compromised your sources. Matters can only take a turn for the worse if that Jacobin on Guadeloupe has two frigates at hand. I suggest we send someone to the nearest island to investigate."

"Captain Poynton, such an act would compromise my people. Then there will be no intelligence coming in at all. The presence of those two frigates makes it even more desirable that we keep those channels untainted."

"It is rude to eavesdrop, Harry," said James softly.

His brother merely smiled at him and cocked his head a touch closer to the open door. Poynton, it seemed, had been fired even more by the implied rebuke the Irishman had delivered, causing him to heap as much abuse on Dillon and his "supposed" intelligence as he'd heaped on them. The officer catalogued each failure in detail, listing the captains who'd returned empty-handed, plus the way such events had reduced everyone on the station to penury, something which was to be exacerbated by the arrival of these "damned Ludlows." But the flow came to an abrupt end when Dillon, exposed to a piece of personal abuse, rather than that related to his responsibilities, cut across Poynton's ravings in an icy tone.

"You will withdraw that remark, Captain, or send me your second."

"Enough of this," said Bessborough, petulantly. "Things are at a sorry enough pass without my subordinates duelling. Poynton, you have gone too far and you will withdraw. That is a direct order."

A low mumbling followed, which Harry couldn't hear.

"And you, Dillon, must allow the truth of Captain Poynton's words. We are simply not carrying out our allotted task. It now seems to be common knowledge that I was subjected to the most intolerable abuse at the governor's dinner the other afternoon by a bunch of low-life factors and merchant captains. You would wonder at some of them in the servants' hall, never mind the dining-room. It's not something I want to suffer a second time. I was minded to let matters rest, since Hugues avoided attacking our own shipping. That is no longer the case. If the intelligence does not answer, and Toner returns empty-handed, then I will order someone to go to St Eustatius or St Thomas myself. I leave up to you what method you choose to avoid that eventuality."

"And Ludlow?" asked Poynton.

Bessborough dropped his voice then. Harry had to strain to hear him. "He wants his men back. He cannot operate effectively as a privateer with half a crew. So, we must accede to his request with seeming good grace, write out the orders and keep Toner and *Endymion* away from English Harbour so that they cannot be delivered."

"I cannot say which is worse, Admiral Bessborough. You give us the choice between lining the pockets of a newly arrived upstart, or a newly arrived thief."

"You're a reckless man, Captain," said Dillon, his voice still carrying the cold tone of his earlier challenge. "I don't know this Ludlow well. But I don't think he'd take to the insulting tone of your remarks. And he's been known to call people out before."

"He can damn well take them or leave them, sir. I stand by what I say."

"Enough!" snapped Bessborough. The scraping of chairs had Harry tiptoeing away from the French windows, to stand beside his brother by the wrought-iron fence.

"Eavesdropping may be bad manners, James. But I recommend it to you when dealing with such devious people. And I might add, there are none more devious than the admirals of the king's navy."

"Gentlemen," boomed Bessborough, exiting into the sunlight, a huge smile on his face. "I hope Cram has taken good care
of you."

"He has, sir," answered James, holding up his goblet.

The admiral spread his arms. "Then you must allow me to
introduce you to my wife and daughters. Apart from a love of
society, they will welcome any news you have from England."

"Toner's orders?" asked Harry coldly.

"Are being drawn up at this very moment, Captain Ludlow,"
he replied, turning away to lead them back into the building. "And
rest assured I will make haste to append my signature to them.
Why, one wonders what Toner was thinking about, pressing your
men in the first place."

Harry glared at Bessborough's back.

Yet for all his opinion of admirals, Harry was apparently happy
to accept an invitation to dine the following evening in the
company of Bessborough, his wife, and some newly arrived ar
my officers on condition that their young French prisoner would
come along as well. Lady Bessborough, a woman who clearly dominated her husband, was present when this request was made, and
asked if he was the right sort, alluding to the number of Jacobins
who'd achieved rank in the French service. James, adopting a
knowing air, stretched the truth by a mile as he mentioned the
boy's name.

"He's a St Pol, Lady Bessborough, from the Artois. The house
is exceedingly ancient. Why, one of his ancestors fought King Hal
at Agincourt."

The brothers had a laugh about that as they left. Brissot was
indeed from a northern French town called St-Pol-en-Ternoise, but
that was his sole connection with the aristocratic title. But the
smile disappeared from James's face when Harry insisted he come
to Bessborough's dinner.

"Whatever for, Harry?" asked James, aware that it would
very likely be an affair dominated by serving officers. He was not

overfond of such gatherings, being disinclined to share the high opinion that naval types had of themselves. Nor did he readily take to the way that the conversation invariably turned to sea battles, or to tales of heroic deeds, much embellished.

"He cannot be said to be your sort. And you've heard the pretensions of his wife. I have come across the name, mentioned by my friends. She's apparently a distant cousin to the Sackvilles of Knole, and has, even on such a short acquaintance, all the hallmarks of a tremendous bore."

"Why do you think we've been invited, brother? It's not out of love or respect. While we are at Bessborough's table we pose no threat to Toner. He knows where *Endymion* is, James. Perhaps, in his cups, he will let something drop. Then there's that Dillon fellow, though he looks tight-lipped. But there will be other officers who might know Toner's orders. I need you there as an extra pair of ears."

They were walking down the hill towards the harbour and the Duke of Clarence, where they'd taken rooms. Harry pointed towards a frigate entering the outer roads under topsails. Set against the deep blue water trapped by the rim of the extinct volcano, with her sails bleached snow white by the tropical sun, it was an imposing sight. Harry stopped a passing midshipman.

"*Diomede,* sir, sixth-rate." The boy's red face, which had carried a cheerful look, clouded over. "She's come in empty-handed, like all the others."

"She was out here in '82. Who has her now?"

"Captain Sandford, sir."

"Marcus Sandford?"

The sails on the *Diomede* disappeared in a flash as she dropped her anchor, which brought back an earnest look to the boy's face. "That's him, sir. A crack frigate, sir, and no error. Best on the station by a mile. Captain Sandford is a fine commander by all accounts."

"Aren't they all?" added James sourly, still angry at the prospect of the admiral's dinner. He turned to look at a poster on the wall of a house, behind the boy. It offered a reward for the apprehension of one Nathan Caufield, of Sag Harbour, Long Island, for robbery and the murder of a Mr Stephen Norrington.

"It's true this time, James," said Harry, after he'd thanked the midshipman. "I served with him as a youngster and he was on the *Barfleur* with me. Even then he had the gift. He's bound to be on the invitation list for tomorrow. I must send him a message before Bessborough's feast."

That startled James. Normally Harry avoided those who'd known him as a serving naval officer. Their presence tended to remind him of what he was missing. Harry picked up the look and grinned.

"I have no secrets from Marcus Sandford, James. He was my second when I fought my duel. And as for seeing him beforehand, I doubt he'd discuss matters relating to me without my express permission. But it would be as well to make sure."

As they entered the Duke of Clarence, they observed a young man in deep conversation with the proprietor, Mr Gracewell. Noting their arrival, he raised his hand and pointed. The young man shook his head hurriedly and without another word made his way past them and out into the street. James favoured the owner of the inn with a quizzical look.

"He was enquiring about the death of Mr Norrington, sir."

"Who?" asked Harry.

"Is that the fellow on the poster?" asked James.

"That be the one, your honour," Gracewell replied, emerging from behind his hatch. "He had your rooms, gentlemen. And the man who did him in came in here that night."

"Did this Norrington expire on the premises, then?" James enquired.

"Never in life, sir, if'n you'll forgive the expression. He was done in outside the admiral's garden wall, the night that Mr Dillon was robbed."

The brothers made to move on towards the tap-room, since

the subject was of limited interest to them. But Gracewell was a garrulous soul, who clearly had a deep fascination with the darker side of human behaviour. The sheer enthusiasm of his account kept the brothers pinned in the hallway. "Nathan Caufield his name was. He was a black-hearted scully an' no mistake, brought in by one of the naval captains after his ship was taken by that other villain, Victor Hugues."

"That's all very interesting, Mr Gracewell—" James didn't get as far as the "but" that would release them, since Gracewell continued as though he hadn't spoken.

"Imagine the gall, gentlemen, breaking into Admiralty House in the middle of the night, and that after he'd had high words with Mr Norrington, right above our heads, about the insurance on his ship. I watched him follow the poor man out of the door, though that was much earlier. He sandbagged Mr Dillon and ransacked his strongbox, then took a crowbar to Mr Norrington's head. I had it all from the marine sentry."

"I require pen and paper," said Harry, swiftly, lest Gracewell be tempted to continue. "And a messenger standing by to take a note." He turned to James. "Sandford will have instructions to report to Bessborough."

The inference was plain enough. Harry would want him to know of his presence beforehand.

"If you'll step this way, your honour." Gracewell indicated his private quarters.

James wandered into the tap-room and was surprised to see Dreaver there, tankard in hand, in the act of swigging rum. Harry had issued strict instructions for his men to stay aboard ship till he'd found out how the land lay. The last thing he wanted was more impressment. Their temporary servant put his tankard down hastily, using his sleeve to rub the residue of drink off his lips, and headed across the room to accost him, speaking hurriedly.

"I came ashore sharp, your honour, 'cause there's a fact that you ought to know. A cove in one o' them traders' bumboats said that *Endymion* is a hell ship, an' tipped us the wink that we should have a word with some others in the harbour. So I took the jolly-boat across to the *Redoubtable* an' sought out the lower-deck gunners. Seems that bastard Toner has flogged every man aboard during the crossing, some more'n once, paying particular attention to those he pressed. There's floggin' an' floggin', your honour. By all accounts Toner is a right sod and over-free. Word has it that one man's already died at the grating, though they thinks that happened afore they cleared the Needles."

James wanted to ask about Pender. But he couldn't do so without giving the impression of an apparent indifference to the others in the crew.

"How reliable is this?" he asked.

"Horse's mouth, your honour. They used the men from *Bucephalas* to crew the bastard's barge and they shaded themselves by the gunports. They reckon, with all that punishment, *Endymion* is ripe for mutiny. An' you've got to recall most of these men have seen the lash afore. They'd not go moaning if'n it weren't serious."

James glanced round, happy to see that Harry was still engaged in penning his message. "Any idea where Toner has gone?"

"Not a clue, your honour," said Dreaver. "Seems that any ship gone a-cruising ups anchor with its course a dark secret, only gettin' its orders when they're set to weigh."

"Back aboard ship, Dreaver."

"But Captain Ludlow?"

"I will tell my brother." He patted the man on the shoulder. His desire to inform Harry stemmed from concern, not a wish to claim credit. "But I think I'll have to pour him a stiff drink before I do so."

"One more thing, your honour. Seems that there was a petition written to the admiral, as well as a letter to the captain. Hands that bespoke the Redoubtables didn't know if it was delivered."

"Go by *Redoubtable*," said James, slipping Dreaver a few gold coins. "Use these to check if they're telling the truth about Toner's whereabouts."

"Aye, aye, your honour."

James watched Dreaver leave, unobserved by his brother. He sat down heavily and ordered two rum punches, wondering if he should tell Harry or not. He had seen his temper and he knew how much he cared for the welfare of his crew. Given this information he'd likely explode. He was glad Toner wasn't here. Given news like this, Harry might kill him.

CHAPTER TWENTY-THREE

JAMES WAS right about Harry's initial reaction to Dreaver's information, though it didn't take the form of an explosion. But the grip he had on his tankard threatened to crush it, for all that it was made of stout pewter.

"A petition, you say?"

"That's what Dreaver said. But we have no way of knowing if it's true, and if it is, if it was delivered."

"He also mentioned a letter," said Harry. "Which surely would not yet be aboard a mail packet?"

James leant forward and tapped the table. "If that letter is with the man who owns the postal service . . ."

"Then Bessborough must have the petition. Which means he knew all about our crew before we ever arrived."

"The address is in Kent, sir," said the shopkeeper, giving Harry a sly look. He was a small man, bent with servitude, and the possessor of a slippery demeanour. He held the postal sinecure on Antigua, plus several others judging by the myriad signs outside his door.

"The superscription states quite clearly that it is for me, Mr Bridge. And I am not in Kent, sir. I am, as you can very well see, here in the West Indies!"

"That's as maybe, Mr Ludlow. An' I don't doubt you's who you says you are. But the man who will take this from Deal to your house has bought his office, just as I have. Good money paid out to a government that knows nothing about the difficulties of handling the mails. Nor do they know how hard it is for a decent man to turn an honest penny. Now it stands to reason that if I pass this to you, then him who has the Kent office will not receive payment for delivery. Having invested his coin, how would he feel to know that his colleague, which is me, sir, your humble servant, had dunned him out of his shillings?"

"Are you saying that my brother has to pay for this letter, even though it has not been sent?"

The shopkeeper looked at James and beamed, his head tilted sideways, before turning back to address Harry. "Now there's a gent that sees things plain an' no mistake. An' has a sense of justice t'go with it, too."

"Who gave you this letter?" asked Harry.

He was quick, this slimy shopkeeper, to see an advantage. Bridge didn't even pause for breath before upping his price. "Now that's what we, in the postal trade, calls confidential. An' where would folks be if we didn't know when to speak and when to keep mum?"

Harry reached for his purse as he spoke to James. "How often do they hang postmasters?"

James fixed the shopkeeper with his coldest stare. "Not often enough, brother."

If they'd hoped to dent the man's assurance, they failed. He just gave them a toothy grin and held out his stained, long-fingered hands. "Gents are pleased to jest, which is all right as long as they're prepared to pay. The person who brought this was a midshipman, who by his voice I would take to be a Scottish man."

"Did he have a name?" asked Harry.

The shopkeeper shook his head. "No. But he was a tall lad, fair haired, and given to the blush."

Harry read the letter in the street, his own face becoming redder by the minute. His lips moved as he worked his way through Pender's stilted prose, then he handed the letter to James and set off down the street, his heels kicking up the dust from the roadway. James merely looked at Pender's signature and, folding the letter, followed his brother.

"That smug overblown sack of gold-braided shit," said Harry, in an uncharacteristic burst of foul language. "He knew this. As he sat there and talked to us he knew what our men have gone through. And then he had the gall to get that streak of piss Dillon to ask us to leave them be."

"Well at least we shan't have to suffer their company at dinner."

Harry stopped dead, but didn't reply. Instead he spun on his heel and dashed back into the shop. He was gone but a few seconds, then he came out and rejoined James.

"A couple of guineas will ensure Mr Bridge's continued silence."

"I don't follow, Harry?"

The icy look in his eye testified to the depth of his feeling. Even James was shocked by the intensity. "I don't want Bessborough to know that we have any knowledge of that petition. So the fellow back there knows nothing at all about any letter delivered by a fair-haired blushing midshipman. The only way we can help our men is to get them off that ship. We can't find Toner without information and we can't wait here, unless, in his blood lust, he kills someone. It will be hard, James. But we will attend their dinner and smile. We must find out where Toner has gone."

James put his hand on Harry's arm, for in his passion his voice had risen till, loud and harsh, it alarmed those people passing by. "We will, Harry. We will."

"It was as well you sent me that note, Harry. I have little time ashore. I must say the sight of your ship anchored out in the bay set a few tongues wagging. None of them had much to say in the way of compliments."

"You saw the admiral, I take it, Marcus?"

"I certainly did. Bessborough asked me about you before he even enquired about the results of my cruise."

"Did he tell you about Toner?"

"He did."

"Do you know where he's gone?"

"I do not!" replied Sandford, in a tone that almost said that even if he knew, he wouldn't say.

"Then let us put that out of our minds," said Harry, smiling at his old friend.

Marcus Sandford sat in one of the tap-room booths, his hat and coat off, clutching a large tankard of rum punch. He was a huge man, with a pink, open countenance, scarred here and there with the results of numerous bloody encounters. He wore his fair hair loose and long, and spoke with the deep voice of a natural baritone. Lacking the accoutrements of his rank, gold thread and broadcloth, sat against the high back of the bench seat, he looked less like a naval captain than anyone could imagine.

"What did you tell him about me?"

"I couldn't deny that we were acquainted, Harry. He knows I was out here in '82, as well as which ship I served on. So I acknowledged that I knew you well, and that I esteemed you highly. Bessborough replied with a string of questions which can only be termed personal. I informed him that I had no wish to hold a conversation that might require me to break a confidence, and that he showed a want of manners in interrogating me on the subject."

Harry grinned, wondering if he too had shown a want of manners in asking about Toner. "I'm obliged, Marcus."

He could imagine that his old friend had said just that to the admiral. From being a shy, easily put upon youth, slight of build, Marcus Sandford had grown to his present imposing stature. In the process he'd lost his reserve and acquired the habit of speaking his mind. He was known throughout the service as a famously forthright personality, which probably accounted for his continued presence in a frigate, when he certainly had the seniority to command a ship of the line.

"That's no way to talk to an admiral, even if you are the captain of a crack frigate."

Sandford took an elaborate swig of his rum punch, the tankard covering half of his face. He was proud of his ship and the way he ran it, but modest enough to blush when someone alluded to the subject.

"Almost word for word what Bessborough said. He was exceedingly put out. He then tried to cover his prying by alluding to his desire to engage you in a special service."

"Service?" said James, his voice rising in disbelief.

"His very expression," replied Sandford, sharply.

Apart from the initial greeting, these were the first words he'd exchanged with James since they'd sat down. He looked from one to the other, noticing the likeness between the two brothers, as well as the differences. This James, slim and handsome, was a much more urbane creature than Harry. His attention, while they'd talked, had seemed to reside elsewhere, as though he found the company uncongenial and the talk dull, and this patent lack of regard had riled him. Much as he liked Harry Ludlow, Marcus Sandford had mentally prepared himself to bridle at James if he was exposed to the slightest degree of condescension.

"Forgive me if I sounded surprised, Captain," said James, picking up the change in the man's voice. "It is not that I doubt your word in any way. But for Bessborough to seek to engage Harry in a service is somewhat singular."

"You would not call it singular, sir, if you knew the man or his problems. These, I must represent to you, are manifold. A prime example is the loss of Guadeloupe, which weighs heavily on his office."

Much to Sandford's annoyance, James had glanced away again, as if unwilling to meet the officer's eye. His deep voice dropped an angry octave. "But I see none of this holds any interest for you."

"It interests me, Marcus," said Harry, unwittingly cutting off the apology James was about to pronounce. "Tell me about Guadeloupe. I hear it was a disaster of the first magnitude."

Sandford's huge leonine head swung back to Harry, the glare he'd reserved for James disappearing as quickly as it had come. He then recounted the tale of the arrival of Victor Hugues and the trouble it had caused Bessborough.

"We managed to save no more than fifty of the Royalists, and only because they were mariners, not soldiers. Trethgowan was all for sending them back, till the Jacobin started with his guillotine."

"So they watched too?"

Sandford nodded. "It was hard for them, Harry. Much more so than it was for us. They were a low crew in the main, bondsmen who'd yet to finish their time. Their officer was a gentleman, though. A most engaging fellow who had only one fault in my eyes: he kept a pet mongoose, which as you know is very close to being a rat."

Harry jerked forward slightly as the high back of his seat moved. It was as if someone very bulky, in the act of sitting down, had thrown themselves against the other side.

"Do they make pets?" he asked, with a backwards glance that revealed nothing.

"I never thought of them as such. But Monsieur de la Mery had tamed it enough to provide the creature with a home in his pocket. Not that it stayed there. Damned thing turned up in all sorts of places, like my cot. Forever rushing around the place like a demon. Apparently the fellow amuses himself by handling snakes. He has some novel ideas regarding antidotes. Claims that the venom of a snake contains the very seeds of its own cure. Same for spiders and the like. Can't say I agree with him and I have no desire to put his theories to the test." He took another swig of rum punch, his fair hair tumbling halfway down his back as he tilted his head.

"What a singular fellow."

"Lord, Harry, singular or not I was glad he was aboard. I had Trethgowan and his entire staff to accommodate. Soldiers, to my way of thinking, are poor company at the best of times. But they're even worse when they've just had a thorough drubbing. My Frenchman, at the dinner table, precluded too much discussion of anything military, especially recent events. And his hands proved very able as supernumerary crewmen. I fetched them back to Antigua and, being forever short-handed, offered a place in our ships to any Frenchman who wished to serve. Naturally, they declined. Quite apart from a desire to avoid killing their own countrymen, I think after what they saw on that beach they'd had enough of the British and their unfulfilled promises. I went off to sea again and when I returned they'd decamped."

"How very wise," said James.

Observing, out of the corner of one eye, that James Ludlow's attention, for all his languid interjection, was still adrift, Sandford assumed it to be a character trait. But he noticed that Harry had picked it up too, and was now showing some annoyance at the cavalier way his brother was behaving to one of his oldest friends.

"Bessborough took a heavy portion of the blame, of course, though it was hardly his fault. Trethgowan went home and bleated that the navy had let him down by letting the Jacobin ashore in the first place, a tale the Horse Guards is only too ready to endorse. The admiral didn't even know Hugues was on the way. And matters are not entirely resolved as far as I know."

"It was Howe that missed him, Marcus."

Sandford nodded. "Sitting in Torbay, most like."

"He missed the French grain fleet as well," said James with some relish, his attention returning to their table. "For all the ballyhoo about the Glorious First, in going after Villaret-Joyeuse, Howe ignored his orders. They'd be right, in France, to count that date as a victory. The French lured Howe away deliberately so that the American grain shipment could get through. If he'd done what he was employed to do, France would have suffered a devastating famine and the war would be over. The bells should have rung in Paris, not London."

"He still thumped them," said Harry, sharply. He was aware that James was merely repeating words he'd heard from his own lips, and having no desire that such open criticism of the service should be attributed to him by his old friend, he abruptly changed the subject. "But Guadeloupe was nine months ago. Surely the dust must have settled by now?"

"Never in life. Hugues has not been content to just sit on one island. He set in train a rebellion in Dominica and is busy trying to take back Grenada. One more reverse and Bessborough will be on the way home. Can you imagine the number of people queuing up to hound him out of his command? And to cap it all, it seems there's a degree of trouble with the illegals."

"What trouble?" asked Harry, his eyes bland and his face and voice the very epitome of innocent enquiry.

James jerked his head round and looked at his brother hard. He'd heard a very full discussion of that very problem when he'd eavesdropped, that morning, outside the admiral's windows. For all his deep friendship with Sandford, Harry still maintained that reserve, in possession of information, which sometimes made him manipulative. Nor had he mentioned anything about Pender's letter, or the petition that they suspected had been delivered to Bessborough. Still, it was not his place to interfere. If Harry wished to reserve his hand, that was his own affair.

He went back to the subject that occupied his main attention: the young American who'd been speaking to Gracewell when they'd arrived at the inn after seeing the admiral. If the youth was hoping to disguise his blatant eavesdropping it was a singular failure, since his body was half in, half out of the next booth. Harry, with his back to him, couldn't see. Neither could Sandford because of the angle of the high-backed seating. James, perched on the very end of the table, had a clear view of the American's back. Such behaviour was bad manners and he was sorely tempted to say something to the youngster. And what was it, pray, about a pet mongoose, that could produce such an overtly physical reaction?

Only half his mind was on what Sandford was saying as he continued his litany of the admiral's problems. He heard much about Bessborough's manifold tasks, work that had to be accomplished with too few vessels. Victor Hugues was mentioned several times, as well as ships, captains, and various islands, including Dominica. Then Sandford gave a description of his own recent adventures. This part of the naval captain's conversation obviously had great interest to the American. He hardly kept contact with the seat of his bench as he strained to catch every word Sandford said.

"My cruise was a waste of time. I was given rendezvous, names, and dates, with a brief to sweep wide in the hope of catching the fellow."

"Is that normal?" asked Harry.

"The orders are," he replied.

"And you obeyed them?"

Sandford avoided Harry's eye, unwilling to meet a look which would imply that his friend knew just how many of his fellow officers would interpret such orders differently.

"I think I caught sight of his topsails, but the wind favoured him. Worse than that, I missed the illegals. So much so that I half feared to enter such a miserable report, in case I risked some form of official censure. Yet now I find that I'm not alone. Poynton was in the harbour preparing for a refit but he's been ordered back to sea. He rowed across to *Diomede* as soon as I anchored. He informs me that he suffered likewise, and that Effingham, who put back to sea yesterday, came in with a similar result."

"Don't you spend any time in port?" said Harry, with an angry scowl. "Toner barely touched before the admiral sent him to sea again."

"There's nothing unusual in that. We all have the same orders. We anchor, revictual, receive outline instructions, and if all proceeds according to plan, weigh within 24 hours. Our final orders, with the exact location of our targets, are often given to us when we're at single anchor. I almost feel sorry for Bessborough, especially with Vandegut writing to everyone he knows complaining loudly of the admiral's abilities. The quick turnarounds are Captain Vandegut's idea. He maintains we lose fewer men at sea than we do when they come ashore. And it also helps cover what is too large a canvas. If we doubled the ships we have we'd still be short.

"So, goaded by Vandegut and prompted by necessity, Bessborough's harried every captain on the station since Guadeloupe.

Not that such a procedure does not suit him. It makes him look exceedingly zealous. I presume he wishes to ensure his reputation has a decent bulwark, should the business of Hugues continue to plague him. And there's no doubt, Harry, that he's right. Who knows what mischief the French would get up to without his vigilance? Trouble is, the enemy has shifted his ground. He finds that while he's sought to contain them territorially, Hugues has turned his attention to playing the corsair. Now he's got your two French frigates to contend with and given all the other things he must guard against, the poor man is at his wits' end to know what to do about it."

"So this is not a new phenomenon?"

"No. It's been going on for months, I'm told. And if he hadn't started taking our own shipping we might have never known. Poynton picked up the crews from the illegals he was set to intercept, so we know for sure about them. But reports are coming in from the other islands now listing just how many ships Hugues is taking, including those that we are set to intercept. He must have his own spies in the islands. Rumour has it that he's taken near a quarter of a million in three months."

Harry was surprised. But there was an element of admiration in his voice as well. "That's quite staggering."

Marcus Standford snorted angrily as he pulled out his watch and looked at it. "The staggering thing is the bloodless way he does it. I had words with Poynton, who informs me that not only did the man release the crews of his captures, he apologized for his behaviour, shared a glass of wine, then directed them to a point where Poynton would pick them up. I cannot find it in my heart to believe that the ogre I saw on the beach at Guadeloupe is the very same person who takes these ships without harming a soul. The Victor Hugues I saw wasn't like that at all. He was just the type to string them all up from the yards, cut out their vitals, then toss them to the sharks."

"Perhaps he fears a hue and cry," said Harry. "Too many bodies spells a different kind of trouble."

"Perhaps you're right, Harry. Anyway, I have my orders. I am, unusually, allowed a little time ashore to attend this dinner the admiral is giving for some general. But I dare say once the port has been passed I'll be told to revictual and put to sea immediately. So, much as I am happy to see you again, I must return aboard."

Sandford stood up, towering over the two seated brothers. "Bessborough told me about your run-in with those frigates. He doubts they'll do more than touch at Guadeloupe, since Hugues is secure there. We have a lookout on Pigeon Island just in case. Bessborough's considering sending his nephew to join Effingham with orders to take station off Grenada and Poynton's refit has been postponed so that he can join him. I've to cruise to the south of Dominica, intercept them if they appear, and bottle them up in Roseau harbour if I can't."

Harry's voice had a sad note as he replied. "Then I wish you joy, Marcus."

Sandford picked it up, knowing it was the voice of a man who'd like nothing more than an equal contest with such a foe. "Come out to *Diomede* tomorrow, Harry. We shan't weigh till late in the day. I would be mighty pleased to have you look her over. Then you can tell me all about those frigates. How they sail, their officers, and their gunnery."

"This service you alluded to, sir," said James, turning back to face the pair. "Do you have any notion of what Admiral Bessborough meant?"

"None at all. Yet you have a fast, well-armed ship and no responsibilities. It takes no great leap of the imagination to see the way his mind may be working."

There was a long silence which brought James's mind back to what had been said earlier. He realized immediately that something was amiss. He felt his original supposition, the absurdity of Bessborough asking Harry for a service, to be correct. If anything the admiral owed a great deal more than he was entitled to ask for. He looked at Harry to see if he'd spotted the anomaly, only to observe that Marcus Sandford was the object of a very enquiring stare. Then he made the connection. Judging by the look in his brother's eye, he'd clearly made it already. That it was Sandford who'd put his name forward, not Bessborough.

"Was that Irishman Dillon consulted about this proposed service?" asked James.

Sandford looked relieved to be able to turn away from Harry's look. "He was. Bessborough makes few moves these days without asking someone's opinion. Vandegut was involved, though I wouldn't trust that his advice is above board. Damn me, the admiral even asked his nephew, who's barely breached, which is damned insultin'."

"And?"

"None really offered an opinion, either for the idea or against."

"Were they there when the idea was originally proposed?" asked James.

Sandford blushed as he shook his head.

"You are aware, Marcus, that Toner has illegally impressed half my crew?"

"Indeed I am, Harry. And I said, despite his arguments to the contrary, that the good of the service demanded that they be released."

"Yet you also proposed, did you not, that I undertake a task which should fall to the navy, a task that will bring me no discernible gain?"

Sandford grinned as he picked up his hat and coat. "I don't know about that, Harry. If you nobble a cove like Hugues you'll be the toast of the nation. You might even get a call to tell your story to the king. Charm him enough and he might just give you a post captain's commission."

Harry's face closed up. "Right now, Marcus, I'd settle for my crew."

CHAPTER TWENTY-FOUR

THE MESSAGE caught Antoine de la Mery just as he was about to weigh anchor. The sight of the aviso heading flat out into the bay turned his stomach for a moment, since it smacked of impending danger. *Diomede,* even if she hadn't come close, had definitely been looking for him, since he knew the ship was well off the station necessary to intercept illegals. The mongoose was in the shrouds, playing with a loose piece of hemp. He barely had time to pluck if off and hide it in the coach. As the two mulattos came alongside he could see no hint of panic in their dark-skinned faces. The one who climbed aboard had another oilskin pouch in his hand, which he handed to the Frenchman. Given a peremptory signal, his mate in the boat pushed off to a point where conversation with the *Ariadne*'s crew was impossible. Both men headed into his cabin, staying on deck would only expose them to curiosity. The pet, not being caged, was sniffing along the slight gap at the bottom the door, and scratching at it as if trying to gain access to the main cabin. De la Mery ignored it, which forced his visitor to do likewise. On the other side of the cabin the door to his sleeping cabin was open, exposing a cot swinging on the gentle swell, a cot which seemed to be occupied, judging by the naked foot hanging out at the bottom.

The Frenchman ripped the seals on the letter and began to read the coded Latin. His correspondent explained that given the burden of their work he was under great strain. A new arrival merely added to this, but that they could deflect the growing criticism if he was allowed a measure of freedom. Therefore, as far as he was concerned, the following masses were cancelled. But it was

vital that he carry out the other masses listed at the second destination. The final passage went on to say that their success in
converting the English heathens had incurred the wrath of the local
bishops, an anger so great that they might be forced to desist completely. So, after this temporary alteration, one last effort should
be made to rescue as many indigenous souls as possible. Then,
if his fears proved correct, they could retire knowing that they
had, to the best of their ability, carried out God's holy work. As
to the relics in his possession, they would be better returned to
Europe than left to rot in the tropics; and he should propose a
rendezvous where the responsibility for their passage home could
be shared out.

His eyes stayed with the words *passage home*. Here was the
moment of truth. The message might hint at doubt and be short
on any details of how much of a threat existed. But, reading
between the lines, he had none. Attacking those British merchantmen had been a mistake. The pieces of a puzzle that had
been sustained by time, distance, and antipathy were combining
to create a dangerous situation, one that should end quickly. His
men would make up their own minds, but his opinion was clear.
They should repair the ship and sail as a body to some convenient
European destination, then, having secured a safe place for their
funds, head home to France. But putting that to them would have
to wait. First there were the ships listed at the bottom of the page,
with dates a week hence. They were easily deciphered, and de la
Mery was heartened to see that they were all neutrals. More telling
still was the fact that his final act of piracy would take place off
Guadeloupe, taking ships destined for Pointe-à-Pitre. He had a
fleeting vision of his going ashore and taking vengeance on Victor Hugues, but he put it aside as a fantasy. Perhaps, when he
took these ships, Hugues would be watching from the shore. That
would go some way to providing a feeling of revenge, an emotion
that Antoine de la Mery conjured up every time he thought of the
Jacobin murderer.

Forcing his thoughts back to the present, he realized that his rendezvous at Martinique had been cancelled. He penned a swift acknowledgement, sealed it, then led the mulatto back on to the deck. As soon as he appeared his companion hauled his sail round to bring the aviso alongside the *Ariadne*. As soon as they were out of earshot he ordered his men to warp the ship into the jetty again. Once they'd taken to the boats, and had started to haul the ship's head round towards the shore, he went back into his cabin. He had several days to kill, which would give him time to continue his experiments, as well as make arrangement for his final departure.

The *Endymion*'s marine drummer beat to quarters before first light, rousing out the watch below. The hands tumbled from their hammocks, then, harried by the curses and ropes' ends of their warrant officers, they rolled them round their few personal possessions. Hustled up the companion-ways on to the deck, they proceeded to place them in the nettings that lined the side of the frigate, before rushing to take up their allotted stations. Some made for the shrouds, ready to go aloft and shorten sail, while others cast off the guns. Bulkheads disappeared as the carpenters' mates struck them into the hold. The boats were being hauled over the side by the watch on deck, to be towed behind *Endymion* as she went into action. The master-at-arms unlocked the chains that secured the cutlasses and pikes, arranged in racks under the taffrail. Dunlop handed out pistols and shot to the officers, but kept secure the muskets that stood like sentinels outside Toner's cabin. They would only be issued, if at all, to members of the lower deck at the last moment. The carpenter sorted out tools and plugs, and heated tar, all to fill leaks in the planking should the ship be holed; the surgeon arranged his instruments to deal with human wounds while his loblolly boy pushed the chests together in the cockpit to form a makeshift operating table. Meanwhile the gunner, surrounded by dampened screens, lit the lengths of slowmatch and filled bags of powder, handing them to the ship's boys, who scurried about, delivering them to the guns. Down in the hold the servants packed away every stick of cabin furniture, and moved the animals from the manger. With the bulkheads down, and every-thing that wasn't needed removed, *Endymion* had a clean sweep fore and aft.

The stars still shone overhead, but they were fading rapidly as the sun tinged the eastern horizon, throwing the black bulk of the island of Martinique into silhouette. The winds were light and the *Endymion* slid along, steering due south under reefed topsails towards the first of the places where Toner had been advised he could intercept some illegal shipping. Pender knew they must be close inshore, for Toner had a leadsman in the chains, calling off the depth of water below the ship's keel. The top of the island began to turn bright green as the tropical forest was illuminated by the rapidly rising sun. There was a palpable air of excitement along the whole deck. After such a voyage, the prospect of some action played on the crew's imagination. Garmond would have found few listeners for his seditious ideas at a moment like this. All the talk aboard was of booty and a run ashore with some money to spend. The voice from the masthead, with a better view than those on the deck, called out urgently.

"Three o' sail in the bay, Captain, with boats plying to and fro. Shifting cargo by the look of it."

"Mr Dunlop! It's time tae man our boats. Issue cutlasses and boarding pikes. Take Mr Callander and his division. If those ille-gals have landed any cargo, I want it found and impounded. That is your paramount concern, sir. Prisoners are of secondary con-cern. I want a file of marines ashore an' aw, to play on those ships, with musket fire from the shore."

"Aye, aye, sir," cried Dunlop, rushing towards the waist and shouting to his party to gather by the gangway.

Mr Midshipman Callander was already issuing his commands before the premier arrived. Half the men were busy hauling the hemp lines that would bring the boats alongside, while the oth-ers, under Pender's direction, sorted out their armoury. The clink of metal was loud in the clear morning air as the swords, axes,

and pikes were pulled from their racks. The light increased sufficiently for the crew to see the tops of three masts, the first sight
of their quarry. Eager glances, and pointing fingers, were aimed
towards the shore. Callander ordered ropes to be cast over the
side and the men scrambled down. Being topmen, and therefore
nimble, the seamen filled the boats in seconds. Without a word of
command, Pender had taken to the barge, followed by the same
group of men who'd rowed ashore with him at English Harbour.
The air of quiet efficiency brought forth a surge of pleasure. It
was the same in the other boats, with Harry Ludlow's contingent
needing no commands to sort out their respective stations. But
quick as they were, they had to sit idle, waiting for the marines.
With their muskets and rigid drill they were forced to come aboard
through the gangway, a tedious and time-consuming manoeuvre
accompanied by loud cursing from the impatient sailors. Finally
Dunlop, who was to command the boats, took up station in the
rear of the barge.

"Haul away, lads," cried Callander, as soon as the premier
nodded.

The oars bit into the water in unison, propelling the boat away
from the side of the ship. Here, to leeward of Martinique, the
swell was gentle, with no hint of that dangerous surf which came
roaring in on the windward side from the deep Atlantic, propelled
by the strength of the trade winds. Pender, acting as coxswain and
steering the barge, now had a good view of the illegals riding at
anchor with their sails furled. But the increasing light had alerted
them to danger. The sound of agitated voices floated over the dark
sea towards them. Boats were putting off from the shore in panic,
with men falling over each other to get aboard.

The rumble of gun carriages filled the air, as the ports swung
open and the *Endymion*'s cannon were run out. The row of black
guns, appearing suddenly, looked sinister in the morning light, having the appearance of deadly teeth on some fearsome monster.
Pender heard the shout of command just before the first gun fired,
sending a long red flash out of the muzzle. The ball flew over their

heads with a whoosh that made everyone crouch down. The passing ball was followed by a cloud of dense black smoke, which
filled the air with the acrid smell of burnt powder.

Another command followed and the whole side of the ship
erupted. The broadside, from men unused to aiming and firing
their guns, fell either well short of the target or carried on to land
soundlessly and uselessly on the soft white sand of the beach. Not
a single ball came close to touching those three ships. It was terrible gunnery, given that they were firing from a reasonably steady
platform. But that very inaccuracy worked in the barge crew's
favour. It convinced the men on the beach, who'd just pushed off
in their boats, and whose numbers nearly matched the Endymions,
that they were the prime target. The passing balls had made a loud
enough crack in their ears to terrify them, and make them think
twice about intercepting their assailants.

They hauled their bows round in panic and ran their boats
back in to the sand, jumping out in a confused mass, then rushing up the beach to disappear in the lush undergrowth that lined
the shore. The three small ships, trading ketches, were cutting their
cables. The rigging on each ship was full of sailors and scraps of
sail were now visible on their masts. Young Struan Callander, his
face alight with excitement, stood up and, waving his sword, called
to the premier.

"Those on the shore seem to have abandoned any idea of a
fight. Should we not steer for those vessels, sir? I'm sure we could
board them before they get under way."

"Did you not hear the captain's orders regarding the cargo,
Mr Callander? Steer for the shore as he instructed."

"Aye, aye, sir," said Callander, slightly crestfallen.

The first shot from the leading illegal, aimed at the youth standing upright, was an example to the men of the *Endymion*. It hit
the water some five feet from the bows of the barge, and only the
angle of fire prevented the ball from holing them below the waterline. As it was, the spray drenched everyone aboard, causing them
to bend their backs that much harder, long before Dunlop screamed

at them to do so. They were in shoal water now, with the waves breaking to their right and left. Pender called the orders that would keep them true, with their bows aimed straight for the shore. The surf wasn't huge, but to an inattentive crew it still represented a risk. Poorly handled, it would have them broaching to. Without consulting either of the officers, Pender called: "Boat your oars," and ordered the leading oarsmen to jump overboard, which earned him a glare from Dunlop. Formed up to await their officers, they chafed as the marines came ashore at the same unhurried pace. Pender cursed under his breath. He would have rushed straight up the beach as soon as they landed, using the element of fear to overcome their enemies. So far, the whole affair, the gunnery as much as the behaviour of the lobsters, highlighted the lack of training of everyone aboard. That is, everyone who'd not previously been under the command of a captain like Harry Ludlow.

Dunlop finally ordered Callander up the beach, taking command of the marines himself, who formed up to fire their muskets on the ships. To Pender's way of thinking, it was the exact opposite of what the premier should have done. The main threat to the shore party still lay with the men who'd been on the beach. As the senior and most experienced officer, Dunlop should have taken command of the pursuit. He obviously apprehended danger in that thick, tangled undergrowth, and wanted no part of it. He prized the greater safety on the open beach, surrounded by men armed with muskets. The sun was full up now, already hot, making the white sand gleam with a blinding light. The middle section of the beach was full of cargo, piled neatly awaiting further transport. Hoofprints led inland, testifying to the mode of transport that the locals had adopted to shift their goods.

"Mules, sir," said Pender. "Which means that there are wide trails we can probably follow."

Callander stopped by the cargo, the confusion plain on his face. The captain's orders, as relayed by Dunlop, were quite specific. Take possession of the cargo. Yet here was a chance to capture the perpetrators as well, surely a desirable prospect.

"Right, Pender," said the midshipman. "Tally off half the men to guard this stuff, the rest follow me."

He turned towards the line of trees, just as Dunlop screeched out new orders, his voice betraying a note of panic. "Mr Callander, back to the boats, at the double."

Callander only hesitated for a split second. Despite his own inclinations there was no choice but to obey. As they ran back down the beach they could see why such an order had been given. With the *Endymion*'s poor gunnery, the illegals had obviously decided that they could confound her. Well-aimed cannon fire would have kept them attached to their anchor, too afraid to move. But the frigate's wild shooting had exposed her weakness. And once their quarry realized that the attacking boats were on course for the beach, instead of intent on boarding, they took their chance to escape. The three ships were all heading out of the bay, each on a different heading. Toner fired one useless broadside after another in a vain attempt to frighten them. But this was no hard-pounding fleet action, where mere proximity was enough to bring success. It was pinpoint gunnery aimed at accelerating targets. Since the Endymions had never even been trained for the former, it was hardly surprising that they could not perform the latter.

The fully manned boats, pushing off from the beach, were now too far away to affect the outcome. Toner, faced with three possible targets, was left with no choice. He was forced to confine his attention to a single ship, choosing the slowest sailer, merely to avoid a fiasco. But even that involved him in a stern chase. The *Endymion* headed out to sea in the light morning airs, firing off her bow-chasers. Perhaps Toner was aiming them himself. The gunnery was certainly more accurate than it had been in the bay. He brought the ketch to, just as the others, clearing the bulk of Martinique, picked up a decent wind and headed off into the empty blue Caribbean.

CHAPTER TWENTY-FIVE

TONER HAD the one ketch he'd managed to capture under his lee. She was the *Fortitude* of four hundred tons out of Baltimore, with a crew of eight, carrying a cargo which made the captain's mouth water. It consisted of French delicacies, from brandy through delectable cheeses to pipes of fine wine. There was flour and butter as well, fresh from the American mainland, all of which he had ordered loaded into the *Endymion*'s hold. He also had in his possession most of the trade goods that the three ships had been planning to load, mainly coffee, sugar, and sacks of valuable spices. The whole would run to several thousands of pounds in value, of which Toner would receive two-eighths. The crew of the *Fortitude* were put back to work, loading their own ship in the manner they'd intended before the Royal Navy had disturbed them.

Pender had expected him to be angry. After all, two of his quarry had made good their escape. But Toner was in high spirits, with a grin that exposed both the upper and lower molars, and a flushed face. Nearly every item that came aboard was subject to a gentle touch of his hand before being taken below. The sour looks on the faces of his crew didn't dent his happiness, simply because he failed to observe it. The other officers, contemplating their profits, were likewise blinkered. Callander alone suspected the mood, even if he, in his naïvety, had no idea why it was so. Every item that was being loaded into the frigate was being stored in the captain's private lockers. He was already hinting at the capital dinners he could host, telling Dunlop in a loud voice that he would entertain the admiral. It didn't take a sharp mind to guess that Toner meant to use these delicacies for his own consumption. They would not be sold, as they should, on the dockside in Antigua, under the label of prize goods. That in turn meant that the crew would not get their share, which would amount to a fair portion of the total. True, they'd have their two-eighths of the *Fortitude* and the rest of her cargo, but a good third of the value of the total haul was going to disappear down the officers' gullets, a sure cause for dissent. On top of that, their captain had, through poor tactics, and worse seamanship, let those two other ships get away. Garmond, labouring away on the deck, wasn't slow to point this out to those not quick enough to see it for themselves, which meant that Toner was the subject of many a malevolent glare as he whispered in their ears. This resulted in the loading being carried out in a lacklustre fashion. Distracted as he was by this addition to his income, it was some time before Toner observed the lack of enthusiasm. To his mind the crew should be as pleased as he was. In time they would have gold in their pockets. But it was clear to him, once he chose to look, that his men did not share his feelings. At first he was perplexed, and then he was angry. The grin disappeared, to be replaced by his habitual frown. The teeth, now grinding together again, seemed unchanged.

"Belay!" he shouted to the party working on deck.

Some of the men, including Pender and the crew captured from the *Fortitude,* were in the boats below. Those on deck were hauling up a pallet full of cheeses, slung from a whip on the yard. The cargo was stopped halfway, still over the side above the barge, which rocked gently on the clear blue water of the bay. Those who'd been glaring at their captain, seeing him heading towards them, immediately adopted a bland expression, bovine stupidity being the best defence against arbitrary authority.

"What's the matter wi' you scullies?" demanded Toner.

No one answered, for the question had been general. The captain grabbed the nearest man and spun him round to look him in the eye. The sailor kept his gaze fixed on the deck, not daring to look up. But the lack of the jubilation that Toner was seeking seemed proven by the man's listless bearing. Toner grabbed another one and repeated the question, only to earn the same response.

"Damn the lot of you. Don't you take to the idea of having some money in your poke?"

Every eye was on the deck now. Toner looked over the side of the ship. Those men who'd been looking up, wondering what was going on, adopted the same pose as their shipboard fellows, casting their eyes down to avoid the captain's glare.

"Mr Dunlop."

"Sir?" shouted the premier.

"These scullies don't seem too pleased with the work we've done today. Well, since they've taken no pleasure in the success of their ship, they'll take no pleasure at all. No grog until further notice."

"Aye, aye, sir."

"And let's have them working at a proper pace, Mr Dunlop. Enough of this pussyfooting around. Start them, sir, and let's see their backs bend."

Toner only heard the quiet voice say, "Let go, lads." Then, as he saw the look of shock on his first lieutenant's face, he heard the sound of the ropes running free through the block. By the time he turned round, the men in the boats below were diving into the clear blue water for their lives. The fully laden pallet dropped like a stone, hitting the captain's barge right amidships. The boat tipped on to its beam ends, which emptied the rest of its valuable cargo into the deep blue sea.

All hell broke loose, with those in the water who couldn't swim crying out to be saved and Toner shouting a mixture of imprecations and orders. Men on the deck were ducking away from the blows that were suddenly aimed at them by their officers, instead of doing what was required, which was to cast lines to those in peril. Callander shouted to those close by to save Flowers, who had been thrown some distance from the nearest boat and was clearly incapable of even floating. He threw off his hat and coat and jumped into the water.

The mayhem seemed to last for several minutes. But order was finally restored, both on the deck and down on the waterline, as men were hauled, dripping wet, into the remaining boats. Toner paid little attention to this, occupied as he was with watching his cheeses sink. The whole pipe of fine Burgundy that he'd seen loaded on to his own barge had already disappeared from sight. The boat itself, under the pressure of the falling pallet, had turned turtle. That sight only served to fuel his anger. He turned to face his sullen crew, only to be greeted by a whole row of looks that were openly triumphant.

"Who gave the order to let go?"

"It was an accident, your honour," replied Garmond.

Toner lost all control at that point. He screamed at the man. "An accident? Do you take me for a gleckit fool, man? I heard the order as clear as I can hear you!"

"T'weren't no one's fault," said Garmond, stubbornly.

Pender, standing to one side, knew that Garmond, normally a cautious soul in the presence of authority, was trying to take the blame himself. It was probably his command that had caused the trouble, so that was in some ways fitting. But he would never admit to having given the order, for that could see him hanged.

"If it wasn't anyone's fault, then it was the whole gang of you, which sounds like mutiny to me."

They should have dropped their heads then, cowed by such a threat, since it could be the rope for the whole party if that was the case. But they didn't do as Toner expected, and the cold looks of hatred in their eyes, plus the direct way in which they were delivered, shocked him to the marrow. His officers stood around the men, at the ready, waiting to seize anyone he indicated, perhaps even all of them if so desired. But their captain didn't know which command to give. For the first time since they'd set out from Portsmouth he hesitated to order punishment.

It was partly fear at the collective nature of the seamen's protest. But another factor was at work. Toner rarely thought of his standing with the crew, naturally assuming, in his ignorance, that they saw him as stern but fair. Those cold looks gave him an inkling of how he was really perceived, and the knowledge seemed to drain him of the power to act. His voice was low, and the hesitant nature of his response uncharacteristic.

"An accident, you say?"

Garmond could not keep the look out of his eyes, which was part triumph, part surprise. He'd been expecting the worst. He'd sensed Toner's doubt, yet hadn't dared to hope. He fought to maintain a steady tone of voice, so as to hold open that which surprised him, an avenue of escape.

"That's right, Captain. An accident."

The face was set, the teeth grinding slowly, as Toner squeezed his response out. "We have had good fortune today. It is not to be spoiled by a minor accident."

Toner turned and made for the entrance to his cabin. "Carry on, Mr Dunlop. As soon as the *Fortitude* is loaded, put a prize crew aboard her and shape her a course for English Harbour."

"And the crew, sir?"

Toner seemed to recover some of his fire. "They are in the Royal Navy now, Mr Callander."

"They will claim they are Americans, sir."

"I dare say they will, Mr Dunlop. If they demur, offer them the choice of the noose."

Toner started drinking well before the hour allotted for the officers' dinner. The feast he'd planned to entertain the wardroom had been cancelled, the host suddenly in no mood to entertain. Dunlop, taking advantage of his position, and lacking clear instructions, had allotted his favourite midshipman, Hemmings, the task of taking the prize into English Harbour. Callander had been given the watch in his place. The premier now stood before his commander awaiting further orders. Toner gave him a course for the frigate, but seemed curiously reluctant to allow him to leave, while being equally at a loss to find the means to detain him. The glass of brandy he'd poured for his visitor lay untouched between them.

"There'll be a few cracked faces at English Harbour when they see our prize sail in."

"Yes, sir," replied Dunlop, without enthusiasm, his eyes fixed on a point just above his captain's head.

Toner's nonplussed expression clearly showed that he'd expected more from his premier.

"Three would be better, of course." The lieutenant's tawny eyes flicked down for a split second, then dropped further till he was looking at the top of the desk. This changed the note in his captain's voice from one of forced jollity to something approaching desperation. "They were bonny sailers, those illegals, Dunlop. Stands to reason, man. We'd have needed two ships to cage them."

Dunlop's lack of response was as telling as a verbal rebuke. Eventually the silence in the cabin grew oppressive, and Dunlop, seeking permission to carry on, was relieved when it was granted.

"Send me the purser, wi' a list of the goods we took today."

When the purser arrived, Toner avoided the subject of captures completely. For the same reason he'd been unable to discuss discipline with his first lieutenant, he now found himself constrained in the presence of this man, not wishing to make any allusion to the quantity of cargo they might have taken with a better-trained crew. But at least the purser consumed his drink, finishing each glass with an audible smack of the lips that indicated his desire for a refill. Toner obliged, keeping pace himself, which, given what he'd started earlier, began to affect his speech. He made several stabs at the subject of discipline, all received with supportive grunts from behind the purser's raised glass.

"A captain sometimes disna see what's really happening below decks. He needs good officers, wi' a sharp eye, to keep him aware."

"Heaven knows that they're not ten a penny, sir."

"How right you are. What happened on deck today . . . ?"

"I was below, Captain," replied the purser, suddenly wary. For the first time his wine glass stayed close to his ample paunch. But Toner, in his cups, didn't notice.

"I'm curious to know how you see the condition of the crew, Purser, an' no too proud to take a bit o' guidance."

"Oafs to a man, sir. Never off complaining about what we see fit to supply them. Every cask of beef is rotten to their ill-bred noses."

"That's common stuff."

"It's all I see, sir. What happens elsewhere I pay no heed to." He got to his feet quickly. "If that will be all, Captain?"

Toner nodded angrily. The purser had put down his glass before he'd had a chance to respond. He was left to finish the bottle himself. It seemed only moments later that he heard the laughter float up from the gunroom below. In his inebriated mind he conjured up the image of his first lieutenant, or the purser, indeed any of his officers engaging in some critical sally, a witticism directed against himself. He had failed to act decisively on deck, and that fact had been public. His crew had defied him and survived. Never had the loneliness of Toner's position borne down on him so heavily. He knew he had to make a decision, and that it had to be done alone. Dunlop had known it too, which is why his premier had stood silently and awkwardly before his desk. The purser had been worse than useless. Toner couldn't ask for help or advice anywhere. He was the captain. Only he could decide the course he should follow.

The defiant looks of his crew had wounded him deeply. Not that he'd ever supposed himself loved. That was something he was prepared to forgo until the laurels of success were fitted to his name. But he had, for all his recourse to a ready discipline, expected a degree of loyalty. Surely those who served before the mast understood that they were engaged in a harsh occupation; that the punishments he delivered were as much for their sake as the good of the service, or the ship. He did not spare himself, so it would be folly to spare anyone else. He poured another goblet of captured brandy and held it up to the light. The brown liquid glinted in the crystal, which, being patterned, threw out a myriad small points of light. Toner fancied that these pinpoints were the defiant looks of his crew, and that roused him to a loud curse. He pushed himself upright and staggered out on to the quarterdeck. Midshipman Callander stood by the binnacle, conversing quietly with the man at the helm.

"You!" spat Toner.

"Sir," Callander replied, standing to attention, his hat raised.

"Is that all you can say, laddie?" the captain barked, in a voice that could be heard throughout the ship. The man at the wheel jerked his head, trying to take a quick look. "Attend to the wheel, man, while I attend to this . . . this. What should I call you, laddie? For you're no gentleman, to my mind."

The youngster's reply carried with it all the disingenuous honesty of a confused youth. "Mr Callander, sir."

"Callander eh! Just like that arse of an uncle of yours. I'll see him off, boy, as soon as a prize agent sells our captures. Then, maybe, I'll be spared the need to have you on my ship. You're like a standing reminder of debt bondage. Get out of my sight."

"I'm the officer of the watch, sir," Callander replied.

"Do as I command, sir!" yelled Toner.

The boy turned away abruptly and ran aft to the rail. Toner walked over to the man conning the ship, laying a hand on his shoulder in a way meant to transmit friendship. Drunk, he didn't feel the shudder of fear that ran through the sailor's body.

"Stick wi' me, laddie, an' we'll aw be rich. Fiddler's Green will be yours for the asking." The ship jibbed a little as, in turning to reply, the wheel slipped a strake. The note of camaraderie disappeared immediately. "Hold her steady, man."

"Aye, aye, Capt'n."

Callander saw Toner stagger back to his cabin. He was just about to return to the wheel when he heard his voice through the open skylight. Toner was talking to himself again, berating his own person, cursing himself for a weak-livered fool and enumerating the dire punishments he intended to inflict on those who failed to serve him. Then the voice dropped away, till it seemed like an uneven whisper that Callander couldn't quite hear. The young midshipman didn't know that his captain, that stern unbending man who seemed so often like a malignant God, was weeping with self-pity, cursing his past life and his prospects ahead, exposing every nerve end of his secret fears. The thought of failure loomed large, the idea that he might be beached again, to eke out an existence on half pay. Callander edged closer to the skylight, drawn inexorably by the rasping voice, and listened transfixed as Toner ran through the story of his miserable life. Bullied as a mid, passed over time and again in favour of men with influence, and finally denied the comfort of a proper home, either as a child or an adult.

"Love. I've lived without that all my days . . . A wet nurse, no a mother, and a father who cared for his cards more than his bairns. A toy for the sodomites as a ship's boy and life no better in the mids' berth. Always hungry, always cold, and scarce a penny in ma poke when I ran ashore. What lassie has ever looked at John Toner and seen a prospect? And me, I've never had the words to engage their fancy . . . No wife, no children . . . and scant affection. The only warmth of flesh I've ever felt has been a whore's rotten hide, with the stink of other men still on her . . ."

The voice changed, becoming harsher and rising slowly to a terrible crescendo. "And have I withered in the face of this? Never in life. And I'll not bend now . . . So they hate me, do they, those stinking scum? Do they think I care about that? Captain John Toner stands beholden to no man!"

The sound of shattering glass made Callander move away. But the voice, rising again, pursued him.

"I'll not seek affection from those scullies any more than I sought it from my own father. I took a fist to his face in my time. I should have flogged them all, the insolent sods, the very minute they let go of that rope. Lying bastards to a man. Accident, say they! I'll give them a fuckin' accident. I'll accidentally flog them till they beg to be thrown into hell. This is my ship, my command.

Every man jack aboard will do what I tell them to do. I'll make the *Endymion* the envy of the king's navy. And if the bastards won't smile when I do it, then they can die to make it happen!"

The crash of Toner's cabin door smashing against the bulkhead reverberated throughout the ship. The midshipman quickly made for the companion ladder, but stopped when he saw his captain swaying in the light from the binnacle. Callander wasn't the only one to hear the next shout. So did the whole ship, it being loud enough to be heard in the tops.

"Boatswain! On the double. And break out the cat-o'-nine-tails!"

There was a mad light in Toner's eyes, which showed up in the lanterns that were slung in the rigging. He was still affected by drink, though what had happened before his eyes these last hours was enough to sober even the most hardened sot. The marines, lined up on the quarterdeck, muskets at the ready, were nearly dropping with fatigue. But they kept their station, just as the junior warrant officers did. There were so many men to flog, each one with a punishment so severe, that they had to work in relays. Fifty lashes per man. Blood had flowed copiously from the torn backs. It had run off the canvas set to contain it, and out through the scuppers and into the sea, mixed with sweat, vomit, and salt water. Those of the crew not brought to the grating stood silently watching the drama before them, as their captain sought to ensure that his authority could never again be challenged. What they witnessed sickened them. Yet their stoic faces mirrored those of the officers, which were set like masks. But anyone who'd looked would have observed that their gaze was aimed above the bloody business, to a point in the rigging that avoided the sights before them.

He left Garmond till last. The man who had given the order to "let go" had been allotted the greatest number of strokes, being given an extra twenty for insubordination. Yet Toner's attempt to single him out backfired. Those involved in this terrible work were tired. They had long since lost enthusiasm for the task, and after a while their strength had ebbed as well. Yet it looked good enough, for the cat was so soaked with the blood of others that the first few lashes created a criss-cross of bloody weals on the man's back that finally brought a grim smile to Toner's lips.

The sound was different too, softer, and Pender guessed it wasn't just fatigue that made it so. Garmond might think his seditious talk had gone unnoticed. But there wasn't a junior warrant officer aboard the ship who was unaware of his position with the men. So they'd flog him, with a good appearance of venom. But they'd avoid the charge of laying it on, since Garmond was the type to take note of a bullying boatswain's name, and see him over the side one dark and stormy night, with not a cry raised, nor a tear shed, for the man's passing.

Garmond suffered nevertheless, evidenced by the cries that accompanied each crack of the whip. He wasn't the type to be silent under pain, and his screams filled the night air, which brought echoes from the thick jungle of Martinique, which lay no more than two cables distant. The air, so close inshore, was hot and humid, which added to the vision that many men had already dubbed hell. The last stroke of the lash hit Garmond's back, the last scream shot from his throat, and the bosun's mate who'd delivered the final blow sank to his knees in exhaustion.

"Punishment completed, sir," said Dunlop, without waiting for the man to report.

"The deck is a disgrace, Mr Dunlop," said Toner coldly. The captain swayed slightly, as though the effort of holding himself upright was no longer necessary. "I shall retire for the night. But I expect to be up during the morning watch. I also expect the deck to look less like that of an abattoir, and more like that of a king's ship."

"Aye, aye, sir," said Dunlop, to Toner's receding back. "Mr Callander. Put your men to cleaning the deck."

"With respect, sir," said Callander, "they are topmen, not waisters."

For once Dunlop didn't growl his reply. If anything his voice sounded unnaturally soft, as though he too had been affected by the brutality he'd witnessed.

"With respect, sir, they are sailors, like any other. We shan't be setting any canvas till daylight. And Mr Callander, do the deck well. Make it spotless. I would hate to see your work ruined by the sight of a topman at the grating in the morning."

In the great cabin, Captain Toner was talking to himself again, almost in the rhythm of the holystones which were trying to wear the planking of the deck down, so that the evidence of his night's work would disappear, repeating over and over that "the men would know their place, or by damn they'd meet their maker." Two decks below, amidships, as the surgeon and his assistant dressed the bloody backs, they wondered at the unnatural silence and the distracted stares of the men they were treating.

In the gunroom the conversation had a stilted quality, as the officers sought to maintain communication without making reference to the day's events. That proved difficult enough. But each inadvertent allusion carried with it some implied question as to the actions of the captain. In the midshipmen's berth they were silent. Normally boisterous, they'd been struck dumb by the carnage. Mrs Wallington, the gunner's wife, sewed steadily, repairing the torn shirts of her young gentlemen, her head swaying back and forth as she tutted in disapproval. Her husband was with the other warrant officers in the galley, watching the one-legged cook scraping the grease off his coppers that would be used to dress torn flesh. Less careful than their seniors, they openly berated Toner for his wayward behaviour. In their hammocks, those off-watch who'd escaped the lash whispered quietly, each punishment that had been inflicted since they'd left Portsmouth reprised and condemned.

The *Endymion* rocked gently on the swell, ropes straining and creaking as men gathered in small knots to exchange opinions. The officers, with the exception of the man on watch, had now retired for the night, knowing that their captain would expect them to be particularly alert in the morning, so there was no one to break up their small seditious gatherings. Then the rumbling started, as a piece of round shot, taken out of a ring of ropes that lay beside each gun, rolled across the deck. There was a thud as it struck the bulwarks. But as the ship pitched on the swell, the ball careered, with the same ominous rumble, back to where it started. Everyone aboard, from the highest to the lowest, recognized the sound that heralded true naval dissent, the signal since time immemorial, that a vessel in the king's service was ripe for mutiny.

CHAPTER TWENTY-SIX

ADMIRAL Bessborough, as host, had set himself to be nice to the Ludlows, and his welcome was effusive, in sharp contrast to the one he accorded to General Driffield, who'd come out to take over the governorship of Dominica. Lady Bessborough took her cue from her husband and proceeded to monopolize them, having obviously discovered, in the course of her enquiries, that Harry Ludlow was a bachelor, the heir to large estates in Kent, as well as the holder of two rotten-borough seats in Parliament. To a mother of two unmarried daughters this represented an opportunity not to be missed. As a well-known portrait painter much esteemed in London society, James was likewise cosseted, with the offer of her ladyship's assistance should he wish for commissions in the islands, all the while plied with numerous crystal goblets full of a fruity rum punch. The admiral's wife was a creature with a sharp eye for her own advantage. She was also a woman of trenchant opinions, forcibly delivered.

"You must catch your commissions after the harvest, Mr Ludlow, when the planters are flush with the profits of their cane. The sowing season always throws them into debt. They mortgage their properties to the hilt, which is not an inducement to luxury. It shows a want of acumen to be rich at one part of the year and in penury a few months later." This remark was made, loudly, in the presence of several wealthy planters, to whose feelings Lady Bessborough was clearly indifferent. "Then the trick is to find the mortgagees, for they are the true nabobs of the islands."

The two daughters were introduced, the contrast to their formidable mother very obvious in both their appearance and reserved demeanour. Harry was called to meet the general as James introduced their young French prisoner to the Bessborough family. De Brissot was then treated to a demonstration of execrable French from his hostess, who bemoaned the nature of the war, which debarred her daughters, as well as her nephew, from visiting France and polishing their knowledge of the language. James was tempted to ask which war had interfered with Lady Bessborough's education, but good manners, and the lack of a true opportunity, prevented him. Their hostess was not one to pause for breath. She began to praise the Frenchman for his lineage. The confusion on de Brissot's face was not just because of her lack of linguistic skill. The problems were associated with the continual reference to the noble name St-Pol, not to mention the battle of Agincourt. It was a situation which taxed all of James's powers of self-control, though he missed some of the exchange through the constant demands of accepting introductions.

"The French showed great nobility that day, sir," said Lady Bessborough, "dying, as they did, in droves. One cannot help but be saddened that archery, the province of the common man, should wreak such havoc amongst the quality. Such a pity that the comte de St-Pol had to perish. It must have come as a great shock to the family."

This remark was delivered as though young Thierry had known his supposed ancestor personally, and accompanied with a look that almost enquired why he wasn't in mourning. "We are, of course, accustomed to the better class of Frenchman here at Admiralty House. We had a Monsieur de la Mery here for near a month. A perfect gentleman, though unfortunate in his choice of pet. It would not let off ravaging the brocades for thinkin' them pythons."

She turned in James's direction, only to find him partially occupied in another conversation. But in a voice that overbore all others, she made her enquiry, forcing him to break off and attend to her.

"Are you acquainted with the family de la Mery?" she asked the Frenchman.

Thierry de Brissot, who'd only understood a fraction of what Lady Bessborough had said, shook his head. His hostess fixed James with a stern look.

"De la Mery, Mr Ludlow. That is surely a most noble appendage?"

"Oh yes, Lady Bessborough," lied James smoothly. "A whole tribe were early victims of the Terror, entirely due, I assure you, to their social prominence."

"Terror indeed, sir!" she snapped. Her ample bosom swelled with indignation as she peered into de Brissot's face. "And not confined to the faubourgs of Paris. Poor Monsieur de la Mery lost his estates in St-Domingue to that horrible creature l'Ouverture. The French disease has spread by the most damnable hands, black, white, and mulatto."

"Lady Bessborough," said James quickly, taking the lady's arm and steering her away. The young Frenchman had understood enough of that last statement to be insulted on behalf of the nation, and looked set to say so. He placed him beside Harry for safety's sake. He, in turn, guided the young man in the opposite direction, away from the eager eyes of the two daughters, only to find himself, after a nod to Marcus Sandford, face to face with Dillon.

"Good evening to you, sir," he said, before bowing to de Brissot. "*Et vous,* Monsieur."

Harry introduced them formally and listened with half an ear to Dillon's exquisitely phrased questions, delivered in impeccable French. They didn't quite constitute an interrogation, more a reaffirmation of what the Irishman already knew. But at a social gathering they bordered on the over-inquisitive, which Harry put down to the nature of his office.

"I doubt that Monsieur de Brissot has much to add to what he has already told us," said Harry, aware that he would be leaving the French prisoner ashore after the dinner, at the mercy of Dillon's curiosity. "And he has already given us his parole, which I'm sure he will renew for the admiral."

"An exchange of prisoners could take some time, Monsieur.

There is little suitable accommodation on the island for enemy officers. Perhaps, if I intercede with the admiral, you will accept an offer to stay here at Admiralty House."

De Brissot looked at Harry, who'd provided him with more than enough funds to accommodate himself till a cartel could be arranged. But Dillon was still talking, quietly but forcefully, so he couldn't say anything.

"I know that the admiral esteems the company of your race, sir. That applies also to his family. I had little difficulty, previously, in persuading him to accommodate one of your fellow country-men, though his pet tried the admiral's wife somewhat. He, like me, finds it adds to the gaiety of what can be a dull office. A quiet conversation with a cultured man is to be welcomed when one's surrounded by serving officers. Besides, you've clearly impressed Lady Bessborough, not to mention her daughters, in the same man-ner as Monsieur de la Mery."

Cram's loud voice announced that dinner was served and the guests filed into the admiral's quarters, which, with both sets of doors thrown open, ran the entire length of the rear of the build-ing. The long mahogany table, with its deep polish, was ablaze with silver. The candles glinted off the plate, and both were reflected in the burnished wood. Each portrait on the wall, mostly of Bessborough's predecessors, had to illuminate it a many-branched candlestick. It was James, with his quick painter's eye, that spotted the portrait of their father, which had been given pride of place above the mantelpiece. He elbowed Harry gently and directed his attention to it.

"He'll expect us to be flattered. Though it's such a poor effort that I could, if you wish, affect to be insulted."

Harry just smiled. "Your manners are too refined, brother. I'm the one for mortifying behaviour at social gatherings."

"Really," replied James, archly. "Lady Bessborough barely sur-vived me. How did she escape censure from you?"

"The long game, brother."

Their sudden elevation to the position of favoured guests was highlighted in the seating arrangements. Not only had the admiral given the brothers precedence over the military, he'd put them above Vandegut. This officer, seeing his place card, looked mightily displeased. Bessborough was taking care that the Ludlows would be close enough to feel the effects of his charm. Lady Bessborough was relegated to the opposite end of the table. She'd seated their young, supposedly aristocratic prisoner there, along with her daughters and her nephew, Caddick. Marcus Sandford was on hand to amuse her, with Captain Poynton added to ensure that she shared the social burden. The servants, under the careful eye of Cram, were all black and exceedingly well proportioned, with that arrogance redolent of a permanent household staff, a group that would outlast the occupancy of any temporary major domo.

"Your first visit to the Indies, sir?" said Bessborough to James over the turtle soup. By the time he'd emptied the bowl the admiral had blessed the climate and cursed the disease, which he called the obverse side of paradise. "Was a time, sir, when we could pull our ships out and send them north to Chesapeake Bay to avoid both the yellow jack and the hurricanes."

"A hurricane. I long to see one, Admiral. The elements at their most ferocious, I believe."

Harry cut in as Bessborough's white eyebrows lifted at such an odd notion. "My brother would stand at the lip of an active volcano, sir, just so that he could record it accurately with his brush."

"Then I recommend Martinique to you, Mr Ludlow, if you can abide the smell of sulphur. St-Pierre is a delightful town and Mont Pelée is forever bubbling."

"You would scarce need to make the journey to Martinique in order to experience a sulphureous smell. There is enough devilry on Antigua to provide an abundance."

Harry turned and looked at Vandegut, who'd made this rather lame remark. He sat two places down on his left, his face a picture of wounded pride.

"The devil resides in us all, Captain Vandegut. It is in the nature of the place," said Bessborough coldly, as a servant removed his soup plate. Then he turned to Harry, in a way that was clearly designed to cut Vandegut. "The next dish we shall savour is testimony to that. It is called black crab pepper pot."

It was hot and spicy, just as the admiral said, its smell wafting out of the huge urn borne by two negroes. Eager to demonstrate his culinary knowledge, Bessborough described the ingredients.

"A capon stewed down added to a ham that's been stewed to a jelly. Six dozen land crabs with their eggs and fat, cooked in onions, okra, and sweet herbs, and the season's vegetables. I had it off a Jamaica planter, sir, and it is just the dish to set you up for the rest of your dinner."

It was delicious, if too rich, and the slight feeling of discomfort it engendered was heightened as the dish was followed by removes of turtle, mutton, beef, turkey, goose, duck, chickens, more capons, ham, tongue, and crab patties, all of this washed down with either fine wine or more fruity rum punch, the whole finished off with various cheeses, sweets, and fruits. James ate sparingly, though he was careful to comment favourably on the little he consumed. Noticing this, Bessborough was at great pains to keep his glass full. The conversation was as varied as the meal, with everyone except Vandegut careful of their subject. With the Frenchman safe at the other end of the table the state of his country was a reasonable matter for discussion, with special reference to her navy. Harry was pressed to explain the situation off the enemy coast, which led to a general discussion of the merits of close blockade. The general, during this, was tactless enough to allude to the quality of the basic weapon, with the French being praised for their ability to build better ships.

"They'll never rebuild their fleet in a lifetime, sir," said Bessborough, sharply. "No matter how many ships they commission. They've guillotined or chased off their best officers. And if I may say, from experience, it takes time to turn a mere lieutenant into an admiral. It can't be achieved overnight. So let us put Howe's

great victory in that perspective. I have no wish to dim the light
of his achievements, sir. But I would like it remembered that Villaret-Joyeuse is not yet a comte de Grasse."

His fork was aimed at de Brissot. Then Vandegut spoiled matters by his interjection. "They seem to train their civilians quite
adequately for the military tasks, sir."

This was an obvious reference to Hugues and Guadeloupe,
a gibe that Vandegut generally avoided. But he was clearly
smarting at what he saw as his commander's condescension.
Bessborough flushed angrily. But he didn't allow his temper to
interfere with the wit needed for a reply.

"If only we could teach some of our officers to be civil, Captain Vandegut, then perhaps we would achieve great deeds."

"Very droll, Admiral," said the new governor of Dominica, a
portly individual, so red-faced and gross that he looked like a master baker.

From that point on, if Vandegut interrupted at all, he was more
careful in his choice of sally. But he did engage Harry in conversation, eager to know what opinion in England said about the
navy's efforts in the West Indies.

"The war goes badly everywhere, Captain," Harry replied, well
aware, after his cutting remark, of the true nature of Vandegut's
interest. "The French seem fired by a zeal that we cannot counter."

"Except at sea."

"I don't think this command, or your service, can be singled
out for opprobrium. The confusion rests in the higher direction
of the war. There are too many plans being pursued at once, while
our enemies have simple aims; that is to feed their population and
secure their borders."

"I cannot agree with you, sir. Our aims are simple enough.
And I take leave to say that if they were vigorously pursued, then
they could be brought to a speedy conclusion. The want of direction in warfare is not confined to Whitehall."

Harry glanced quickly at the top of the table, to ensure that
Bessborough was fully engaged in talking to James. He even

dropped his voice to ensure the admiral would not hear his next remark.

"I find it odd, with two enemy frigates in the offing, that Toner was sent on his present mission."

Vandegut dropped his voice as well. "You could not wonder, sir, if you were stationed here. You allude to the very confusion to which I referred. My superior may cut a fine figure socially, Captain Ludlow, but he is less impressive in the execution of his office."

"Illegal cargoes are tempting, mind."

"Perhaps they are, sir, to a man of your persuasion. But my own view is that they are a distraction at any time, more so with what has occurred these last few months. Yet I cannot make my view prevail. My commander is more concerned with the possibility of profit and the good opinion of his client officers than he is in confounding the French."

"Is Toner a client officer?"

"Certainly not!"

"Yet he has sent him off to . . ." Harry left the rest of the sentence hanging in the air, hoping that Vandegut would complete it. But the man was too taken with his own concerns to accept the bait.

"If only Dillon would back me, we might get somewhere. But he does just the opposite. He almost encourages the practice." Harry opened his mouth to speak, to pose another question that might trap the other man, but Vandegut kept speaking. "You might be tempted to ask why, sir, as I am, since he profits not one jot by it. Perhaps it is the Irish in him. They are, as I'm sure you're aware, a quixotic race."

"Captain Ludlow," called Bessborough. "Your brother is making a good fist of describing your action with Monsieur d'Albret. But he lacks a sailor's eye. I half fear he's confusing starboard with larboard."

"You mean that there's a difference?" said James, with mock seriousness.

That remark was received with much hilarity, but it didn't avert discussion of the subject. That, in turn, effectively killed his private conversation with Vandegut. Even he was eager to hear details of how *Bucephalas* had escaped the Frenchman's trap.

It was time to say goodbye to the opposite sex. Lady Bessborough claimed de Brissot as a companion, assuring the Frenchman that he would be bored rigid in Anglo-Saxon company. Caddick, likewise, was dragged away to provide company, something that, judging by his face, was unwelcome. His quiet protest was easily overborne by his aunt.

"He has no head for port, sir. Besides, his *Français* has lapsed since our previous French guest took it in hand to improve him. Perhaps Monsieur de Brissot can rekindle his interest."

She shepherded both young men out into the hallway with a loud aside that her husband spoke such indifferent French as to be near useless. The port was produced, with a dish of nuts to go with it. Once they'd gone out of the door, with everyone moving up to the admiral's end of the table, Bessborough promptly surprised everyone by getting to his feet, his eyes fixed firmly on the Ludlow brothers.

"I plead duty, gentlemen. Captain and Mr Ludlow. I'd be obliged if you'd join me upstairs in my private quarters for a moment. Captain Vandegut, I know that you will take great pleasure in doing the honours at what is, after all, an admiral's table."

There was no opportunity to demur. For all he'd consumed the older man met Harry's eye with a steady gaze. James said nothing, hoping that Harry would politely refuse. He was feeling slightly inebriated, having drunk steadily as he ate sparingly. Bessborough could only want to ask Harry for that service which Sandford had mentioned. A request delivered personally, after a fine dinner, might be hard to refuse. But as he formed these thoughts James knew that Harry's endemic curiosity wouldn't allow him to adopt such a course. He got to his feet at the same time as his brother. Dillon stood too, only to be ordered back to his seat by a peremptory wave that brought a flush to his normally pallid cheeks.

Bessborough led them out of the open French windows, explaining that he had a separate outside staircase, which would avoid disturbing the ladies, who now occupied the rooms that opened to the hallway. This ran up the side of the building to the first floor. At the top, Bessborough produced a key. The door opened on to his bedroom, but he carried on through that and entered a small study which he explained was his private office. Cram stood ready to serve and a decanter of port stood on the table. The servant, with an air of superiority that bordered on condescension, poured three glasses before Bessborough indicated that his guests should sit down. With that, he began to pace between the two doors.

"I find myself in an awkward position, gentlemen, at a stand so to speak, and it is only the arrival of Captain Sandford, a man I trust implicitly, that has allowed me to see daylight. He has represented to me that given the current circumstances I should enlist your aid in a delicate matter."

"Admiral Bessborough."

"Please, Captain Ludlow. It may be that I cannot ask for that, nor shall I if it proves to be the case." Harry waved his arm to indicate the depth of his confusion. Cram mistook the signal and stepped forward to top up his glass, which allowed Bessborough to continue. "I dare say your friend Sandford has waxed indiscreet about the trouble we are having with this damned Jacobin, Victor Hugues."

James cut in. "Perhaps my brother should be more concerned about what the good captain said to you."

Bessborough ignored that and carried on as if James hadn't spoken. "Not that all this is new. We've known about the fellow's activities for months. But things have taken an unwelcome turn recently. This gives credibility to a notion hinted at some time ago. It was something I set aside as impossible, but Hugues's continued success demands that I examine matters without sentiment."

"He seems to have enjoyed rare good fortune," said Harry.

"It is perhaps more than that, sir. I was minded to ignore the fellow as being no more dangerous than a gnat. After all, he never laid a hand on a single English vessel. But what would you say if I told you that the Jacobin takes every ship we know of?"

"Every ship, Admiral Bessborough?"

"Damn near, Captain Ludlow," replied Bessborough, pausing for a moment. When he was sure that he'd made the point he began pacing again. "I was in St John's a few days ago. I had a chance, a rare one, to bespeak some of the businessmen and merchant captains who use that port. If they'd heard of Hugues in the past they'd ignored him, seeing the villain as an asset not a liability. After all, he never laid a finger on their ships. Then I sat down to the governor's dinner only to find out that our friend has changed his tune. Some of the owners who'd suffered losses were at that very feast, and were quick to demand that the navy do something."

"All of which makes perfect sense," said Harry.

"If only they'd come forward sooner. These men sail to all the islands of the Caribbean. They know more about what is happening than we do."

"Why interfere? They were happy to let him ruin any competition from neutral traders."

"Well, they're not happy now, sir, and neither am I. Because as they named his successes, every ship they identified struck a chord with me. Why? Because each one had been listed on our intelligence reports. Now we take great care of those, and only release them to our captains when they're set to weigh. You can, I'm sure, see how gallin' that is. If that ain't bad enough he also seems to have the rare knack of avoiding my frigates, which are cruising in search of the same vessels. Indeed, from the little we know, he takes them just short of our arranged rendezvous. That, sir, is more than good fortune."

Bessborough stopped his pacing and looked from one to the other, his green eyes as hard as agate. Harry and James reacted in a similar way. Neither said a word and it was only by the slight stiffening of their bodies that Bessborough could detect that his words had some effect. The silence lasted for several seconds before Harry finally spoke.

"With respect, Admiral, I cannot see what all this has to do with my brother and me."

"I would not wish to allude to your reputation, Captain Ludlow. But word gets about in the service: from Gibraltar, Genoa, and the Downs. It seems you have a particular skill in uncovering things. And here you are, in my bailiwick, with a freedom of action denied to serving officers."

"I sail as a privateer, Admiral, which I would remind you is short on her complement."

"Oh, you'll have them back, Ludlow, never fear. You have a written order. You can present Toner with it just as soon as he comes in."

"When will that be?"

Bessborough was so smooth, as though the matter was of small moment. "He is, as I told you, his own master. It could be tomorrow or it could be a month. I just thought, with some time on your hands, you might put your mind to my little problem."

"I have no interest in your problem, Admiral."

That made the admiral's voice sharper. Yet for all that he didn't seem very upset by what was a downright refusal to assist him.

"Then you're not the man that was represented to me earlier. So be it. But I would ask you one thing. Should you come across anything that arouses your suspicions, I would be obliged if you'd let me know."

"That is a very odd request to make of a civilian, Admiral," said James, "when you have the whole resources of the service at your disposal."

Bessborough's eyes became watery and his voice soft, like a man recalling a favoured pet. "It is those very resources, as you call them, Mr Ludlow, that seem intent on bringing me down. For I tell you this. The loss of Guadeloupe still hounds me. Now this threatens to get out of control. My officers don't signify. Indeed Vandegut undermines me with their Lordships and Poynton is a pompous jackass. Of those that have gone to sea only Sandford has seen fit to obey my instructions."

"I think we should rejoin the other guests now, sir," said James, interrupting. He could see the wetness around the admiral's eyes and the man's whole demeanour smacked of the onset of self-pity. It was not something either he or Harry would wish to be exposed to.

"Yes," sniffed Bessborough, acknowledging the futility of continuing. Then his whole manner changed abruptly as he seemed to slough off his depression. James looked at Cram, who seemed on the verge of a smile.

"It's not all a waste. You see, I couldn't help wonderin' if just speaking with you would not unlock something. If one of the people in whom I repose my trust, seeing us heading off to be closeted alone, hearing, as I have, of your reputation, might not be a trifle alarmed."

"Alarmed enough to betray themselves?" asked James.

"Precisely, Mr Ludlow."

"Reputations are easily exaggerated, sir," said Harry, coldly.

"They are more easily destroyed," snapped Bessborough.

CHAPTER TWENTY-SEVEN

THE LUDLOW brothers declined to return to Bessborough's dinner, taking the option instead of departing by the postern gate, having asked that it be unlocked specially. The ill grace with which Cram performed this menial task did nothing for their temper. James, who'd drunk more than he'd realized, was affected by the fresh air, becoming unsteady on his feet. He was aware that Harry was quietly seething. Under normal circumstances he might have kept silent, but his condition affected his judgement as well as his legs. Once they were out in the street and heading down the hill towards the twinkling lights of the harbour, he could not contain himself.

"I don't think we've ever been exposed to such bare-faced affrontery."

Encouraged to speak by this remark, Harry showed equal disgust. "He thinks he has a spy in his headquarters and rather than sully any naval hands with the task of finding out who it is, he tries to engage me. Then when I refuse, he calmly informs me that it was all a ploy. Damn it, he didn't even offer to speed up the return of my crew."

"Not a word about Sandford, Harry? No approbation for him?"

Harry stopped suddenly. "What's Marcus got to do with this?"

James staggered slightly as he stopped, which made him wonder just how much of those rum punches he'd consumed had been made up of fruit. "Your old friend has been a little less than frank, Harry, as you know very well."

In the dark it was hard to know if Harry was angry or

confused. "I'm sure if he said anything, he was only trying to help us."

With that, he started walking again.

"Us, or the navy?" said James. "He told you this afternoon that he'd had news of you these last few years. Where do you think Bessborough got the information to hint at what happened off Gibraltar and Genoa? And if any of the people downstairs were to be alarmed by a private interview, they too must be privy to our recent past."

"The navy has its own way of conveying news. It is, as you've observed more than once, prone to gossip. It's quite common to talk of friends and ex-shipmates."

"To those who have an interest, Harry. Bessborough doesn't know you, barring a brief glimpse at your court martial. Neither, I think, does anyone else. Marcus Sandford is an old friend who acted as your second. And that is probably common knowledge. Anyone hearing about your exploits, good or bad, would be bound to tell him. Someone even mentioning your name would be pressed by him for news. The idea that you take a hand came from him, not his commander."

"He must have had his reasons," said Harry stubbornly.

"I don't doubt it. And there may be a perfectly honourable explanation why he chose to imply otherwise. But I do doubt that."

"I think you're allowing your dislike of the man to cloud your view."

"Dislike?" James spluttered. "Who said anything about disliking him? I hardly know the fellow."

"You made that perfectly plain this morning. I must tell you, James, I was close to checking you for the way you behaved."

"Harry, for the life of me I don't know what you're talking about."

"You acted as if he was the most tedious man in the world. Every time he opened his mouth to speak your attention wandered. It was damned insulting and he noticed."

James laughed out loud, which in his inebriated state and in the narrow roadway sounded more raucous than he intended.

"It's not funny, brother."

"But it is, Harry. My attention was taken up with the young American fellow. Do you recall the one who was talking to Gracewell and asking about our rooms? He was in the next booth to us, eavesdropping on your conversation with Sandford in the most obvious way."

Harry stopped again, just as he reached the entrance to the Duke of Clarence, and turned to look at James. "The young fair-haired fellow?"

"Yes."

"Did you see him tonight?" he asked. James shook his head, an action which unbalanced him, forcing him to steady himself against the wall. "He trailed us up to Admiralty House. You, in your usual manner, were dawdling, pointing out the flora and fauna. He kept having to stop himself. Otherwise I wouldn't have spotted him."

"I do not dawdle, brother," said James, his hand still against the wall.

Harry smiled broadly. "Yes, you do. And you also have too little regard for rum punch. But let's put that aside and turn our minds to this Jonathan. I wonder where he is now?"

James waved a hand at the well-lit doorway. "Here at the Clarence?"

"No, I'll wager he's standing outside the front of Admiralty House waiting for us to come out."

"Then he's in for a long night, which only serves him out. Shall we go back?"

"No," replied Harry. "I think you need to sit down. Let's go inside and see if he turns up here."

As they entered the tap-room they ran straight into Mr Gracewell, his arms full of empty tankards.

"A word with you, sir," said James, with a wave of his hand.

The slight frown of anger, no doubt because of being accosted when busy, was fleeting. As befitted a good host the man was quick to smile, even if his guest's eye did look a touch bleary. "If'n you'd care to sit down, gentlemen, I'll free my hands and attend upon you directly."

Which he did, bearing as gifts two large tankards of rum punch. Harry took his without much enthusiasm. But James was loud in his thanks, pronounced himself parched, and took a great gulp to prove it.

"That young Jonathan, Mr Gracewell, who enquired about our rooms. Did he have a name?" asked Harry.

"If he gave me one, sir, I do not recall it."

"Did he say why he wanted to know about this fellow Norrington's murder?"

Gracewell growled angrily. "He hinted that there might be a clue still there, Mr Ludlow. To which I took great exception. Every room in the Duke of Clarence is cleaned thorough, by the day, as I hope you've observed."

"A clue to what?" said James, with a puzzled expression.

"Only that young fellow knows, sir."

On cue, the young man appeared in the doorway of the tap-room. Of medium build, with fair hair, he was rather thin, looking as though he'd yet to fill out properly. Harry guessed his age to be around sixteen or seventeen. He glanced at Gracewell, gave the Ludlow brothers a sour look, as if they had no right to be here, then made a move to slide into the next booth. James's voice, loud through drink, made him freeze.

"Come, sir. Would it not be more convenient to join us?"

A moment's confused silence followed the invitation, before he replied. "Convenient?"

"You was enquiring about the rooms these gents occupy," said Gracewell. "I told you then to talk to them if you wanted a look-see."

"What is it that you expect to find there?" asked Harry, standing up.

The young man looked from one to the other, clearly at a loss for a reply. "Nothing in particular."

"And in following us this evening. Was that for nothing in particular?"

"Following you?"

"Your neck must be sore from your eavesdropping as well," slurred James. "And you must tell me what is so interesting about a pet mongoose."

The stranger had been puffing himself up for a denial. But these last few words seemed to rob him of the power of delivery. He looked at Gracewell, who seemed more confused than anyone. Harry understood that look immediately.

"Thank you, Mr Gracewell. The gentleman will join us."

Harry moved to take a position that made refusal impossible. The American hesitated for a second, then complied.

"Let's have another drink, Mr Gracewell," said James, loudly. Then he peered at the new arrival, with a slight hint of belligerence. "I am drinking rum punch, sir. What will you have?"

"Perhaps a glass of port," he replied.

That produced a lopsided grin. "A capital notion. My brother and I shall join you."

Harry sat down opposite as Gracewell moved away. "I believe you know our name. I'd be obliged if you'd respond with yours."

"That's not something I'm inclined to offer."

Harry looked thoughtful for a moment. But that look was replaced by a warm smile. "Perhaps, now that Mr Gracewell has departed, you will tell us what you hoped to find in our rooms."

The youngster's brow furrowed and he bunched his fists. The effort to control his reply exaggerated both his slight frame and his Yankee accent. "I told you, sir. Nothing in particular. And I would add that I do not take kindly to being questioned in this fashion."

"You are from the United States?"

"I should have thought, sir, that was obvious."

"The northern colonies . . ." Harry paused and quickly corrected himself. "Forgive me, northern states, judging by the accent. May I enquire as to which part?"

"Long Island."

Gracewell arrived with a decanter of port and three glasses, which he immediately filled to the brim. Harry addressed his next enquiry to him. "Remind me, Mr Gracewell, of the details on that poster outside relating to the murder of Mr Norrington."

The proprietor rolled his eyes and spoke with relish as he reprised the story, from the very moment that his visitor arrived to the vision of the victim marching through the tap-room, letter in hand, to be followed out of the door by the man who later killed him. His demonic delivery had a noticeable effect on their guest, especially his closing sentence. "There's a reward for the villain that done it."

"Who is?" asked Harry.

"Why it's on that there poster, Captain Ludlow. Nathan Caufield, his name be. A native of Sag Harbor, which, I'm informed, is a nest of smugglers and thieves." Gracewell shook his head, like a man wondering at his own good fortune. "An' to think I stood an inch away from the miscreant's murdering hand."

"Thank you," said Harry, quickly, anxious to avoid a peroration on the vagaries of fate. Then, as Gracewell shuffled away, he smiled at the American. "Sag Harbor is, if I'm not mistaken, at the very northern tip of Long Island."

"So?"

"Come, sir," replied Harry earnestly. "You have an interest in the events leading to the death of Mr Norrington. So much so that you wish to search the rooms he occupied. You come from the same part of the United States as the man who stands accused. You refuse to reveal your name, which must in some way be significant. Why? Because to do so would entail some risk. Only one name would do that. I must therefore deduce that your name is the same as that on the poster outside."

"And what if I said you're wrong?"

"You could have said any name you chose a few minutes ago, since I had no grounds to disbelieve you. But your very reluctance to answer has betrayed you. If you claim now that your name is not Caufield, I cannot say I will accept it. Are you a brother or a son?"

The young man looked hard at Harry for several seconds. Then, suddenly, his thin shoulders slumped. "Son. Matthew Caufield."

Harry held out his hand. "I am pleased to meet you, Mr Matthew Caufield."

"The son of a man accused of murder."

James cut in, leaning forward eagerly. "If it would help you, sir, let me tell you that events in my life have cured me of the desire to believe that a man accused of murder is therefore guilty."

"That, too, applies to me," said Harry. "And I deduce from your wish to seek clues in our rooms, visited on the night the murder took place, that you do not think your father guilty, either."

"He's not!" said Caufield emphatically, returning Harry's stare.

"Such certainty, in a son, is very commendable. But can you prove it?"

"It is a fact, Captain Ludlow."

"Whether that is true or false, you may certainly look and see if you can find anything."

"I'm much obliged, sir."

Harry gave him a wolfish smile. "On one condition."

Caufield's eyes narrowed. "Which is?"

"Simple, Mr Caufield. My brother tells me you showed great interest in our conversation with Captain Sandford yesterday. Due to his infuriating habit of stopping every few seconds, your attempts to follow us were very obvious. I'll let you examine our rooms if you, in turn, tell us what interests you so much about us."

Caufield lifted his glass and took a hurried swig of port. "I was gnawing on the idea of asking you for a look at your rooms. But then that captain started talking and what he said was a lot more interesting."

"Like when he mentioned a pet, for instance," said James.

Harry, who could not see the significance of this topic, brushed the question aside and pursued his own line of questioning. "That does not square with following us this evening."

"After what that navy fellow said, I asked about you, Captain Ludlow. Every tongue in English Harbour is wagging as to how you lost your crew to *Endymion*. Most are betting you'll never get them back again."

"Then they'll lose," snapped Harry.

"My mind has been in a stew all day, after what I heard yesterday. I have a piece of information to trade, something that would set those fellows up at Admiralty House on their ears. It might also get my pa off the hook for Mr Norrington's murder."

"What information?"

"That's the problem. Who do I tell? And with my name, would telling get me anything other than a long time in gaol or a share of the family rope?"

"I can't answer that without knowing what you have to say."

"That Sandford fellow told you yesterday how much luck he and the other captains are having. What if I was to tell you that there's more'n a fair chance that a person here on Antigua, quite likely someone up at Admiralty House, is responsible for that?"

Harry put his hand on James, under the table, and squeezed in an effort to ensure that he said nothing about their conversation with Bessborough, then shot his brother an anxious glance. He needn't have worried. James was very drunk, sitting back with his eyes closed, and in some danger of falling asleep. Caufield couldn't see the way Harry sought to control his own features. His face was a disinterested mask by the time he looked back at the young American.

"I would be forced to ask why you think so."

Caufield sucked in a deep breath, clearly still not utterly convinced that he was doing the right thing.

"My pa's ship was taken. He wrote me all about it. How they took him by surprise, calling out his name and home port. Then the guns appeared when he was too close to get clear and this Frenchman came aboard. Man was all apologies, especially with Pa being wounded. He dressed that and poured him a drink. Then he set him adrift, with his crew, in the cutter, with a course to intercept a Royal Navy frigate."

"*Andromache,* Captain Poynton."

"That's right."

"What was your father's destination?" asked Harry.

"Martinique. He had struck a deal with an agent for the French planters on the island, to trade his goods for theirs."

"An illegal in other words."

The young man grinned for the first time since he'd sat down. "That depends on where you're sitting, Captain Ludlow. From Sag Harbor it looks like normal trade. Dare say it looked the same to all those other captains that Poynton picked up, every one happening to be a so-called illegal."

"That's hardly grounds for what you said earlier."

"I know that. But my pa was sure enough."

"Then he must have had more to go on."

"He did."

"Was Norrington involved in some way?"

"Not that I know of. All I do know is that my pa tripped over his body on the way out of the Admiralty House garden, just after he clambered over the wall." Seeing the look of confusion on Harry's face, Caufield continued: "The man was already dead by another's hand. And if my pa was set to kill him, he could have done it as easily in the rooms upstairs. Why wait till later?"

"Dillon?" said James, without opening his eyes. "Who robbed Dillon?"

"That was a blind, the robbery. Pa was lookin' for information that might lead him to the man who took his ship."

"I should have thought that was easy," said Harry. "All he had to do was to go to Guadeloupe. There can hardly be any doubt that the island is where Victor Hugues resides."

"Just one problem, Mr Ludlow. The man who took my father's ship was not Victor Hugues."

"How can you be so sure?"

"Pa was trading out of Guadeloupe when the new governor

arrived. He's seen him, close to. He even wrote me a description. The man is fat, with piglike eyes and a pock-marked skin. Dressed for the part he might be, but Pa's adamant in his letter that it wasn't Hugues that captured him."

"Then who was it?" asked James, still with his eyes closed.

The youngster's voice was steady as he replied. "All I can tell you is what I know. He's French, young, and well set with an unmarked complexion. And as for damn near breaking the furniture when Captain Sandford was talking, my pa said that the man that took his ship kept a pet mongoose."

"Could this be the same fellow that Sandford mentioned?" whispered James. "He stayed at Admiralty House. I think his name was de la Mery."

They were negotiating the stairs, something which James found difficult. It wasn't hard to knock him slightly off balance and thus interrupt the flow of his words. His whisper was not as soft as he supposed and there was some danger that Caufield, behind them, would hear. Harry apologized and took an elbow to assist him. They reached the door and entered their rooms. James sat down heavily in an armchair. Harry stood in the centre and waved his arms to their companion. Matthew Caufield talked as he searched the room, looking behind cupboards and under the furniture.

"The last name they found in Norrington's ledger was the name Nathan Caufield, with a fair copy of a certificate confirming the nature of his loss. Pa said in his letter that Norrington, when he arrived, had just penned a letter for a man called Dillon at Admiralty House, which he waved in his face."

"So what are you looking for?" asked James, forced to move so that Caufield could look under his armchair.

"A note, perhaps. An *aide mémoire*. Something that he wrote before the finished article."

"Still here after all these months?" snapped Harry. "This is nonsense. What are you really after?"

Neither brother had gleaned how on edge the young man was,

James because he'd drunk too much and Harry because of his temperament. His outburst cracked the thin veneer of Caufield's self-control. He had a slightly deranged quality in his voice, which made him seem extremely young and vunerable.

"I know it looks crazy, sir, after all this time. But what choice do I have? If the British pick up my pa they'll hang him, no matter what he pleads."

"But you have the information you've just passed to us. Take it to Admiralty House."

Even as he spoke Harry knew that would be pointless. Who'd believe the written testimony of a man accused of murder and robbery, a man who'd been positively identified as Dillon's assailant? The same thought had occurred to the young man, whose voice was full of despair.

"Who am I to lay it before? The very people who've accused him of murder? He openly admits to attacking Dillon. Norrington was found close. He could have been done in by someone in that very building, Captain Ludlow. Now since my pa reckons he was killed because of what he'd told him, who's to say I won't suffer the same fate?"

Harry had moved to lay a reassuring hand on Matthew's shoulder. But the boy hadn't finished. He pulled a crumpled letter from his coat pocket. "This is the last word I had from him, sent from St Eustatius and it's months old. I don't even know if he's still alive."

Harry edged him towards a chair, then poured him a glass of brandy. Caufield, as if seeking some form of catharsis, told them all about his father. His voice was cracking with emotion and his mind lacked sufficient concentration for a neat narrative.

"His affairs are in a mess, Captain. Have been ever since '76. He was true to King George, for his sins. Lots of the colonial Tories went to Canada or fled back to England. Not Nathan Caufield. He stayed to brazen it out. Did it too, but he lost most everything in the process. While others bought up cheap land he found himself hemmed in at every turn, without the means to trade his goods or sell abroad. And there was no money around after the British left. No one wanted to barter with a Tory, lest they suffer by association. The West Indies trade was suddenly ruined by our being subject to the Navigation Acts."

Caufield sniffed loudly, following that with a humourless laugh. "Pa didn't exactly help his case. He was fond of pointing out to the Patriots what they'd achieved as they watched their goods rot on the quayside."

"That was twenty years ago."

"Things are better now, but not much. Don't get me wrong. I support the Republic, just as I favour the Revolution in France. But my father never has and it's cost us dear. He's moved mountains to pay for my education, just as he has to keep us lookin' respectable. This trip, successful, would only have cleared the debt on his ship. The idea of a man who'd taken as much money as the owner of that pet mongoose excited him, especially since he figured that he could find him."

He didn't have to elaborate on that to Harry Ludlow, who could easily see the temptation in one thief relieving another of a quantity of treasure. Caufield had relapsed into silence, his head bowed, the crumpled letter in his fingers.

"You said the letter was from St Eustatius."

Caufield nodded. "That's where he went after he left Antigua."

"Why did he head there?"

"He reckoned he had the name of Dillon's informant on the island, who could tell him about the destinations of the illegal cargoes. Stealing the money was only a blind. That was what he was really after."

"Dillon's informant?" asked Harry slowly.

"Another Irishman called O'Dwyer. Pa figured that anything Dillon had would be in a code he couldn't read. His idea was to blackmail O'Dwyer into telling him who was sailing where. He did get to him, as well. It was the first thing I checked up on when I arrived in the West Indies."

"You talked to him?"

"No. But I watched him plenty. And my pa's as well known

in St Eustatius as O'Dwyer himself. They have done business in the past."

Looking down at the floorboards, Caufield hadn't observed the way Harry slowly stiffened. But the change in the tone of his voice made the young man look up.

"And did your father establish if he was right or wrong?"

"He sure did. I even followed his messengers to a bay on the north side of the island and saw them hand over the intelligence to Dillon in person."

"Mr Caufield, I think you'd be safer aboard my ship."

"Why?"

"I've no time to explain, sir. But you have unwittingly rendered me a service. I also have good grounds to believe that you're not safe here. If I can deduce your name from such a short acquaintance, so may others."

"And the information I have?"

"May be as damaging to your person as you expect. Even I could offer the same tale and excite disbelief. So, we must check its veracity. Once we have done that things will be easier. If you do consent to come aboard *Bucephalas,* I promise that I will do everything in my power to help you clear your father's name."

"I don't see how."

"There is a way," said Harry, without the faintest idea if he was right or wrong.

"The only sure way is to find the true culprit, sir, and force him to confess."

Harry smiled. "That is so. But saying it is one thing, achieving it another. And I suspect it's something you'd find near impossible to accomplish without help."

"And you will render me that help?"

"Have I not already said I will?" Harry looked at James, now asleep in the chair. There was a double blessing in that. First, James was not awake to observe his dissimulation. Secondly, he provided a handy physical task that would end Caufield's questions. "But first you must help me get my brother out of here. I fear he will prove a heavy burden."

CHAPTER TWENTY-EIGHT

"GONE?" asked Bessborough, sitting up in bed. His nightcap had slipped to the side of his head, which made him look very like a cuckolded husband in a Restoration comedy. "Gone where?"

Dillon shrugged and his voice was filled with irony as he replied. After all, he had no idea what Bessborough had said to the brothers out of his hearing.

"Who knows? I most certainly don't. Ludlow slipped his cable during the night. He was observed from the deck of *Diomede*. Sandford was here with us, and his officers had no instructions to interfere. We can only assume he's gone after Captain Toner. Perhaps, in hindsight, it was unwise to issue those orders quite so quickly."

"I had a choice, Dillon. You said so yourself. They are his men by right. I cannot stand between Captain Toner and the law."

"I fear you wasted a good dinner, sir."

"Should we send someone after him?" asked the admiral. His political assistant raised one of his thin ginger eyebrows in a quizzical way. "Perhaps we can demand that he remains in port till Toner returns. For the good of the service. I do represent the law around here and have the power to detain any ship I please."

Dillon shook his head. "I doubt he'd agree, just as I fear it would be unwise to insist. I think Captain Ludlow has smoked your game and decided to engage in a touch of duplicity."

Bessborough frowned and straightened his nightcap. "So there is nothing we can do?"

"No, sir."

Both Dillon and the admiral had supped copiously themselves.

The older man's slightly puffy appearance and bloodshot eyes testified to the condition of his head. His political assistant, on the other hand, blessed with a Celtic liver, showed no ill effects from the previous day's debauch. His apparent immunity to the after-effects of black crab pepper pot and the bottle annoyed Bessborough, which was obvious by the tone of his next remark.

"If there is nothing we can do, Dillon, why the devil did you bother to wake me at this hour?"

Dillon smiled at what was clearly intended as a rebuke. His voice had all the silken irony of his race when he replied.

"I had a choice, sir. You'd either berate me at a later hour for not waking you, or do so now. I chose the course that afforded us both a degree of discomfort."

James yawned as he came on deck. He felt heavy and listless, with a dry mouth and a foul-tasting tongue, adding to that a dull ache in his temples that would not go away. He had certainly drunk too much, thus ensuring a disturbed night's sleep, staying abed in a vain effort to compensate. Now as he saw the sails aloft, full of wind, he realized that it was not only drink that had interrupted his slumbers.

"Good morning, James," cried Harry, from the windward side of the deck, his blond hair flapping in the fresh breeze.

This earned him a dyspeptic look from the younger Ludlow, who was annoyed at his older brother's apparent immunity to nature's revenge. Harry was the picture of rude good health, with a pink face and sparkling eyes. James looked around the deck, noticing that the yards were braced right round, lying almost fore and aft, as the *Bucephalas* beat up, close-hauled into the wind. Then his eyes swept around the horizon and observed the obvious fact that they were out of sight of land.

"We are at sea?"

Harry laughed at that. "Your nautical education proceeds at a snail's pace, brother; but it does proceed."

James put his fingers to his temples and rubbed them slowly.

"Do not bait me, Harry. I am not in the mood."

His brother laughed even louder, then called out the orders that set his ship round in a long sweep to larboard. The deck was full of running men, sprinting aloft or hauling on ropes. Harry called his instructions in a continuous stream and James watched as the bowsprit swung steadily through an arc until the *Bucephalas* settled on to her new heading. Immediately the motion of the ship eased, as the waves, the current, and the wind all favoured her passage, instead of opposing it.

"You need some coffee, some food, and plenty of fresh air," called Harry.

The deck tilted as the *Bucephalas* increased speed, her bows dipping in and out of the Atlantic swell. James felt an unaccustomed queasiness in his stomach as he lurched across to join Harry. His brother, taking an arm, proceeded to examine him closely, a smile playing around his lips.

"That's the truth, James, and no mistake. In fact, you seem a trifle green around the gills. Surely you've not lost your sea-legs after two days ashore?"

"Bessborough's local cuisine, I don't doubt. That pepper and crab dish, particularly."

James using both hands, steadied himself by the rail and took several deep breaths. A mug of steaming coffee was pushed into his hand and the combined effect of these two tonics meant that he could listen to Harry order their breakfast with something approaching equanimity.

"I take it that we are going after Toner," he said.

"We are."

"How do you know where Toner is?"

"Right now, I don't."

James frowned and looked around the empty horizon. "But you have some notion of his whereabouts."

Harry grinned at him. "Not the faintest."

"So are we to wander the seas and rely on luck? I cannot believe it. You are endlessly lecturing me on how large, not to mention how unforgiving, the ocean is."

James saw that Harry's grin had widened, something which produced an exactly contrary expression in him. "You know how that smug air infuriates me, brother."

"Do I?"

"Yes, you do! So please enlighten me as to our destination."

"How much do you remember of last night?"

James's face screwed up as he tried to remember. "The dinner. Going back to the inn."

"And Matthew Caufield?"

"Who?"

Harry pointed aloft, to a solitary figure sitting in the crosstrees. "The young American eavesdropper. And what about the pet mongoose, do you recall that?"

James groaned, though it was impossible to tell if that reaction was brought about by pain or a search for his missing memories. Harry kindly filled him in, though leaving out of his explanation the parts he'd missed, especially the exact contents of Nathan Caufield's letter, which the youngster had allowed him to read.

"So we're following in his father's footsteps."

"To St Eustatius. Do you know of it?"

James intoned his reply like a particularly dogmatic pedagogue. "It's mentioned in a book I bought in the Canaries, penned by a Frenchman called Père Labatt. It claims to be a history of West Indian islands. St Eustatius is, according to the good Father, a Dutch possession, a trading post, rather dull and earnest in the tradition of the race."

"That it is. And along with the Danish Virgin Islands, St Bartholomew and St Croix, it's a prime landfall for illegal traders."

"You think Toner will be there?"

"What an absurd notion, James!" replied Harry. "Few ships carrying illegal cargoes would risk putting to sea with a British frigate in the offing."

"Do I have to drag an explanation out of you with a crowbar, brother!" snapped James.

"Too much port and rum punch, James. I should have warned

you of its deleterious effects. It may taste like fruit . . ."

James closed his eyes and rubbed his forehead again, squeezing the skin between extended fingers. "It's the very devil, Harry. I never normally suffer like this. I wish I'd stayed at the Clarence with my books."

Harry decided that his brother had suffered enough. Matthew Caufield came down from the tops and joined them just as James was discussing Bessborough's dinner and his wife's reference to their French guest de la Mery. Then suddenly he stopped, rubbing his aching forehead.

"You know I think even she mentioned that damned mongoose to de Brissot. I was only half listening, unfortunately, being engaged in another conversation. Not that she mentioned it by name. But she said something about his pet treating her brocades like pythons."

Dreaver called them to their breakfast. Harry led the way into the cabin. There, under the young American's eager gaze, he outlined his plans, which were simple. Suborn O'Dwyer, by bluff or by threat, then catch this filibuster.

"Whose name, we are now all agreed, is Antoine de la Mery?" said Matthew Caufield, turning to James.

"I don't think we enjoy the luxury of certainty," James replied.

"What about coincidence?"

James began to nod, but stopped himself before the pain became too much to bear. Had he not been suffering still he would have picked up the obvious omission in what had just been said. Harry had made no mention, while Caufield was present, of Bessborough. Nor had he alluded to his primary reason for being in the West Indies, Toner, Pender, or the recovery of his crew.

"Are you not over-simplifying things, brother? This fellow has eluded the entire squadron. He will not be so easy to find."

Harry merely shrugged. "It's simpler than it would be elsewhere. First of all, we're not a navy frigate, so if he spots us, he'll be less tempted to run."

"That assumes you can get close enough in the first place."

"The Caribbean differs from other seas. The winds are generally steady in the north-east, except around the islands, and the trade routes have a regularity lacking in other oceans. Ships arriving in the West Indies still sail along lines of latitude to their destination. Those leaving can only do so by three routes: the Mona passage, the Windward passage, and the Florida channel."

"Is not this illegal trade mainly carried out between islands? And have you not told me yourself, many times, the difficulties in making a rendezvous at sea?"

Harry frowned. "Yes. But that does not alter the wind. The only variable is time and destination. This de la Mery, vouchsafed similar intelligence, is finding his targets and taking ships by the dozen, well ahead of Bessborough's cruisers. Given the same information I think I can find him."

James pointed to the young American. "Then you believe what our young friend told you about the contents of his father's letter?"

Matthew Caufield didn't bridle at this because it was a reasonable question, and one he'd asked himself many times. Besides, James Ludlow hadn't read it, as his brother had. The obvious answer was that taken with Bessborough's request, Nathan Caufield's suspicions were a near certainty. But Harry hadn't told the young man about the admiral's worries, or his ham-fisted attempt to engage their help. Nor had he bothered to enlighten his brother on the matter of what he intended to do about such knowledge. Given his condition, James had also failed to make the connection.

"I don't have to believe any more than this. That O'Dwyer is Dillon's agent. That is a secret he will want kept. The price will be to provide us with the intelligence that is, by methods we don't know, being made available to this Frenchman."

The mention of the name O'Dwyer cleared James's thinking. He appeared angry with himself. But at the same moment he caught the look in Harry's eyes that begged him not to enquire too deeply, lest by doing so he reveal more than the young American needed to know. Mentally he cursed his brother's devious nature, which left him somewhat adrift, unaware of which information was damaging and which was not. That knowledge, and the irritation it engendered, made him keep talking in a situation where Harry probably required silence. Partly it became an indirect attempt to lever him into being more open.

"The supposition that it is de la Mery is, as Matthew just pointed out, based on coincidence. Even proven, who's to say he isn't operating alone? If Dillon can find the routes these ships take, so can a Frenchman."

"But you must allow that Matthew's father has a point, James. Let us assume for a moment that it is the man we think. He has not only the location of the illegals, but the precise rendezvous that has been arranged for our cruisers, which means he can avoid them."

"Is that so very significant?" demanded James, doggedly.

Harry missed the tone of disquiet, hearing only another example of James's ignorance in nautical matters. "Yes. Without certain knowledge of their position, and sailing in the same waters, he'd be bound to come up against one of them at some time. The clear fact that he never does quite explodes the notion of mere luck."

"Are you basing all of this entirely on the contents of my father's letter?" asked Matthew.

Harry replied forcibly, and with a lack of sincerity which was obvious to his brother. "Didn't Marcus Sandford not say something regarding that? Poynton certainly did. You remember him, James, the man with the loud voice who damned our arrival."

"I know who Poynton is, Harry, and so does Matthew."

"Everyone seems to have missed what Nathan Caufield spotted months ago. Yet if anybody should have seen it, Poynton was the one."

James rubbed his temples again. "You will have to go on, brother. My brain is lamentably slow this morning."

"Come, James. It must be clear to even the most muddled head. That was the only occasion when a British frigate picked up the crews. At all other times, barring Effingham's fluke, they've landed up on other islands, all well away from their home ports. Hence the delay in information coming together. In the case Matthew's father cited, either de la Mery realized that such a policy was folly, or his contact in Antigua, aware of the damage that could be done, told him to desist."

"You are leaping, Harry. You go from speculating on a contact in Antigua to a certainty so well placed as to be able to warn this filibuster that he must change his ways. Bessborough—"

"Let us leave him out of this," said Harry quickly. "I must go on deck and see to the needs of the ship."

James caught him alone as soon as he could get away from Matthew Caufield. "I have finally realized what you are about, brother. Does the young man know that you have quite different priorities?"

"I hope not," said Harry, coldly.

"Would it not have been simpler to take young Caufield to Bessborough with the information in his father's letter?"

"That letter tells him nothing he doesn't already suspect. And even if it points a finger, it uncovers no secrets. It also exposes us as being in possession of information regarding some of Dillon's network."

"I was wondering if Bessborough would be grateful enough to give you Toner's course?"

"I was foolish enough to think that news of d'Albret's frigates would help us, but it didn't. Given that Matthew came ashore with the messengers, whatever orders Toner was given were probably based on intelligence received from St Eustatius. That information will not be divulged to us. Therefore we must go to the island, find out what we can from O'Dwyer, calculate the point of contact for *Endymion,* and be there at the right time."

"I still think we might have done better to have stayed in English Harbour."

"Can you imagine me sitting there, James, swapping yarns with the other captains and twiddling my thumbs for months on end?"

"Surely not months?"

"You heard Bessborough yourself. *Endymion* is well victualled. There is no gain to Toner being in port. In fact, to his mind, the minute he returns he's beached, with or without prizes. The admiral can hardly send him out on his own again. The very best he can hope for is convoy duty. Bessborough will send someone else on patrol, one of his favourites. To make matters worse, Bessborough is bound to find a way of informing him that we are in these waters. No, brother. It all favours him staying at sea. The only thing we'd observe, if we'd stayed tied up in Antigua, is assembling convoys, weed growing on our hull, and perhaps, if he's lucky, Toner's prizes sailing into the harbour."

"We might also have unmasked Bessborough's spy."

"That's his job, James, not ours."

"We have to get our crew back?"

"That's right. And before Toner kills someone."

"Land ho! Islands fine on both bows."

Harry looked up to the masthead before he took out the telescope.

"St Eustatius?" asked James, well aware that he'd receive no answer to his previous proposition.

"No. We would have to sail north-east past St Kitts," said Harry grimly. "I sailed south-east from Antigua, just in case they were tempted to send Marcus Sandford to shadow me."

Harry pointed with his telescope to the two extinct volcanoes that were now old Caribbean islands.

"Guadeloupe is the island to the north. The other, smaller one is Marie Galante. And dead ahead, if you care to go aloft and look, you will spy a long chain of rocky islets. They, James, are Les Isles des Saintes. This is the very channel where Rodney and Admiral Hood beat de Grasse in '82."

James looked eagerly over the side, for the first time like a man without a hangover. "So, brother, this is the place you fought your duel?"

CHAPTER TWENTY-NINE

GARMOND flogged was a different creature. Gone was the wry smile that looked upon the folly of his fellow sailors with disinterested amusement. His words of complaint now had a harder edge. And his efforts to engage Pender took on an urgency that had been lacking previously. He never stopped alluding to their fate, determined to undermine any prospect of relief. And since their mess tables were back to back he was a hard man to avoid. They were below decks, off watch, sweating in the heat despite the breeze coming in through the open scuttles. All he had to do was turn round. This he did frequently, despite the pain he must be feeling from his lacerated back.

"So, Pious Pender. Where would you say your old captain is today? No doubt your Mr Ludlow is wearing out the pavements between Billy Pitt's and the Admiralty to get you back, pounding on doors and usin' them rotten boroughs you told me about to issue all manner of threats. Happen he's got the First Lord by the scruff this very minute."

"The one thing he won't be doin', Garmond, is sitting around idle, which is what you're hintin' at. The trouble is you don't know him like I do. He'll set the whole of London aflame if he has to."

"Like as not, Pender, like as not. Not a man of his aboard that don't praise him to the skies for his care and attention. They all think like you. That he'll move heaven and earth and sup with the devil to get you set loose. Only trouble is that they can see what you're missin'. That he's on one side of the briny and we're three months away on the other."

This had become Garmond's persistent theme, one that being

the plain truth worried Pender. "You don't miss any chance to point that out, do you?"

"They can reckon their own odds, mate. They don't need the likes of me to do it for 'em. Given Toner's habits, they can work out how many of them might be set to meet their maker before their precious captain can get word out to the Caribbee to save 'em. Just as they can see, with their own two eyes, not to mention their back skin, how much good you did with your letters and petitions."

"How'd you know about that, Garmond?"

"You can keep the likes of that from the officers, mate. I got a keener eye."

"Don't give yourself airs, Garmond. Someone talked. Like as not the same mouth that mentioned the captain's rotten boroughs, for I never did."

Garmond winked at him. "Happen they did. Happen I knew afore I was appraised. Happen that there's more of your men keen to talk to me than you'd like."

"It's easy to spout about mutiny, friend," said Pender. "A lot harder to do it." Garmond opened his mouth to speak, but Pender cut him off, his voice full of passion. "But the hardest thing to do is survive after. There's nothin' the navy hates more'n mutiny. They'll hound every man aboard this ship, exempt or no, till their dying day, just for the pleasure of seeing them swing."

"Mutiny, Pender. Now there's a notion."

"Don't you josh me, Garmond. It's what you've been on about since we came aboard."

Garmond grinned and spun a little further on his bench seat. The act caused him to pull a face, as the pain in his torn back intensified. "Mutiny? I don't recall ever using the word, myself, mate. But I'll grant it's a good one."

Pender stood up abruptly and took his mess kit over to the butt kept for scraps. The foul odour that rose from this stood testimony to the rotten state of their provisions, pork and beef which had been years in the cask. Perhaps even the pigs in the manger would turn up their snouts at such feed, leaving it to be tossed over the side, an act which, in deep water, rapidly brought sharks into their wake. These creatures seemed to thrive on food that was putrid. The water in the scuttlebutt was equally bad. In this climate it turned brackish in no time, having been in casks since they left Portsmouth. He was troubled by the heat as much as Garmond's words. The real difficulty being that the man had a point, to which his own painful shoulders bore witness.

The way Toner had behaved these last few days, since he'd flogged Garmond and the men who'd dropped his goods, had made matters worse. The captain was rarely off the deck now. Officers who'd shown scant gentility in the past knew that they were expected to work the men even harder. Under the baleful eye of their commander, eager to please, there was no act which did not earn a crack of the rope's end. They too could hear the shot rolling round the ship at night and knew what threatened. If any of them concluded that their captain was to blame they were in no position to do anything about it. Only Dunlop could relieve Toner, an unlikely scenario since he shared his captain's tastes. Added to that he risked being beached for the rest of his days if a subsequent court, manned entirely by naval captains, failed to uphold his actions.

Only two officers, Mr Wheeler and young Callander, sought to evade this addition to the already harsh discipline. Toner, observing this, had openly upbraided Wheeler, threatening him with being confined to quarters. The third lieutenant had stood up for himself, refusing to be cowed as he challenged Toner to call a court martial. This had infuriated the captain. His jaw became so clenched it seemed close to breaking. Callander had paid the price for Wheeler's intransigence. He, upbraided for the same offence, was laid across a quarterdeck gun, his breeches around his ankles. Toner took the vine sapling himself to administer this public humiliation to the recalcitrant midshipman. The boy, his face bright red and his fair hair stuck to his scalp by sweat, had not uttered a sound through this painful ordeal. Oddly enough, this act had infuriated a number of the Bucephalases more than their own frequent punishments. These men, sailors to their fingertips, had formed the backbone of Pender's resistance to Garmond and his influence. They had a very strong sense of right and wrong which went beyond their own concerns. Captains might punish, even to excess, and still hold their loyalty, if not their trust. But what Toner had done to Callander, a kindly youngster and a lad willing to learn, was plainly, to their way of thinking, downright criminal.

Pender made his way up on to the deck, where the watch on duty was going about its work. Several officers, aware of Toner by the windward gangway, were loudly abusing their divisions. Pender heard the crack of knotted rope on skin several times as he continued on to the heads, clambering out on to the thick beam that stretched out over the nettings that were slung above the deep blue water. Flowers was already there, along with several others, his crescent-shaped face filled with that contemplative look common to men at their ablutions. They were well away from Martinique now with just a ghostly shape visible over the stern, half hidden by the heat haze and, for once, in a place they could talk without any danger of being overheard.

"I made it just in time," said Pender, as the commands rang out to man the falls, preparatory to a change of course. Men were going aloft to reef the topsails, a necessary manoeuvre sailing into this wind on the larboard tack.

"I hope we're a-heading back for English Harbour soon, Pious. Maybe with an admiral in the offin' that bastard will leave the cat in the bag."

"I wouldn't swear to it, mate," Pender replied gloomily. Toner was not one to share his plans. But Pender had it from his steward that they were sailing in a wide arc, to return to the island and surprise some more illegals. After that they were off someplace else on the same errand.

"I'm beginning to think that our sea-lawyer has the right of it."

"Not you as well!" said Pender.

"The captain is a long way away, Pious. And who's to say that them bastards who has the power will heed his plea?"

"They'll do it 'cause o' the law, Flowers. I told you that a dozen times."

"So you say. But who's to be sure the news will ever reach us? It wouldn't be so bad in any old king's ship, but this here Scotchman has got me rattled an' no mistake. There's a devil in the man. An' I tell you, Pious, I ain't alone in thinkin' that."

"Happen Captain Ludlow will bring it personal. I can see him gettin' right mad when he gets my letter."

"If'n he gets it."

"He'll get it, Flowers. I know it was posted. It was confirmed by the man that did it."

The yell made them both jerk their heads up. The body falling through the clear sky was jerking like a doll, as the man tried to grab at some imaginary means of salvation. For a moment the movements stopped, as the wide-eyed victim stared at them. It was Lowden, one of the youngest and nimblest of the Bucephalases. As he dropped, he yelled Pender's name and shut his eyes. Both Flowers and Pender responded with reassuring calls. Being out on the heads they could see that he was set to miss the ship's side. The helmsman had put the wheel down anyway, to take the bows away from the area of his descent. Lowden hit the water with a huge splash and went right under as the bulk of the frigate ploughed on. Everyone watching held their breath to see if he'd be sucked in by the undertow, and emitted a collective sigh of relief when he surfaced several feet away from the side. One sailor, with more presence of mind than his mates, threw him a line, then rushed to attach another length to it so that it could be paid out for the necessary distance to keep Lowden out of the ship's turbulence.

The yelling of orders had commenced as soon as he'd parted company from the yard. But Lowden was in the wake before they started their turn. Pender and Flowers were back inboard, rushing to the opposite bulwark to see if he was safe. He had the rope in one hand. But it wasn't taut enough to keep him afloat and every so often his head slipped under the water. Callander had his coat off and looked set to go in after him.

"Belay, Mr Callander!" yelled Toner. "And I will have you properly dressed, sir, on my quarterdeck, if you please."

Toner had clearly decided against launching a boat. These were inboard, filled with water to keep the seams tight in the tropical heat. They would need to be baled or tipped before they could be hauled out and into the sea. *Endymion* came round in a tight arc, slowing as she turned, until she was wallowing on the swell. Pender took the line and called on those who'd cast the rope. They started to haul away. Lowden was pulled in towards the side of the ship, the pace of his tow being enough to keep him afloat. Aloft his mates were already lowering a whip from the main-yard, which could be used to haul him aboard.

Pender, looking over the side, could see that Lowden was bleeding on one side of his head. Perhaps he'd brushed against the barnacles which encrusted the waterline. But his hold on the rope was secure, just as the look of relief on his face was obvious. It was only then that Pender's mind turned to an obvious thought. How was it that an experienced topman, known to be nimble, had lost his footing and fallen into the sea on such a calm day, doing a job which posed no difficulty at all? And he missed the side of the ship for sure. If Lowden had been close enough to sustain a cut, then he should have been dragged under the keel. He was ruminating on this when the whip from the yard slid past his face, on its way to the outstretched hand of Lowden. He put one arm through then the other and lay back as if exhausted as the sling took his weight. Half a dozen men were on the other end, ready to haul away. Pender, looking round, saw that Toner was standing right beside them, his sword in his hand. Another line snaked down to the deck, with a hitch round the one that held Lowden so that it could be hauled inboard. Toner stepped forward and picked it up.

"Weel now. It'll be of interest to see if you can haul this cargo inboard without dropping it." Toner turned and shouted to the premier, standing on the quarterdeck. "We'll get under way again, Mr Dunlop."

"Lowden's bleeding, sir," called Pender.

Toner didn't even look at him. The watch on deck obeyed Dunlop's orders and hauled on the yards to bring the ship before the winds. Every rope creaked and strained as the frigate started to move, inching forward as Dunlop, under Toner's instructions, spun the wheel to bring the breeze in just abaft the beam. The captain's voice was low and compelling as he gave his orders to the men next to him.

"You'll haul him halfway, then treat him the same way you treated that contraband. A topman doesn't fall over the side aboard a crack frigate. And that is what this ship is going to be, the envy of the squadron. So we'll teach this grease-footed sod a wee lesson, and let him drink some more sea water once or twice. Then he'll know next time that skylarking in the tops is not to be borne."

The men on the rope couldn't allow their eyes to meet, lest by a glance they indicate their feelings on being handed such an order. Instead they looked past each other as they calculated that, unpleasant as it appeared, Lowden was secure in his sling. He might go under a few times, but he wouldn't drown. They knew he was bleeding, Pender had said so. But he'd had the strength to hang on to his rope, so it wasn't worth the skin on their backs to deny the captain his pleasure. They took the strain and pulled, hand over hand, lifting the slight body-weight of the slim topman with ease. His inert form, lying back in the sling, came above the height of the bulwarks. He dropped his head and, as his eyes caught those of his shipmates, every man on deck caught sight the great gash on his forehead. Blood mixed with sea water from his hair ran into his eyes, forcing them shut, just at the moment when Toner ordered the men to let go.

"Give him plenty of line," snapped Toner, as the men looked set to haul him up short. The heads lining the bulwarks, nearly every man off watch and a good many on, followed him down until he splashed back into the sea. Then the captain hauled on his rope, which pulled the main line in towards the side of the ship. Toner wasn't quiet now. His voice, made more sinister by the effort of pulling on the line, was loud enough to be heard the entire length of the deck.

"Now let's have him feel the kiss o' the keel."

He held the line inboard for a full minute before he let go. A nod to the hauliers had them pulling like crazy as they brought Lowden up again. He wasn't lying back this time. His hands were above his head, clutching the rope that held him, trying feebly to inch his way higher. His shirt had been torn off his back by the rough planking and his side was raw flesh. Pender glared at Toner and started to move towards him. A hand grabbed his arm and pulled him back. He swung round and found himself face to face with Garmond.

"Don't even think on it," he whispered. "That bastard has a sword. An' if you go anywhere near him, in the mood he's in, he'll run you through."

"Let him go, I tell ye."

The voice rang out and Pender turned to see that Toner had his sword raised. It was hard to tell if he was threatening the sailors or the line they held. Either way the men had no choice. Even their hesitation might cause trouble enough. They released the line and Lowden's squirming body was dropped back into the water. Toner kept his sword raised to ensure that they paid out enough rope. With the ship now moving steadily through the water, there was no need for Toner to haul Lowden in. The undertow would accomplish that without assistance.

"Shark!"

That single cry from the men still aloft made them take a grip on the line. Those nearest slid past Toner's upraised arm to help. Everyone's head was over the side, their gaze following the pointed finger of the topman. The ship's wake seemed suddenly full of them, all but one seemingly intent on other things. A single dark blue fin sliced through the water at speed, heading for the writhing

body of Lowden, still beneath the waves. His shipmates were hauling like mad, trying to take up the slack of the line that Toner had
made them drop. Pender and Garmond saw Lowden emerge dripping from the sea, first his head, then his bloody chest. They also
saw how close the fin was. Pender screamed at his shipmates, uselessly, for they were already doing their best. Lowden's feet cleared
the sea just as the shark, turning sideways, rose out of the water.
Time seemed to stand still as the men aboard the ship gazed into
those open jaws, those jagged teeth in uneven rows above the soft
white flesh of the creature's underbelly. It took Lowden just above
the thigh, the soft squish of its teeth sinking into the flesh audible from the deck.

The men on the line felt the extra weight and increased their
efforts. The shark, half its body hauled clear of the water by the
effect, started to tear at Lowden, swinging in a frenzy. The combination pulled him apart. A great gush of blood followed the
shark as it suddenly dropped back into the sea, half of the victim's body in its jaws. The sudden loss of weight brought the
remainder of the stricken sailor shooting up past their eyes. His
mouth was open and he was screaming. Blood ran down the trails
of viscera straggling from the great wound that lay open where
his hips had been. Then the scream died as the loss of so much
took away the power to remain conscious. Toner had stepped back
in horror at the sight, and it was left to another to haul on the
rope he'd dropped and pull the half of Lowden that remained
inboard, there to be laid gently on to the deck. He gave a few
spasmodic jerks, his eyes opened in a wild stare that cursed his
captain. Then with a final shudder, he died, right at Toner's feet.

"I'll kill him for this," growled Pender. "So help me God, with
my own hand."

"Take it easy, mate," said Garmond, taking hold of him in a
firm grip. "There's a time and there's a place. But this ain't it."

Pender twisted his way out of the grip and made for the companion-way. He knew that if he stayed on deck nothing would
restrain him, not even the prospect of a rope for the murder of

the captain. As he blinked on entering the gloomy interior of the ship, he could feel the stinging of the tears in his eyes. Stumbling, he made his way down to his mess table. The stench of the butt full of rotten meat seemed to fill the air, adding to the feeling of nausea. The image of the remains of Lowden filled his mind and he fought back the heaving in his stomach. He stood up and leant against the side of the ship. Then his eyes caught sight of the greasy trail that led from the butt to the open scuttle. Slowly, transfixed, he walked its path, until his nostrils picked up the odour of the open sea. He forced himself to go back to the butt and look in. It was now half full. Yet it had been near the rim when he threw away the remains of his dinner.

That was why the sharks had come. Someone, below decks, had slopped the contents of that putrid butt out into the sea, attracting those great fish to feed. And when they'd come they'd found an even more attractive prospect, one that writhed and bled in the water. That took Pender's mind back to Lowden's fall. He was a noted topman amongst a very competent crew. And he was a Bucephalas. Anyone could slip and fall. That was the nature of the work they performed. But if Pender had been asked to bet his pay warrant on anyone, he would have plumped for Lowden to keep his feet. Then there was that gash on his forehead. Perhaps he hadn't fallen, after all. Perhaps he'd been knocked off his perch, while down below someone had fed that rancid brew into the sea to make sure that when he did so, he would not survive. Pender swung round and rushed back up to the deck. The men were gathered round the remains, listening as Toner instructed them to sew him in canvas.

"Let that be a lesson to all," he cried. He was glancing around the cold faces that surrounded him, again displaying, in his look and manner, a trace of that uncertainty he'd shown the day Garmond and the others dropped the contraband. "He was lucky not to land on the deck, which would have made his end quicker. But death comes to us aw, and rest assured he shall be afforded a decent burial."

Pender had moved up to stand beside Garmond. The other man looked at him, taking in the white face and the cold glare. "I'm with you now, Garmond. It's time to stop rolling shot, and start breaking heads."

"I'm glad it's come, an' I won't say different. But it saddens me that it's taken this to bring it about."

Pender wouldn't look at him. His eyes were fixed on Toner. "Never fear, Garmond. The man who did this will pay, and pray to be thrown to the sharks himself, instead of bearing the fate I have in mind for him."

CHAPTER THIRTY

BUCEPHALAS passed the looming bulk of St Kitts at first light, staying well clear of the island. Harry was on the quarterdeck, telescope in hand, scanning the horizon all around. All he saw for his trouble were small fishing boats rocking on the swell, with the shellfish catchers closer inshore. The illegals would weigh anchor at night, so as to be out of sight by daybreak. He lifted his glass to take in the bulk of Brimstone Hill, which rose eight hundred feet above the surface of the sea. The battlements of the Fort of St George were still ruined, having been destroyed by the French during the last conflict. Then he swung his glass northwards to take in St Eustatius. The little Dutch possession looked tiny from here, more of an outcrop than a proper island. But Harry knew what level of trade would pass through the port in wartime, a trade that would earn a blind eye from the British navy even if the Dutch, in support of their new masters, did declare war.

The island had no garrison and the harbour was purely commercial. The illegals were only taken when they'd cleared the port, which could be seen clearly from the top of Brimstone Hill. Thus St Eustatius represented a known entity which posed no military threat to Britain's position in the Caribbean. To subdue it would not stop the trade, merely move it to another, less observable location. The island had only suffered in the American War because of Admiral Rodney's naked greed, a greed which, as Harry explained to the others, had distracted the man from his primary duty and had cost the king his American colonies. The Dutch colonists had angered the admiral by saluting the new flag of the Continental Confederation. This was construed as open support for the rebellious American colonists fighting King George. Rodney descended without warning and sacked the town, then delayed here for a month, flying a Dutch flag above the harbour, so that incoming ships would be unaware of the danger. Meanwhile the comte de Grasse, shadowed by the inferior forces of Admiral Grave, had sailed into Chesapeake Bay and blockaded the British army. Rodney made a fortune out of the sack of St Eustatius. That was small comfort to General Cornwallis at Saratoga, forced to surrender by the blockading French fleet. Or to his sovereign, King George, who lost all hope of retaining his American colonies hard on the heels of that defeat.

"Well I, for one, thank the good Lord for that," said Matthew Caufield. "My pa told me all about it, Captain Ludlow. And given how much Rodney made, with a bit of the corsair in him to boot, he could never decide whether to curse the man or praise him."

"Harry has no such difficulty," said James with a wicked grin. "He will bore you rigid, given half a chance, telling you that if Admiral Hood had been in command, he would have met de Grasse with the whole fleet, and you'd still be a British subject."

"I shall say no more on the subject," Harry replied, smiling.

He was well aware of his tendency to thump the table when discussing Rodney. He couldn't help himself. The man's actions still made him angry even after all these years. Worse still was the fact that he'd got away with such blatant chicanery, being recalled to action and leading the combined fleets against the French at the Saintes. Following that brilliant victory, his position as Britain's premier mariner was unassailable.

He headed for the shrouds again with his telescope. Soon he was up in the crosstrees, telescope trained on the approaching island. Rodney notwithstanding, it was wise to be cautious when entering a Caribbean harbour. The West Indies operated like a see-saw when it came to who possessed what. The British would take a French island only to find the enemy had attacked one of theirs. Or an expedition would suddenly arrive from Europe intent on capturing a particularly important source of sugar or trade. It had something to do with territory and everything to do with wealth. Good harbours, like St Lucia and Antigua, were prized for themselves. But often it was the greed of the sugar lobby that directed the varying military moves. The expression "as rich as a creole," originally French, had crept into usage in England. The eastern fortunes of the "nabobs," like Warren Hastings and Clive, paled beside the total amount of money to be earned in the lush Caribbean. Some of the greatest fortunes in England had been earned out here, based on the burgeoning desire in an expansionist England for coffee, cocoa, and tea, products sweetened by sugar. Easy to make a profit when your labour was black and not in receipt of a wage.

The ever present trade wind suddenly made the *Bucephalas* heel over as she cleared the lee of St Kitts. The sails cracked sharply as she took the breeze and Harry heard the orders given to get aloft and shorten sail. Tucking the telescope in his breeches he slid down a backstay to the deck, then went below to join his brother and Caufield for a late breakfast.

"It's not a very inspiring place, Harry," said James as they entered the roadstead. "I preferred the other islands."

"It's a damn sight more inspiring than the last time I was here. Rodney's men burnt every building on the shoreline before they left."

"Pilot boat approaching, Captain," said Dreaver.

"Then we'd best break out a bottle of our finest claret, lest we get stung for another exorbitant mooring fee."

"For God's sake let's get some food inside us," said James, "before we risk a drink."

Conlon O'Dwyer stood on the steps of his warehouse watching as the newcomer moored in the roadstead. He was a prosperous-looking man, with a round, cheerful face and bright blue eyes. His skin had a high colour that indicated a love of the bottle, which was exaggerated by his near-white hair. The ship was unfamiliar and that itself made it an object of curiosity. But more to ponder was its lines. It was not a vessel designed to carry much in the way of cargo, and the rows of gunports told of a level of armament superior to that borne by a proper merchant ship. So, a warship, with seven ports a side, about a hundred feet in length, displacing perhaps three hundred tons. But not a national one, since the ship flew no flag at the mainmast to identify the country of origin. His was not the only eye on the *Bucephalas*. In a world full of danger it paid to be alert. Every ship's captain in the harbour, and every other factor, had taken note of her as she came in, just as Harry knew they would. If he sought to engage in privateering, then these would be the very ships, as a Letter of Marque, that he would be entitled to prey on. In other circumstances, to preserve his anonymity, he would never have come near the place. But that quality of mystery had to be sacrificed to a more important consideration.

The pilot spoke English in the Dutch manner, slowly and with too much emphasis on each word. Not that his conversation interfered much with his drinking. But, like pilots all over the world, he was a garrulous soul, and a great source of local information. For instance he not only informed them of the fact that ships went missing, with the minimum encouragement he went on to name them, one by one, unaware that Matthew Caufield was behind him, writing them down. And the Hollander had no doubt, at all, where the blame lay.

"The trade is close to ruin, man. That Victor Hugues fellow is taking ship after ship. No one dares sail in daylight, yet still we hear that our cargoes are intercepted. He's worse than the Englanders, damn him."

James picked up the third bottle and emptied it into the pilot's tankard. Then he shook it with a deliberate air, meant to convey a message that there was no more to follow. The Dutchman took the hint, calmly drained his drink, and stood up, making his way out of the cabin in such a steady fashion that anyone would wonder if he was an abstainer. Harry went out to see him over the side, then returned to the cabin, where James and Caufield waited.

"Time to go ashore, I think, and see if Mr O'Dwyer will oblige us with some of the same kind of information."

"Hail fellow well met is the easiest way to describe him," said Matthew, as they were rowed ashore. "Conlon O'Dwyer's welcome in every tavern, for he's an amusing man, if a mite loud in his jocularity for my taste. And he's loud in the way he condemns King George, with many a toast raised to a free Ireland."

"That's probably how he gets his information," said Harry. "There's nothing like rum to loosen the tongue."

That remark was made with a knowing look towards his brother, who responded with a slight grimace.

"Getting it is one thing, Captain Ludlow. Retaining it is quite another. He is a trencherman of the first rank, who both eats and drinks to excess. He can barely get to his feet after a drinking bout. Were it not for his faithful servant, a Cormorante negro called Joseph, he'd spend most nights in the gutter."

"This negro," said James. "Is he of the sort that the Codrington family tried to breed?"

"The very same," Caufield replied. "I'm surprised that you have knowledge of them."

"A most amazing phenomenon. They are mentioned in a tract I picked up in the Canaries. Do you know of them, Harry?"

"I'm ashamed to admit I do not," he replied, as the barge crew boated oars and glided alongside the harbour wall.

James's attention had moved to other things, judging by the worried look on his face. "That ladder looks a mite slippery."

He was right. The wooden frame that ran up the harbour wall, exposed because of the low tide, was barnacle encrusted and covered in slime. Harry had two sailors follow his brother up, to make sure he didn't end up in the debris-filled water that washed against the jetty. He climbed it with practised ease, as did Matthew Caufield. The three men stood on the top of the harbour wall, rubbing the marks of slime from their coats, aware that every eye that could observe them was firmly fixed on their persons. Harry gave Dreaver some money, told him to keep the boat crew both sober and chaste. He also warned them to guard their tongues, then indicated to Matthew to lead the way, and with an exaggerated air of ease, engaged his brother in loud conversation.

"You were about to tell me about these negroes, James."

James was aware that his brother's interest was minimal. But he entered into the game with a reply that was louder than necessary.

"Cormorantes are African, brother, but of a height and build superior to most of their fellows. They are also intractable and extremely fractious, according to my correspondent. So much so that they make poor slaves. They refuse to work manually and only consent to undertake other duties with marked reluctance."

"Look, James. Close to you can still see the scars of Rodney's raid." James followed Harry's pointed finger, towards the black marks that showed where the flames had licked at the outside walls of the factories. Indeed there were still gaps in the line of warehouses where some of the buildings had collapsed. Harry scowled, before returning to the subject. "Why did Codrington bother with them?"

"He felt that they were misunderstood. That educated and properly trained they would make excellent overseers. They have, it seems, scant regard for their fellow Africans. It was a reasonable notion. Indeed, even though he failed, Codrington came to admire them greatly, claiming that every man would do well to treat them as a friend, since they had one positive trait to add to their less worthy ones, and that was loyalty."

Caufield had dropped back slightly, close enough to join in the conversation. "O'Dwyer bought three of them at auction some years back. He uses two of them to sail to Antigua and back, those are the ones I followed, while Joseph acts as his personal servant. I even followed them ashore and saw them hand their package to Dillon."

"You've observed this Joseph at close quarters, it seems?"

"Hard not to, Captain Ludlow. He's near six and a half feet tall and built like a brick chimney-breast. They say that he has the gift of second sight, as well."

"What about his language?"

Matthew laughed. "He has better English than me. The Codringtons raised them to speak like men of parts."

"And can Joseph write?" Caufield snapped his head round quickly, to observe Harry's smile. "With such a servant O'Dwyer need not worry about his drinking. And it's a habit in these parts, a bad one, to act as if negroes do not exist, even men six and half feet tall."

They were on the main thoroughfare now, hemmed in by the crowds that lined the route. Every building, tall and Dutch gabled, was for business, each having stalls in front manned by vendors loud in their proclamations of fair play and bargain prices. Such assurances were delivered in every language used in the Caribbean, the same as the bargains being struck in every tavern. As they passed each warehouse the smell advertised its function. The air was full of the odour of spices one second and coffee the next. Tobacco would then predominate only to be overborne by the sickly sweet smell of molasses. The Portuguese Jews, in their long robes and decorated hats, traded in gold, silver, and jewellery, or in luxuries like silk, lace, and fine wines, which eased the life of all these wealthy planters, and their wives, far from their native land. There were bookshops and bakers, filling their nostrils with the familiar smell of fresh bread and ship's biscuit. Costermongers sat behind heaps of vegetables and fruit, while to the rear stacked casks of lime juice stood ready for purchase. Butchers had open warehouses, with sides of beef, pork, and lamb hanging in dark caverns, with barely observable negroes, squatting in the gloom, employed to keep the flies at bay. They passed the abattoir, and held their noses against the reek of rotting flesh that emanated from the insect-filled interior.

Nearer the quayside the smell was of fish, with tables groaning under the astounding variety of brightly coloured produce dragged from the surrounding sea. Live crabs and lobsters climbed across each other in damp casks, while near the water's edge, under a canopy of screaming frigate birds, men were skinning and gutting, preparatory to salting and barrelling food that would feed those who manned the ships in the harbour. And all this activity was happening under a blazing sun and a deep blue sky free of clouds. James pronounced himself entranced and Harry noticed that his observant eye was in constant motion, as if storing these sights in some special place, to be retrieved and placed on canvas at some future date.

"O'Dwyer's place is at the far end," said Matthew. "Do you wish to go straight there?"

"You know him better than I. Should we pin him now, or wait till he's in his cups? He may be more amenable in drink."

"I dare say," replied the American with feeling. "But, sober, he controls Joseph. His negro has as much regard for a white man as he does for an African. If we upset O'Dwyer when he's drunk, we might have to deal with his slave."

CHAPTER THIRTY-ONE

HARRY entered the front portion of O'Dwyer's warehouse ahead of the others, blinking slightly as his eyes, after such brilliant sunshine, adjusted to the gloom. The place was heaped with ships' stores, and the wind blowing in through the open front doorway picked up the dust from the floor and swirled it about. At the far end of the building the man he took to be Joseph was standing with his back to a door, one that looked as though it led to some form of office. Given what Caufield had said, he imagined O'Dwyer's giant negro would have a touch of the pugilist about his features. Nothing could have been further from the truth. He had the build certainly, barely concealed by a fine white linen shirt. But his smooth unblemished skin shone even in the half-light, while his facial features showed a degree of refinement. His carriage, as he moved a few paces to greet them, was that of a very superior person. And the way in which they were examined by his huge brown eyes was more like the act of a major-domo at some ducal establishment than the servitor of a lowly West Indian factor. The voice likewise, when Harry asked after the owner, was deep and refined.

"And who should I say is calling, sir?"

Harry introduced himself, leaving the others out since the use of the name Caufield might ring some alarm in his master's mind.

"And might I enquire as to the nature of your business, sir?"

That stalled Harry for a moment. He hadn't expected the question, assuming that his use of the title "captain" would explain quite adequately his presence in the establishment of a ship's chandler. His hesitation made the negro smile, which exposed a set of perfect teeth so large and white that they eclipsed every other feature. As Joseph turned away, which he did without waiting for a response, Harry heard the soft laugh, deep and throaty, which made the muscular shoulders under the white shirt twitch. Then he was gone through the door.

"An imposing creature, Harry," said James.

"Indeed."

The slightly terse note in Harry's voice made Caufield laugh. "That's his way, Captain Ludlow. He thinks himself a cut above us mere whites. It's a favourite sport of his to humble men who think they are his masters."

It was now James's turn to be terse. "Judging by some of the specimens I've seen engaged in the slave trade, Mr Caufield, he may well have a point."

O'Dwyer appeared in the doorway and examined them silently. Even without a smile, his face had the engaging look of a man prepared to laugh. But given that they might be potential customers his demeanour had none of that welcome which presaged the possibility of doing business. It was more the look of a man on his guard. Neither James nor Matthew spoke since it was Harry's place to do so. He didn't speak because he was determined that the factor should do so first.

"And what can I be doing for you?"

"Perhaps you may be able to do a great deal, sir," said Harry, his eyes sweeping the untidy warehouse. "But I doubt this is the place to conduct a conversation."

"Joseph tells me you're called Ludlow, so you'll be off that jackass frigate in the harbour."

"The *Bucephalas* is neither jackass nor a frigate. It is, nevertheless, a ship. And you, Mr O'Dwyer, are a chandler."

"Would that be it then? You're in search of stores?"

"We might be."

O'Dwyer's eyes looked troubled, even if his lips parted in a smile. "My man Joseph doesn't think so. He says that you represent a bit o' danger."

"That is a curious assumption, sir," said James, "on such a short acquaintance."

"Maybe to you. But where I come from second sight is a common thing, and not to be sneered at. I've learned, over the years, to trust his inner eye."

Harry took a couple of paces forward. Keeping his voice low to avoid his words being mistaken for a threat. "If your servant is correct, sir, the level of danger we represent will not be tempered by a refusal to talk to us."

O'Dwyer grinned then, which made him look very cheerful. But the eyes were still suspicious. "That's what he's just told me."

Harry turned and introduced the others. But he made sure his eyes were on O'Dwyer when he said the name Caufield. The grin disappeared abruptly.

"Is Nathan Caufield a relation, boy?"

"My father," snapped Matthew. Like young men everywhere he hated to be addressed as boy.

"Then you're the sprig of a rogue, boy." The grin that accompanied this belied the words. The way that O'Dwyer said them, in his thick Irish brogue, made the expression sound like praise. "I saw a poster, some time back, that says he's been in a touch of bother."

"He came to see you right after the events that poster described."

"He did at that."

"I think perhaps we have come upon the same errand as Nathan Caufield," said Harry.

"Would that be right, now?"

Matthew pulled the crumpled letter from his pocket. "My father wrote to me, Mr O'Dwyer."

"Before or after we spoke, boy?"

Matthew flushed angrily. "I'd be obliged if you would stop calling me boy."

The factor grinned from ear to ear. "And I'd be obliged if you'd answer the question, young sir."

Harry interrupted. "Mr O'Dwyer. It makes little difference, surely? His letter exposes you as a close associate and correspondent of a certain Eamon Dillon."

"So?"

"He also opines that you supply King George's navy with information about potential illegal traders," said James.

"A man's opinion is not proof."

Harry smiled. "On an island like St Eustatius, I doubt that proof is a requirement. Rumour would be quite sufficient to entirely destroy you. Your bellicose Irish condemnation of King George would be seen for what it is, a smokescreen to hide your true occupation."

"Believe me, sir, when I say that I loathe everything that your nation has ever done in Ireland with every bone in my body. But that is neither here nor there, now. Let us look to the matter at hand. I would say that allowing a man like you, in that ship, to prey on the illegal trade, would sink a man just as quick as laid information, true or false."

"I have no intention of preying on the illegal trade."

That lifted his eyebrows, and brought an expression of disbelief to his ruddy face. But it also presented Harry with a dilemma. He had got this far by promising Matthew Caufield that he would help him find his father. But the only way to convince O'Dwyer that he represented no risk was to tell the truth. Even that might be insufficient, leading him to threaten exposure.

"Would it be possible for us to have a word alone?"

"There's no need, Captain Ludlow. You can tell him you're after your crew, not the whereabouts of my pa."

Harry blushed, which was obvious, even in the shadows of the warehouse. Then he glared at James, suspecting that he had said something to the youngster. Caufield obviously read the look.

"I worked it out for myself, Captain Ludlow. Not that it took much figurin' with a talkative crew an' all. But I think that you're a man who's true to your word. So after you've got your crew, I reckon that you'll do what you promised."

"What a perceptive young man you are, Matthew," said James, wickedly. "It's exceedingly clever of you to spot honour in so devious a breast."

Finally allowed into the inner sanctum of O'Dwyer's office, Harry, carefully watched by his brother and Caufield, sought to bargain. The negro Joseph was present as well, making coffee in the background, then serving it, clearly listening to every word. His master would glance at him occasionally, as if seeking his opinion, through eye contact, of the veracity of Harry's tale. All the while the Irishman kept a cheerful expression on his face, which, given the threat the Ludlows posed, was equally disconcerting.

"You feel that you have a strong hand, Captain Ludlow," said O'Dwyer, finally. "But if you expose me, then you will as they say kill the goose."

"You'll be finished here. They may even hang you."

"I have the means to ensure my own survival, Captain. I cannot believe that you'd actually hand me over to the Dutch governor with a rope threatening."

"Believe me, Mr O'Dwyer, I would. I have a motive that is more compelling than your survival."

The look that the Irishman gave his servant was different, like some form of signal. Harry's hand automatically went to the hilt of his sword. But the factor's voice remained even and his cherubic face lost none of its good humour.

"A compelling motive. And what, sir, would that be?"

Harry was aware that he was in danger of losing this argument, perhaps even of being placed in a position where they'd end up in a fight. That was undesirable, not least because his earnest presentation of his case meant that he had his back to Joseph, a man who could break his neck before his sword left its scabbard. It was the thought of the negro, and the relationship with his master, that gave him the idea of how to continue. It also allowed him to half turn in his chair, so that Joseph was in view.

"You repose great faith in your man."

"I do. I doubt I'd be here talking to you if it wasn't for him and the care he takes of my person."

"Well, a certain Captain Toner has aboard a frigate called *Endymion* someone that I esteem very highly, along with forty other men he took from my ship off the coast of Brittany."

"You've come a long way, then, Captain Ludlow?"

"He left English Harbour four days ago to intercept a batch of illegals, with my men aboard. I believe the intelligence he is using came from you, having first been delivered to Eamon Dillon. I have an order from Admiral Bessborough telling Captain Toner to give my crew back. I'm prepared to swear that once I have my own servant and the rest of my crew back on my ship, and when I have fulfilled my promise to young Matthew, that I will depart from the Caribbean."

"Indeed. That seems a strange thing to be doing after you've only just got here."

"It is, nevertheless, true. I will also undertake to put out of my mind this conversation I'm having with you. I have no desire to interfere with your activities."

"So for information that would help you find this frigate, you'll leave things be." Harry nodded as the Irishman's blue eyes flicked past him again. "Captain Ludlow, have you ever heard of *vaudoux?*"

"I've heard of it."

"Do you have any faith in such a thing?"

"How would I know, since I've never been exposed? It's the religion of slaves, not civilized men."

"There you are, Joseph," said O'Dwyer, laughing. "For all your airs you're nothing but a barbarian. Now, Captain Ludlow, would you oblige me by looking at my servant?"

"Why?"

"Because I cannot tell if you are talking the truth. But I have every faith that this barbarian will know."

The thought of refusal, of a claim that such an act was undignified, even dangerous, he quickly suppressed. Harry spun right round and found himself looking into the eyes of the negro, who walked forward and held both his hands. Slowly he repeated what he'd said to O'Dwyer, using Pender's name for the first time. It was odd the way that Joseph's eyes seemed to grow larger, as though he was sucking Harry towards him. Yet neither man was physically moving. He was forced to speak quickly by the desire to break away from that look, something he did as he restated, emphatically, Pender's name. With a sharp nod the negro indicated the result of this examination to his master. O'Dwyer looked thoughtful for a moment.

"Well, now, Captain Ludlow. Joseph here believes you."

"I must say, Mr O'Dwyer, you choose a singular method of verification," said James.

"It's proved reliable in the past, sir. But I have one further question to ask if you don't mind. You said that you thought the intelligence you require came from me. Might I be permitted to ask how you came by that opinion?"

"My pa's letter put me on your tracks," said Matthew. "I followed your messengers to Antigua. It was a clear night, and calm. I watched those niggers hand their oilskin packages to Dillon. He gave them a despatch in return, plus some flagons of rum."

That caused O'Dwyer to throw his servant another meaningful look. "You're sure it was Dillon?"

"I didn't know who it was at the time, but I found out afterwards it was Dillon."

Joseph's deep voice came from behind. "And did you see them depart?"

Matthew spun round to answer. "Yes, I did. They put to sea immediately."

"Why do you ask?" said Harry. He addressed the question to O'Dwyer, which caused the chandler to shrug. Then he realized the import of Joseph's enquiry. The distance between Antigua and St Eustatius was less than a hundred miles. If he needed to ask about their departure it meant that they had yet to return. "Is it perhaps that you suspect your position to be insecure anyway?"

"The work I do has its risks, Captain. I should have thought that was plain."

"How much greater those risks would be if you discovered that you had enemies in English Harbour, as well as here. I have already told you what we have come to find out. One thing Matthew's father didn't say in his letter is whether you told him anything in the same line."

"All I did for Nathan Caufield was discount a certificate he had for the loss of his ship and help him spend some of the money on drink."

"For how much?" asked Matthew, cutting across Harry's next question.

"Thirty per cent."

"And have you redeemed it?"

"I agreed that transaction before I knew how he'd come about it, boy. I only found out later that he'd killed the man who gave it to him."

Matthew positively barked at him. "He didn't kill anyone!"

"Makes no odds, boy. I didn't even send it off to London on the half-chance. Can't see Lloyd's paying out on a policy that cost one of their agents his life."

"So you still have it?" asked James.

"Right by my hand," said O'Dwyer. He bent down and opened one of the doors of his desk. Harry, ever alert to danger, stiffened. But when he came up O'Dwyer was holding a piece of paper, not a pistol. He threw it down on the desk. "There it is, for all it's worth."

"My father didn't kill Norrington."

Harry listened impatiently to the story tumbling out as Matthew told O'Dwyer the details of that part of his father's letter.

"I hope and pray you have the truth of it, boy. I've known him for years and though we're not bosom companions, I reckon I know him. It's not the kind of thing I'd be for laying at his door."

Harry finally interrupted, closing off Matthew's desire to

pursue this reassuring statement. "Did you know Nathan Caufield well enough to believe him when he said there was a spy in Admiralty House?"

The bright blue eyes were steady as the Irishman answered, but his body stiffened. "He never told me any such thing. I've told you. All he did was discount this certificate, assigning it to me. We spent some money getting drunk and that was the last I saw of him."

"What if I was to tell you?" asked Harry. "Information that you are sending to Antigua is being passed to a certain person, who is intercepting the illegal cargoes before any of the admiral's cruisers see them."

O'Dwyer leant forward, his eyes narrowing. "I'd say I was interested."

"Have you heard anything of the number of ships taken by a certain Victor Hugues?" asked James.

"What happened to my father?" said Matthew.

"I don't know, boy," the Irishman replied emphatically.

"Where will I find Captain Toner, Mr O'Dwyer?"

There was a long pause. Only Matthew, still worried about his father, seemed set to speak. But James laid a restraining hand on his arm. O'Dwyer tapped his fingers on the plain deal desk, beating out a tattoo which, after Joseph's activities, seemed like *vaudoux* drums.

"If he's acting on the information I sent in, he'll be in off Guadeloupe in four days and then the island of Dominica right after. I'll give you precise landfalls once we've transacted our business."

"What business?" asked Harry.

"Your ship is a letter of marque, is it not?" Harry's nod produced a grin. "Then when a man like you, a privateer, visits a ship's chandler, people in this part of the world might be asking what he was doing if he re-emerged empty handed. So if you'll give me a list of stores you need, including fresh produce, I'll have Joseph make sure they're on your ship before the tide turns."

Then he looked at Matthew. "And if you're so convinced your papa is innocent, boy, you can buy this damned certificate back off me."

"I'll cover that," said Harry, aware that young Caufield lacked the money to pay. "Just as soon as you give me a list of those illegal rendezvous."

The grin on the Irishman's face grew even wider. "Not to be, Captain Ludlow. The details you want will come aboard with Joseph and your victuals. He, in the mean time, will accompany you to your ship. I'll be obliged if you don't so much as bid anyone the time of day. And I'll be having your parole, sworn public, that you'll not set foot on the island of St Eustatius again, once you have them."

"Tell me, Mr O'Dwyer," said Harry, just before he left. "How can you be so sure that Joseph knows I'm honest?"

"There's many an occasion that would provide proof, Captain Ludlow."

"For instance?"

"For instance he told me, a few nights ago, that a question I asked would never receive an answer. That was just before he told me that some strangers would arrive soon who had the power to destroy me."

CHAPTER THIRTY-TWO

"COME, DILLON, and look at this. It is a sight to gladden an admiral's eye."

Dillon looked out over the harbour, to the outer roadstead and the frigate that was beating its way up towards the anchorage. Even at this distance he could see the British flag flying above the Stars and Stripes, the signal that the ship was an American, and a captured prize. *Endymion*'s number flew from the signal halyards.

"It seems Toner has a touch denied to your other officers," said the Irishman softly. "But one swallow does not, I believe, make a summer. Especially since our information pointed to three potential illegals."

"Are you going to bleat, Dillon?"

"Why should I do that, sir? I have no cause. It seems that, in part, the intelligence that I passed on to Captain Toner has paid the proper dividend. No, sir. I think your bleating will emanate from other throats. Uniformed ones, especially when they calculate the value."

"They are towing their pinnace, Dillon. Write me out a despatch to Toner that will bring him up to date regarding Ludlow and those French frigates. And fetch me my nephew."

Dillon, as usual, ignored the evident haste in his superior's request and sauntered out of the room. Bessborough, who'd long since given up trying to chivvy his political assistant, heard him ask a servant to fetch Mr Caddick. But his mind was elsewhere, so that when his nephew did arrive he had to stand silently behind his uncle for some time, before a polite cough caught his attention.

"Ah, there you are. I want you to double down to the harbour and take some of your men out to that prize that's coming in." Bessborough paused, as if to give his nephew a chance to pose a question, but the boy stood silent. "Dillon is penning a note for Toner, detailing the latest intelligence. Tell whoever has charge of that prize to hand it over to you. It will go to the master attendant under my personal supervision and I will oversee the buying in, so they needn't worry about being dunned out of their rightful reward."

"I am alone in wondering whether they deserve it, uncle," said Caddick.

"As a member of my family, Charles, I expect your support. As your commanding officer I demand it. *Endymion* has to be warned about those two frigates. Toner also needs to be told that Ludlow is on the loose, and about the orders I was forced to sign."

"So you intend that he should remain at sea?" asked Caddick, with a slightly sour look.

Bessborough turned slowly, his handsome features arranged in as haughty a way as he could manage. "He's taken a prize, on his first cruise, within 48 hours of weighing anchor. He also seems to have outmanoeuvred Victor Hugues. Toner might be a Caledonian bore, but he runs a tight ship. When you show evidence of the same ability, Charles, you too will be allowed to cruise at will."

"I believe experience is gained at sea, uncle."

The boy was right, of course, which made his relation even more angry. Bessborough had dithered in that area. He'd promoted the boy ahead of his skills, yet could not bring himself to assign an officer to *Percival* who'd have the knowledge and the tact to act as a captain *in locum*.

"Just do as I ask, Charles, and do it quickly."

"Aye, aye, sir," replied Caddick slowly. Then he turned and left the room with no more alacrity than Dillon.

"Insolent pup," said Bessborough, as he turned to look once more at the prize coming in. The sight of that brought a smile to his lips.

◆ ◆ ◆

The natives were lined up on the beach, their crinkly ginger hair, which stood in sharp contrast to their dark skin, very evident in the strong sunlight. Out in the harbour *Ariadne* was at single anchor, ready for sea. Antoine de la Mery approached the chieftain first. He was a shrunken, wrinkled individual with a gaunt face and deep eye sockets. Even painted and feathered he lacked a regal bearing. But the Frenchman placed the gaudily decorated cross round his neck and added several rows of brightly coloured beads. The boat party laid a pile of stores at his feet, a keg of rum, flour, salt pork and beef plus various tools which some of his tribe had learned to use while the French had been ashore. Possession of these would enhance his status and hold off the inevitable challenge of a younger man for his position.

The tribesmen were treated likewise, care being exercised to ensure that a proper hierarchy was maintained, with the number of beads and provender strictly related to the man's position in the tribe. Behind the men the women huddled mournfully. Some of the younger girls were pregnant by his sailors, which would, in years to come, make this already hybrid group even more interesting in the variety of its features. Fortunately this caused no rancour. The Caribs had a lax attitude in such matters. Finally, with an air of ceremony, the chief stepped forward. In his hand he had a finely woven basket which he laid at de la Mery's feet. Standing back and using his staff he flicked open the lid. The sudden light made the creatures inside, who preferred darkness, respond swiftly. The three fer de lances writhed and slithered over each other. One poked its head up above the rim, which caused the French sailors who remained ashore to take a step back. De la Mery's pet was struggling to free itself from the folds of his pocket. The old chieftain gave them a toothless smile then flicked the lid shut again, trapping the protruding head on the rim. It disappeared back into the dark interior of the basket before the mongoose got close.

The ceremonial lighting of a torch was the last act. Once this was accomplished, and the other torches had been lit from the original, de la Mery presented his flints to the chief, a gift that clearly delighted him more than any other. Patiently, for his command of Carib was as limited as the language itself, the Frenchman repeated the reasons why he must leave no trace. The chief understood only too well. He'd never met a Spaniard or a priest. But they were held to be a great terror throughout the islands, as much in those they'd subdued as those they'd left alone. The presence of a wooden encampment, de la Mery's pavilion, and particularly the jetty that jutted out into the mouth of the river could cause some passing ship to investigate. These Frenchmen had lived amongst the islanders in relative peace, taken little from them that would destroy their way of life, and in the main respected their customs. There was no guarantee that anyone following on would be so benign. Antoine de la Mery torched the pavilion himself. Bone dry, the flames took hold of the tarred wood in seconds. The trail of turpentine carried the fire to the thicker poles of the jetty. Soon the whole was ablaze, sending a column of black smoke into the clear morning air.

His men were already in the boats, uncomfortable in the presence of the basket full of snakes. He made his way down the beach and climbed aboard, turning to wave farewell to the tribe which had come to the water's edge to say farewell. There had been a moment, very early in the morning, when he'd contemplated staying, of handing over his ship and all the treasure to another, with instructions as to the last rendezvous. But even as he contemplated such a course, de la Mery knew that he could not stay on this island. He craved the company of his own kind too much. The natives were still on the beach when he cleared the coral reef and headed out to sea. He set the course himself, checked that his sails were properly set, then went into his cabin.

The voice from the sleeping cabin, on hearing his footsteps, called to him. He opened the door and looked at the pale invalid lying on the cot, favouring him with a warm smile.

"We are under way, my friend, and for the last time. Soon you will be on your way home to Long Island."

Toner read the first part of Bessborough's despatch with a mounting sense of excitement. The news of the two French frigates in the vicinity acted like a drug on his ambitions, bringing a hint of colour to his normally pallid face. The admiral's instructions to stay well clear of these enemies could safely be ignored. No British sailor risked censure for putting himself yard-arm to yard-arm with the enemy. He shouted for the requisite charts to be brought to his cabin and examined them closely. His next rendezvous with potential illegals was to the north-west coast of Dominica. By standing off a little further east than necessary Toner would be in a good position to cover Pointe-à-Pitre. With his topsails showing to an enemy with the weather-gage, he might tempt them into a battle before they made their landfall. Failing that he could stand off Pointe-à-Pitre and tempt them out to fight once they'd revictualled.

Money was one thing. But Toner longed for fame as well. The best way for a frigate captain to achieve that was in a single-ship action. True, he might find himself facing two Frenchmen instead of one. But he had nothing but faith in the traditions of his service, which held that any British warship was a match for two of any other nation. And the glory that would attach to his name with success! In his mind's eye he could already see the *Gazette* that would announce his victory. He imagined himself standing before the king, while his monarch pinned upon his proud breast the insignia of the Order of the Bath. There would be a knighthood to go with that, a gold-and-jewel-encrusted sword subscribed for by the Patriotic Fund. Thanks would be voted in Parliament, with a pension to augment the money he made from his captures. Crowds, delirious with joy, would drag his carriage through the streets of London and Edinburgh. The most eligible women in the land would faint away at a mere glance from such a puissant hero.

Success would breed success. He could look the Lord Commissioners of the Admiralty square in the eye and demand a command
that befitted his new-won status. And there would be no tiresome
search for a crew. Proper sailors, aware of his reputation, would
flock to join him.

He was still in a state of euphoria when he turned to the second page. The name Ludlow leapt out at him, acting like a
thunderbolt to bring down his flimsy edifice of impending glory.
Slowly Toner read the incredible news that the man he'd robbed
of half his crew had not only followed him across three thousand
miles of ocean, but was at sea, searching for him with an order
from his own commander instructing him to hand back the men
from the *Bucephalas*. It was no great moment for one so given to
luxuriating in such flights of fantasy to plunge just as swiftly to
the depths of despair. There would be no fight with those two
French frigates if he lost those men. Through them, and his own
imposition of proper discipline, his original draft of landsmen had
improved immeasurably, but the Ludlow men were still the most
efficient section of the *Endymion*'s crew. Lost to him, he would-
n't have enough of a complement to engage in an action against
a fishing boat.

This image was as much of an exaggeration as the glory he'd
contemplated a few minutes before. Yet that alone shaped his decision. He might well find another chance to make money from
prize-taking, and God knew that with his debts he needed it. But
Toner had been afloat long enough to know how slim the chances
were for the kind of action that made men such as himself national
heroes. An opportunity such as the one presented to him might
never occur again, even if the war lasted his entire lifetime. With
another quick glance at the chart, he yelled for the master and
gave him instructions to set a course for the eastern approaches
to Pointe-à-Pitre.

It was an agony waiting for O'Dwyer's stores to be loaded, one
made worse by the constant presence of the tall negro. Every time

one of the trio seemed set to speak, he'd turn and look at them with those huge compelling eyes. No great effort was put into hurrying Harry to sea, but finally his purchases were in the hold and he could at last ask for the information. In a prodigious feat of memory, Joseph reeled off the times, dates, courses, and landfalls without ever once having recourse to the piece of paper in his hand. Then, despite all the questions that the events of the day had thrown up, it was time to get to sea. Harry left St Eustatius at night and, after going north about the island, headed out into the Atlantic, beating up into the Trade winds to avoid detection from Brimstone Hill on St Kitts. Those lookouts would have observed his arrival. With a regular aviso plying between the island and Antigua it wouldn't be very long before everyone in English Harbour knew his whereabouts. They might detach a frigate like *Diomede* to shadow him. So much the better. If they sent someone to St Eustatius, only to discover that he'd gone, that would be one less ship he might have to avoid in his search for Toner. He was reasonably sure that O'Dwyer would not want to compromise himself by letting English Harbour know that he had given Harry information.

In the morning, well out to sea, James, acting as his usual conduit of information to the curious, had matters explained as the *Bucephalas* pitched into the Atlantic rollers.

"I can't tell you what opened O'Dwyer up," said Harry.

"I can't believe it was the threat to expose him," James replied, the perfect picture, with his hand rubbing his chin, of a man struggling with a dilemma.

"We could speculate for hours without drawing any conclusion. We have the information we wanted."

"Is it genuine, Harry?"

"James, I learned as a nipper that there were certain things I could do nothing about, things that only time and no amount of asking would solve. This is such a case. Now I would be obliged if you'd take that expression off your face, and adopt one that gives the crew the impression that I know what I'm about."

James grinned. "Not even I can conjure up such dramatic skill, brother."

"I think I preferred you with a sore head," said Harry.

"You'd best tell me what we're about. After all, I have a reputation to protect that isn't already in tatters."

Harry laughed out loud, which in itself had the crew nodding with approval, it being a sound they'd scarcely heard since the Downs. And when they observed the two brothers locked in conversation, all seemed well in their world. James listened with great care, aware that he must impart what Harry told him accurately. The calculations regarding Toner's position must put him to windward of the illegals, which placed him at the western end of the Saintes channel. Likewise, Harry wanted them to be to windward of Toner. There was every chance that Bessborough had sent him the news that Harry was in the West Indies. Coming into that channel, which ran between Guadeloupe and Dominica, he should have the weather-gage as he approached the anticipated rendezvous. Given that advantage, in such confined waters, his quarry would find it near impossible to evade him.

"Just as long as he doesn't aim off a broadside as soon as we get within hailing distance."

"If he does, James, you'll live to see him hang. I intend to ensure that we encounter no trouble. I'm tempted to put an Admiralty flag at the masthead, with his ship's number, along with a signal which tells him we bear official orders from his commanding officer."

"I would have thought that would be likely to inflame him, brother."

Harry laughed out loud again, just to show that the thought of annoying Toner didn't bother him at all. "Given his habit of gnashing his teeth, James, it might just cause him to break his jaw."

"I rather fancied that you had such a thing in mind yourself."

"Not at sea, James. But if I get him on land I will most certainly be tempted."

"Even if, as we have heard, he has flogged every one of our men."

"I don't say that inaction will be easy, brother. But I know that nothing would suit Toner better than a display of violence from me or any member of my crew. In fact, it is my intention to disguise the ship by taking out my upper poles."

"That promise you gave O'Dwyer?" asked James.

"I shall keep it, of course."

"Even though the pickings in this part of the world appear quite rich?"

Harry looked at James with slight surprise. "You're not suggesting that I break my word?"

"No, Harry, I am not," said James, serious once more. "I am checking what you intend. I have the same concerns for when you meet Toner face to face. Just as I would naturally wish you to keep that promise, as well as the one you gave to young Matthew about helping him to find, and clear, his father. Deep down I have the feeling that there's something you're not being open about, even to me."

"I cannot think what you mean, brother."

"But you will grant that it's not the first time in your life that you've said one thing, only to do the complete opposite when the time comes to act."

Harry fixed him with a quizzical look. "A family trait, perhaps, James?"

"No, Harry. I think it's confined to you."

Harry looked aloft, partly to avoid commenting, and partly to check on the set of his sails. Satisfied, he handed the wheel over to the quartermaster, giving him instructions to hold their course, before finally turning to look at James.

"I think our breakfast is ready."

CHAPTER THIRTY-THREE

O'DWYER had done them proud in the article of fresh food. With time to spare, Harry could turn his mind to the major problem that James had just identified: how he was going to aid young Caufield. The first question, and one he was unable to answer, was this: was the boy's father still alive? Gentle questioning over the tender American beefsteak had established that Nathan Caufield was an indifferent correspondent, who had often been at sea for eighteen months with no written word of his welfare. That opened up a flood of the young man's reminiscences.

"He's always sailed the West Indies, Captain Ludlow. He was doing it at my age, before the Revolution in '76. I came south with him as a nipper on a couple of trips."

"I'd noticed you had little difficulty in climbing into the tops."

"Pa wanted me to be a sailor. It was my mother who insisted that I study law."

"I can imagine the family worries being multiplied with you both at sea," said James. "How did your father send news home?"

"Word of mouth was the best method, since we'd generally run into a ship heading for those parts as he made his landfall."

"So the letter you have is unusual?"

"It's not unique," replied Matthew, with a trace of stubbornness, pressing the missive out on the table till it was flat.

"I have yet to read it," said James. The American passed it to him and he engrossed himself in the words while Harry ruminated silently. James looked up after a few minutes. "There's nothing here asking you to come to his aid."

"No."

"So he apprehended no danger?"

"I can't say about that. But he's not the type to bleat."

"Yet you abandoned your studies to come to the Caribbean. Might I be permitted to ask what prompted you to do so?"

"My mother and sister were anxious."

"Matthew," said Harry, suddenly, "the same night you told us your story we had a private meeting with Admiral Bessborough."

"So?"

"He tried to engage us to help him," said James. "He said that there was a spy in his headquarters and that Harry was just the man to root him out."

"Why you?" asked Matthew, clearly struggling to comprehend why neither brother had told him this before.

Harry shrugged. "I'm not a naval officer. But I understand the way they think."

"An arcane skill, indeed," added James.

"Odd you didn't say. I had you both down as straight up and down folk."

"I'd like to think that you were right," replied Harry. "I won't apologize, Matthew. But there was no malice in retaining that information. It came as quite a shock to us to hear you say more or less the same words in the Clarence that we'd heard from Bessborough a mere hour before."

"There's been time since."

"I do intend to keep my word. But I'm troubled as to how to go about it."

"The first thing I want done is Pa's name cleared. Then we might not have to go looking for him. He might just surface as soon as he hears."

"I'm no surer how to go about that," said Harry emphatically.

"You said it yourself, Captain Ludlow. The only way to clear my pa is to nail the true culprit. At least with what your admiral told you, it's clear that Pa was right."

"Knowing he was right is one thing," said James, "proving it quite another."

"And is the man responsible the same person who murdered Norrington?" asked Harry.

"If you want to drop me back on Antigua . . ." The youngster left the rest of that sentence hanging in the air.

Harry held up his hand. "Don't be impetuous. I'm merely thinking out loud. And the chances of there being two people are too far-fetched, unless there is more than one person involved in the espionage. Thankfully, we have a little time to ponder on that."

"I understand about your crew, Captain Ludlow." There was a slight trace of bitterness in those words as Matthew lifted the letter off the desk. "But my pa's facing the rope."

"I have a letter too," said Harry, reaching into his desk. "My servant left it to be posted in English Harbour. Only I came in before it was sent. I'd like you to read it."

Reluctantly, Matthew Caufield took the letter from Harry. His reading was swift, but he had the habit, from childhood, of moving his lips as he did so, which made him appear less competent.

"Can you understand it?" asked James.

He just responded with a quick nod, his lips stopped moving but he continued to stare at the page for several seconds. Then he lifted his head and looked at each brother in turn.

"If ever anyone wondered why we Americans wanted to get away from King George, they'd only have to read this."

"Does it go some way to explaining my behaviour?" asked Harry.

"All the way, Captain Ludlow. All the way!"

"Good. Now let's turn our mind to what Bessborough calls his bailiwick and see if we can find any indication of who is responsible for . . ." It was Harry's turn to hesitate. He was faced with two different mysteries, with no guarantee that the same person was the culprit. He pulled a clear sheet of paper towards him and picked up a pen. "Let's start with the Frenchman, what do we know about him?"

"He has a pet mongoose," said James, facetiously.

Harry glared at him and began to write. "He was picked

up from Guadeloupe. Bessborough and Dillon were on board *Diomede* at the time."

"So was Marcus Sandford."

"Come along, James. He suggested we look into this. You said so yourself. He would hardly do that if he was guilty."

"After what you just told me, that applies to your admiral as well."

"True," replied Harry.

"I don't think it matters who was on the ship," said James. "If de la Mery is our man, then he stayed in Admiralty House for over a month, a welcome guest who repaid their kindness by teaching half the household how to improve their French."

"Didn't Dillon say he persuaded the admiral to accommodate him?"

"Not to me."

Harry rubbed the feather top of his quill along his lips. "No, he said it to me, when I introduced him to de Brissot."

"Who's he?" asked Matthew.

"A Frenchman we took prisoner. Dillon spoke perfect French as well. He certainly required no instruction in the language."

"That's a man I would find hard to trust," said James.

"What about Lady Bessborough, James. Would you trust her?"

"I sincerely hope you're joking, brother. Besides, she lacks the wit for such subterfuge."

"It was in the nature of a jest. But how can you tell? We have no knowledge of the way they manage things at Admiralty House. For all we know the information could be lying around for anyone to look at."

"No," said James. "That day Dreaver came ashore to tell us about Pender's petition, I asked him if he had any notion of where Toner had gone. He said, quite clearly, that the men on the *Redoubtable* had no idea, because the orders for cruising warships were kept secret. I sent him back to enquire further, with the means to bribe. He gave me back the money the morning we cleared English Harbour."

"I don't think when your brother said anyone, Mr Ludlow, he had in mind the lower-deck hands on a warship."

"Never underestimate them, Matthew. I would be at a loss to know how they manage it, but sailors are dab hands at sniffing out secrets."

"There's always a loose tongue aboard every vessel," said Harry, maliciously. "Even this one."

"All I'm saying, Harry, is that if the orders were lying about for all to see, with sailors being the gossips they are then the men aboard any ship in the harbour would soon be appraised of their contents. And if it was common gossip, why would your good friend Marcus Sandford not inform you?"

"Didn't he actually say that the intelligence regarding the illegals was delivered when they were about to leave harbour?"

"He did, but given the way he's behaved, who knows if it's true?"

"Because it flies in the face of all logic to go to the trouble of gathering secret intelligence only to leave it lying about for everyone to see."

"My pa said that Dillon had a strongbox with a lot of stuff inside he couldn't read."

Harry didn't respond to that. He was pursuing his own train of thought. "Whoever is supplying the information has to have access to both the information from the likes of O'Dwyer and the orders to the frigate captains. If we assume that they are careful with that, how many people would have an opportunity to see both?"

"Bessborough and Dillon, certainly," said James.

"What about Vandegut?" asked Harry. "He's Bessborough's second in command, with quarters in the house."

"As I recall, there's no love lost between them. Vandegut was very unhappy at being placed below us at the table."

"Money!" said Harry.

"Sorry?" Both Matthew Caufield and James looked equally mystified.

Harry looked at them in turn. "Whoever is doing this, it's for the money. They said that Hugues had taken a quarter of a million in prizes by the latest estimates. Now we know it's not Hugues. We suspect it is a man called Antoine de la Mery, who stayed at Admiralty House for a month. Didn't Lady Bessborough say he'd lost his plantation in St Domingue?"

"It's a fair wager he departed from Guadeloupe with nothing but his clothes and his pet," added Matthew.

"So, we have a French sailor, a royalist supporter."

"At least no supporter of Hugues," said James, with a trace of pedantry.

"He's fallen on hard times," Harry continued. "He's in English Harbour, penniless and living on charity, when someone suggests to him a method of repairing his lost fortune."

"Who might well be someone intent on acquiring one," said James.

"Bessborough gets an eighth of every penny his captains earn."

"He's been getting precious little since this started."

Harry looked at James. "He's hardly likely to cut off his nose to spite his own face. But Vandegut, as captain-of-the-fleet, gets nothing. Nor does Dillon."

"Would Vandegut be privy to everything?"

"I can't see how Bessborough could justify excluding him," Harry replied. "But another thought occurs. If the pilot in the harbour at St Eustatius knew about the ships Victor Hugues was allegedly taking, then so did O'Dwyer."

Matthew Caufield pulled a folded sheet out of his coat. It contained the names he'd written down while the pilot had been sinking his claret.

"He could hardly fail to tally the names. And some of them are bound to match those he sent to Dillon. If he's in correspondence with him, he could hardly fail to pass on such information."

"Well done, Matthew," said Harry. "O'Dwyer said something about an unanswered question. Perhaps those two negroes you saw on the beach weren't meant to survive. I have to say I didn't

take to Vandegut. But for a serving naval officer to risk everything—"

James interrupted. "For a quarter of a million pounds, Harry?"

"My guess would still be Dillon. He has all the strings of the
situation in the whole Caribbean by his fingertips. His commander is a bit of a buffoon, and the whole surrounding sea is awash
with valuable cargoes."

"It must be galling for an intelligent man to watch others
prosper."

"Nor just galling, brother," said Harry. "Tempting."

"Almost as tempting as supposition," said Matthew.

Harry blinked at that, which brought a smile to the youngster's lips. "I'm studying law at Yale, Captain Ludlow. I should be
there at this very moment, in fact. Now I haven't got very far, but
one thing I do know: I wouldn't want to go into a court of law
with all this speculation. Admiralty House is full of possible suspects, especially since we don't know if their information is as
secure as they suppose. And if money is the motive you might as
well include everyone on Antigua."

"Do you have any ideas on how we should go about getting
proof?" asked James.

"Not many."

"Bessborough asked us to help him out," said Harry. "If we
enlist his aid, that's one way."

"After that little tête-à-tête, if we start snooping around, will
that not scare off the man responsible?"

"Very likely."

"Then I don't see how that helps."

Harry smiled. "There is another avenue, of course."

"Don't respond, Matthew," said James quickly. "I've seen that
smile before. It's my brother being smug."

"At least two people know everything, Bessborough's spy
and the man we think is Antoine de la Mery. O'Dwyer has
given us the location of the illegals so that we can find *Endymion*.
Toner will proceed directly to the rendezvous itself, unaware that

the ships will not be there to take. While he's so engaged, our filibuster, Monsieur de la Mery, will be busy catching the illegals at a different location."

"Of which we have no knowledge."

Harry stood up and went to his chart locker. The one he wanted was near the top. Extracting it, he brought it back and laid it out on the table.

"I've told you, brother, that the winds in these parts blow steady and true north-east to south-west for most of the year. St Eustatius, like all the ports the illegals use, lies to the north. They have to, or they'd find themselves beating into the wind to make their landfall. Given that they're making for the Saintes channel to land cargoes in Guadeloupe and Dominica, de la Mery, if it is him, must take them before the narrows or he'll be observed. He won't want to take them in completely open water, so that cuts down his options considerably."

Harry was pointing to the chart, his finger to the east of the island of Guadeloupe. Then he moved it to the narrow point of the channel with a string of small outcrops between the group of bigger islands. "Toner must hold his position here. If he ventures out into the open he risks being spotted and scaring them off."

"That applies to us as well, brother."

"Not if we disguise the ship, James. Which I had intended to do anyway, as a way of getting close to Toner without alarming him. Once we've got Pender and our crew back, we can reverse our course and hunt for de la Mery."

"There's an element of chance in all this, Harry."

"There is an element of chance in everything we do, James. How much of a chance is someone taking in Admiralty House? What element of chance had us in that bay in Brittany at the same time as Toner? How did we miss *Endymion* by a mere 36 hours?"

"A considerable one, I grant you."

"It's more than that, brother!"

Harry started pacing to and fro in the confined space of his cabin, his voice betraying clear evidence of the excitement generated by the flow of his ideas.

"Let us assume, just for a moment, despite your reservations Matthew, that it's Dillon. Regardless of how he controls the flow of information he can't account for everything. The whole edifice rests on time, distance, and the competing interests of the various trading islands. No one in St Croix cares if a ship trading out of St Thomas is taken and *vice versa*. So our man has a sure notion of how much time it will take for de la Mery's depredations to become a major problem shared by all the illegals' bases, with the certainty that even if they're alarmed none of them will come anywhere near English Harbour to complain."

"A thief preying on people breaking the law," said James.

"Exactly! But there are other factors. What are the chances of someone seeing through the disguise of Victor Hugues? Matthew, your father guessed the truth only because he'd seen Hugues. He also named the one unusual fact about his man that could identify him, namely his pet. That was chance. And then he told Norrington. Now there's a dangerous fellow. He'd know as much about what's going on in the area as anyone. As an insurer he has to have an eye on all the losses to assess the risk. That presents him with a picture very different to that afforded to any one person concerned with events in his own locality. How much of a chance was it that both he and a victim with the knowledge of Nathan Caufield were in the same place at the same time? Bessborough, who relies to a large extent on Dillon for information, goes to the governor's house in St John's just after several English vessels have been taken. He is then surrounded by merchant captains detailing not only their own losses, but all the rumours they've hitherto ignored. Worse, they list the ships lost so comprehensively by name that even a fool like Bessborough can remember them."

"There is one other thing, Harry," said James. "As well as a way of informing de la Mery, there has to be a way of stopping him. That would be very necessary."

Harry looked hard at his brother. "And given that things are unravelling . . ."

"A wise man wouldn't take a chance."

"What you're saying, Mr Ludlow," said Matthew, "is that it might already be too late."

Harry put his hand on the youngster's shoulder. "That's one thing about an element of chance, Matthew. You have as much possibility of being right as of being wrong. I intend to assume that you are wrong, because the time to stop was when Norrington was murdered. Whoever the villain is at Admiralty House, he's not perfect. In fact, I suspect, like most thieves he's fallen prey to greed. Things might, as my brother says, be unravelling. But he may just go for one more throw, the one that sees him trapped."

A head poked through the cabin door. "Mr Patcham's compliments. Time to go about, Captain Ludlow."

CHAPTER THIRTY-FOUR

IT WAS difficult on a ship like *Endymion,* being so closely watched by the warrant and commissioned officers, to foment any kind of concerted action which, happening spontaneously, would produce a positive result. As in most ships, the men with a little authority, like the master-at-arms, the boatswain, the gunner, and the carpenter, tended to respect and obey anyone who wielded more power than they did. And having risen from the mass of the crew to achieve some status they had more to lose than the men beneath them. Besides that, the kind of persons who sought and achieved such positions were rarely the men most qualified. Slavish behaviour in the past had won them their warrants over better-qualified candidates, men who spoke their mind. Some of them might be sympathetic to the men's plight but there was no way of knowing without broaching the subject openly, a dangerous thing to do since a misplaced choice would inevitably lead to the initiator being clapped in irons. Likewise, the marines were an unknown quantity. Toner had been careful not to flog them excessively. Being in permanent possession of firearms they would either have to be won over or taken by surprise. Below decks the majority of the crew had no opinion, one way or the other, whether they should act to take over the ship. Certainly they grumbled, and with good cause. But they were careful to show their superiors a submissive face, to laugh at any joke they made, and in some cases to act as conduits of information about what was happening below decks.

The backbone of dissent was the leadership of Garmond. The hard core numbered about forty souls, some who were malcontents by nature, others men who would have found naval discipline too hard to bear in any circumstances. One or two even had notions about a proper revolution, having belonged to debating clubs ashore. They were prone to quote from Tom Paine and the "Rights of Man." But even in the most favourable circumstances these men were too few, and too inefficient, to achieve anything. Given their basic antipathy to the service, months at sea had not turned them into proper seamen. Thus they were allotted the most menial tasks, which made them even more surly. Such an attitude did not go unobserved by the officers, careful to keep an eye on the obvious trouble-makers.

The key to success lay with Harry Ludlow's men, blue-water sailors who formed a cohesive body that would, under Pender's leadership, act in unison. They also preserved their exclusivity in the nature of their contacts, so any plan they made was likely to remain a secret. A careful eye would have noted that Pender had changed in the few days since Lowden's death. Now, instead of avoiding Garmond, he sought his company in a way that he'd previously been subjected to himself. Quietly in the carpenter's walk, or in the manger and the heads, with men posted to ensure they were not disturbed, the two discussed various strategies. Every action aboard the ship was dissected to see what opportunities it presented. The major stumbling block was simply a lack of weapons. Unsure of the marines, they'd have to be armed themselves to achieve anything. The only time that was likely to occur was within sight of a prize, when the men were issued with weapons for boarding.

"Then it's simple," said Garmond. "We take over the ship the first time Toner orders it cleared for action."

"No," said Pender, slightly too loudly, for his voice echoed in the narrow confines of the carpenter's walk. "When that happens the crew're scattered all over the ship, with most of my lads in the tops. The rest only come together on deck once that's complete. Even then we're scattered. You have to wait until we're on deck, ready to board. Then we're armed an' all in a group. That's the time to turn on Toner."

"I'm looking forward to the sight of his blood," said Garmond.

"No killing!" snapped Pender. "Mutiny is bad enough. If you go murderin' the officers, then you might as well slit your own throat at the same time. Over the side in a boat is enough."

"You're too soft, mate."

Pender stuck his nose close to Garmond's. "Am I? How many men have you killed?"

"What difference do that make?"

"If you have to ask, it makes a difference. Killin' ain't as easy as some think. Besides, if you kill one, you've got to kill 'em all."

"I don't see that as a problem."

"What about the midshipmen?"

Garmond knew that Pender had a soft spot for young Callander, so he took a savage delight in making the sign for a cut throat. "They're officers, ain't they?"

"And the warrants?"

"Slimy bastards they are," snapped Garmond. "Their feet are on our necks too. Only difference is they'll jump on to our side as soon as they see we're winnin'."

"Who gives the order?" asked Pender.

The other man's eyes narrowed. It sounded as though Pender thought it should be him. "We'd never have got any place if'n I hadn't reminded the men of their rights."

"So you want to do it?" Garmond nodded and Pender posed the next question. "Have you given any thought to how?"

"I'll just call on the men and they'll obey, at least the ones on my side will. The others will follow, like the sheep they are."

"I wish I was so sure."

"You got a better idea?"

"I have. I reckon you should rush the captain and grab him. Once you've laid hands on him the rest will know you mean business. And none of the marines will dare use their muskets to stop you for fear of hitting him."

"Officer coming," whispered Flowers, who was a few feet away up the walk, his eye on another lookout.

They'd picked their spot well, with three exits from the narrow walkway that ran round the inside of the ship's hull. They were dispersed before the sound of footsteps reached their ears. Flowers and Jubilee went with Pender. Once they were out of earshot, Flowers pulled at his arm.

"What are you about, Pious?"

Pender looked at him with an innocent expression. "You can't say some of our lads ain't in favour of taking over the ship."

"That's talk, Pious, an' you knows it. The only way they'll do anything is if you tell 'em to."

"So maybe I will."

"Never in life. Toner's a sod, right enough. But he'd have to go further than he has to get you a-mutinyin'. Besides, you's done precious little to excite our lads, or prepare 'em."

"They'll follow me when the time comes," said Pender.

Flowers's crescent-shaped face was very close to Pender now. The way he talked out of the corner of his mouth, it was as if he was addressing a third party. "Not if'n they're not warned. You know like I do that a split second, in this sort of case, can make all the odds."

Pender smiled, though his look lacked any warmth. "What do you think Garmond will do?"

"He'll kill Toner, Pious, that's what he'll do, regardless of what he agrees. It's the only way for the likes of him. He'll put every man aboard beyond the pale so that the only way they can see to survive will be the wholesale murder of every officer on the ship."

"I want you to keep what I say to yourself," said Pender. He looked at Jubilee, the squat Pole, but he had little English, so posed no problem. But Flowers was offended by that and he growled his reply.

"I don't know where you go gettin' the idea that I'd do owt else, mate."

"Don't you go gettin' on your high horse, Ben Flowers. I've taken a leaf from the captain in this. I'm telling no one what I intend. And I'm right too, for if it goes amiss we'll all hang, instead of him that deserves it. I reckon that Garmond had a hand in the killing of Lowden."

"Don't be daft. It was Toner on the rope."

"Lowden didn't fall, mate, he was pushed. An' that there shark didn't just happen by, it was there by invite. Somebody was ladling the slops out of the scuttle long before Lowden went overboard. Toner did his bit, though how Garmond knew he would beats me. Happen it was more ill luck than anything else. But with them slops and Lowden's blood in the water . . ."

Pender paused. Flowers would see the flaws that made what he was saying such a long shot. He gnawed at them often enough himself, without ever resolving a method that didn't depend on sheer chance. "Whatever, there's two who has to pay for that death. I think you're right. I reckon that Garmond will try to kill Toner."

Flowers stepped back slightly. "What happens then?"

Pender was so angry he spat the next words. "I'll be right next to him, Ben, with no mind to become a mutineer or a pirate."

"Is that what Garmond intends?"

"I reckon he'll make for Guadeloupe and hand the ship over to the French. Let him kill that Scots bastard. But as soon as he does I'll fetch him a swift clout round the ear with a marlinspike. He might not hang for Lowden, as he should. But, by God, I'll make sure he swings for Toner, with us getting the credit for savin' the ship."

As they walked away, Pender prayed that he was right, that the Bucephalases would follow him instinctively. He knew that some of them had succumbed to the blandishments of Garmond. That was another reason he was playing things so close to his chest. It grieved him to even think it, but he wasn't sure, amongst Harry Ludlow's men, whom he could trust any more.

The pipes sounded their shrill call for all hands on deck. That was followed by the booming voices of the warrant officers, going through the ship with their ropes' ends lashing at anyone laggardly enough to be caught standing still. Pender took in the sight of men jamming bars into the capstan, then rushed up the companion-way, hearing Mr Callander give the orders for his topmen to get aloft. Men were already uncoiling the falls while others hauled sails and booms into position on the deck. As he ran up the shrouds with his mates he could see that all the officers were on deck, with Toner, grim-faced as usual, issuing a stream of orders. Aloft, above the heat haze that lay on the sea, he could see the islands to right and left of *Endymion*. There was little time to examine them. Booms were coming aloft and he had to rush to set the chains that would hold them in place. They were followed by a succession of sails, all of which had to be bent on and furled.

Down below Toner gave the order to come about. Pender saw the master spin the wheel and watched the rows of men holding ropes, who looked like worker ants from this height. First they released the falls paying them out to let the sails spill their wind. That same wind, plus the forward motion and the action of the rudder, brought the ship round on to the new course. Once *Endymion* had come round sufficiently they ran in lines to haul the yards into position. The yards were set nearly fore and aft as Toner put his ship as close to the wind as she would sail. Then he called aloft, and in a series of commands that seemed to go on for an age, the captain set sail after sail as he sought to coax an extra half-knot out of his ship. The motion was greater now, as *Endymion* ploughed into waves that had come across three thousand miles of open sea before entering the Saintes channel. Still Toner kept at it, trying and discarding options at a bewildering pace. Finally, satisfied that he was making the best possible speed, the men were sent below. It was only then that Pender had the time to wonder at what all the fuss was about. What were they after to windward that was so important? That thought wasn't given long to mature. The whistles blew again and he was on his way to the shrouds, ready to shift the sails as their captain came around on another tack.

Aboard the *Ariadne* they were busy disguising the ship, covering

the gunports with painted canvas and adding the useless sail
booms, which when dressed made the sleek schooner look like a
merchant ship. To the south-west lay the bulk of Guadeloupe,
while due south, a mere two miles distant, the tiny uninhabited
island of de Sirade rose sheer from the sea. This was the first landfall for the illegals who intended to supply the entire group of
French islands. Laying to, in the lee of de Sirade, they could recon-
noitre the main channel off Pointe-à-Pitre in daylight, ensure that
there were no British warships close enough to threaten danger,
then make their arrangements to run their cargoes ashore at night.
De la Mery would be there before them, with a lookout on the
top of the island. Sailing from de Sirade on a converging course
he would take them one by one. This time he would put the crews
ashore on Guadeloupe itself. And since this was to be his last interception he would tell them his true name and something of his
background. It would be good to let Victor Hugues know that
some of those he'd intended to butcher by the banks of the Rivière Salée had survived.

Harry Ludlow, having swung farther out into the deep Atlantic,
had set his bowsprit for the centre of the Saintes channel. With
the steady wind abaft the starboard beam he was sailing easy,
aware that he had ample time before any of the illegals would
arrive. Toner, in possession of the same information, would not
want to be on station too early himself, lest by his presence he
gave the game away. He too was busy disguising his ship, though
he didn't feel the need for too much elaboration. Harry just wanted
to get close enough to *Endymion* to make any attempt to ignore
him impossible. With luck Toner would take him for one of his
illegals and make an attempt to come alongside. At a major cost
in available speed he'd struck down his upper poles, which made
Bucephalas so easy to recognize.

The lookout on the top of de Sirade, with his huge mounted
telescope, could see him quite easily. But when he lifted his instrument to look due east all thoughts of that original sighting faded.

The topsails of the two warships were clear on the horizon. He swung round to tell his companion and that's when he spotted *Endymion,* hull up, emerging out of the rocky outcrops of the Isles des Saintes. Something had gone badly wrong. *Ariadne* was caught in a trap, with ships, clearly men-o'-war, converging on the island from three different directions.

His instructions to fetch de la Mery were quickly obeyed, once the runner had appraised himself of the situation. The captain might not like the idea of a long climb, but he would need to see this for himself before deciding what to do. Maybe they could escape to the south and hide in one of the bays of Marie-Galante. Or perhaps they should go north, and fight their way out of the trap by taking on what looked to be the smallest of the four ships.

The lookout aboard *Bucephalas,* seated lower than usual because of the absent topmasts, was the same man who'd been aloft the first time he'd sighted those two sets of sails. He didn't have a second's doubt as to their identity. Thus his call to the deck was a screech rather than a shout, as he named them and their position. He looked down to see if Harry was coming aloft to look for himself. But his captain was too busy giving orders to reset his upper masts. Without them, and the sails they would carry, and with an enemy to windward, he would be taken for certain.

It took de la Mery an hour to get to the top of the only hill on de Sirade. By that time matters were much clearer. He saw the ship to the north, shaped like a cut-down frigate, hurriedly resetting his top hamper. Whoever commanded her had just changed course and was making for the narrows that separated de Sirade from Guadeloupe. He was flying no national flags but de la Mery suspected that he was British. He was clearly keen to avoid the two real frigates to the west, which had the French tricolour steaming forward from their mainmasts. Spinning his telescope to look down the Saintes channel he focused on *Endymion,* beating up into the wind, tack after tack, with her red ensign standing proudly to the rear.

He knew the men were looking at him, waiting for him to say what they must do. There was an eagerness in their stance, as if they wished nothing more than the order to run downhill to the ship. But de la Mery hesitated. He was tempted to wait here and see what happened. There might be a battle, with him in a grandstand position to watch the whole affair. But even as he formed the idea he knew it was impossible. He must get aboard the *Ariadne* and make her ready for sea. No one could tell if there would be a contest, and if there was how it would turn out. But one thing was certain. As soon as a gap opened between the approaching ships, an opportunity to escape, he would seize it with both hands. Antoine de la Mery had no intention of staying around to exchange pleasantries with the victors.

CHAPTER THIRTY-FIVE

HARRY Ludlow was heading for the Pointe des Châteaux, intending to shave the shore in order to recover a little of the ground he'd already lost. Up above his head the topmen were toiling under the most difficult circumstances. Seating upper masts in their caps was not a job to be undertaken under sail. He wouldn't have attempted such a task were they not in so much danger. Others were working flat out preparing the slings for his topgallant yards, which had been hoisted up in preparation. Matthew and James had taken a turn at the capstan until all the wood was aloft, then come to join Harry on the quarterdeck. In the waist and along the gangway the sails were ready, lashed on to the lines that would haul them into place. The two Frenchmen seemed intent on following him into the narrows, and had gained enough on *Bucephalas* to give themselves the option of sitting in his wake, or altering course to the south of de Sirade. Ahead lay Guadeloupe. Really two islands, it was joined in the middle by a narrow causeway. The nearest section, Grand Terre, was mountainous and green. The other part, Basse Terre, was barren and flat with a volcano, Mont La Soufrière, rising near the southern shore.

The causeway sat at the head of a deep bay which was subject to variable currents and the looming bulk of Grand Terre deadened the steady north-east wind. At the other extremity, the southernmost point of Basse Terre formed one corner of a triangle, completed by his enemies, from which Harry had to escape. The French frigates could hold their course, shortening their side of the triangle, with the aim of driving him into the great bight, at the head of which sat the main harbour of Pointe-à-Pitre. Once trapped in there, with the current setting in towards the shore, they would be able to deal with him at their leisure.

Harry watched them closely through his telescope, praying that they'd take the longer route and stay in his wake. Once he had his upper sails set, a task which would be much easier once the land mass killed the wind, he'd stand a fair chance of emerging into the Saintes channel fully rigged. The two frigates would have closed the gap by then and might even be in range to try a broadside. But they'd suffer the same effect from the island, and the gap should open again. Then it would be a race for the narrows between the Isles des Saintes and the town of Basse Terre. He'd outrun them before in open water. Here, though, things were not so simple. Though the wind entered the channel at a steady pace, it could prove freakish, being affected by the proximity of so many islands, so he had no guarantee that it would favour him over his enemies.

If things looked bad, and he felt that he couldn't get clear, he could always use the narrows between the tiny Saintes archipelago, or bear up to larboard and use the larger island of Marie-Galante as a buffer between him and the pursuit. In that case they'd have to split up, going either side of the island to pin him. That, at least, would shorten the odds to a point where, if he must fight, then he'd have a chance against a single enemy. Not that he sought such a thing. Given a wind he could run for the Martinique passage and escape entirely.

"Damn!" he said as the sound of the signal gun died away.

The curse was soft but heartfelt. Both James and Matthew Caufield waited, knowing that Harry would explain as soon as he was sure. They could see the white puff of smoke being blown to leeward of d'Albret's ship, *Persephone*. The signal had both Frenchmen altering course to the south. They'd waited till he was close to de Sirade before doing so, aware that if he decided to come up into the wind, his only option, he would do so at a terrible disadvantage without his upper sails.

"He's no fool, this Monsieur d'Albret."

"Man-o'-war, hull up and dead ahead, Capt'n."

All three men spun round at once, their hearts in their mouths. Even a lubber like James Ludlow knew that if she was French they were doomed. The voice called down again, this time with something approaching a whelp of excitement. "*Endymion,* your honour!"

Whatever joy this engendered was killed quick enough by one of the older hands, who yelled ferociously at those who stopped work to look. "No slackin' there, you swabs. Ain't you seen a king's ship afore? Get crackin' with that there gammonin' or you'll be a-learning French afore the day's out."

"What is Toner doing here?" said Harry, shaking his head.

"That's not important," said James. "The question is, does he know the danger he's in?"

"I guess he can't see the Frenchmen," said Matthew. "The island is in the way."

Harry had his glass on *Endymion* now. She was a fine sight, her yards braced near fore and aft, with the red flag that denoted her squadron blowing stiffly towards the stern. He watched her for a full minute before turning to his brother.

"James, you've done this before, so I expect you to be quick. Raise *Endymion*'s number then signal *Enemy in sight, due east.* Run up the numbers 32 and 28. That will tell them they are frigates. If he's had any contact with Antigua he'll know just who they are."

James ran to the flag locker and started sorting out the message while Harry saw to the loading of the signal gun.

"Do you think he'll come on?" asked Matthew.

Harry turned and looked at him. His eyes were alight, no doubt because of the prospect of action. But the voice was dead calm. "You'd be better employed helping my brother, Mr Caufield."

Matthew smiled and turned to do as he was asked. "Always used to annoy my pa when I was aboard his ship, the way I expected him to know the answer to everything."

Harry instructed Dreaver to handle the signal gun and waited while the flags were bent on. Toner would be on *Endymion*'s deck, with his own telescope trained on *Bucephalas*. He could hardly fail to recognize her at this distance, now that her upper masts were nearly back in place. Harry half hoped that he hadn't heard from Bessborough. The sight of a ship he'd last seen three thousand miles away might give him a seizure. He heard the sharp crack as the furled flags broke open in the wind. What would Toner say to see naval signals on a privateer? Harry knew from experience that it was not the kind of thing likely to please a king's officer.

A nod to Dreaver and the signal gun went off. Harry counted off a full minute then called to James to change the flags. The new signal, 32, swept aloft as the old one came in. Dreaver had reloaded and the signal gun spoke again. Another minute and that was replaced by the number 28. Harry held his breath, wondering what Toner would do. He would be well within his rights to decline an action. The enemy, sailing into confined waters, had the weather-gage and superior force. But somehow, much as he despised the man, he knew that he wouldn't turn away. He'd been a king's officer himself, proud to wear the uniform. It would go against the grain for anyone in a captain's coat in King George's navy to decline a battle, even at these odds.

The signal gun aboard *Endymion* sent out a puff of smoke and a series of flags broke out at the mast-head.

"Enemy in sight!" shouted Harry. That disappeared and, after a short pause, the gun spoke again. Another group of flags replaced the first. Harry's shout now had a note of jubilation. *"Am engaging!"*

"What now, Harry?" asked James, who'd come up beside him.

Harry looked at his brother, aware that, up to a point, he could do as he pleased. He was sure if he chose to assist Toner his men would follow him. But to take James into the maelstrom of a battle without consulting him was beyond his powers. Then there was Matthew Caufield. What he wanted to do, which was no more than following his own natural instincts, could get them all killed.

"Pender is aboard *Endymion*," he said softly.

James smiled. "That, brother, is a mere excuse. But it will suffice. Much as I despise that damned Scot, we can't stand by and watch a British ship go down in defeat. What signal should I send?"

"Permission to take station on flag," said Harry.

"Flag!" barked James.

It was now Harry's turn to smile. "Yes, brother. Your damned Scotsman is about to become a commodore."

The confusion aboard *Endymion* was almost total. Toner had ordered the ship cleared for action as soon as he sighted *Bucephalas*. But giving that order and seeing it carried out were two different things. It wasn't only Harry Ludlow's men who couldn't keep their mind on their work. Every hand on the ship kept running to the rail to point and have a look. It was as though the sight of that ship promised salvation to them all. Toner barked and yelled for more speed. Dunlop and McPartland responded with a harshness that achieved new heights of fury, lashing at any bare back that passed within reach. Pender, halfway out on the maincourse yard with his mates, taking in the sail, was yelling too, happily reminding every one of his party that they'd soon be at home aboard their own ship. He knew his captain wouldn't be here if he didn't have orders to take them off, orders so specific that Toner couldn't ignore them. All this clearing for action, as though he was going to fight, was mere frippery.

The first of Harry Ludlow's signals broke out, the gun making sure every eye aboard the frigate was drawn to look. Only the officers had the faintest idea what it portended, and even they had to wait until Midshipman Hemmings, book in hand, translated the flags into a clear message. His voice was high and squeaking as he informed the captain and his words caused amazement on more than the quarterdeck. They sent an audible buzz around the whole ship. Toner, grey faced, had his telescope up, sweeping the horizon ahead. The gun from the *Bucephalas* boomed twice more, adding to the confusion. But whatever message those flags contained was confined to Toner's ears. Aloft every eye followed the direction of their captain's long glass. Had they been looking at him they'd have seen it jerk as the bowsprit of the *Marianne* poked out from behind the mass of de Sirade.

The whole ship fell silent now, with not a voice emitting so much as a whisper. The first French frigate was in full view when the second one emerged. Toner stood stock still for a full two minutes before he spoke.

"Mr Dunlop, make a note of what has occurred here. I'll bring charges against Ludlow for the illegal use of navy signals."

That was not what any man aboard, from officer to lowly waister, wanted to hear. Wise heads dismissed it as just an excuse so that the captain could give himself time to think. Everyone would have to be patient while Toner assessed the situation. Finally, he shouted at Hemmings, who ran to the flag locker. Without being asked, men were loading powder into the signal gun. As it went off, and the flags broke out, Midshipman Hemmings, his voice still shrill, shouted to confirm the message.

"Enemy in sight," muttered Pender, his earlier jubilation tempered by this unforeseen development. The next signal did nothing to cheer him up. Toner was about to take on odds of two to one, with a crew that had been given no real practice at gunnery, and who, moreover, despised him.

"Privateer signalling, sir," yelled Hemmings, quickly thumbing through his manual. *"Permission to take station on flag."*

It was stupid for Harry Ludlow's men to cheer. The odds had shortened but they were still bad. Yet they did so, their enthusiastic response inflaming the rest of the crew, who joined in heartily.

"Belay that damned racket," yelled Toner, aiming a swipe with his telescope at a passing seaman. "Mr Dunlop, a word to the gunner. If he doesn't fill those sacks with more speed I'll have his warrant. And get those topgallants in. We'll engage under topsails only."

The stream of orders went on and on: extra chains on the yards to prevent them being shot out; more wet sand on the deck; gunners to chip any rust off their shot so that it would fly true; bow-chasers to be loaded and run out right away; a party to man the relieving tackles in case the rudder was shot through; marine sharpshooters to take station in the fore and mainmast caps and play their muskets on the enemy deck, with another party on the quarterdeck to seek out and prevent the enemy doing the same to *Endymion;* deadlights to be rigged across the stern casements to prevent boarding; leather buckets of fresh water for the gunners, who, in this heat, would pass out without it.

Garmond, once he got the squealing, screeching animals out of the manger and into the hold, was harried up to the deck, running a steady gauntlet of ropes' ends, the blows of which opened wounds that had only just started to heal. He was soon informed of what had happened, but before he could speak to any of his mates he was set to rigging nets below the yards. These would catch anything except a complete mast that was shot away above the deck, and prevent it falling on the heads of the men below. His mind was in a turmoil, since these were the very conditions which he and Pender had discussed for taking over the ship. Unable to recognize the *Bucephalas* himself, he was nevertheless in no doubt of its identity. The name was being called out with jubilation every few seconds.

"We're to have a battle, Pender," said Midshipman Callander breathlessly.

His lack of breath had nothing to do with fear, more to do with the effort of furling and lashing off the upper sails. He lay over the yard, his feet in the horses below, continually glancing along to ensure that all his division were working at the same pace.

"We are that, Mr Callander," replied Pender, lifting his eyes to the sight of the two enemy frigates, now well clear of the island ahead.

"Have you been in a battle before?"

Pender didn't stop labouring as he tried to reassure the young man. To do so would only affect the work of every man on the yard. And the effort of his task, toiling flat out eighty feet in the air, robbed his voice of the certainty he sought to convey.

"It don't make no odds, your honour, if'n you've done it before or not. If I had enough breath to think I'd have enough to curse the feeling in my belly. All you can do is stand and be shot at half the time, with no idea whether God has decided to spare you or not. So the best thing to do is what you're supposed to, without paying any mind to whether you're going to live or die."

The work was suddenly complete, and it was time to descend and man the guns. Callander blushed as he addressed his final words to Pender. "I don't know that I mind dying."

"Don't you fret, Mr Callander. You'll do your duty just like you always have."

"Mr Callander," shouted McPartland. "Are we to wait all day for you to resume your rightful position?"

Still at the crest of the hill on de Sirade, Antoine de la Mery watched the scene unfolding before him. The activities of the smallest vessel intrigued him. Clearly she was no warship. The three men-o'-war, French and British, had their huge battle flags flying. The wisdom of one frigate engaging two was interesting enough, but it looked as though this other vessel, rigged and armed like a letter of marque, was going to join in. That flew in the face of all precedent. It was the business of navies to fight each other. But privateering ships had no business expending blood for anything other than profit.

He could see that all the yards and sails were now aloft, but the smaller vessel was making no attempt to escape. Instead she was beginning to turn in a wide arc that would bring her round behind the British frigate's stern. This action, plus the obvious intention of the other ships to engage, was opening up his avenue of escape. He raised the large mounted telescope. At this distance he had no difficulty in seeing what was happening on the deck of the privateer. The three men by the wheel, all with fair hair flapping in the breeze, leapt into focus. But the one who had command stood out from the trio. To a sailor like de la Mery it was obvious just by his carriage, an air of easy authority that permeated the prisms of his glass, that he was the captain.

"Are you a fool, *mon ami,* or a hero?" he asked himself softly.

Then he turned the glass round to the French ships. Their discoloured and worn canvas informed him that they had just crossed the Atlantic. The huge tricolour battle flags, their colours fresh and bright, streamed out to windward from the mizzen, while the larger of the two sported a long commodore's pennant at the main. His mind went back to that day on the beach near Pointe-à-Pitre, to the way that Victor Hugues had butchered his fellow colonists with both guillotine and musket. Would he stand still again and watch the forces of revolution triumph, watch while these French captains provided more ammunition with which that odious man in Guadeloupe could celebrate? Certainly they were his fellow-countrymen aboard those frigates. But they were men prepared to kill to maintain an idea, a notion of freedom so misplaced that it had cost Antoine de la Mery, and his crew, all that they owned.

He allowed himself one last long look at what was developing before his eyes, then turned and ran down the hill.

CHAPTER THIRTY-SIX

THE LOSS of wind in the lee of Grand Terre, bringing with it a reduction in the motion of the ship, allowed Harry to complete the bulk of the work on his upper sails. *Bucephalas* emerged into more open water with nearly everything she required set aloft. The difference, as they rediscovered the breeze, was immediate and the ship raced towards *Endymion*. Harry kept his eyes to the south, eager for another sighting of the enemy. Given his increase in speed, he didn't have long to wait.

"So, brother. Do we have a plan, or are we operating on your instincts?"

"At this stage, James, neither Toner nor I are in control. Nor are we likely to be if our enemies have any sense."

"That doesn't sound like a situation to suit you."

"Monsieur d'Albret will do everything in his power to hold the weather-gage. By keeping to windward he can dictate the course of events."

They'd passed *Endymion* now and begun to swing round. A ragged cheer, quickly suppressed, floated across from the frigate as *Bucephalas* came across her wake and bore up into the wind. Matthew Caufield, standing right up in the bows, waved as the view of the enemy frigates was shut out by *Endymion*'s rigging.

"I wonder if our presence is as welcome on the quarterdeck as it is to the hands?" asked James, flicking at a large sheet of drawing paper.

Harry called aloft to shorten sail before he answered. "I think so, brother, albeit with reservations. Toner has got some extra firepower at no cost, from someone who will not be able to contest any of the fruits of victory."

"Your sanguine temperament is showing again, Harry. I cannot believe that the use of the word victory is anything other than tempting Providence."

Harry Ludlow grinned. "You may be right, James. And I will appease the deities with a raft full of doubts."

"No one demands a complete shift of nature, not even the gods. But a little humility works wonders."

"Just the one, then. I admit that I'm worried about Toner's gunnery," said Harry. "Do you remember how poor it was off the coast of Brittany?"

"I do not. But he must have corrected it by now, otherwise he'd be a fool to accept battle."

"How little you know about the navy, James. I never doubted for a moment that Toner would engage. He's the type to face death rather than bear the slightest hint of dishonour."

"How can you use a word like honour about a man like that, especially after the way he's behaved? Have you so quickly forgotten Pender's letter?"

"I was thinking in the professional sense, brother. He cares not one whit what you and I think of him, but any fellow officer's opinion ranks very high in his concerns. And might I add that few of them would damn him for being a flogger."

"And to think you were once cut from the same mould."

Harry looked down at his brother, secure in his captain's chair, to see if he was being practised on. But James had his eyes set steadily to the front, all his attention seemingly engaged in recording the details of each ship as they steadily approached each other. It was galling to be ribbed. But if that was what it took to get James back to his true occupation, drawing and painting, then Harry would gladly pay the price. The men had come down from the tops now and gone about the task of preparing *Bucephalas* for the coming fight without instructions. If anything was designed to bring home to Harry the problems he faced, it was this. Though it would never do to enumerate them, he had many more worries than the one he'd just explained to James. Of paramount concern was the fact that he had too few men to manoeuvre the ship and man the guns. The irony of his being short-handed when he was in the process of aiding the man responsible, did not escape him. Perhaps Pender and the rest, all well-trained gunners, were better off on *Endymion*. There they had the larger-bore cannon of the frigate to fire. But, allowing himself a touch of vanity, he doubted they'd be as effective under Toner's supervision as they were under his.

He'd avoided responding to James's gibe about a plan because all he had, at this moment, was an aim. And there was no doubting that it was a difficult one: to aid his fellow-countryman, ensuring that Toner only had to fight one of his enemies at a time, without over-exposing himself. But if ever Harry Ludlow was in his element, this was it. He loved nothing more than to be presented with a series of complex problems requiring a simple, direct solution. Now, nearly in position, the pieces were falling into place, and the first germ of an idea was taking shape. He issued his first order, telling every man he could spare to get back aloft.

"What will Monsieur d'Albret do next?" asked James, looking up from his sketching.

Harry looked down at the pad on his brother's lap. It never ceased to amaze him, how, with so few strokes of his charcoal, James could create such solid shapes. He had drawn the bowsprit, the jib, and the stays running to the foremast. Two groups of men were working to load the bow-chasers. The enemy frigates stood out beyond that. Having picked out the salient features that separated their differing designs, Harry could tell which was *Persephone* and which was *Marianne* without raising his eyes.

"He'll change course soon, and come up into the wind. Villemin in *Marianne* will take station slightly to the rear to ensure that *Endymion* doesn't try to sneak past his stern."

"Why?"

"Well, as I said, d'Albret keeps the wind. Also the smoke from his guns will blow right across *Endymion*'s deck, so the Frenchman will be able to see what damage he's doing, while denying

Toner the same luxury. If *Endymion* gets in a lucky shot, and wounds a mast, then d'Albret can pull out of the action and let Villemin come up to engage. At the appropriate moment, they'll attempt to attack her simultaneously, with one on her beam and the other athwart her stern or her bows. Several broadsides will follow and then they'll begin to board."

"Should our mad Scot not strike now?" asked James in mock alarm.

"Of course not, brother. We are here to prevent any of that happening. Which is why, if you look carefully, you will observe that a number of our men have gone aloft."

The Frenchmen had also shortened sail, thus extending the time it took to close the gap between the combatants. Sailing into the wind, with so very little set, *Endymion* and *Bucephalas* had barely any way on them. The advantage of the weather-gage was never more striking than on an occasion like this. For Toner, the option to turn away was there, so that all four vessels, sailing down the Saintes channel, would have the same force of wind playing on their sails. But that would open up new avenues to d'Albret. Once they'd cleared de Sirade, which would happen very swiftly, he could choose to fight, or decide to make for the safety of the harbour at Pointe-à-Pitre. This far from home, with no dockyard available to effect repairs, part of the French commodore's duty was to keep his ships intact. Toner knew this as well as Harry and was clearly determined to deny him any opportunity to disengage.

Not that there seemed to be any reluctance on d'Albret's part. Barring the possibility of sustained damage, he, on the face of it, held all the cards: firepower, wind, and a well worked-up crew that had now been together for three months. Against that Toner had a tradition of victory and a well-found ship, though a question mark hung over his crew. In the end it would all come down to raw courage, gunnery, and sheer bloody-mindedness. Toner, certainly, was relying on his men being steadfast in the face of a superior assault. Harry wasn't like that. He hated the idea of sitting off the beam of a well-armed foe, exchanging broadsides.

Besides, unless he was lucky, if such a circumstance arose the difference in weight of metal would presage only one outcome. Toner would have to beat *Persephone* then turn and come to the rescue of *Bucephalas,* which would, if the fight went on, be nothing more than a dismasted hulk.

The natural thing to do, for two ships planning to fight together, would be to co-ordinate their actions. Toner, who had to have some plan, knew that Harry had a naval signal book aboard. Not that he needed it. *Bucephalas* was within hailing distance now. All the man had to do was bring a speaking trumpet to the stern rail and he could engage in conversation. But such a request, by either method, would be made in public. No doubt fearing a snub, the captain of *Endymion* declined to invite him to act in unison. Harry was grateful. He was not prepared to act as a sacrificial lamb so that Toner could garner all the glory. Despite the gentle ribbing from James he was here because his men were aboard that ship and they had the right to expect his best efforts to aid them.

The first ball from *Persephone* was fired from a single bow-chaser, just as she began her turn to starboard, coming up into the wind in such a way as to invite Toner to follow suit. It was not an action designed to do much damage, more the throwing down of the gauntlet, an invitation to fight. Harry, still shielded by Toner's rigging, shouted to the men aloft to reset his upper sails. As soon as they were sheeted home *Bucephalas* picked up speed and began to overhaul *Endymion.* With the wind now some twenty points free the sailing qualities of his ship showed immediately. Toner had in the mean time started his turn, certainly intending to oblige Monsieur d'Albret. Harry was alongside before that was completed, his eyes searching the rigging for a sight of Pender. So many arms were waving that it took a while to distinguish him from the mass. But Harry saw him eventually, hanging on the weather shrouds on his way to or from trimming the sails. He yelled to James, his finger pointing as the stern of the frigate swung towards them, and shouted out some words of encouragement, even though he knew they'd be unlikely to carry.

Marianne was just where he expected her, coming on a touch more than the commodore with the intention of brushing Harry aside on his way to the assistance of *Persephone.* Having shaved bowsprits in mid-Atlantic by aiming straight for her, Harry reckoned it wasn't a game he could risk again. Villemin, having been humbugged once, would hold his course this time and it would be *Bucephalas* that would have to sheer off to avoid a collision. But there was space between *Persephone*'s stern and *Marianne*'s bows which a slick sailor might exploit. The gap he intended to go through was desperately narrow. Even worse, it would begin to close once the enemy realized his intentions. But he was counting on the personality of the *Marianne*'s captain. After their brush in deep water, Harry reckoned the man opposing him to be a slow thinker. If he could succeed in exploiting that fault, and could get to windward of *Persephone,* then it would be Monsieur d'Albret, not Toner, who'd end up caught between two fires.

He spun the wheel, bringing *Bucephalas* as close to the wind as she would bear. No ship, even the most nimble, could expect to make much headway into the teeth of the trade winds. But Villemin had a problem, just as he'd had before. His orders were at odds with the actions of his enemy, and he had to decide to either risk compliance or institute a complete change of plan. It was the time he took to decide that made the difference. Harry had pushed *Bucephalas* into the gap before his opponent showed any sign of reacting. But he did act eventually. The gun from his commodore came just after he'd begun to bear up, proving that d'Albret saw what Harry was about long before his subordinate. But, as luck would have it, both men were now compounding the original error. Given the firepower that the French ship possessed it would have been more deadly if he'd held his course, then borne up to sweep across Harry's unprotected stern.

Villemin, now committed, had to come up into the wind, so there was nothing swift about her manoeuvre. But her captain had the presence of mind to fire off both his bow-chasers in an attempt to slow his opponent down. Harry had most of his men aloft and the rest manning the falls that controlled the yards. He could only reply with three of his starboard cannon. Had he declined to man those ropes he could have favoured the *Marianne* with most of a broadside. But he was manoeuvring in difficult circumstances and the ability to maintain that advantage was more vital than the chance to show off his gunnery.

One shot from the Frenchman struck the bows above the waterline, which pushed *Bucephalas*'s head around just enough to check her progress. Here was where Harry's caution paid off, for the men on the falls could ease the braces, which, combined with his movement of the wheel, allowed the ship to keep some forward motion. *Marianne*'s bows were following *Bucephalas* round, so those two cannon constituted the Frenchman's entire available strength. He'd fired off guns that were already loaded, hence the round shot and the low trajectory. But his next attempt was more in the Gallic tradition. He used bar shot aimed at Harry's rigging. Though it went wide this was dangerous indeed. Sailing so close to the wind was a most delicate operation in which continued stability in the sail plan was paramount. A well-aimed volley of two small ingots connected by chain could slice through some vital set of ropes and throw all his hopes into disarray.

The guns that he'd fired in reply were now ready, while those left idle were still loaded and run out. He shouted a string of orders and his men, having lashed off their ropes, raced to their stations. With such well-trained gunners aiming the hands were in the air signalling that they were ready to fire within a minute. He gave the command and the whole side of the *Bucephalas* erupted, just as his opponent fired off a third volley. The Frenchmen, seeing what was coming their way, had fired too quickly, their guns going off on the downroll. Another shot struck the hull, doing no damage. But one of the bars attached to the chain came in above the bulwarks, dragging its companion piece behind it. This swept across his deck like a scythe, decapitating one of the men on the forward carronade. Blood gushed from the headless body, which first staggered around before crumpling on to the deck. James threw down his drawing materials and, with a couple of gunner's mates, ran forward with a tarpaulin to cover him over.

Another gun from *Persephone* called attention to a new signal at the mast-head. Harry couldn't read it but the message was soon clear; d'Albret wanted Villemin to take station to windward of *Bucephalas,* even if that meant the sacrifice of time, vital minutes when the commodore would have to face both his enemies at once. But it was a shrewd manoeuvre, since it nullified most of the advantage that Harry had gained from cutting across *Marianne*'s bows. It was only a matter of time before Harry Ludlow was in the position that he'd prepared for the French commander. And given that he faced the prospect of doing battle with two frigates, he'd have no choice but to hurry on past *Persephone* in order to gain a degree of safety, an act which would remove him from the engagement for some considerable time.

Harry wondered what they were making of all this on *Endymion.* Nothing probably, since they were coming up to commence their own battle. Both frigates, French and British, were holding their fire, clearly determined that their first broadside, by being delivered whole, would have the maximum effect. Villemin had ceased to trouble *Bucephalas* with his bow-chasers, so all the noise had ceased. An eerie silence, punctured only by the creaking of ropes and the whistling of the wind, reigned supreme as the two biggest ships edged towards each other, with *Endymion* overhauling the Frenchman inch by inch. In moments they would open fire, and the gap between them would be filled with black, acrid smoke and hurtling metal death.

CHAPTER THIRTY-SEVEN

ABOARD *Ariadne,* Antoine de la Mery harried his men as they removed the disguise he'd used to alter the shape of his ship. Others were aloft setting the sails, while the remainder toiled on the capstan to haul the ship over her anchor. Sure that everything was being done with maximum effort, he walked into his cabin and opened a foot locker used to store flags. Every nationality that sailed the Caribbean was represented, a riot of coloured silk that hid the ensign he sought. Pulling it out, and looking at the blue and gold, he felt a strange sensation. The Frenchman had never thought the day would dawn when he'd sail again under these colours. He wanted to be properly identified, while well aware that such a thing was impossible. So this would have to suffice. Even as an officer in the French navy he'd had little regard for the Bourbons who ruled France, seeing them as an obstacle to the kind of progress that had made the old enemy, Great Britain, master of the seas. But Antoine de la Mery had no time, either, for a revolution that had run out of control till it consumed the lives and loved ones of people who had initially welcomed the idea of change. A revolution that had thrown up butchers like Victor Hugues.

Back on deck he was informed that the anchor was thick and dry, ready to be plucked from the soft sand of the bay. He took the wheel, smiling as his pet mongoose jumped on to the rim. No need to hide him now. Orders followed to let go the upper sails. Men hauled round on the yards to catch the breeze and the ship began to move gently forward. As it eased over the cable the anchor came clear, to be catted and fished. More orders followed as de la Mery increased sail, tacking out of the bay into the north-east wind. Once clear he swung the wheel to bring the wind on to his quarter, then stepped towards the mainmast with the flag in his hand. His ship cleared the island quickly enough and he was able to see the state of the battle. He observed that the smaller ship had, surprisingly, got ahead of one of the French frigates and was now overhauling the other, which bore the commodore's pennant. Meanwhile the British frigate was down to topsails, trying to come abreast and engage the same ship. He wondered, as he tied the knots, if anyone had raised their eyes from their own concerns to notice his approach.

No matter. He was his own man and would take what action he deemed necessary. As long as every other vessel in sight knew who he was and the tradition he represented. He called the orders to clear for action, then tied the final knot on to the flag. Finally he stepped back, pulled the rope so that the folded flag flew aloft, then jerked it hard. It opened with a crack, streaming out in the breeze. Every eye on the deck was looking aloft, to see the gold fleur-de-lis on a pale blue background, the ensign of Royal France, streaming from the mast-head.

"Who's that?" said Harry, his telescope swinging wildly to the north as this new arrival showed itself to the east of de Sirade. He watched closely, seeing the flag being hauled aloft. When it opened he gasped with surprise.

"What is it?" asked James. "Another enemy?"

"No, brother. I would say it is a friend."

"Topsail schooner," said Matthew Caufield. "Six gunports a side and chasers bow and stern. She's clearing for action by the look of it."

"Have you seen the flag, Matthew?" asked Harry, passing the telescope to James.

"Not for many years, Captain Ludlow. And I never thought to see it again."

"The fleur-de-lis," added James, equally surprised. "Who would fly that these days?"

"I can think of only one man in an armed ship at sea in these waters who might raise such a pennant."

"De la Mery!" replied James.

Harry nodded, and looked towards the stern of *Endymion.* "I don't know what it is about our Scotsman, James, but he seems to be able to conjure up allies out of thin air."

Aboard *Endymion* all eyes were concentrated on the *Persephone,* now only a cable's length ahead. Toner and the other officers had donned their best uniform coats and the sunlight gleamed off the captain's epaulettes and buttons. Red-coated marines were lined up on the quarterdeck, silently fiddling as they checked their muskets for the tenth time. Each lieutenant stood behind his division, ready to pass on the commands. Hemmings, who would act as a messenger once the noise of battle commenced, stood beside his captain, his face as pale as the white collar patch on his uniform coat. The gunners were crouched in anticipation, their weapons trained at right angles to the ship. Toner had declined to heave his cannon forward. He wanted no delay between broadsides, with men using their rammers to lever the guns round. The damp sand on the deck steamed in the heat blurring the outlines of this silent tableau.

Pender, standing by the mizzen shrouds, formed part of a group under the command of Mr Callander, designated to go aloft at the first sign of damage to the rigging, there to effect emergency repairs. They knew that they'd be prime targets for enemy muskets. The French, too, would have marksmen stationed in the caps. Out of the corner of his eye, he was watching Garmond, who'd used the excuse of wetting the rapidly drying sand to get within striking distance of Toner and young Hemmings. He turned to look along the deck, and was suddenly aware that Dunlop, McPartland, and Wheeler were similarly threatened, each having one of Garmond's associates, bucket in hand, standing near by.

This was all wrong. They'd discussed the right time to take over the ship and agreed, as far as Garmond was concerned, that it should happen after they were cleared for action. But that had supposed their enemy to be an illegal merchantman. Pender, for all his subterfuge, had never envisaged that such an event would occur in the presence of a French warship. Garmond, if he intended to go ahead with his plan now, in circumstances very different from those they'd discussed, should have found a way of telling him. His supposed accomplice wasn't even looking in his direction. Then he saw Sloman, another malcontent and a slavish adherent of Garmond, by the base of the mizzen. And it was only because he moved, when everyone else was still, that Pender spotted him. He was easing a knife in his belt with one hand while the other tested the halyards that held aloft *Endymion*'s battle flags.

"He's plannin' to do them all," he whispered, angered by the idea that Garmond had out-manoeuvred him.

"What?" said Flowers, bending forward and, as usual, speaking out of the corner of his mouth. Callander jerked his head as well, surprised that anyone could speak in such a tense situation.

Pender's eyes were searching his own party. If Garmond had decided to attack all the officers and midshipmen, that would include Mr Callander. But these were all men from the *Bucephalas*. Surely with their own ship in sight they'd be mad to do Garmond's bidding! That thought brought enlightenment. The malcontents had no choice but to act now, and do so without assistance, unless they wished to abandon the idea completely. Garmond could see as well as Pender that if Harry Ludlow was here then he had the power to take back his men. Depleted in numbers, with the most cohesive group gone, they might never be presented with another opportunity to take over the ship. And if they did so in the presence of these French warships, striking the flag as soon as battle commenced, then they could be sure of a warm welcome from their Jacobin counterparts, and an even warmer one in Guadeloupe when they went ashore.

He'd always had mixed feelings about the idea of a mutiny. If ever a captain deserved to have his ship taken off him it was Toner.

Had he not seen that streak of offal leading to the scuttle the day Lowden was killed, perhaps he could have been persuaded to join in, regardless of the near certainty of retribution by the navy. But the idea of surrendering one of his own nation's ships to the enemy, just before they were set to fight, was anathema. It had nothing to do with his own captain being close by. If he ever wanted to hold his own head up again this had to be stopped. Pender turned away slightly from the others, so that only Flowers could hear him clearly.

"Garmond's decided to do the dirty on us all by surrendering the ship. That's not somethin' he'll succeed in as long as there's an officer left standing. So he plans to get them all at once. Look where his men are."

"Holy Christ," said Flowers softly, as his eyes ranged along the deck.

"One of our lads might be daft enough to try for Mr Callander," added Pender.

"Silence there," said the youngster, aware that their whispering had attracted the attention of the quarterdeck.

"Aye, aye, sir," replied Pender, pushing Flowers forward till he was right behind the midshipman's back. The man needed no telling what was required. He pushed everyone else out of the way until the only route by which an assailant could attack the youngster was head on. Jubilee was standing slightly apart from the rest of the men. Pender tugged at his sleeve and edged him further back. He put his mouth right by the Pole's ear. "See that bugger Sloman, hoverin' by the mizzen, Jubilee. If you look close you'll see he's got a knife in his belt. As soon as he takes it out, get over there and belt him hard. Make sure he goes down, an' stays down."

The Pole looked at him in disbelief. Such an act aboard a ship like *Endymion* would mean a flogging that even he couldn't endure. But he trusted Pender, who'd always looked after him, making sure that his limited command of English didn't get him into trouble. The square head moved in an almost imperceptible nod and the man's small blue eyes fixed on Sloman like a bird of prey on a dormouse.

Pender cast his eyes around the rest of Callander's party. He saw good seamen, all of whom he'd trust with his life aloft, or in the middle of a boarding mêlée. But there were no quick brains amongst them, men who would see what he could see and act without asking questions. That left him with a real problem. If he went anywhere near Toner, Garmond wouldn't wait. Likewise Dunlop. McPartland, with his love of the cat and the rope's end, who was also a poorly qualified officer, wasn't worth saving. Only Mr Wheeler, the third lieutenant, had any credit with the crew, having proved more gentle than his fellows. And he'd publicly stood up to his captain over the question of excessive punishment. He was in command of the larboard gunners, who would take no part in the opening of the action, but who would be directed to take the place of any casualties on the starboard side.

That turned Pender's mind to what the rest of the crew would do. Most, true to their nature, would act like sheep. But like sheep they'd also do nothing to protect their officers. If Garmond gained the upper hand then they'd follow him. But if Pender could take charge, just for a few seconds, then with his own men certainly behind him and Mr Wheeler in charge he could very likely carry the majority of the crew. Looking over the rail, with the French-man coming closer, he knew he couldn't wait. Garmond was hanging for some kind of signal, which would most likely come from the Frenchman. He might hold off until the first broadside was fired. But he could also start his assault as soon as the first muskets opened up, and this, with the ships edging closer, could only be a matter of minutes at the very most.

Unlike Harry Ludlow, Pender was not the type to take the bull by the horns. Sizing things up carefully before moving was more his line. But could he wait for whatever signal they'd worked out? If he did he'd be too late. The best thing he could do was to goad them into action. The man standing behind Wheeler, ladling water on to the deck, looked up as he shot across to the larboard side.

His hand reached back into the bucket. But it emerged holding a marlinspike, not a ladle. He lifted it to swipe at Wheeler's head. The third lieutenant, who'd looked with disapproval at the man rushing towards him, must have observed what was happening behind Pender.

Every man on the deck heard the cry of "Look out!" Most would have seen Toner, clubbed hard around the ear by Garmond, drop to the ground like a felled gamebird. While such a fate might please them, it would also cause alarm. Vaguely, Pender heard Garmond's shout.

"Come on, you swabs, we're takin' over the barky."

They would have seen Garmond swipe young Mr Hemmings across the face as the other men posted to attack took out McPartland and Dunlop. The marines swung their muskets, but with that many officers attacked, and the rest of Garmond's malcontents crowding round them, they were at a loss to know what to do. Sloman had his knife out, and had begun to hack at the first of the halyards when Jubilee hit him with an uppercut to the chin that lifted his feet clear of the deck. The crack of his bone breaking cut through the shouts of panic and alarm.

All of this, occurring in the space of a few seconds, was hidden from Pender. Wheeler's eyes had opened wide at what he'd seen, even more as Garmond's shout shattered the silence. No doubt assuming that Pender was intent on doing the same to him, he stepped forward to defend himself. The man behind him swung and missed, then pulled back his club for another strike. Pender threw up his arms to deflect those of Wheeler and pushed him to one side. He was under the lieutenant's guard before the officer knew it, taking the assailant in a tackle round the waist that drove him straight back into one of the cannon. He screamed with agony as the huge metal button on the base dug into his spine. Pender dropped him and turned to shout to the rest of the crew. He saw that McPartland had fended off his attacker and was now struggling with him. But whatever words Pender had formed were drowned out by the crash of the French cannon, as Monsieur d'Albret, having heaved his guns round to point to the rear, opened up with a full broadside.

The deck of the *Endymion* suddenly descended into chaos, with men who should have stood their ground flinging themselves to the deck. The shot hit the ship hard, making it shudder. Splinters flew from the bulwarks, slicing across the deck like huge deadly knives. One took McPartland in the back with a fatal blow of such force that it went right through his body and killed the man he was fighting. The quartermaster and his mates had let go of the wheel, allowing the head of the ship to fall off from the wind, which brought the guns on the larboard side to bear on the Frenchman. Some fired and others didn't, all of the shot expended heading straight into the sea. This brought forth a volley from the marines, who'd been pushed back by the gesticulating crew towards the larboard bulwark.

Garmond, who'd been hurtling across the deck to sort out Pender, went down rapidly, right beside McPartland's twitching body, as the balls whistled past his ears. A great cloud of black smoke billowed out, half from their own guns, but more from *Persephone,* and streamed across *Endymion*'s quarterdeck. Pender took advantage of this to propel the stunned Lieutenant Wheeler towards the wheel, shouting above the din to Flowers, ordering him to do likewise with Mr Callander. They had to step over the inert forms of Toner and Hemmings, and Pender had to yell at the quartermaster to get a grip on the wheel.

As the smoke cleared, Garmond, who'd raised himself, grabbed at the dead officer's sword. The naval hanger came out of its scabbard with an audible swish and Garmond held it aloft, as if in triumph. Matters hung in the balance as he began to approach the group by the wheel. The second French broadside swept by, this time above their heads. The rigging was sliced by the bar shot, with blocks and ropes falling to the deck. Garmond ignored it all, intent only on killing Pender. Wheeler, for his own protection, pulled out his sword and faced Garmond. The untrained clerk, who'd never even become an efficient sailor, was no match with such a weapon for the skilled officer. The swords clashed together twice, Garmond's being easily swept to one side by Wheeler's expert swing. The mutineer jumped backwards, so avoiding the third lieutenant's thrust. But Wheeler was quickly on him. Garmond would have died then, if Jubilee, at a signal from Pender, hadn't fetched him a clout as he passed him by. Garmond was poleaxed and crumpled in a heap at the officer's feet.

"Leave him, your honour," shouted Pender. "You must take command, Mr Wheeler."

Flowers pushed a bemused Callander to stand beside the wheel. "You too, Mr Callander."

"What happened?" demanded Wheeler.

Another broadside swept across the deck as *Persephone* fired again.

"There's no time for words, Mr Wheeler. If we don't sort ourselves out on this deck we'll be boarded and taken."

Years of discipline told then. Wheeler turned away from Pender and began to call out the orders that sent men to their rightful places.

"Man your guns, damn you. Load them and bring them to bear on the enemy. Mr Callander, take charge of the forward division on both sides. Quartermaster, resume our course and set me alongside that Frenchman."

He turned to give Pender an order. But the man was already gone, making his way down the deck pushing and cajoling the sailors to take their stations.

CHAPTER THIRTY-EIGHT

HARRY LUDLOW, ignoring the fire from *Marianne*'s bow-chasers, watched the actions of *Endymion* with mounting horror. The way she yawed off to windward, followed by that half-broadside in reply to Monsieur d'Albret's opening salvo, would have been risible to anyone in a less exposed position. All the shot had done was to churn up some water between the ships. As *Persephone* fired off her second discharge he lifted his telescope to focus it on *Endymion*'s quarterdeck. But he dropped it again. The smoke from the Frenchman's guns obscured the view. He did see that the British frigate was steadily coming back on to its original course. The bowsprit was now abreast of the Frenchman's taffrail. Some of the smoke cleared so he could see that Toner's marines had moved forward and opened up, playing their muskets on to d'Albret's quarterdeck. The commodore replied to this with another broadside, firing on the downroll, which sent wood flying in all directions. Harry observed *Endymion* stagger as the weight of metal pounded into her hull. Beside him, James, still seated, worked like a demon to record as many of the details as he could.

"Why doesn't she reply?" asked Matthew Caufield.

Harry's answer, with Toner firmly in his mind, had a bitterness that he'd hitherto managed to conceal. "If that last effort was anything to go by, they'd do better to try fishing."

Finally *Endymion*'s guns opened up. It was clearly intended to be a rolling broadside aimed at *Persephone*'s decorated stern, with each gun firing in turn. But, while it achieved a limited degree of success, it fell lamentably short by Harry Ludlow's standards. The gaps were uneven and the aim poor, though at such short range nearly every shot struck home. Only the last few guns showed any proficiency in aim and timing.

"At last," cried the young American, quite forgetting whose side he should be on. "They've done some real damage to those deadlights."

Harry refused to be cheered by this. "Make a note on your drawing, brother, that in three months and as many thousand miles, Toner's gunnery is of the same appalling standard as it was previously."

The crash as *Marianne* with a well-aimed shot removed Harry's stern lantern made them all spin round.

"Carpenter!" he yelled. "Check the rudder and report."

Some of his men were removing the headless corpse from the blood-stained deck, an act which finally made James pause. He laid aside his charcoal and pad then stood up. "Shall I go below now, to assist in the cockpit?"

Harry nodded. With what he had in mind he expected more casualties than that one he'd just sustained. "Mr Caufield, you are welcome to remain on deck, or to assist my brother in tending the wounded."

"Before I go, Harry?"

"I shan't risk more than is wise, brother. Pender wouldn't want to get all his mates killed just to rescue him. Besides, we've already achieved much. We have pinned *Persephone* in place and prevented Villemin from coming up on Toner's larboard side at a time of his own choosing. My intention is to occupy enough of Monsieur d'Albret's men to prevent them making a swift attempt at boarding *Endymion*. That will permit Toner to inflict some damage. I cannot trade broadsides with him, since his guns are of a heavier calibre than mine. So, as soon as I have stung him, and before his consort can interfere, I intend to come about, with the wind behind me, and try and place some round shot in his living quarters. What happens after that will depend on how things turn out."

"What about that ship with the Bourbon flag?" asked Matthew Caufield.

"I have even less knowledge of his plans than I do of Toner's. If he comes within range of my guns before he's declared himself, I shall treat him as hostile."

"Matthew?" asked James.

"I shall remain here, if I may, Mr Ludlow."

"Good luck, Harry," said James, as he turned away to go below.

Pender, as he hauled on the tackle that brought the 18-pounder cannon back into its firing position, was looking over the rail of *Endymion* wondering how he could tell Harry Ludlow what had happened. The actions of Mr Wheeler had surprised him. He'd fully expected the third lieutenant, with most of the other officers out of commission, to break off the action. But he hadn't. Instead, he sent the unconscious officers to the cockpit, called for Overton, the youngster in charge of the party on the relieving tackles, to come up on deck and take charge of his division, and after a word to Callander, he'd set about calming the men and preparing them to respond to the enemy's gunfire. This was no easy task with round shot, musket balls, grapeshot, and bar shot flying in all directions. Most of the crew had never seen action and there were a few who cowered in the scuppers. Wheeler took time to encourage them and get them back to their places. Having twice walked the length of the deck, he paced it a third time, personally ordering each gun to fire as he passed.

The art of a rolling broadside was that with the ship in motion and gaining on the enemy each shot landed in close proximity to its predecessor. Properly timed, it was a sure way to wound the opposition. At the very least it would do the kind of damage that would keep a good section of the opposing crew occupied in repairs. But this, for all Wheeler's efforts, proved to be a ragged affair. And the aim of the guns, barring the rearward section, was as variable as the timing of the firing. Still, it wasn't all wasted. With what could only be termed luck, the forward cannon smashed d'Albret's deadlights. Number six, amidships, sent another ball into what had been his cabin. The rearmost guns, manned by men from the *Bucephalas,* made a much better fist of their task, sending their shot, accurately, through the existing gap. The angle of fire precluded the kind of carnage that would have occurred had they been sitting across their opponent's stern. But the sound of tearing wood, accompanied by the odd scream, settled the less experienced men and satisfied them that they were not complete tyros.

D'Albret put his helm down and let the wind bring him closer to *Endymion.* This also allowed him to concentrate the fire of his cannon on the forward guns of his enemy. Clearly, he'd noticed that they were less of a threat than the rest. Destroying them, when his rate of fire was probably faster, would open up an undefended area through which he could board. Wheeler, aware that Harry's men would reload faster than their fellows, ordered them to fire at will, then stationed himself behind the forward cannon to co-ordinate their efforts. The two frigates were now abreast of each other, separated from the rest of existence in a maelstrom of flying metal and wood, with the shouts of men at war mixed with the screams of the wounded, all overborne by the near-deafening noise of booming cannon. The inexperienced men on the *Endymion*'s deck were learning as they worked and within half a dozen firings they were keeping pace with their French counterparts. This was nothing to do with instruction. The quantity of smoke and the level of noise was so great that it became impossible for a man to see, or think, beyond his own little area of the battle. Pender, acting as gun captain on the rearmost cannon, felt himself tugged by the shoulder as Wheeler pushed another man in to take his place.

"Do you have any idea what your captain intends?" he yelled.

Pender, too, had to shout in reply. "None, your honour. All I can tell you is he's a fighter. He wouldn't be sitting where he is without a mind to do some mischief."

"If I seek to board the Frenchman on this side, will he attack from the other?"

Pender pointed through the smoke to the dim outline of *Marianne*. "Not with that other sod in the offin', beggin' your pardon."

"Would he obey me if I signalled him to do so?"

Pender shook his head emphatically. Whatever else his captain was, he was not one to take any orders he didn't agree with. He put his mouth next to Wheeler's ear. "If you trust him, your honour, I can swear he won't let you down."

Wheeler smiled at that. Given what Pender had done it would be a fool who disbelieved him. "Then I shall just have to do as you say, Pender, and put my faith in his good judgement."

"Sir," shouted Callander, running towards them with a telescope in his hand. "Mr Overton has spotted another ship to windward of *Persephone*. You will observe her from the foredeck. She's flying the old French flag, the royal one."

Wheeler grabbed the telescope and ran towards the bows. Callander, his face blackened by smoke, grinned at Pender. The older man, in strict contravention of the Articles of War, patted him on the shoulder. "Some of the gunners on the starboard side are getting weary, Mr Callander. Permission to replace them in ones and twos from Mr Overton's division?"

The boy didn't hesitate, or even throw a glance forward towards his superior. "Carry on, Pender." Then he was gone, yelling to the men on the starboard guns to keep firing.

"He's coming round, Captain Ludlow," cried Matthew Caufield. "And he's run out his larboard cannon. I think he aims to put himself across the commodore's bows."

Harry, who'd detailed the youngster to keep an eye on the stranger, turned to look. He sincerely hoped that Matthew had the right of it. *Endymion,* while dishing out a great deal of destruction, was getting more in return. Her rigging was in tatters, with ropes and tackle dropping on to the protective netting. Given that d'Albret was directing a full fifty per cent of his fire into the tops, it was only a matter of time before he hit something serious. It was essential to tip the balance in Toner's favour. He'd been watching the *Marianne,* as she failed to make any gain on *Bucepha-las.* In fact, the gap had opened slightly, which might just give him enough time to do something really effective. What he'd said to James, at the time, had been a hope rather than a certainty. Something too close to call. Now with the gap opening it was becoming more of a possibility. He wanted to favour *Persephone* with just one broadside, then, by coming up into the wind, use that to make a very fast turn. By boxing the compass, and bringing the wind in at his best point of sailing, he could cross *Persephone*'s stern and bring his carronades into play.

Nothing was more telling than an attack from such a quarter. The problem was his shortage of men. There would be a delay, after he'd fired off and reloaded his larboard guns, before his men could get to their stations in the tops. His opponent, observing this, might guess what he was about. Villemin, if he was quick enough, could swing broadside on, bringing all his power to bear on the weaker ship. A vessel in the process of tacking through 275°, when she was nearly stationary, was extremely vunerable. The distraction of this stranger, dead ahead, would place Villemin in two minds, something which had proved advantageous in the past.

Matthew Caufield jumped backwards as the rearmost guns of *Persephone*'s starboard division opened up, churning up the water in front of *Bucephalas.* He looked at Harry, who smiled in return. "He's merely trying to scare us off. How's that Bourbon schooner faring?"

It was as if the captain of the schooner heard. At that moment, though they were at extreme range, he fired off his cannon. Light guns, at such a distance, did little in the way of damage. In fact, a goodly number didn't cover the distance, merely drenching *Perse-phone*'s side as they fell short. But they did have one very positive result. There was now no doubt at all about which side this strange ship was on.

"Stand by on the larboard guns!" yelled Harry as he took a firm grip on the wheel.

◆ ◆ ◆

Antoine de la Mery had fired off his guns to steady his men, who were showing signs of nervousness at the approaching battle. He knew it wasn't fear. They were Frenchmen firing on their fellow countrymen. It was necessary to remind them of what had happened on the beach the previous year. He asked them to remember how Victor Hugues had murdered their fellows, merely because they wore a white coat. Then, as the sound of cannon fire boomed across the intervening sea, he pointed to the flag above their heads.

"I am no lover of kings. But I am even less a lover of the kind of tyranny that men like Victor Hugues spread. Some of you come from Brittany. Need I remind you what rumour says Hugues did in Brest? How many of you hail from the Vendée? You have heard what the Committee of Public Safety did in Nantes. They are Frenchmen under that tricolour. But they are not like us. Anyone who does not wish to fight them, who wishes to see Victor Hugues strengthened, favours the idea of an increased tyranny, can go below and take no part in what is about to happen."

He toyed with the idea of telling them that their cruising days were over, but decided against it. Those with any wit would realize, and those without would not be swayed by such a statement. The loud murmuring that followed was prolonged but gratifying. Not one of his men moved.

"Good. What we do, we do for our country. For the France of 1789, not the France of Robespierre, King Louis, or Victor Hugues."

As he took the wheel, to turn *Ariadne* back to a heading that would take her into the heat of the battle, he saw the ship dead ahead begin to swing into the wind.

Harry had got himself close enough to *Persephone*'s side casements to rip the starboard windows apart. The cannon that poked out from d'Albret's sleeping quarters, one of the few the commodore could bring to bear on *Bucephalas,* took a carronade ball right on the muzzle. A long nine, it simply burst apart, the metal being driven backwards into the confined space of the interior, there to combine with the flying glass from the windows, all to wreak a terrible harvest of soft human flesh. The men who'd fired that deadly broadside were working feverishly to reload, while their captain calculated the amount of headway he'd lost in relation to Villemin. The cannon were run out and lashed off at commendable speed and the topmen ran for the shrouds, racing aloft. They were well aware that their lives could depend on it, while their shipmates, with equal alacrity, took station on the braces. Only when they were in position, and he was sure that what he was attempting stood a fair chance of success, did Harry spin the wheel.

Bucephalas, brought right up into the wind, still with the topsails set, stopped as though some great hand had placed itself on the bow. The men on the braces hauled the yards round and the ship started to spin as others let spill the jibs so that the force of the breeze could push the ship's head round. As soon as she had begun to turn they hauled them tight again, adding their canvas to the effort. The equatorial current, running towards the Saintes channel, was against *Bucephalas,* but the steady trades proved powerful enough to overcome the deadening effect of the leeway. Aloft the topmen waited, hunched over the yards, ready to do their part.

Harry watched as his bows edged round, till they were aimed at *Marianne.* Villemin had seen what he was about and begun to turn to starboard. That was when the Bourbon schooner, still sitting at an angle to *Persephone*'s bows, fired her second broadside. She was much closer this time and the gunfire, closely concentrated, shot half of d'Albret's forward sails away. Villemin hesitated, and started to reverse his movement to bring him back on his original course. No doubt he hoped he could get across Harry's stern on the way past, give him a broadside through his rear, then go on to engage the Bourbon. That was the calculation that had so worried his opponent. Harry had no intention of being there when *Marianne* went by. With the wind on his best point of sailing, he was going to cross *Persephone*'s hawse, inflict the maximum damage, then sail on out of harm's way.

Bucephalas was still swinging. Now the guns that had fired at *Persephone* were aimed at the on-coming *Marianne*. He called out for more sail and the topmen let go the courses, while at the same time the men on deck hauled the topsails till they drew. The wind took his ship beautifully and she eased forward, picking up speed. The shrouds and the deck were, yet again, full of running men as the crew made their way to the loaded starboard guns. No broadside this time, but the kind of rolling affair that did so much internal damage when fired through the unprotected stern. The first cannon, fired at point-blank range, put round shot through the already smashed deadlights, a ball that with nothing to impede its progress would travel all the way from stern to bows of the French ship, killing or maiming anyone who got in its path.

D'Albret had sent his sharpshooters to the taffrail. Harry saw two of his gunners, on the second cannon, spin suddenly and fall to the deck. Number three fired as those on *Persephone*'s quarterdeck began to reload. He handed over the wheel to the quartermaster, grabbed a musket, and passed it to Matthew Caufield as he ran by.

"Those fellows on the quarterdeck. Take one of them if you can. But at the very least, keep their heads down."

Harry ran down the deck calling to the remaining men on the cannon that had fired, stopping them from reloading and directing them to take up muskets so as to protect their fellows. The French sharpshooters got off one more volley before they themselves came under musket fire. That forced them to duck their heads down behind the rail and reduced their efforts to single shots. Even that died away as they discovered that a raised head immediately became the target of several well-aimed muskets. All the time the noise continued, as the two battling frigates exchanged broadsides. Harry, making his way back to the wheel, was now looking straight up the narrowing gap between the ships. The sea was full of debris from both vessels, with great clouds of smoke alternately masking everything before being torn away by the wind to reveal yet more destruction. Half of *Endymion*'s forward bulwarks were shot away and the rigging showed even more signs of damage. The battle was reaching the climax, the moment when one or the other must board and seek to effect a conclusion.

Another broadside erupted from *Persephone*. This time, either by accident or design, they'd fired their round shot high, and Harry saw the mizzen-mast cap take the full effect of the salvo, saw the marines posted there blown into oblivion. The topmast began to sway backwards just as his own bows were passing *Endymion*'s stern. There was nothing he could do. The man on the wheel did his best to get them out of danger. But the time to do so was simply not available. The mizzen toppled, just as the first of his deadly carronades fired. The ball smashed through the remaining stern-lights and a huge wail of screams emerged from *Persephone*'s upper deck. But Harry wasn't looking, or listening. Time took on a new, slow dimension as the mizen-mast collapsed, bringing with it a mass of spars and cables. The great boom that held the lateen sail crashed into the sea. But the upper section, with the topsail and top-gallant yards, came down across Harry's jib-boom, smashing it down and tangling itself in the skein of sheets and blocks. Any forward motion of the *Bucephalas* was now a danger to both ships. Harry, ordering the other guns to fire off, jumped for the shrouds, followed by every man that was spare. Others could deal with clearing the bows. At this moment his sails were acting like a great rudder, forcing *Endymion* round so that her bows would crash into *Persephone*.

Half the Frenchman's stern disappeared as the last of Harry's guns fired. The interior of the ship would be a bloodbath. He succeeded admirably in what he'd set out to do. But that was small compensation for the peril he was in. Villemin was coming on and he would soon be in position to do to *Bucephalas* what Harry Ludlow had done to his commodore.

CHAPTER THIRTY-NINE

PENDER had been working his cannon, close to the mizzen shrouds, when the round shot smashed into the mast. He'd vaguely registered that *Bucephalas* was crossing her opponent's stern, but had been too busy with working his gun to pay much heed, only registering that the opposing fire had slackened somewhat. But the sound of falling timber, plus the deluge of blocks and pulleys that this released, forced him to abandon his task and rush forward to seek safety. Looking back from amidships he saw what the Frenchman's last salvo had achieved. The falling rigging had engulfed the men conning the ship but the wheel was intact, so she was still capable of steering if the debris could be cleared. Shouting, with all the noise of battle around him, was useless. Instead he grabbed an axe, pushed it into a nearby pair of hands, then propelled the man forward, making gestures to tell him what to do. Some of his shipmates reacted to this dumb show and made their own way aft. Others had to be driven to the task, their first job being to clear the wheel.

The effect this drag was having on *Endymion* was immediately obvious to Mr Wheeler, still forward of the waist directing the gunfire. His first assumption was that the wheel had been shot away, something that could be rectified by the use of the relieving tackles, ropes which could operate the rudder from below decks. It wasn't till he'd passed the mainmast that he saw the true cause. Pender and his party were already there, gathered around the companion-way that led to Toner's cabin, hacking at the heavy stays which held the mizzen fast to the ship. Part of the problem was that, lying across the quarterdeck, it was not heavy enough in any one direction to drag itself over the side, so that even when they sliced through a rope, it did nothing to carry the mast any further to the point where it would either drop into the sea, or be carried clear by *Bucephalas*.

"Belay, there!" shouted Wheeler. This was done to very little purpose. But his physical attempts to stop the men came to the notice of enough to render the efforts of the rest pointless. One of these was Pender, halfway up the companion ladder and well ahead of his mates, hacking away like a demon at a whole tangle of ropes. Wheeler grabbed him and spun him round, an act which nearly earned him a clout with the boarding axe.

"Crawl through to the taffrail and call to your captain. Tell him that we are going to board across the bows in ten minutes' time."

Pender, who'd looked out of control when Wheeler grabbed him, suddenly grinned, which made his white teeth look like pearls in his blackened face. The lieutenant lip-read his response of "Aye, aye, sir."

Wheeler grabbed at the remainder of the men who had been working with him and pushed them back towards the bows. As he passed Mr Callander he gave him his orders. He instructed the young Scotsman to take his division forward and attack over the bows. Then he crossed the deck to tell young Overton to assemble his division by the smashed bulwarks. Pender, meanwhile, was crawling along the damaged mizzen, praying that it wouldn't suddenly decide to free itself and carry him with it into the sea. By the taffrail he dropped through the mass of ropes and crawled underneath till he reached a clear space. With some difficulty he threaded himself through the rigging and strips of torn canvas till he was standing upright.

Harry had watched his men trying to free his ship with mounting frustration. Given that Villemin was close by he stood no chance of getting clear in time to avoid a severe drubbing. But he was not one to cry surrender. His mind was still clear and he realized that some chance still remained to affect the outcome of the fight. Close to the battle, he had as much difficulty making himself heard as those aboard *Endymion*. He grabbed a speaking trumpet to magnify his voice and called for his men to be prepared to board, just as Pender's blackened face popped up through the skein of ropes twenty yards away. He saw the lips moving, but could make no sense of the words. He raised his trumpet and shouted out the information that he was about to board through the Frenchman's damaged stern, which brought a blackamoor's grin to his servant's face. Then with a wave, Pender was gone.

"Mr Caufield. Would you oblige me by going below and informing my brother that we are going to board. I doubt that Monsieur Villemin will go by without giving us his compliments. But I hope his main concern will be to save his commodore. Should this prove to be the case I will leave someone aboard with instructions to haul down our colours."

"What shall I do then, Captain?"

"You will stay below," snapped Harry. "On no account come back up on to the deck when Villemin is crossing our hawse."

"I'd rather join you, sir."

Harry put his hand on the boy's shoulder. "That's bravely said, Matthew. But this is not your fight, and if things do not go well aboard *Persephone* I rather fear there will be little quarter, given or taken."

"But . . ."

"Please tell James not to be depressed. The element of chance dictates that there still exists a way to put matters right."

His men had obeyed handsomely, and were already throwing the grappling irons that would haul the ship round till they made contact by the stern. D'Albret was wise to the danger, and a few men had already begun to gather in his smashed cabin to oppose such a move. Some of Harry's crew had climbed up the shrouds so that they could leap directly on to the quarterdeck. Their captain was busy issuing orders to those who would stay aboard. Since his guns were loaded and run out they were to fire each one in turn, doing as much to deter Villemin as possible. He gave a final look towards the looming bulk of the *Marianne,* then set himself at the head of his party, just before the two vessels collided.

It was de la Mery's American invalid who pointed out what had happened. Thrown out of his cot by the impending fight he'd declined to go below. Not having time to argue, the men sent to help him left him to his own devices. With some difficulty, he dragged himself up on to the quarterdeck so that he could observe the action. At this distance, with the wind blowing away from him, the smoke only obscured part of the unfolding events. He could see, clearly, the French gunners loading and running out their guns. Through the smoke that followed their discharge, billowing up as well as out, he saw the top of the British frigate's mizzen begin to go. Then, observing how the forward motion of the smaller ship ceased, he turned and made his way to the wheel, a point where he could inform de la Mery.

The Frenchman ran to take a look, well aware that such an event threatened him as much as those to whom he'd allied himself. At all costs something must be done to keep that 28-gun frigate out of the fight. Even as he watched the situation was changing, with the two battling ships seemingly destined to collide broadside on. Who would attempt to board first was an irrelevance, since it was a contest in which morale counted as much as any other factor. If that 28 came up on the commodore's open side, he'd be able to add his men to the fight, which would almost ensure a triumph. If there had been any lingering doubts, the thought that the two frigates might separate, they were laid to rest. The mainmast, with the commodore's pennant flying proudly at the top, leant drunkenly to one side, then majestically, under pressure from the wind, it toppled over and fouled in the British ship's rigging. They were locked together now, in an embrace that could only have one outcome.

De la Mery was shouting the orders to come about before he

turned away. Whatever doubts his crew had harboured before, they were with him now. Perhaps the mere smell of battle was enough to ignite them. They rushed to their stations willingly and hauled like maniacs to bring the *Ariadne* on to a new heading. Her bottom might be foul and her timbers a touch weak, but she answered well. He set himself straight for the 28-gun ship, determined to draw her away from the fight. Together, the other two ships should muster enough of a crew to defeat the commodore. If they could achieve that quickly enough, and cut down that damned tricolour, then the other captain would sheer off and look to save his own ship rather than risk it being taken.

The great gap in *Endymion*'s bulwarks provided an obvious avenue of attack for either commander. Usually the attacking boarder, with morale high, held the advantage, even if the numbers were even. Wheeler, aware of this, could not understand why those opposite him, instead of carrying the fight to his deck, had adopted a purely defensive posture. He was unaware, of course, that d'Albret, who would dearly have loved to forestall him, was stymied by what was happening at the stern. With a strong party of men attacking from that direction he dare not leave his ship. If that flank collapsed, then no matter how much he achieved on *Endymion*'s deck, the outcome would still be defeat. The gap between the two ships was now a matter of yards, with men throwing buckets of water, trying to soak the touch-holes of the opposing cannon so they couldn't be fired. Not that anyone seemed to be in a hurry to go near them. The remaining marines had abandoned any other targets since the last broadside and were occupied shooting any gunner who attempted to reload.

The French sharpshooters were equally busy trying to decimate the boarders. In such a crowd they could hardly miss. Wheeler, reacting to a particularly loud scream, turned round. He saw Callander lead his party up the larboard side towards the forecastle. The youngster had ordered his men to stay close to the back of the main party, then hunch down so that their progress would not be observed. Pender, bringing up the rear, pushed his way through the throng towards the third lieutenant and shouted Harry's message. He could see the effect these words had on the young man. The shoulders went back and the lines of worry disappeared from his brow. He'd seen his intended attack as a forlorn hope, a last throw that with luck might produce a result. Now, with the news that Pender had brought, he could see a real chance of victory.

"Permission to join Mr Callander, your honour?"

"Granted! And Pender, take good care of him." He turned to the other midshipman, Overton, and smiled. "You are lucky, boy. There are admirals who've never had an opportunity like this."

Getting through the smashed sternlights had been a bloody affair, with close-quarter fighting of the most deadly kind. No progress could be made without stepping over those who'd already fallen. Harry had a deep cut across his cheek and another where a boarding pike had slashed through the arm of his shirt. Yet a glance at his men would have shown that he was no exception. It seemed that none of them had got through the casements without a wound. Yet the heat of the fight sustained them, suppressing any feelings of pain. And they had succeeded in their main aim, which was to drive the defenders far enough back to deploy their full strength. Now they stood shoulder to shoulder, a solid wall which was proving hard to resist. Behind them they could hear the sound of cannon fire as those left aboard *Bucephalas* carried out Harry's instructions, while Villemin responded in kind. But the firing on the main-deck, ahead of them, had died away, a clear indication that Toner had boarded.

That also explained their own progress. They could never have got aboard in the face of resistance by the whole crew. Not that they were making much headway now. The advance that allowed them to deploy also had certain advantages for the defence. They'd suffered at the casements by their inability to bring maximum pressure to bear. Now, on the open deck, their numbers, considerably greater than Harry's, could count for something. But retreat was not to be contemplated. There wasn't a man in Harry's party who didn't know that should they falter, and surrender even one strake of planking, retreating by way of the sternlights would be a lot more dangerous.

Above their heads the fighting was even more desperate as those who'd landed on the quarterdeck struggled to prevent their opponents from dropping down behind the party below. James, bearing a brace of pistols and accompanied by Matthew Caufield, had come up just as *Marianne* fired off her last cannon. It was as well that few men had stayed to man the deck. The rigging was in tatters and great chunks of wood were missing from her stern. Two of the forward cannon had been blasted off their trucks, killing one of the gunners and wounding three others. A sustained attack of this nature would have reduced *Bucephalas* to a hulk. But the Frenchman had eschewed such a course and passed by. The side of his ship was now lined with men, all waving weapons and cheering madly. Villemin was putting his helm down, to join in the fighting on *Persephone*'s deck. James turned to look himself and spotted that the men on the quarterdeck were struggling to maintain their foothold. Since Harry's guns were now useless he ordered everyone aboard to follow him and provide assistance.

Not being a sailor, James arrived long after the others. Their intervention had obviously been welcome since the fighting had receded somewhat. He could see Matthew Caufield swinging his cutlass with as much abandon as any crew member. James made his way forward, pistol held out, looking for a gap through which he could contribute. His wish was provided in the most unfortunate manner as one of Harry's crew fell in front of him. The rammer from a musket, fired in panic, had buried itself in his chest. James stepped over him and moved into the gap, only to find himself threatened by a great bearded fellow with yellow, stained teeth intent on separating his head from his body with a cleaver. The way he fired his guns owed more to fear than ability but the effect was the same. One took the man in the eye and another on the chin, throwing his head back in a ferocious jerk. As he dropped, his companion to the right thrust at James with the butt end of a pike, taking him in the ribs. The blow was painful. Worse than that, it drove him backwards. When he recovered and tried to re-enter the fray, the gap had closed.

The sound of cannon fire distracted him and dragged his attention to what was happening over the starboard rail. The sight of the ship mystified him until he spotted the fleur-de-lis. He'd completely forgotten about the Bourbon schooner, which had obviously come up hand over fist, intent on interposing herself between *Marianne* and *Persephone*. It would have been a near suicidal idea if Villemin had his guns manned. As it was, this stranger was doing better than he could possibly have hoped or imagined.

As he sailed into action, it became clear to de la Mery that the captain of the 28-gun frigate intended to ignore him. He'd watched with dismay as the cannon tore great chunks out of the ship, now lashed and near stationary by the commodore's stern. He'd fully expected the smaller frigate to back her topsails and finish the job, allowing him to come up and engage. But whoever commanded the 28 had decided instead to board his consort, with the aim of forcing a conclusion. This information, and the sight of the men leaving their guns to fetch their boarding weapons, was relayed to him from a lookout in the tops. The angle caused by the differing heights of the two decks prevented him from having a clear view of his own. In possession of such information, he issued new orders to his gunners.

"When you've fired off your cannon, reload with grape."

Then he spun the wheel. It would be useless to stay to windward with what he had in mind. He must get to leeward of the 28, between him and his commodore.

James observed the result better than de la Mery. From his higher elevation on d'Albret's quarterdeck he saw the effect of the first salvo of round shot, fired at long range. Firstly, it forced Villemin to back his topsails, so that he came to a virtual standstill. Men who'd been crowding the side ducked for cover as the balls whistled past the point where their heads had been. But that was as nothing to the carnage caused by the next broadside. Those same men had raised their heads to jeer. The grapeshot, fired at a rate they'd never anticipated, took them by surprise. Many were too slow to react, and paid the price. The yelling from up ahead made James jump on to the shattered taffrail, holding the flagstaff to support himself. From that vantage point he could see the whole of the maindeck, covered with a struggling mass of bodies, weaving to and fro by the larboard side. Regardless of what happened here, that was where matters would be resolved.

CHAPTER FORTY

AS HE THRUST and parried Wheeler decided that there could be few more dangerous modes of conflict than the mayhem inherent in boarding an enemy ship. Discipline, in the military sense, was non-existent. As a commander he was in the thick of it, finding it very difficult, no matter how hard he tried, to disengage and take enough backward steps to direct the efforts of others. Every time he downed one enemy a new one appeared to take his place. Beside him, Midshipman Overton was doing his best. But the lieutenant realized that the boy was physically too immature for such an affair, a fact that was made plain by the way his own left side was constantly being exposed as the youngster was driven back. He opened his mouth to give him new orders, no easy matter since his tongue and throat were too dry to speak properly.

"A message to Mr Callander," he croaked. He had to stop then, to parry a man with a spiked club, which had been raised to crush his skull. Wheeler's sword flashed upwards and cut into the wood, holding the whole upright, including the attacker's arm. Overton, for the first time, achieved a worthwhile result, as he thrust up into the man's belly with his dirk. Somehow Wheeler found the spit and the breath to thank him.

"Obliged to you, young sir. Now carry out my instructions. Bid him make haste, or he'll arrive in time to see us back on our own deck."

Overton, covered by his superior, slipped away easily, his position being filled immediately as the line closed up. The man who took his place, being tall, could see over the heads of the enemy, a scene he conveyed to his commander.

"They're getting set to charge us, your honour. They's got their muskets lining up at the rear. An' they're fixin' their bayonets, an' all."

Wheeler knew that whatever the risk, he had to see for himself.

"Cover me, men," he yelled. Those either side obliged him without having the faintest idea what he intended. But Wheeler didn't, as they expected, attempt to go forward to almost certain death. Instead, with a vicious thrust at the man before him, he jumped backwards and made for an intact bulwark. At last he could raise himself and get some idea, both of the state of the battle, as well as an appreciation of the danger this new development posed. It was worse than his crewman had said. Monsieur d'Albret had gathered not only his sharpshooters, who stood in a disciplined line. He was also fetching men from below, which would indicate that he'd contained the attack from that direction. The men at stern seemed to be in stalemate, neither making nor losing ground. He looked along his own wavering line, painfully thin in places. A determined attack by the French, in the right spot, would break it in two. Once that happened the cohesion which had sustained them until now would be broken. Defeat wasn't certain to follow, but it was probable in a situation where, because of the tangled rigging, he could not discontinue the action by sheering off. The only hope he could still muster, which was a slim one given their numbers, was that Callander and his party, struggling to scale the forward bulwarks, would arrive in time to break up this threat.

Those fighting below decks noticed that their situation had eased. Even then progress was painfully slow, an inch at a time. But they were at last moving forward at a satisfactory pace. Harry was bemused by this till he actually saw some men disengaging and running up the companion-way. He was too experienced to see this as anything other than a tactic. D'Albret wasn't beaten yet. But the Frenchman was clearly willing to trade ground below, in order to strengthen his numbers on the maindeck. That could mean only one thing; that matters had reached crisis point with the main boarding party, and that the commodore expected a major thrust would hurl them back. At first he tried to increase the pressure, in an attempt to break through. But the men in front of him had taken a defensive posture, which made it even harder to dent their line. The route to the deck was coming tantalizingly close, a mere twenty feet away. But with the force between him and his goal, whose sole object was to hold the continuity of their place, it might as well have been a mile.

"Bucephalases, fall back!" he yelled, a shout which echoed in the confined space.

The order took every man fighting with him by surprise. But it was here that their experience, their faith in their captain, plus all the training he'd put them through, paid off. They stepped back as a unit, drawing some of the defenders with them, who, in the heat of the moment, and seeing only a retreating enemy, ignored the command to hold fast. Harry now had what he wanted. The line he faced was no longer solid. Taking a firmer grip on both his sword and his knife, he yelled the order to return to the attack and rushed forward to take the nearest man in the flank.

Overton found Callander on the forecastle, so heavily engaged as to be incapable of receiving orders. The young Scotsman was yelling wildly in his heathen Gaelic, either ignoring or unaware of the great bloody gash on his forehead. He and three others were holding off a superior force of at least a dozen Frenchmen while Pender hacked at the breechings holding one of the bow-chasers. The thick soft ropes were more difficult to cut than wet cable. If curses would have helped, the stream emanating from Pender's lips would have severed them in a second.

They'd been repulsed on their first attempt to get aboard. *Endymion* had a slightly lower forecastle than *Persephone*. Added to that they were attempting to make progress over a section of the bulwarks untouched by the recent gunfire. Worse still, with the sweep of the bows, there was a dangerous gap to jump across, making it difficult to enter the fight in any co-ordinated fashion. Leaving the two groups stabbing at each other across the divide, Callander and Pender had taken Flowers, Jubilee, and a massive brute called Fogarty and tried further forward, where the gap between the vessels was even greater. The French were unprepared for this, which had allowed them to achieve this slender foothold. But they weren't winning, they were retreating. Pender was aware that they were fighting right above his head as the last of the breechings parted.

"Jubilee!" he shouted. "On the gun."

The Pole stepped back and grabbed the frayed rope that was thrust into his hand. Pender leapt across the black metal barrel to take the other side himself. "Watch your back, Mr Callander, Flowers. Heave away, Jubilee."

The deck was canted at this point, which meant as soon as the two men got the wheels of the gun carriage moving, it continued, gathering speed, under its own momentum. Callander and Flowers jumped aside as it trundled past them. The men who'd been trying to force them back did not have the luxury of room, crowded as they were by their sheer numbers. Some of them tried to jump the gun, only to fall victim to a sword thrust from the trio following up. Two men went down under it, screaming in panic and pain as the great carriage swept across their unprotected legs, crushing the bones to pulp. Pender had his head over the side, yelling to the men further down to break off and make their way to join him through the now empty gun port. The first head through was that of Mr Overton.

"Mr Wheeler's compliments, Pender, to Mr Callander," he gasped. "There's an attack bein' prepared and could he make haste."

Pender was gasping himself, with the effort he'd just expended, and was in no mood to be polite to a shaver like Overton. "If you would oblige me by moving your arse, young sir, my men are trying to get through the hole you're fillin' at this very minute."

Overton opened his mouth to put Pender in his place. But the words died as he was grabbed by his collar and hauled out of the way with such force that he fetched up on to his feet. Pender was pointing down the deck with his free hand. "If you have your sword, young sir, Mr Callander requires assistance."

No sooner was Overton through the gunport than a steady stream of men followed him, pushing him ahead as they made their way down the deck to join in the fight. The midshipman was involved before he could deliver his message. Pender was alongside the last men through, cajoling them to move steady, fight hard, and hold their line. But what he saw over the heads of those in front caused him to pause. He forbade the late arrivals to enter the fight, instead forming them up behind in a tight group. Then, having ordered a couple of men to stand by to take his place, he grabbed Mr Callander's shirt collar with as much ceremony as he had shown Overton, and dragged the youngster out of the fight.

"Look there, your honour," he cried, pointing towards the line of sharpshooters gathering on the main-deck, with a small group of sailors armed with axes and cutlasses forming up at their rear. "You've got to mount a proper assault right now or they'll chuck Mr Wheeler back aboard *Endymion*. I've got most of the men ready."

A flap of skin had fallen forward over the deep cut in his forehead. Pender whipped off the bandana he'd been wearing while firing the cannon and wrapped it untidily round Callander's head. "Are you up to this, boy?"

"I am, Pender, never fear," he replied, in his clear, slow English. The eyes had a distant quality, as though he was drunk. But there was no doubting his resolve. He turned and put himself at the head of the party gathered behind, yelled an incomprehensible oath in Gaelic that carried above every other noise on the deck, and charged forward shouting for his own sailors to get out of the way.

Harry's ploy had paid off. He'd split the French force and driven them down either side of the companion-way, which left the way clear for his men to ascend. Now the position was reversed as his rear-guard fought to stop the enemy following them up on to the maindeck. Harry emerged into the sunlight, yelling, at the head of his party, to see a middle-aged officer with his sword raised. The man's head spun round in alarm, which revealed a lined greyish face with deep-set brown eyes. Judging by his coat and decorations, plus his position by the wheel, this was Monsieur d'Albret himself. He was just about to order a body of men to advance into the fight that was going on in front of them, when Harry's arrival threw his plans into disarray. The crowd of sailors behind, at a shouted command from their commodore, rushed to intercept. Once more Harry's party found themselves stopped by the sheer number of their opponents. And not just halted, pushed back towards the companion-way. He was now in quite desperate straits, with one party trying to force him back down the stairwell, while down below those he'd been fighting earlier were trying to push their way up.

Even above the din, the shouts of triumph and loss, the clash of wood and metal, he heard the outlandish Gaelic cry of young Callander. Raising his eyes from his own fight he saw Pender beside the blond hair and swinging cutlass of a young officer. His men were sweeping down the gangway, brushing aside those Frenchmen taken in the flank. Harry tried to match the quality of the hellish cry as he urged his own men forward. Wheeler likewise took heart from this sudden assault and leapt back into the fight.

Pender, Jubilee, and Flowers were in amongst the sharpshooters now. The tight formation they'd adopted worked to their disadvantage, allowing them to be broken into piecemeal pockets. And at such close quarters their bayoneted muskets, which would have scythed through any opposing line of sailors who stood before them, couldn't swing. So they were useless, either as blades or clubs. They went down in numbers as Callander's party literally swept over them. Harry had to drop his sword in a hurry as the filthy young midshipman, in a tattered shirt, wearing a sweat-stained bandana, careered straight into him. The boy, whose eyes seemed as mad as his yelling, raised his weapon to strike, but Pender was quick enough to grab his upraised arm and prevent him from killing his own captain.

Suddenly the fight had gone out of the French. Assaulted on three sides and feeling outnumbered, they made haste to discard their weapons and surrender. Lieutenant Wheeler, catapulted forward with as much ceremony as Callander, stumbled into d'Albret, who, knowing that all was lost, dropped his sword to his side. The silence that fell and the speed that it did so, surprised everyone. Within seconds Harry, James, Matthew Caufield, Callander, and Wheeler stood together in a space that had been cleared by their victorious men. Monsieur d'Albret stepped forward, his sword flat in his hands, his eyes searching the tattered group before him for some sign of the person to whom he should surrender his sword.

The crash of cannon fire shattered the illusion that matters were concluded. Headed by Harry, the entire party rushed to the starboard side. There they saw that the Bourbon schooner was in some difficulties. Villemin had put aside the idea of boarding and, stung by the casualties he'd suffered, remanned his guns to rid himself of this pest. Harry was the first to understand that the *Marianne*'s captain had no idea that his commodore had surrendered. He forced his way through the crowd and slashed at the halyard holding the tricolour. A hoarse and spontaneous cheer came from every British throat as the flag fluttered down towards the deck.

Antoine de la Mery was nearly clear. Having peppered the 28-gun frigate with several salvoes of grape, he'd swung round to slip past the rear of the other ships. But in doing so he presented his stern to his opponent. This would not have mattered if the frigate captain had not been so quick. His guns were ready before *Ariadne* could bear up and hide behind his commodore. He only got off one broadside, but it was enough. One ball entered the coach, smashing its way along the glass cases on the wall as it ploughed

through the bulkhead. Those creatures that survived the ball and
the shock were scattered across the deck. Another ball swept in
across the bulwarks and reduced the wheel to matchwood, cutting the man conning the ship in two and rebounding off one of
the guns to maim two others. One of the spokes of that wheel
flew off like a javelin and hit de la Mery in the back of the neck
at the point where it joined his spine. He collapsed in a heap. It
was only good fortune that held the ship on its course. *Ariadne*
drifted into the lee of the British frigate, out of danger.

His pet mongoose, which had hidden in the cabin to escape
the noise, now faced three fer de lances. Those in the glass cases
had escaped harm, and being deaf creatures they were immune to
the noise. These were from the basket presented by the Carib chief.
No rodent, however swift, could face such odds, but he took out
the biggest one of the three, breaking its neck, before the invalid
American, coming into the cabin leading the two men who were
carrying their maimed captain, saw one of the others shoot forward and sink its fangs into the animal's thigh. The mongoose
didn't lie down to die, but spun round, and as a last act of its life,
it broke the neck of its nemesis. The American stepped forward
with a degree of purpose that he had not been capable of for
months. He had taken de la Mery's sword from his useless hand
when the Frenchman had fallen and used it now, to decapitate the
third snake. Behind him the others had laid de la Mery on the
bare cabin floor and fled.

Harry had called to his men to man the guns on the *Persephone*'s
starboard side. With no pretence at ceremony, they pushed their
French captives out of the way and rushed to obey. These cannon,
loaded when d'Albret cleared for action, had hardly been used
during the battle. The man intent on firing them had his full complement now, barring casualties. In fact, there were too many
gunners to man the available cannon. Pender stepped forward to
sort out the jostling mass. With the efficiency that he'd taken so
much trouble to instil, the Bucephalases, both pressed and free,

heaved the cannon round, ran them out smartly, and at a word of command from Harry Ludlow fired off a telling broadside at Captain Villemin. On a stationary ship, with no return fire to distract them, they took a terrible toll of the *Marianne*'s woodwork. The guns came in smartly and even though on an unfamiliar deck, they were reloaded and run out within the minute.

Having fired his own broadside at the Bourbon schooner, Captain Villemin had to wait until the smoke cleared before someone pointed out that *Persephone* had struck her colours. As indecisive as usual he'd held his course, sailing right into the salvo that Harry's men aimed at him. What happened to his ship, with that one example of proficient gunnery, was enough to convince him that discretion was the better part of valour. He put up his helm, took the effect of two more broadsides as he turned, and, setting everything he could bear, he headreached the entangled ships then turned to run down the Saintes channel, heading for the safety of Pointe-à-Pitre.

Lieutenant Wheeler was finally able to accept Monsieur d'Albret's sword. Now the horrible business of clearing up after the carnage of the battle began. The sound of men in pain filled men's ears, sailors who, shifting their wounded mates, had good cause to be thankful that the incessant gunfire of the past hours had dimmed their hearing.

CHAPTER FORTY-ONE

HARRY went back aboard *Bucephalas* to assess the damage, with James and Matthew Caufield in tow. Pender was left to check how many men from their ship had suffered, and to gather up those whole and fit and send them back aboard. *Ariadne* had drifted off on the current, wallowing down towards the Saintes channel, seemingly with no one to con her. Monsieur d'Albret and his officers had been confined to their quarters while their men were put to duty as stretcher bearers. Toner, now that the battle had ended, had been shifted to his own cabin. Likewise Dunlop and Hemmings. The captain could at least speak, though he remained groggy, confused about what had happened, and seemingly incapable of comprehending that his ship had taken a Frenchman in prize. The other two were still out cold with the harassed surgeon's opinion being that their fate was in God's hands. He'd known men to stay in that condition for days and even weeks. Garmond had fetched up in the cockpit for a while, only to be turfed out as soon as the more serious casualties began to arrive. Pender found him wandering aimlessly on the lower deck, with no idea what to do.

"There's boats over the side, one with the last of my captain's men at the oars. I intend to call it in. If'n I were you I'd get hold of them sods who crowned the other officers, and anyone else that thinks they might face a rope, then stand by to take their place."

Garmond just looked at him blankly, as though bereft of any idea of the danger he was in. "Rope?"

"Toner's talking already, though not with much sense. The other two could snuff it at any minute, and Mr Wheeler is too busy to think about what happened. You either get off this ship now, and row for shore, or stay here and face a noose as soon as we get back to English Harbour."

"I never trusted you, truth be known," replied Garmond sourly. "Yet now you're getting set to save my hide."

"Trouble with you, mate," snapped Pender, "is that you don't see further than the end of your nose."

"We could have had the ship."

"You never listened, did you? I hate the likes of Toner as much as you, with no time at all for the king's navy." He pointed out of the open scuttle. "But there's nowhere out there to go, for the likes of you or me, ship or no ship."

"Then why are you talking about a boat?"

"There's a French island over there, with the current running right into it. If'n I thought you could stay and bluff it out, I'd tell you to do that. But Toner knows full well you clobbered him and he's not going to let it pass, is he? Get in the boat, make for the island, give yourself up to the French, but!" Pender held up a warning finger. "Get yourself something to do that keeps you on shore. Don't even go fishin', mate. 'Cause if you're picked up, even ten years hence, they'll still string you up. Now get your lads together and move your arse. You ain't got much time."

There was so much happening on the deck of the two frigates, and so few people in authority to direct everyone's actions, that Pender was able to effect the switch without being observed. His own men, coming up the side, adopted a blank look when they saw what he was about and milled around a few feet away acting as a shield. One by one, Garmond's men slipped over the side. Their leader was the last to go and just before his head disappeared below the bulwark Pender stopped him.

"What happened with Lowden?" he asked.

"Lowden?" he replied, as though the name meant nothing. He somehow conjured up that irritating grin, the first feature about the man that Pender had really noticed, and it worked on his temper, despite exhaustion and his resolve to remain calm. He finally knew, clearly, what he didn't like about this blethering ex-clerk: his so-called concern for his fellow man was mere dressing. The shipmates he said he cared about were there just to feed his pride. He was a born troublemaker who would have been active even if Harry Ludlow had been his captain. Here was a man who would have seen everyone on the ship flogged just to further a personal aim: to be seen as better than his fellows, a leader who wielded power by use of the tongue.

"Did he fall, Garmond, or was he pushed?"

"He was unlucky, Pender, that's all. Happen if you'd been like-wise I'd be taking this ship as a gift to yonder Frenchmen."

Garmond started to duck, but he was too slow. Pender's fist took him square on the nose, which erupted in a fount of blood as he tumbled backwards, to land in a heap on top of his mates in the boat.

"Come on, lads, let's get back aboard our own ship."

The quickest way was over *Persephone*'s shattered taffrail. They filed along the deck, their eyes taking in the mess of broken wood, smashed cannon, and the blood that stained the deck. Callander was by the mainmast, supervising the hoisting aloft of a set of spars to act as a jury rig. Pender stopped by him and grinned.

"I reckon it was that yell of yours that did the trick, Mr Callander. It was a heathen sound and no error."

"Will you be making for English Harbour?" asked the young-ster, with a blush.

"Don't rightly know what my captain intends, your honour. But just in case I don't see you again . . ." Pender held out his hand, which Struan Callander gripped tightly.

"Good luck," he said, with a slight catch in his throat.

Pender, who thought himself immune to blubbing, had to set-tle for a nod, afraid that his voice would betray the same emotion. There were many words to say. He just hoped the look conveyed them.

◆　◆　◆

As soon as Harry Ludlow had his own men aboard he cut the ropes holding his ship to the Frenchman, as well as the cat's cradle of ropes from *Endymion* that had trapped his bowsprit. This allowed him to drift clear. Men had been working steadily to repair the rigging, fetching new sails from the locker to replace those tattered by Villemin's broadside. Some of his yards were too damaged to bear canvas and the stern was a mess. But the carpenter reported little water in the well, which meant that the hull was sound. As soon as he could get any way on the ship he steered for the Bourbon schooner, still with the fleur-de-lis at the mast-head, coming alongside and hailing the man who'd finally taken the wheel. Being French, he either didn't or wouldn't understand, so Harry let *Bucephalas* drift gently into the side. James came on deck with Matthew, but despite their glum looks he insisted on going on board himself. Once his men had lashed the two ships together, he clambered over the rail, wondering at the lack of activity on the untidy deck. Pender followed, but Harry indicated that the rest of the men should stay still.

"*Où est le capitaine?*" he asked.

The man pointed to the open door and Harry walked in. The left-hand side of the cabin was a mess, with the blue sea visible through the opening which had been the door of the coach. The floor was covered in glass and debris. And in the middle lay a mongoose, obviously dead, with a snake clamped in its jaws. Two others lay beside it, one of them sliced into two. A small knot of men stood at the other side of the cabin, crowding round the door. Harry softly touched those at the back until they allowed him through. Once they'd parted he could see the invalid in the cot, lying with his eyes closed. Another man, with a big frame which looked slightly undernourished, leant over him. The face was pale and gaunt, but somehow familiar. He was talking quietly and holding a small mirror.

"Is he dead?" he asked. When the man just stared at him he asked in French: "*Est-il mort?*"

"No, friend. There's still breath showing on the mirror."

"You're not English?"

"American. And who might you be?"

"Harry Ludlow."

"Navy?"

"No!" He pointed to the man in the cot. "This gentleman is Antoine de la Mery."

"Yes."

"There are two surgeons, one French, one British, aboard those frigates."

"Don't reckon he'd care for that much."

"He looks as though he requires attention."

"He was hit by the blunt end of a flying splinter, friend, which if I'm not mistaken has broken his neck. He opened his eyes about twenty minutes ago and said he could feel nothing in his body. We tried to move him and he passed out again."

Harry turned and closed the door, forcibly shutting out the curious members of the crew.

"Might I be permitted to ask your name, sir?"

"That's of no account."

"The last person who seemed disinclined to give me his name was a young fellow called Matthew Caufield."

"Matthew!"

Harry smiled. "There is a likeness, sir, which though not immediately obvious is still there. Added to that, your face is, I believe, plastered all over the Caribbean."

"You all right in there, your honour?" called Pender.

"Yes," he replied. "Put someone to watch on *Endymion*. I want to know the minute she's ready to get under way."

"Where did you see Matthew?" demanded Nathan Caufield.

"In English Harbour, originally."

"What in hell's name was he doing there?"

"Trying, unsuccessfully, to clear your name."

"And where is he now?"

Harry held up his hand. "I will be happy to take you to him, sir. But that will be a favour granted in return for a certain amount of information."

"Such as?"

"Is this the gentleman you sought, the man who, calling himself Victor Hugues, took your ship and cargo six months ago?" Caufield looked at him suspiciously. "Your son was good enough to allow me to peruse your letter. It would be as well to add that we arrived here, in this stretch of water, due to information supplied to us by a Mr Conlon O'Dwyer."

"I'm not much given to trusting people I've only just met."

"Your son shows more sense, Captain Caufield," said Harry, showing a brusque quality that stood in sharp contrast to his previous politeness. "After what I've just said, I hardly think you will be imparting anything I can't guess."

Caufield nodded to the patient. "How did you know his name?"

"I was told of him by an admiral's wife, who said he had a singular pet. Another man told me of his snake hobby. And there is a dead mongoose outside with three dead reptiles. So please oblige me by answering my previous enquiry."

"Yes," said Caufield, his gaunt shoulders slumping. "He's the man who took my ship. But he's also the man who saved my life."

"And the ship is called?"

"*Ariadne,*" he replied. "And I've no mind to see either the ship or its master put in any danger."

"Then might I suggest that someone take charge on the deck and get this ship under way. You asked if I was navy, sir. It can only be a matter of time before they send a boat over to ask some questions."

The American stood up abruptly, looking at him. "What kind of questions?"

"The same kind he wouldn't want to answer in a sick bay. The men over yonder have no idea of either Monsieur de la Mery's name, or, as far as I know, his activities. But after such a victory they will be bound to ask him to return with them to English Harbour."

"Goddamnit!"

"It's not a place that you can go, just yet," Harry continued. The last part of that sentence put some hope into Caufield's eyes. But that was not a subject Harry wanted to pursue at the moment. There were more pressing matters to attend to. "Why are the crew so lackadaisical?"

"I don't rightly know. Maybe they think that without their captain, they are finished."

"Do you feel up to sailing the ship, sir?"

"Not with this crew. They might be docile now, but I don't reckon they'll stay that way."

That statement was accompanied by a singular look which annoyed Harry slightly. "Mr Caufield. You are going to have to trust me. And to avoid hesitation think on this. There's a reward on your head which I could take steps to collect this very minute."

Still he hesitated, sucking in breath as he mulled over the problem. But finally he let go of his breath and his reservations. "If you look in that smashed cabin yonder, you'll see a great brass-bound chest. That French ball just missed it."

"Full of his profits?" Caufield nodded. "I will take the Frenchman on board, Mr Caufield, and give you some men from my ship to sail her."

Caufield pointed his finger at de la Mery. "I feel I'd be betraying a trust. As I said, he saved my life."

"I do not intend to do anything other than take his crew aboard. I then intend that you should sail away from here, to a rendezvous which I will set."

"And you?"

"I will seek to persuade the officers yonder that they should take their prize to English Harbour."

"What about that other frigate, the one that's made for Pointe-à-Pitre?"

"There's a friend of mine cruising south of Dominica, looking for these very ships. I will offer to go south, tell him what has happened, and bring him back to blockade the port."

"That's mighty generous of you."

"Generosity doesn't enter into it, sir."

Caufield's eyes narrowed. "Just how much did you know before you came aboard?"

The question threw Harry for a moment. But he grinned before he replied, amused by what the enquiry had uncovered. "To tell you the truth, Captain Caufield, I couldn't tell you."

"You knew the name of the ship, didn't you?"

He shrugged. "No. But I guessed that it was de la Mery. The location, the nature of the armament, the flag."

"Did you guess that there would be all this money aboard?"

"That letter you sent your son. Do you have any more information to add to that?"

It was the American's turn to be caught slightly off guard by the sudden shift. "If I did, why should I tell you?"

"I take it you told your son the truth. That you didn't kill Norrington."

"No," he replied coldly. "I did not."

Harry nodded, as though that answer was self-evident.

"I promised Matthew that I would help to clear your name. Not of the theft, of course, but of the murder. The only way we can see of achieving such a goal is to nail the true culprit. If you have any information to add, I think it would help."

"When I returned to Antigua . . ."

"What!"

Harry's surprise at such audacity did not evaporate as Caufield explained about the two mulattos and finding de la Mery's base. "But that, you will realize, Captain Ludlow, brings neither of us closer to a solution."

"You said de la Mery saved your life?"

"He did. One of the pet snakes bit me. As if that wasn't the be all, I'd just been nipped by a tarantula." Caufield looked down again, deep concern suddenly etched in his pallid face.

"If it hadn't been for Antoine and his potions, plus his unwavering care, I would have died."

"Given what I've heard already, he seems a gentle creature for a corsair."

"He was," the American replied gently. "It's just like the flag, Captain Ludlow. He was no royalist. But the last thing he wanted was to be bracketed with Victor Hugues."

Then he looked up again and Harry saw that for all his thin frame and pale face, there was steel in the eyes. "By the by, you didn't answer my question."

"Which one?"

"When you reckoned you'd identified the ship, did you figure out he'd be carrying his profits?"

"Why not, Caufield?" said Harry, opening the door. "You did!"

Pender was standing with a raised musket, while the men who'd been shut out by Harry stood with their arms raised. Behind his servant stood several more members of his crew.

"Just in case," said Pender. "Them bein' French an' all."

Harry gestured to the man behind him. "Come, Captain Caufield."

The American looked at Pender's musket, all the suspicion he manifested originally returning to his look. "Where to?"

"Why, on deck, sir. Where, if I'm not mistaken, you may catch sight of your son."

Pender's muskets proved necessary. The Frenchmen weren't happy to be separated from their booty, despite Caufield's attempts at explanation. To mollify them Harry returned four of their number to the *Ariadne,* with the express injunction to guard that brass-bound chest. They agreed to this only when sufficient lashings were put across the glass case holding a fer de lance. His own crew went happily, despite the fact that no one said a word to them about treasure. There wasn't a sailor aboard who spoke French, as far as Harry knew. But every man on the ship knew about that chest before Caufield and his son had finished embracing. Their first task was to secure a heavy bolt of canvas over the gap that Villemin's shot had made.

The lookout Pender had set called out. "They're hauling canvas up to the jury yards on *Endymion*'s mizzen. And that French barky's near rigged, an' all."

"Time to part company, I think," said Harry.

Caufield senior put his arm round his son again. "You'll come with me, Matthew."

Harry cut in quickly. "I think not. Matthew would be better staying aboard *Bucephalas*."

"I really think, brother—"

James got no further, being brutally interrupted. "Since I'm off to see Marcus Sandford, James, you'd be better off sailing with Captain Caufield. And while you're aboard *Ariadne*, you can have a good look for anything that might help us in the small matter of Captain Caufield's innocence."

Harry's look brooked no argument. He didn't yet know how much was in that chest, all of de la Mery's profits or merely part of it. But he was determined that whatever it was, it would stay there.

CHAPTER FORTY-TWO

"**A GRENADIAN** planter, of French extraction, loyal to his monarch, Captain. He sent his compliments, wished you joy of your Jacobin captures, and is yet making haste to return home."

"And his name?" asked Toner.

Harry paused, to conjure up a name. "A Monsieur Gilbert, I believe."

The Scotsman had a lump like a goose egg on his temple. If anything he was even more grey faced than before. He growled and gnashed his teeth, and made little attempt to disguise the fact that he didn't believe Harry Ludlow. This suspicion stemmed from Harry's jovial tone as much as the twinkle in his eye when he answered the questions. And with the ship which had intervened so fortuitously heading south there was nothing he could do about it. Neither *Endymion* nor *Persephone* were in any state to pursue. And, in truth, Harry didn't care if Toner doubted him. Quite the opposite. He was enjoying himself; having come aboard with half a mind to challenge the man to a duel, he'd found this baiting much more satisfying. The humour, however, evaporated when Toner made his next remark.

"You come and take your men off my ship, when I'm laid low. But I see you've taken care to leave me your wounded."

Harry suddenly found he was fighting to control himself. He longed to fetch Toner another clout, this time one that would not have his hat in the way to save him. Pender had told him all about the events preceding the action. He'd issued certain promises to his servant, who was loath to see any man hang. The fellow called

Garmond didn't bother him much. But if he went, he was the type to take others with him. He turned his mind to James, wondering what he'd say exposed to such ingratitude. That saved him. He even went so far as to ape his voice.

"What luck the ship had competent officers in command when she went into action. Otherwise you might have had the dubious honour of giving up your sword while lying flat on your back!"

It wasn't constructed perfectly. James would have done better: avoided the inherent contradiction of the two statements and kept his voice in check at the end. But he could not doubt the effect. He'd struck home with a vengeance. Toner looked set to explode out of his uniform coat.

"Damn you, sir, for a poxed—"

Harry yelled in a voice loud enough to make those on the quarterdeck jump. "Say another word, Toner, and I'll either kill you or see you the laughing stock of the fleet. Remember the prize you have was taken by others!"

"Mutiny!"

"If you mention mutiny, who will you bring forward to punish? No one. A list of names? They could have died in the fight. No, Toner! I'll label you as a man who takes to his bed when action is imminent and snores throughout. You have your prize and I cannot contest the value. But if you want credit, then beware. You will land my wounded in English Harbour and see them given the very best beds in the hospital. Then you can write your despatch. I trust you have enough wit to ensure that you prosper by it!"

Toner's mouth was opening and closing, which made Harry suspect that all his attention had really been taken up with that. And he was right. The Scotsman was wondering how he was going to word his letter in a way that showed him in a superior light. Dunlop he could ignore, putting him down, like McPartland, as early casualties. But Wheeler had really won the fight and taken the prize. He would need to be rewarded if he was not to become a thorn in the creation of the Toner legend. The best reward, one that would not expose his captain to a constant reminder of the truth, was to see him promoted into another ship.

"I intend to do you one more service," said Harry, standing up. "I will find Captain Sandford, who is cruising to the south of Dominica, and ensure that he blockades Villemin in Pointe-à-Pitre."

"Why?" asked Toner suspiciously.

"Don't worry. I shan't tell him of your insurrection. But Sandford is a friend of mine. Perhaps he can winkle Villemin out and, with a little glory attached to his name, get the ship of the line he deserves. You may go home with your prize, composing your fictions on the way. Good day to you, sir."

Harry felt as though he fired each round for a second time. But Marcus was insistent on hearing every detail of the action, from the first broadside to the last sword thrust. His officers were equally enthralled and there was much playing with the cruets and cutlery so that everyone at the table knew the precise location of each ship at every stage. Eyebrows were raised at the identity of the Bourbon schooner, but good manners prevented them from enquiring too deeply, once Harry had made it plain he would be loath to answer. Likewise he deflected any references to *Endymion*'s captain.

"Lord, how I envy Toner," cried Sandford, thumping the table with his huge hand. "A single-ship action and he's only been out here a fortnight. And you tell me he's taken a prize as well."

"Then I raise my glass to *Diomede* and her captain, Marcus. May Monsieur Villemin bring out the *Marianne* for a duel. If he does, you, your officers and men, will cast Toner into the shade."

"Hear him, hear him," cried the diners, the eager eyes flushed with hope and copious wine.

More drink flowed as each remove was placed before the party. Port followed that and it was a merry bunch of men who, having sunk bumper after bumper, bade farewell, some to go to the gunroom to sleep it off, others to take over the watch. Sandford and Harry made for the windward side of the quarterdeck and paced happily up and down in the warm evening air. *Bucephalas* sat in their wake. The sky was a mixture, with banks of cloud, some fluffy white, others dark grey to black, intermingled with shafts of sunlight striking through from the deep blue sky.

"That was a fine dinner, Marcus."

"And a fine tale?" Harry stopped pacing and looked at his friend. "You describe the action most engagingly. I can trace the course of your battle, as I can of Lieutenant Wheeler. That midshipman did well. Even your servant has a role, along with brother James. But not once did you mention Toner or his premier. I find that curious. Doubly so, since you made it plain that enquiry was unwelcome."

"If I tell you, I'm not sure that it's something you can speak about."

"Lord, Harry," he cried, throwing back his head so that the long golden locks bounced off his back. "You've been out of the navy too long. If there's anything untoward in Toner's behaviour, the lower deck will make it common gossip in Portsmouth before the year's out."

"I am well aware of that. But I do not want to be the one to spread the dirt."

"Even when you can't abide the man."

"My assurances were not given to him." Harry stopped and put a hand on Sandford's arm. "I will tell you. But in return I will quiz you about something. And ask you a favour as well; one that you will find no difficulty in granting."

"Very well." They continued their pacing as the sun sank slowly towards the horizon. It was a blaze of colour, from orange through to purple, before Harry finished.

"Lord," said Marcus. "If he gets a *Gazette* it will make interesting reading."

"I'm almost tempted to interfere. The thought of someone like Toner being fêted don't bear thinking about."

"A waste of time, Harry. Their lordships will crown him with the laurel whatever you say. They can't do anything for Wheeler without his captain being praised. Besides every victory is good for the ministry and one like this is a godsend for the naval estimates."

Harry shrugged at the futility. "Now, Marcus, you must pay your forfeit."

"Let's sit down first."

They made their way to the cabin and Sandford stretched himself across the cushioned footlockers by the stern windows. Harry sat in a captain's chair and fixed his friend with a hard look.

"I believe that when we spoke in the Duke of Clarence, you were somewhat circumspect with the truth."

Marcus glared at him. "Are you certain you require a favour?"

"Don't worry. I'm sure your motives were pure. You didn't want to admit to me that you'd suggested my name to Bessborough."

"But I didn't, Harry. True, he asked about you, and while I was vague, I might have alluded to what I'd heard of your doings. Then he pounced on me when I mentioned certain things."

"Mentioned that I'd solved a few ticklish problems?"

"That's it. It was said in passing. But it had a deep effect on him, for he shut me up. Damned if he didn't sit silent for a good two minutes, which I'll have you know, Harry, can seem like an eternity."

"You were alone at this point?"

"We were."

"Yet you told me Dillon and Vandegut were present when he suggested that I be engaged to investigate."

"That was later. After he'd told me what he suspected."

"And they didn't react. Didn't object?"

"Well, to be truthful, Harry, he didn't say to them the same thing as he said to me."

"That there was a spy in his headquarters."

Sandford sat bolt upright, his eyes wide with admiration.

"Damn it, Harry! What I've heard about you is true. How the deuce did you work that out?"

"Bessborough told me."

"Oh!" He lay back on his cushions, patently disappointed. "And I had you down for a genius."

"Sorry to disappoint you. Why didn't he say anything about a spy to Dillon or Vandegut?"

Marcus looked at him with wonder. "You're slipping in my estimation by the minute."

"I want to hear you say it."

"What? That they are the people he suspects?"

"Yes."

"Lord, Harry. You had me worried there. I thought to myself, if he can't deduce that, then he'd best up anchor and head for home."

"Who else?"

"There isn't anybody else."

"You're sure! Another captain?"

"They're at sea most of the time."

"His wife, daughters?"

"Are you mad, Harry?"

"His nephew?"

Sandford yawned. "He has fewer brains than his aunt."

"What about that stiff-necked servant of his?"

"Cram?"

"Yes. I have to say I didn't take to him."

"Harry, Cram may have the staff of a broom up his arse, but it's not him. The spy, whoever he is, has to have information about both the illegals and the cruisers. That's kept locked away. They might get one. But both! And remember it's consistent, day in, day out."

"Are those your words or Bessborough's, Marcus?"

He looked confused for a moment. "Bessborough's, I suppose. But it's common sense, ain't it?"

"Why you! Why did he confide in you?"

"Because it can't be me. Like the other captains, I'm at sea the whole time."

"Poynton was in before you."

"He wouldn't tell Poynton the time if he could avoid it. Or Vandegut for that matter."

"Effingham?"

"Lord, Harry, you ask a lot of questions."

"Effingham?"

Marcus Sandford swung his legs off the cushions and glared at his guest. "Harry. I came in after Hugues had taken his first British ships, and, I might add, after he'd been to that dinner at the governor's. I don't think he realized the true state of affairs till then."

"Marcus," replied Harry, with equal force, "he has intelligence coming in from all over the Caribbean."

The glare disappeared to be replaced by a sad look. "Filtered through Dillon."

"And when, Marcus, did you come to that conclusion?"

Suddenly he was back on his cushions, looking evasive. "I can't rightly remember."

"Before or after you spoke with me at the Duke of Clarence?"

"Before."

"Thank you."

"Pity," he continued, with a sly look. "I rather like Dillon. He's got a brain, which is something I esteem." Harry sat silently, smiling at his friend. The silence lasted for a long time. But finally Sandford could stand it no longer. "Well?"

"Well what?"

"Is it Dillon?" Sandford cried.

"Now how would I know the answer to that?"

"I'm beginnin' to think your reputation is exaggerated, Harry Ludlow."

"Time will tell." He stood up. "This has taken longer than I thought. Can you shorten sail and signal *Bucephalas*?"

He was off the cushions in a flash. "Lord, Harry. I paid no

heed to the time. It's hours since we ate. Can I get you some toasted cheese before you shift?"

Harry walked over and held out his hand. "It's been good to see you, Marcus. A real pleasure."

Sandford grinned with delight. "The same, Harry, the same. Shall we go on deck?"

Diomede shortened sail and Harry's ship did likewise. The boat to take him back to *Bucephalas* was put in the water in near silence, a testimony to the efficiency of the crew.

"Will you be staying in these parts?"

"No, Marcus. I have my crew back, so I suppose I shall take them home."

The moonlight picked out his teeth as he smiled. "Can't say I'm sorry, friend. It would be hard for a naval officer to welcome the presence of a privateer."

"True."

"You said you wanted a favour."

"I do," replied Harry. "That midshipman I told you about, Callander."

"What about him?"

"He'll go to rack and ruin under Toner. He's a willing lad, brave and cheerful, who has a way with the hands. Take him into *Diomede* and look after him. Favour him if you can and see him through to lieutenant."

Sandford's eyebrows went up. "Will Toner surrender him?"

"If he doesn't," growled Harry, "mention the name Garmond."

"Garmond?"

"That will do the trick."

"If you say so, Harry. He must have impressed you, this lad."

"Not me, Marcus. I have exchanged two words with him at most."

"Then why the request?"

"It's a favour to a good and faithful servant."

"Lord, Harry Ludlow. What an odd fish you are."

CHAPTER FORTY-THREE

THEY FOUND *Ariadne* exactly where she was supposed to be, riding at anchor in the secluded Dominican bay. Harry brought *Bucephalas* alongside and came aboard to find that there had been no improvement in de la Mery's condition. It fact it had deteriorated. He was now in the grip of an intense fever during which bouts of silence alternated with wild ramblings, mostly incomprehensible. But one fact was clear. The injured man had some notion that his condition was critical and badly wanted the services of a priest. He uttered the words "find the priest" in Harry's presence, but since he didn't say which one there was no way to oblige. Caufield, damp cloth in hand, was nursing him personally, with little confidence that what he was doing would achieve anything. The worry that Antoine de la Mery wouldn't recover sufficiently, both for the man's own sake as well as to help him, was taking its toll on the American, still suffering from the after-effects of his own brush with death.

"I make you right, Captain Ludlow. It would have been a bad notion to put him aboard one of those frigates. But I reckon he needs the attention of a proper medical man. You know I asked him where he got his information from."

"And?"

"He said he'd sworn on a Bible not to reveal it. Even his crew had no idea."

Caufield rubbed a weary hand over his own forehead, in such a way that made Harry suspect he required the same attention as the man in the cot.

"I had intended to head for Antigua," said Harry. "His condition makes such a course doubly necessary. We can get him ashore and into the hospital." Harry grinned then. "It will be interesting to see what happens when this ship, with this patient, drops anchor within sight of Admiralty House."

"If you're plannin' on berthing in English Harbour, you'd best leave me here. I can't go anywhere near the place."

"You did so once before, sir, which I still consider to be bordering on madness."

Caufield dabbed at de la Mery's brow as he replied. "Then it's as well not to push my luck."

"You can't go ashore there, Captain Caufield! But I think you'll be safe enough aboard ship, provided you keep yourself hidden from view. Besides, the main purpose of going there is to fulfil my promise to your son and clear your name, something which could be severely compromised if you are not at hand."

"And if they search *Ariadne?* Never mind my problems. There'll be hell to pay if they find that chest."

"Search *Ariadne!*" replied Harry. "For what, Captain? She is as far as they are concerned an ally not an enemy. And should they show an inclination to treat her differently, I will claim her as a capture. I am a letter of marque, licensed to sail by the king himself. If I've had the good fortune to take a ship in prize, then all the contents aboard, as well as the crew, are mine to dispose of. They are not subject to legal search by the navy or anyone else."

"There's another matter to consider. I don't have much French, Captain Ludlow. But I have enough to understand that Antoine's crew are a mite concerned about their share of that treasure."

"Then you may tell them I have no intention of touching it," he snapped. Then his face softened as he looked down at the invalid, with his damp face and pale skin. "This man entered into a fight that had nothing to do with him. It is questionable whether the action would have ended successfully without his intervention. The means by which he came by his wealth may be deplorable. But I for one will not lay a finger on their share."

"Then perhaps that message would be best passed to your

brother. He's had more to do with them than I have."

Harry went on deck, pondering on what Caufield had said. The American might well be right. He was also wondering what it was about his brother that attracted people seeking either information or sympathy. He found James talking with Matthew. The youngster, who'd come aboard with him, had steered clear of Harry for the last two days. He moved away as he approached, skirting round him to go and see his father. And the glance he threw him was less than cheerful. Harry, knowing the cause, ignored it.

"Well, James, did you find anything useful in the cabin?"

"Nothing except more venomous creatures. That a man can share his sleeping quarters with toads, spiders, and scorpions beggars belief, but that pales beside the snakes."

"Were there more of those?"

"No, thank God. And I have not dared go near the glass case that contains the survivor. I did search the coach for papers and had Jubilee standing by with a torch and a cutlass, just in case. He has little fear of the creatures, no doubt a product of his fatalistic Papist beliefs. He even found a special instrument with some cane for fixing them to the planking by the neck."

"Is the cabin clear now?"

"I think so. But I berthed below decks in a screened-off cubicle, soaked in vinegar, just to be sure."

"I had hoped some of those papers scattered about the cabin might refer to his activities."

"No, brother. We looked hard, but I think our invalid destroyed everything related to that. The only things we found had notes on his experiments. And his crew know nothing at all. They saw the messengers but never the message. But one interesting fact has emerged. They were set to weigh anchor a week ago when the two mulattos arrived with new instructions and they warped themselves back to the jetty."

"A week ago. Which is just after Toner arrived." Harry looked at the cabin door, just in time to see Matthew Caufield's back. "I seem to have upset our young friend."

"You have. He questions whether you really believe his father innocent. You made little effort to hide your suspicions when we parted company."

"I thought as much."

"He also complained about the way you keep matters to yourself. He hasn't the faintest idea whether Marcus Sandford told you anything of value."

"And what did you reply, brother?"

James waved a dismissive, elegant hand. "I him told it was a character trait, brother, one that he would grow accustomed to if he got to know you better."

"You must have been a great comfort to him," said Harry. "Now, since you are such a samaritan you can explain to de la Mery's crew that we intend to take the chest containing the treasure aboard *Bucephalas*. Matthew's father will come too."

"They won't be pleased, brother."

"They'll be a damn sight less pleased if the ship is impounded."

"Is there a risk of that?"

"Caufield senior has just pointed out that there might be. Whoever the spy is at Admiralty House might recognize this vessel. They won't dare board me, but they might find an excuse to search *Ariadne*. It's not worth the risk. Tell his men they can maintain their guard on it, if they so desire."

James nodded at that. Even the most suspicious *engagé* would see the sense in what Harry was saying.

"Was Sandford helpful?"

"Yes," replied Harry vaguely, looking towards the rigging.

There was a pause before James added a somewhat terse second question. "What did he say?"

Harry affected to be shocked. "You mean I should tell you? You're not suggesting, brother, that I step out of character?"

Harry made James suffer a little more, before outlining what he'd learned and admitting that Sandford shared their opinion of the culprit.

The Frenchman's condition worsened steadily as they beat up towards English Harbour. Once they sighted the island Harry shifted the Caufields and the rest of the Frenchmen to his own ship, leaving Jubilee, a fellow Papist, to look after de la Mery. To all appearances, *Ariadne* was now manned by a prize crew. Toner, if he had returned, might recognize the vessel. But the knowledge that Harry had about his supposed success would ensure his silence.

He'd had many a conversation about how he intended to approach matters, looking in vain for some subtle method that would unmask the murderer. But the more he talked, the more he realized that all he had was supposition. Caufield's two mulattos might help. But he had no way to positively identify the pair, so how to find them in a port full of such people? He was loath to approach Bessborough, as much for the man's character as anything else. Besides, they had little to tell him that the admiral didn't already know. The suspicion that Dillon might be a member of the United Irishmen was interesting, but no one could see how it impinged on their problem, even if it was a proscribed organization. If they did expand the admiral's knowledge, with that snippet or any other, he'd be bound to ask from where they'd acquired it. Finally, he and James had agreed that it was futile, and decided instead that if no one showed their hand after they'd anchored they'd need patience. They would go ashore and tackle Dillon head on.

The first thing they noticed was that *Redoubtable* was not at her moorings, the pilot informing them that she'd gone off to Guadeloupe to blockade Pointe-à-Pitre. But the whole harbour was in festive mood, brought on by the presence of Monsieur d'Albret and *Persephone*, riding at anchor with the red squadron's flag high on the mainmast, and the French tricolour underneath. Not that such an event dented the avarice of the harbour master or his pilots. In fact this increased and Harry found himself paying even more to gain berths. Shifting de la Mery was a sore trial, since every movement affected him deeply. They tried to help him swallow some rum to dull the pain, but the poor man could not keep it down, and was in grave danger of choking through their ministrations. The hospital was full of the casualties from the recent battle, some of them Harry's own men. But a hefty douceur to the man in charge secured the Frenchman a room all to himself, with a good view over the flowerbeds towards the harbour, plus a promise of attention from both physician and surgeons once they were free.

"Whoever attends him is bound to recognize de la Mery," said James, after the sailors who carried his stretcher left the room. "Both medical men must have seen him dozens of times at Bessborough's entertainments. He is the only living soul who can identify the culprit, which will count for very little if he cannot speak."

"I can't see any choice, James, and I'm as aware as you are that it looks like we're using a wounded man as bait. But he needs treatment."

"Let's hope he recovers sufficiently, and is prepared to put aside his oath to give us a name."

"Well, he's in the best possible place," replied Harry sadly.

As they emerged from the hospital, they found a midshipman waiting for them, with a message asking them to call upon Admiral Bessborough. On reaching the ante-room they were subjected to minute scrutiny by Cram, who looked so pinch-faced that Harry half expected to be asked to go round to the tradesmen's entrance. But the admiral was all smiles, going on about the return of their crew as though he'd dragged them out of *Endymion* personally. Part of that could be put down to the prize in the harbour, and it wasn't long before he alluded to that.

"A handsome capture, don't you think?"

"Indeed, Admiral Bessborough."

"I shall buy her in of course, so there's a step going for some lucky fellow. It's a pity Toner's premier took so little part in the affair. But whoever gets her will have Wheeler as their first lieutenant. Toner's despatch demands it. I've rarely known a captain heap such praise on a single officer."

"Such nobility," said James, with a note of profound irony that quite bypassed Bessborough.

"And he has not left you out of the general approbation, Captain Ludlow. The way you distracted the enemy made his victory certain."

Even James was floored by that, while Harry sought to suck in the breath that would stop him exploding. It was a cunning word to choose, distraction, one that could be stretched or narrowed according to the attitude, or even the knowledge, of the listener.

"He also told me about that other ship that got caught up in the action by sailin' too close. Is that the fellow you've come in with?"

Harry nodded. "The captain was wounded in the action."

"I don't have his name, or that of his ship."

"Would it be possible to read Captain Toner's report?" asked James, quickly.

"Why, certainly, sir," the admiral replied, his face beaming as he held up the thick sheaf of parchment. "I shall get my clerks to make you a fair copy. And very pleasant reading it makes too. I believe you and this other fellow both suffered some damage."

"I think 'considerable damage' would be a more appropriate expression."

"How badly wounded is . . . er?"

"Monsieur de la Mery," said Harry slowly.

"What! The fellow who stayed here with us after Guadeloupe?" Bessborough rang the bell on his desk furiously until his servant appeared. "Cram, tell her ladyship that Monsieur de la Mery is at this very moment lying in a hospital bed."

For once the servitor's stiff demeanour cracked and he allowed himself to appear surprised. "Indeed, sir. Her Ladyship will be most upset."

"So will my girls, Cram. My nephew too. Rouse them out and tell 'em. And ask my wife to set us a time for a visit."

Harry cut in quickly. "I'm not sure that would do the patient much good, sir. He is very badly wounded indeed."

Bessborough dropped his voice. "Oh my Lord. Is he likely to expire?"

"It is possible."

"Then we must go. My wife would never forgive herself if he went before she comforted him. See to it, Cram." The servant disappeared, leaving his master looking suddenly very glum, as he shook his head. "I always had him down for an honourable cove. But fancy his cuttin' in to a sea battle against his own kind. Tell me about his wound."

"We think his neck is broken. He has a fever and can't talk."

"Can't talk. That will upset the girls. They were fond of his conversation. What about his ship . . . er. What's the damn thing called?"

"*Ariadne.*"

"Well, if she's suffered some damage in our service, the least we can do is help repair it. Anything below the waterline?"

"No, sir. It's all upperworks and yards."

"And you?"

"The same, Admiral."

"Right. We haven't got a proper dockyard here, as you know. But we've carpenters in abundance and wood for them to plane, plus an inner harbour where the water is rarely ruffled. I don't doubt we can send you both out as good as new."

"That won't be necessary," said Harry quickly. He didn't even want to enter the inner harbour, never mind have a posse of ships' carpenters crawling all over both ships, one of which contained a wanted felon and a chest of treasure.

"Nonsense. I can't give you a share of that Frenchie, but I can do this. And damn the expense. What's the point of bein' an admiral and the law in this harbour, I say, if you can't help such a stalwart pair of friends?"

"That is less pressing, sir, than other matters," said Harry, forced by this possibility to proceed faster than he would have preferred.

"Other matters?" repeated Bessborough, his eyebrows raised.

The door opened and Dillon entered. "The surgeon's here, sir. He has just come up from the hospital and wishes to inform you that Monsieur de la Mery is critically ill and in his care."

Bessborough indicated the Ludlows. "I know, Dillon, I know. We have these two gentlemen to thank for fetching him in."

Harry was looking at Dillon the way the mongoose must have looked at the snakes. But the Irishman seemed to be calmness itself, save that he had a look of concern brought on by the news he'd delivered. The silence of the four men was shattered by the arrival of Lady Bessborough, who swept into the room, followed by her nephew, booming her own response to the news.

"We must go at once, husband."

"The surgeon is here, ma'am," said Dillon. "Perhaps his advice should be sought."

"Nonsense, Dillon," she barked, before turning to her husband. "He merely holds a warrant, does he not, from the Navy Board?"

"Of course," replied Bessborough testily.

"Then he's not of sufficient station to be telling admirals what to do."

Bessborough sighed unhappily. But for a moment he looked set to tell his wife that the surgeon had the right to bar him. But that faded to be replaced by a resigned expression. "I have matters to attend to here. But I will be free in an hour."

"I shall order the carriage," said Caddick, a remark which was greeted by an approving nod from his aunt.

"It's easier, and quicker, to walk, madam. The route down to the harbour is exceedingly tortuous."

"Walk, sir!" she cried, waving her scented handkerchief. "Have you forgotten who we are? It may be in order for you to walk, but the ladies of your house know their place in society."

"Very well," said Bessborough softly, as his wife departed in a cloud of eau-de-toilette. The admiral addressed the Ludlows. "You must forgive me, gentlemen. If you have anything else you wish to discuss with me, then it will have to wait until the morrow. I do however insist that you come ashore as our guests."

Harry, having spoken, was not to be deflected. "The subject I wish to discuss is very important, Admiral, and relates to the last private conversation we had in your study."

Bessborough shot a quick glance at Dillon before replying. "Indeed. Then I can spare you some time in the early evening, say at seven o'clock."

CHAPTER FORTY-FOUR

"**YOU REALLY** are the confusing fellow," said James, once they were out in the hallway. Harry, head on his chest, was in a deep study and his brother wasn't at all sure if he was listening. "I distinctly recall you saying that you had nothing new to tell Bessborough. And if I also remember rightly, the last time we were in this house, we flatly refused to do his bidding."

"True," he replied. "But the news of de la Mery has become common knowledge. And as I was sitting there, looking at Dillon, it suddenly struck me that if there was any written evidence, such news would prompt him to destroy it. I spoke when I did for the benefit of the Irishman, not the admiral."

"What kind of evidence, brother?"

"If the spy in this building wrote to Antoine de la Mery, then it is on the cards that he wrote back."

"No one in their right mind would keep such correspondence."

Harry was quite excited, and put his hands on James's shoulders. "No. But what if those letters carried a statement showing how much money he'd made? A man might be tempted to keep that."

The door to the ante-room opened and Dillon and Caddick came out, both looking grave. Harry turned to face them and was speaking before James could restrain him. "Mr Dillon, I wonder if you might spare us some of your time."

The Irishman took out his watch. "I have engaged to follow the admiral in his visit to Monsieur de la Mery. But that will not be for an hour."

"You're very kind."

Dillon nodded to Caddick, then held up his hand bidding them to follow, proceeding towards his office. James hissed in Harry's ear.

"Are we operating on instinct again, brother?"

Harry ignored him, forcing him to run slightly to catch up. As they entered the room Harry threw a meaningful glance towards the locked strongbox, which earned him a shake of the head from James.

"Be seated, gentlemen." He picked up a small bell and held it, ready to ring. "Can I get you any refreshments?"

Both his guests shook their heads so he dropped the bell and sat back in his chair, waiting for them to speak. Harry obliged.

"How well do you know Monsieur de la Mery?"

"I count him as a friend, esteem him as a gentleman, and have nothing but admiration for his keen intelligence."

"I was wondering if you could tell me where he went when he left Antigua."

"To Grenada, I believe. He and his men went to assist against Hugues's incursion." Dillon dropped his voice to a whisper, which exaggerated his Irish accent. "I fear Monsieur de la Mery found the atmosphere in this house a trifle stifling. I don't think he was, by nature, cut out to be a mere teacher of the French language. Besides that, he was never happy living on charity."

"You were assaulted the night Stephen Norrington was murdered."

The sudden change of subject startled him into an immediate reply. "I was."

"Are you aware that he was actually coming to this house to visit you?"

Dillon looked perplexed. "Me? But I was out till near dawn. There would have been no point."

"Do you mind if I enquire where you were?"

"I most certainly do, sir. Quite apart from the effrontery of the question I was engaged upon the king's business."

Harry looked at James, who added the next statement. "We

have reason to believe that Stephen Norrington was murdered by someone other than Nathan Caufield."

"Indeed, sir," replied Dillon, calmly. "I must say that I would find that hard to credit."

"Are you sure you didn't meet Norrington that evening, say, before you went on the king's business? Or perhaps even on your return?"

He was a quick thinker, able to add up the sum of those questions and reach a conclusion that brought an angry look to his normally impassive face. "I don't like the way this conversation is proceeding. Has someone told you I saw Norrington that evening?"

"He wrote you a letter," said James.

"If he did, it would be an abusive one."

"Why abusive?" asked James.

"Mr Norrington and I were not at all friendly. I think he was aware that I knew of his close association with Captain Vandegut."

"What kind of close association?"

"I believe the good captain to be a passive investor in Lloyd's. What they call a Name."

"Is that significant?" asked Harry.

"It is when on one hand you have a duty to suppress the illegal trade and on the other a clear interest in seeing your insured risks prosper. And I would also say that people normally send letters, sir. They rarely deliver them in person."

"Speaking of letters, Mr Dillon," said Harry, smoothly, "do you have any correspondence with Conlon O'Dwyer outside what you call the king's business?"

"Conlon O'Dwyer?"

"Yes. He provides you with intelligence."

That made Dillon, a pale man anyway, go white. His eyes, involuntarily, flicked past Harry to his strongbox. "Who says he provides intelligence?"

"He does," said James.

"Then he's been exceedingly foolish."

"Let us say, sir, that he had little choice. The night you were assaulted—"

"Are you about to tell me that wasn't Nathan Caufield, either?" he snapped. "Damn you, man, I saw his bloody face."

"Your strongbox was open that night, I think," added Harry.

"For that thieving sod to rob."

"He can read as well, Mr Dillon."

"So can I, sir. I went to collect Norrington's possessions."

Dillon jumped up and pulled a set of keys from his pocket, selecting the one that opened his desk. From one of the cupboards that formed the legs he pulled an expensive calf-skin bag. Opening it, he pulled out a large leather-bound book, throwing it open at the last page and shoving it under Harry's nose.

"There, on his escritoire, lay this ledger. The last name in it was that of Nathan Caufield. And I can add as well as read, sir. The man robs me inside the building and Norrington's body was found outside the back gate. His boat has been shifted that day so that it is ready by the harbour wall. And right after he has finished with his crime he ups and leaves English Harbour as fast as he can. It was not only criminal, gentlemen, it was premeditated."

"What's amiss, Harry?" asked James.

His brother was staring at the ledger as if he'd seen a ghost. He took it out of Dillon's hands and passed it to James. Once his brother had the weight he pointed, rather unnecessarily, to one of the faint ink drawings in the margin.

"This drawing," he said, turning the book towards Dillon. "What would you say it is?"

"Funny, I never really examined it before," replied Dillon, looking closely, "but it looks very like a mongoose."

"Thank the Lord you didn't actually accuse him," said James, blinking in the sunlight.

"It's not conclusive, brother. We had no need to rush out like that."

"Harry. Everyone was quite taken with de la Mery's pet. If he was the man's contact he would hardly be likely to present you with a drawing of one, on a murdered man's ledger, especially when we asked him those sort of questions. If he'd seen Norrington, and heard him pass on Caufield's comments about de la Mery, would he then keep that book, and show it so readily?"

"A double bluff."

"Double vision more like, brother."

"We can't question Vandegut, he's not here." Harry sighed, unwilling to let go of a cherished solution to the problem. They were walking downhill, towards the hospital, well before the time that Bessborough had said he would visit. "Let's look in on de la Mery before we go back to the ship. Caufield, particularly, will want to know how he is."

The whole building smelled of the vinegar used to clean it. The long white-painted corridors were deserted, with the exception of the French sailor Harry had placed outside de la Mery's door lest he recover and require anything. The man was half asleep, hardly surprising in the heat, but jumped quick enough when he heard their footsteps, opening the door so they could enter. De la Mery lay at peace, his head tilted to one side and his eyes wide open in that way that Harry had seen so often in his life. But there was just a chance he was wrong, so James ran to fetch an attendant. Harry leant over and looked at the still features, relaxed in death, reached down with his fingers and pulled the small piece of feather out of the Frenchman's mouth. Then he lifted the head and examined the pillow. The damp patch where the victim's mouth had been, though nearly dry, was still visible, because of the way it had been put back. He walked over to the window, left open to allow the Trade wind to cool the room, and looked out over the flowerbeds to the harbour, his eyes fixed on the empty buoy where *Redoubtable* had been berthed. He was cursing softly as James came back into the room, followed by the sweating surgeon.

"You're wasting your time, brother," he said, holding up the feather. "I'm afraid he's truly dead. And us! We've been taken for fools, James. Well and truly humbugged."

• ◆ •

The detour which took Harry back to the Duke of Clarence had
a serious purpose. Gracewell, both in inclination and position, was
a man who held a fund of information. Several questions he
answered himself. Others required him to tour his tap-room,
bespeaking his customers, especially the marines who drank there
on a nightly basis. The information he gleaned was not in itself
conclusive. But added to what Harry knew, and what he suspected,
it provided an avenue which, followed, might produce the answer
he sought. He returned to the hospital to ensure that his instructions had been carried out, then headed up the hill to the great
white building which overlooked the beautiful bay. He got back
to Admiralty House just as Bessborough was preparing to leave.
The women, even the formidable Lady Bessborough, were very
distressed to be told they were too late, retiring to their rooms
with tears in their eyes. The admiral took it better, patting his
nephew's shoulder and shaking his head like a man who'd seen
too many deaths in his career.

"You and I must go to comfort the ladies, Charles."

Harry watched them depart, then made his way to Dillon's
office to inform him. The Irishman was clearly distressed, indeed
quite distracted, and made no objection when Harry, as he opened
the door to leave, enquired if he could ask one or two more questions.

"Who found the body?"

"Either young Caddick or one of the party he had under his
command."

"Not Vandegut?"

"No," said Dillon, hesitating. "He has formed an attachment
that means he rarely sleeps in his own quarters, so he had to be
fetched in rather a hurry."

"Can you think of any reason why Mr Norrington would write
to you?"

"Several. But I've already informed you that he did not."

"He told Nathan Caufield that he had just done so."

"Then I have two observations to make, Captain Ludlow. First, that I wonder how you came by that knowledge, and secondly, if that villain told you anything, I would advise you to discount it."

"I have, Mr Dillon. Mr Gracewell spoke to one of the marines on duty that night. He remembers, quite clearly, that Norrington called here, bearing a letter, but he asked for Captain Vandegut." Harry waited in vain to see if that statement produced any reaction. "I take it that Captain Vandegut was indeed fetched from the right location."

"Since I was suffering from a severe head wound, I have no idea."

"When you went to collect Norrington's possessions, where was Captain Vandegut?"

"In the admiral's office. In fact, I recall, I asked him if he'd rather undertake the task."

"He declined?"

"Yes."

"And Lieutenant Caddick?"

"I believe he was present too."

"Thank you," said Harry, shutting the door gently.

He was waiting in the ante-room when Bessborough returned from his ministrations.

"Sad day, Ludlow, sad day," he said, shaking his head. "You never know how much you'll miss someone till they're gone."

"Perhaps," said Harry, "since you are not otherwise engaged, we could have that private word now."

"Your brother is not with you?"

"No, Admiral Bessborough, I sent him back to my ship."

"Distressed, I dare say."

"Very."

Harry indicated the route to Bessborough's office.

"By all means, Captain Ludlow, though it grieves me to have the time to spare." He led the way, Cram followed them in and closed the door behind them while the two men comported themselves on either side of the desk. "Now, sir, I trust, since you're so insistent, that you have put aside your prejudices and discovered something of interest regarding the matter we spoke of."

"I have, Admiral," said Harry. "And I have also discovered who was responsible for the death of the Lloyd's man, Norrington."

"That fellow Caufield, Ludlow," interrupted Bessborough. "There's no mystery there. Man's a blackguard."

"And the murder, this very afternoon, of Antoine de la Mery."

The green eyes flew open and his eyebrows shot up. "Murder, sir! You just told me he died."

"He was suffocated by his own pillow, Admiral. Imagine, a man paralysed from the neck down, who couldn't even struggle."

"Are you certain of this, sir?"

"I had dinner with Marcus Sandford aboard *Diomede*."

"A fine officer, Ludlow, if a little free with his opinion. And you, if I may say so, are jumpin' about a bit too much for my old brain."

"And on my travels, I came across your blackguard, Nathan Caufield."

"Then why didn't you bring him in, man? Don't you know there's a reward on his head?"

"Nathan Caufield convinced me that he didn't kill Norrington."

"You don't say?"

"In fact, it was he who tipped Norrington to the possibility that someone in this building was leaking information. Norrington was in the process of writing a letter when Caufield called on him. It was, he was told, addressed to Dillon."

"Dillon!" Bessborough spat that out, and accompanied it with a look of triumph.

"Your political assistant says that he wasn't here, Admiral Bessborough."

The look faded, to be replaced with one of perplexity. "If you can tell me how he got that lump on his head, I'd be obliged. Did he make the whole thing up and point the finger at an innocent man?"

"He claims he came back from a trip across the island just before dawn. There are sentries on the gate. On a night so memorable to everyone, even if it's yet to be confirmed, that shouldn't be too hard to establish. Caufield certainly sandbagged him. But that was just before dawn, and my guess is that Norrington was already dead. Not surprising, considering that he left the Duke of Clarence before seven o'clock the previous evening."

"All this is amazing, Ludlow. And how do you know that, sir, when you were not even here at the time?"

"I asked the man who owns the inn."

Bessborough sat back with a satisfied air. "Captain Sandford was right about you."

"You told Sandford whom you suspected, didn't you?"

"Did I?" he asked guardedly.

"Marcus and I are old friends, with a tendency to be honest with each other."

Bessborough shrugged. "I told him that if my suppositions were correct, only so many people knew enough to make it possible."

"Vandegut and Dillon."

"That's right. And something tells me that you have a bit of proof to lay against one of them."

"Not your nephew?"

"Charles!"

"I've noticed he treats your office as his own."

"Come, Ludlow. Surely you don't suspect that young man."

"On the night he was murdered, Norrington, according to one of your own sentries, certainly met your nephew."

"He met me too, Ludlow, and damned unpleasant it was." The single quizzical eyebrow was enough to make Bessborough continue. "Charles found him wandering the corridors, and brought him to me. He made some allegations which, at the time, I thought a touch wild. It was those I alluded to the first time we spoke alone."

"Anything in writing?"

"No. He adopted a high tone, as usual. He never could see that the interests of his trade and ours are at loggerheads, I'm afraid, and this galls me, Ludlow. I said so in no uncertain terms, which had Norrington using a tone I couldn't tolerate. I was obliged to ask my nephew to show him the door."

"Which door?"

"Even people who insult me are allowed the use of the front entrance."

"Did you see him out?"

"No, sir, I did not. And I'm wonderin' where all this is leading to. Norrington was out of my sight before eight o'clock."

"I don't think there's any doubt that he was murdered long before his body was found."

Bessborough leant forward, a look of deep concern on his face. "You're not suggesting my nephew was to blame."

"No, Admiral Bessborough, I am not. What has been happening with the illegals requires a knowledge of seamanship, plus the vagaries of the Caribbean, that he almost certainly does not possess."

"Thank the Lord for that. You had me concerned for a moment. I curse myself for not listening to Norrington, you know. But he did rub me up the wrong way, so I was short with him. Perhaps if I'd paid more attention to what he was sayin' he'd still be alive." Bessborough shook his head at his own stupidity. "If I had, we could have narrowed it down, or even set some kind of trap. Anyway, that's academic now. Tell me, Ludlow, who do you have your sights on, Vandegut or Dillon?"

"I rather had you in my sights, Admiral Bessborough."

CHAPTER FORTY-FIVE

"ME!"

"Are you not privy to all the same information as those two gentlemen?"

"That's damned offensive, Ludlow, and nothing like the joke you intend."

"It was a neat plot of yours, once you heard from Marcus about my previous exploits. Things were unravelling a bit with what happened to you in St John's and you'd already decided to call a halt. Then I turn up with my ship, free to go where I please, unlike your frigates, when the air is full of rumours. So what better way to ensure that the curious Harry Ludlow didn't upset matters than by first insulting him in the manner of your request, but having him report to you if he was stupid enough to be tempted."

"I think you've caught a touch of the sun, Captain."

"Odd, Admiral Bessborough. I was of the opinion that I'd caught a murderer and a thief. You've already admitted that Norrington came to see you that night, when he found Dillon was out gathering intelligence."

"But he didn't come to see me, Ludlow. He came to see Captain Vandegut. In fact, he specifically asked my nephew where the captain was."

Harry stopped for a moment, but it was no more than a hair's breadth of a pause before he continued. "He came with information supplied to him by Caufield, which I suspected he'd committed to paper."

"If he did, I wasn't aware of it."

"I never met Norrington. But everyone says he was an impatient man. Not finding Vandegut must have frustrated him. Caddick found him and brought him to see you instead. As soon as he told you what he'd deduced, you could see the game was up. That your plan to take more than your eighth would soon fall apart."

Bessborough had sat back in his chair, his green eyes fixed on Harry.

"To think I had Dillon as the man responsible."

"What changed your mind?"

"It helps to be a sailor, Admiral, and one who knows the Caribbean. You were out here, like me, in '82, so you know it well. And then there's the real motive, money. But more than that, I have the impression of someone in a hurry, which is scarcely Dillon's way. What was it that started you off? The idea that you might be superseded after the loss of Guadeloupe? That you might not make as much money from the Leeward Islands command as your predecessors? A neat revenge on Victor Hugues, to get him the blame for all your losses."

"Do you seriously think that I murdered Norrington?"

"Not with your own hand. But he was set to pass some information on to Vandegut that would, in his possession, be lethal. You, your nephew, or perhaps even Cram, employ two low-lifes to carry your messages, as well as an efficient way of contacting them. De la Mery was murdered within half an hour of your discovering he was in that hospital, while I was conversing with Dillon in his office. The oddest thing is, even if he could have talked, he had sworn not to. And your ploy to put Vandegut under suspicion is also meaningless. It was really stupid to kill de la Mery when he was out of the harbour."

"This is all very interesting, Ludlow. And I dare say you're proud of yourself. But it lacks one vital ingredient, barring, that is, credibility. And I say this as the man employed to uphold the law in English Harbour. Proof!"

"I'm sure Dillon, if he put his mind to it, and consulted his papers, could provide some proof. It's a wonder he missed it for this long."

Bessborough grinned, and rang the bell on his desk. "Let's ask him, shall we?"

"By all means," replied Harry uncertainly, this being a development he'd not anticipated. He turned slightly as the door opened, so didn't see Bessborough provide himself with a pistol from his desk drawer as Cram entered.

"Ah! Cram. My compliments to the captain of the marine guard. Ask him to report to me."

Harry had looked back, to see that the pistol was levelled at his chest. They sat in silence for less than a minute, till the red-coated officer appeared. As he did the pistol dropped on to the desk. But the barrel was still pointed in the same direction.

"Captain Metzerhagen. I've just been informed that Mr Dillon is a member of the League of United Irishmen. That, as you know, has recently been named as a proscribed organization, which is especially barred to servants of His Majesty. No doubt he's used his office here to further that damnable cause. Please see that he's taken into custody and held incommunicado 'til I can interrogate him. And put a seal on his papers, this instant."

"Sir!" The captain saluted and marched off, calling for a file of his marines.

"That's one problem solved, Ludlow. You've no idea what power you have when you're an admiral in a place like this. Or maybe you do, having had a father who attained the rank."

"You can't escape justice."

Bessborough grinned again, and some of the handsome look that had earned him his soubriquet "beau" was recaptured. "But here, in English Harbour, I am justice. And I can assure you that should matters become unpleasant they will find amongst Dillon's papers a list of contributions to the League of United Irishmen. Large contributions."

"What about your two mulattos?"

"Rest assured that they are two people I've never met. In fact, only you say that they exist. Who could find them in the Caribbean, when the breed is so numerous? And even having found them, would you really want to take their word against that of a serving senior officer?"

"And me?"

"My next order will be to impound your ship and de la Mery's. You can of course, voluntarily, accept my invitation of a berth in the inner harbour. I shall, of necessity, inspect the damage. Imagine my surprise when I find that one of them contains a small fortune in coin, which neither you nor our late friend's crew can account for."

"I'm not going willingly. So how will you go about impounding my ship?"

"If you look out into the harbour, you will see that I have instructed Toner to load some cannon into his boats, preparatory to an assault on Pointe-à-Pitre harbour. Have you ever tried to avoid a gunboat in a confined space, Ludlow? They can get very close and actually sink you."

Harry laughed. "And of course, if you discover the profits of your crime in the harbour, using your marines to take my ship, then all of the money will accrue to you."

The smile was gone, replaced by a worried look. "I wouldn't have dunned de la Mery had he lived. But he was too soft. I urged him to emulate Hugues, since dead men cannot bear witness, nor carry tales from island to island. And what was he doing assisting Toner?"

As Harry stood up the pistol followed him. "Where are you going, Captain Ludlow?"

"On to your veranda, Admiral. And I urge you to join me."

"Why?"

"I would not want you to miss *Bucephalas* and *Ariadne* clearing the outer roads."

"What?"

Bessborough jumped up and ran out through the double doors. Harry sauntered after him, taking the opportunity to check the time on one of Bessborough's twin chronometers. There was a long telescope on the veranda, mounted on a tripod. Harry lifted it, though he could see both ships, outside the great reef and well into deep water, with the naked eye. After a moment he stood back and offered an opportunity to Bessborough.

"You should have a look through this, Admiral. You might just be able to observe a brass-bound chest on the deck of my ship, with a whip around it from the maincourse yard. They likewise have a glass on this garden. If I don't depart from here within the next half-hour, they'll raise that chest and drop it into a hundred fathoms of water. I don't think even you can manage to get a message that distance in half an hour."

"You've got sick men in my hospital!"

"Correction, sir. I had sick men in your hospital. They've all been shipped out, as has Monsieur de la Mery's body."

The bitterness was in the voice only. All Bessborough's attention was concentrated on the *Bucephalas*. "You'll never clear the Caribbean, Ludlow. I'll have every ship on the station chasing you, with orders to hang you on sight. Remember I am the law in these waters."

"I suspected as much. But right now you are stuck with an under-manned frigate, captained by a man I heartily despise. If you feel you'd like to risk him, send him out after me tomorrow. Nothing would give me greater pleasure than to show him what a battle is like when you're not lying comatose in your cot. If, instead, you go sailing tomorrow, you will be able to collect your share of de la Mery's efforts."

"Share?"

"The rest will go to his crew. Odd that you didn't consider them worthy of any reward."

"They are mere scum," he snapped.

"I'd forgotten, of course, that you are a gentleman."

"I don't trust you, Ludlow. Why offer me half the money, when you now have it all?"

"It may surprise you to know, Admiral Bessborough, that I

care very deeply about what you have done. I think it brings a service I esteem in disrepute. But I'm well aware, as you pointed out earlier, that knowing it, and proving it, are two very different things. You'd probably hang Dillon rather than endanger yourself. You will most certainly destroy me."

"You make me sound like a damned privateer."

"I have no wish to so elevate you, though I dare say that a case could be made to prove that you and I have been engaged in the same trade. All you've done is rob your junior officers and every sailor on the station."

"That doesn't answer the question. Why?"

"I also made a promise which I feel bound to my best to fulfil. So there is something else I require."

"Like what?"

"From you, a pardon for one Nathan Caufield, to be written out before I leave. It will be easy, since there is really no evidence against him except that he left Antigua at an inconvenient time."

"What about robbery?"

"You may hold to the robbery if you wish, but I desire that the capital charge be dropped."

"I could throw you in gaol."

"You forget who I am. The son of an admiral, with two seats in parliament and a brother who is *au fait* with everything you and I have just discussed. He might not get justice, but I wouldn't cherish your career after he's done." Harry's voice changed, became harder. "You must decide now."

"And this?" he said, twitching the pistol.

"Not even you are stupid enough to shoot me in front of your own marine guards. Besides, there's no profit in it."

De la Mery's body was laid out in the cabin of the *Ariadne,* while James and the Caufields discussed what to do. The conversation began in daylight and continued after dark, while the two ships sailed in circles. The argument went round and round as well, with the various options raised time and again. To cut and run, leaving Bessborough to fume in office. To comply with Harry's arrangements and chance that he would leave them be. Throughout, Harry took little part in the discussion, waiting, as he put it, to see what developed. His mind was made up when Pender, sent to keep watch in the harbour, returned to the ship.

"They're piling marines, an' every sailor that can walk, into *Endymion,* your honour, and the captain of that brig that's been here all the while is shifting his men to make up their complement."

"Thank you, Pender."

"Do we run, Harry?" asked James, aware that a fight with king's ships, however it was contrived, would put them beyond the pale in more waters than the Caribbean.

"Justice would be nice," said Caufield *père,* fingering his own pardon.

"He's like a viceroy, friend," said Harry, "and he's absolutely right when he says we've no proof. Vandegut has been maligning him since he arrived, so anything he says will be discounted. Dillon is facing his own charges, with Bessborough prepared to fabricate even more. There's not a court in England that would convict him and not a sailor in the fleet who would believe such a fantastic tale."

"We must decide, Harry. Or rather you must."

He stood up suddenly. "I agree with you, Nathan Caufield. Justice would be nice."

All the doubt seemed to fall away as he pulled himself to his full height. The voice was raised as he issued a string of commands.

"Pender! Ship's boats and a boarding party of twenty with blackened faces. Pistols and knives for each man. Both vessels to shape a course for St John's. Captain Caufield, I will leave you in charge. James, get hold of Jubilee and that damned stick of his and prepare to lower Monsieur de la Mery over the side. Nathan, pen, paper, and a needle and thread, and somebody fetch me that Bourbon flag."

◆ ◆ ◆

Bessborough had denuded his headquarters to man the ships in the harbour. Even Caddick had been granted a chance to take part in an action that would require no seamanship. Now he was pacing up and down in his study, alternately gnawing over the events of the day to ensure he left himself secure, at other times cursing the name Ludlow, then going on to imagine Harry's face when he found himself facing two well-manned frigates. Neither he nor the guards he still maintained heard the party of seamen approach Admiralty House. No one saw Pious Pender, his face blackened, slip a set of picks into the postern gate and open it inside one minute. The men were through and had taken the first sentry within two minutes of their arrival, while six more took up positions to guard them. This poor marine, with a knife at his throat, was persuaded to reveal the whereabouts of two people, the Admiral's servant Cram and Eamon Dillon. Once provided, he was bound and gagged, then left beside the gate.

Cram had a room near the kitchen, which was accessible through a sub-basement door. Two men proceeded in that direction, with instructions to incapacitate the cretin, and an injunction to be as rough as they pleased in the process. Dillon, it seemed, was under the personal supervision of Captain Metzerhagen, whose quarters lay by the main entrance to the building, in a room which, though comfortable, had bars on the window. The captain had gone down to the harbour to supervise the loading of his marines into *Endymion,* leaving a corporal in charge of the prisoner. It was time for pistols, rather than knives. Pender, leading the cutting-out party, made his way round the side of the house to the front. Behind them, four men carrying a stretcher accompanied Harry Ludlow as he cut across the grass to the bottom of the steps leading to Admiral Bessborough's private quarters.

The corporal, seated outside his officer's door in the well-lit hallway, didn't even have time to lift himself off the chair before he had a pistol under his ear. Harry had left his party and come round to ensure that the prisoner complied with his wishes, and made no noise in doing so. Quickly, he reprised his last conversation with Bessborough, looking closely at the Irishman to gauge his reaction. But Dillon was as impassive as ever, betraying nothing.

"I cannot believe that given your position and the intelligence you receive you had no knowledge of Bessborough's actions."

"You'll be saying I was his accomplice next."

"No, Dillon. The admiral did everything in his power, even before I was curious, to point me towards you."

"Then I can only be pleased that you didn't fall for it. Not that being innocent will avail me much now."

"Are you a member of the United Irishmen?"

"What difference does it make, in King George's domains, if I say yes or no? I'll be damned by the mere accusation."

"I'm curious, Dillon. Why did you let him carry on? Was it that you didn't care? Or did you think, perhaps, that when Bessborough had his share, you could then threaten him with exposure?"

Dillon smiled. "It's supposed to be the Irish who're good at making up stories, Captain Ludlow."

"Perhaps by satisfying my curiosity, Dillon, you'll find your way out of here."

The Irishman ran his fingers over his thinning ginger hair. "I think I have already."

"Don't be so sure."

"But I am, Captain Ludlow. Part of my job here in Antigua is to know how other men think. You didn't break in here just for the conversation. I suspect, in some way, my being locked up causes you embarrassment."

The truth of that provoked what Harry considered a lame response. "No man should be damned for merely being Irish."

"Would that some of your fellow countrymen felt the same way, sir," said Dillon, standing up. Harry stood away from the open cell door, indicating he was free to go through. "Tell me,

Captain Ludlow, what do you have in mind for the admiral?"

"Come, Mr Dillon. I'm no more likely to incriminate myself than you."

The Irishman looked him straight in the eye. "I dare say not. If your course takes you anywhere near St Eustatius, I'd be obliged to be dropped there. I've a mind to see my old friend, Conlon O'Dwyer."

Bessborough was still unaware of anything being amiss when he heard the knock at the door. It startled him, certainly, since he'd made no arrangements for anyone to call by that route. But he was the commanding officer of His Britannic Majesty's ships and vessels on the Leeward Island station and he had nothing to fear in his own quarters. He opened the door and looked out. On a dark night, with no one to be seen, it was a moment before he glanced down and saw the silken cloth. Even in the glim he recognized it as the naval flag of Bourbon France, the fleur-de-lis. He bent down, his eye fixing on the large needle that secured this standard around what was clearly a human frame.

The needle came out easily and the wrapping fell open to reveal the body of Antoine de la Mery. Handsome, even in death, his eyes were open, and seemed to stare straight at Bessborough. The admiral had seen too many corpses in his time to be shocked, and understood, as he closed those accusing eyes, that this was a message from Harry Ludlow. The note pinned to the white waistcoat would tell him in detail. He had to tug at it, since it seemed to be sewn on. But it came away eventually, with a slight tearing sound, and the waistcoat fell open. The flash of what looked like a bright metal rod caught his eye, just as the two teeth hit him in the neck. He leapt to his feet. But the fer de lance had sunk its fangs in his jugular vein and the spread of the venom in a major blood vessel was swift. Bessborough staggered back, kicking wildly at the reptile lest it bite him again. He could feel himself going numb and he opened his mouth to scream for help. But his throat was closed,

already so swollen that it was beginning to choke off the supply
of air. Suddenly the local Caribbean nickname for this snake came
into his terrified mind. The slaves called it the three-minute man.
Because, they said, that's how long you had between the bite and
the onset of death.

They found his body the following morning, lying on top of
de la Mery. And in his hand he still had the note, which read: *To
Admiral Bessborough, from his good and faithful servant.*

Motoo Eetee

Shipwrecked at the *Edge of the World*

Swimming for their lives from the senseless wreck of the American sealing ship *Dove*, four men escape—Thomas, a headstrong young sailor; Harrison, the affable, inventive ship's carpenter; Mr. Morgen, the *Dove*'s pedestrian first mate; and the aging Captain Tobit— bungling, short-sighted, and fanatical. Bruised and naked, they find themselves cast away on an uncharted, uninhabited island in the far South Pacific where the bounty and beauty of all that surrounds them are at odds with the old structures of shipboard life. Within the new order dictated by nature and the struggle to secure the simplest food, clothing, and shelter, the old divisions between officers and men, especially between Thomas and Tobit, nevertheless grow deeper. Which voice prevails in the end—nature or human habit—is the essence of this book's gripping climax.

Motoo Eetee

Shipwrecked at the *Edge of the World*

IRV C. ROGERS

ISBN 1-59013-018-9 • 400 pp., maps
$24.95 Hardcover

"**Extraordinary, and very hard to put down.** It's exciting, thought-provoking, and extremely moving, an adventure of Old Testament starkness mixed seamlessly with symbolism and philosophy. The sea and sail-ship elements are impeccable, from the handling and rigging to the characters of the officers and men."

—*Jan Needle author of the Sea Officer William Bentley Novels*

"**Irving Rogers knows about ships and he knows about the sea**. He understands sailors, the good the bad and the mad, and what it is that makes them want to sail the oceans and how they might behave when things go against them. And he can tell a story. I thoroughly enjoyed *Motoo Eetee*."
—*David Donachie, author of The Privateersman Mysteries*

NauticalFiction.com is an inviting harbor for nautical fiction enthusiasts.

This Internet website delivers insightful author interviews and an online bookstore with U.S. and British nautical books at discount prices. It features books from all publishers and all your favorite maritime writers including: O'Brian, Forester, Kent, Reeman, Pope, Woodman, Needle, Nelson, Lambdin, and Marryat.

NEW! *The Royal Marines Saga*

DAVID DONACHIE is an avowed lover of
 naval fiction with a
streak of mischief. A
best-selling author well-
known to European
audiences, Donachie—
as Tom Connery—is the
author of the popular
George Markham of the Marines novels,
also set during the Napoleonic Wars and
telling the land and sea adventures of
His Majesty's Royal Marines. Under his
own name, Donachie is the author of a
multi-volume biographical novel about
Lord Nelson and Lady Emma Hamilton.

A Scot by birth, he lives in Deal on
the Channel coast of England, where he
works to keep his inspirations in motion.